Spectral

Redemption

The Comba Coven Curse

By Joanne Alain Cook

JACbooks

Published, 2022

ISBN 9781737589273

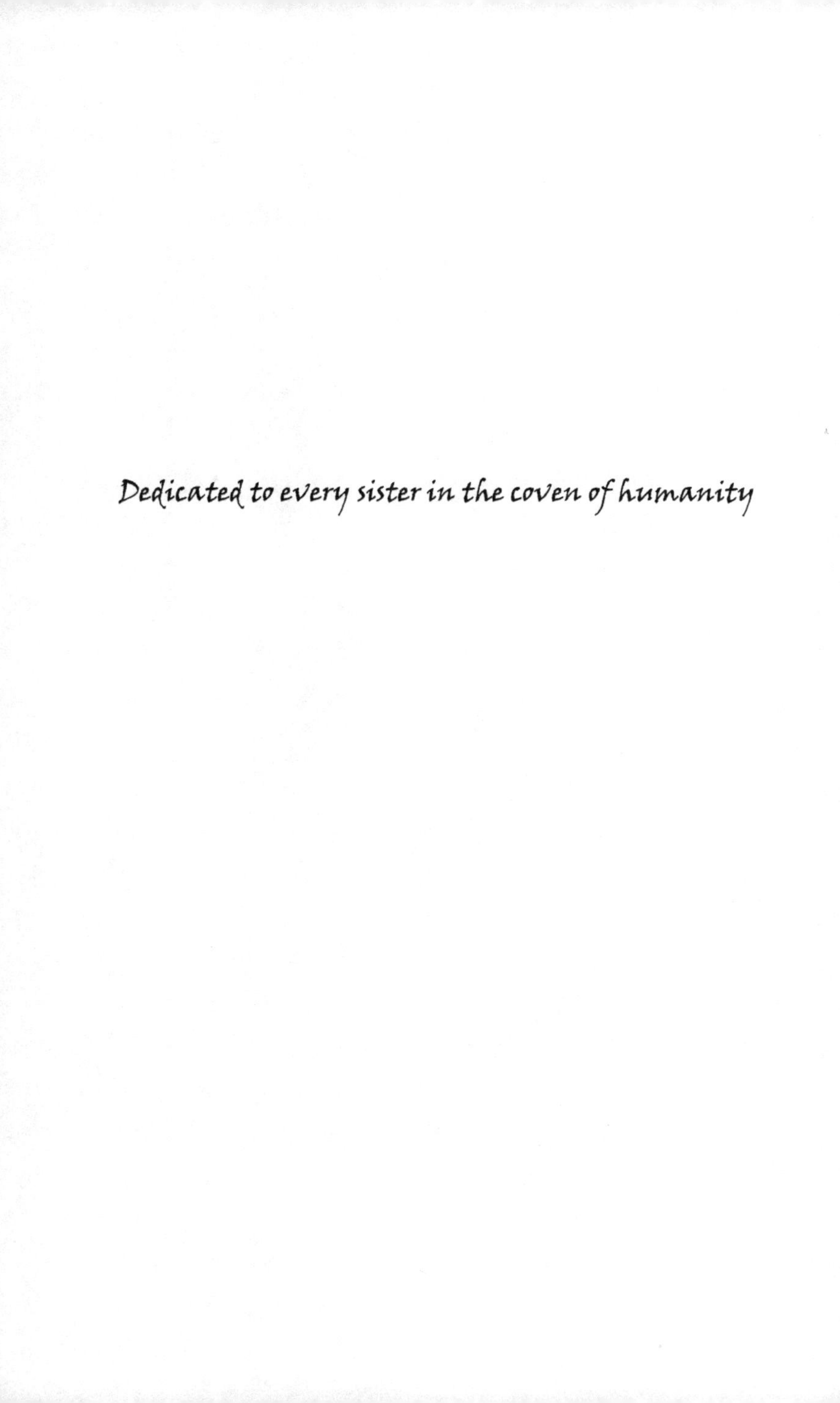

Dedicated to every sister in the coven of humanity

Prologue

Skye

Celeste

On a clear moonlit night, a girl with the right attitude might spy a faery, or even a spirit, while peering through the window of a hagstone.

Celeste and Trinity crept out of the old cottage right under Auntie Meg's sleeping nose, to give it a go. The gibbous moon cast plenty of light and they hoped to glimpse something in the glen before morning. Every summer at Auntie Meg's, their mother took them for at least one midnight hike. *We can spy on those that live in the glen*, she'd wink, but this particular night their mum wasn't there. She was summoned away for a grown up endeavor on one of the other isles.

Celeste, three years older than Trinity, recently turned twelve. Both sisters had long dark hair, ivory skin, and light colored eyes, Trinity green and Celeste blue. Celeste felt plenty old enough to lead her sister into the Faerie Glen. It lay only a scant walk past the far end of the stone wall. They needed to sneak into the glen, if they wanted a tale to tell their mum. She'd delight in hearing about their risky adventure when she fetched them later that week.

"Will Dad let us stay the rest of the summer with Auntie Meg?" Trinity asked.

"Who knows what's in his head." Celeste used a hushed voice. "He doesn't approve of Auntie Meg and the talking of faeries and the like. I heard him call Auntie a silly old bat, and look at how he begged Mum to the lower isle instead. Have you got your hagstone?"

Trinity nodded and held the stone between two fingers. She peeked at her sister through the jagged hole in its center. They followed a border of rocks that snaked gently up the green mound. Most of the land had gone wild since Auntie Meg's companion passed, only the garden near the house stayed presentable. Meg couldn't be bothered with a real crop, she only cared about her herbs. Celeste often wondered about Meg's age. She looked well over a hundred years to young eyes and couldn't be Mum's true sister. Maybe she was a great auntie or other distant relative. Somehow, their true relationship to Auntie Meg was never quite clear to Celeste.

On that dark night, the breeze felt cool and Celeste worried that they left their coats by the entry door. They followed the moss covered wall as it slowly descended into the ground and came upon a large rock preceding the glen. Earlier that day, they left an offering in the nook of that giving rock. They slipped past it and climbed to a higher vantage point.

Never let the wee folk see you, their mother warned, *for they are mischievous and should never be trusted.*

"Stones," Celeste whispered. They each peered through a hagstone.

The waning moon illuminated the entire glen, but not bright enough to wash out the other lights flickering in the grass. Small, luminous, blue-green specks blinked on the far side of the clearing. Will-o-the-Wisps, some called those lights, but Trinity and Celeste knew them as faeries. That's what their mother and auntie insisted. Celeste heard her dad poo-poo that notion, saying they must have seen glow worms or fireflies, but their Mum had admonished him sharply and he never said it again.

Never insult the fae, she warned, *their feelings are sensitive.*

On those former visits, their mother always advised them to stay a distance away and zip their lips near certain areas in the glen. If faeries caught a whiff of a body, they'd flit off for cover or do something to make you pay. So, Celeste and Trinity remained silent as they watched the blue pinpoints dart about, hoping one might pass close enough to see.

Celeste recited a faerie charm in her head, *Come, little faeries, no cause for alarm. We vow to protect you and keep you from harm.*

They observed the flickering lights for nearly an hour before trying to inch closer to the glen floor, but they were too loud. The last of the lights faded into darkness. They waited, but the fair folk must have gone to slumber. Celeste noticed the moon was well past its apex and in a descent. They needed to head back to the cottage. No telling if the old gal would wake in the night. Celeste grasped Trinity's hand and realized the night had gotten very cold, a faint fog hung in the air.

"Come now, Trin," Celeste whispered. "Let's hurry, it's getting cold."

"Maybe we'll glimpse the ghost of the upper wall," Trinity whispered. "Auntie said the old hag can be felt on a cold full moon with the faeries. The moon is mostly full."

Well, that would be something, wouldn't it? Not many have seen the ghost of the wall. Their mum always recited a charm to keep that ghost away, because that one carried the burden of a curse.

Spirits hide, we dare not see, as I command, so mote it be.

No need to scare her wee daughters with such a serious spirit, she always said. Celeste thought about that. At eight and twelve they weren't exactly babes anymore. Pretty soon, Celeste would have her first moon cycle of womanhood and be free to begin a serious study of the ancient feminine teachings.

She might try a little summoning charm to practice. She'd done it before with a bit of success. She had seen ghosts many times. Meg claimed the old spirit belonged to an ancient witch, an old hag who would only manifest for a special charm. Wouldn't that be a tale! Perhaps she could woo the old ghost to appear with a rhyme, so she spun up a clever charm in her head. The air cooled considerably, and the fog grew thicker.

"Say this with me," Celeste whispered to her sister. "*Come, wise soul, to us appear. Show yourself as we come near. Draw us in to make us three, so I command, so mote it be.*"

As Celeste and Trinity strolled along the stone wall, they recited the short summons multiple times. Celeste enjoyed dreaming up the rhymes. She wrote the better ones in her diary, hoping to perfect them later, convinced each would work with a wee bit of fine tuning. Her mum once believed in such things as strongly as Celeste, but like most adults, she developed other concerns to occupy her mind. That was the main reason they always begged to visit Auntie Meg. Meg remained one old lady who took the old beliefs very seriously. As a lifelong practitioner of the old ways, she taught many girls the ancient secrets.

"Look up there, is that a person?" Celeste stopped reciting the poem and pointed into the distant fog where something gathered at the bend in the wall. It sat hunched under the old tree. Through the wet air, Celeste could make out a distinct shadow. Auntie Meg did not bend in a similar way, so clearly this was somebody else. *Could it be the spirit of the wall?*

"Hello?" Celeste called out tentatively. She slowed their pace.

Don't show a spirit fear, her mum always warned, *a spirit will freeze you solid if you show fear.*

Celeste drew a long breath, then let it slowly escape. Perhaps that shadow only resembled a sitting woman, she told herself. As they drew closer and the fog cleared, the woman appeared quite solid, not ghostly at all.

"Hello," Celeste said again. "Are you looking for Auntie Meg?"

The woman's head swiveled, but her body did not sway an inch. Her face met theirs squarely, yet there was something odd about the position of her head and body. It was an unnatural angle to accommodate their face to face situation. This was no regular old woman, Celeste realized, and stopped her sister from moving closer. She calmed herself with another slow breath.

"Who do you see?" Trinity asked, raising the hagstone to her eye, then froze and gasped. Celeste realized that Trinity could not see the old hag, not without her stone.

Celeste turned back to the woman and found that she wasn't old at all. From the distance, she appeared ancient, perhaps due to her hunched posture, but on closer inspection, she looked much younger than their mother. Her hair stuck out in a wild mess, but her luminous skin stretched smooth as porcelain over delicate bones and was creamy white in the moonlight, beautiful. Her eyes hid under that mess of hair, and her hair magically straightened and glossed over the more Celeste peered at it.

Her bulk, Celeste realized, was not due to a thick body, but to the many layers of clothing she wore. The woman might actually be slender. A long thin neck like hers would not be attached to a heavy woman. An elegant hand extended out of a wide sleeve to move flowing wisps from her eyes. Celeste became instantly enchanted. Those eyes glowed like twinkling stars, emerald green, bright and glittering. Plump, pink lips opened over delicate white teeth. She was a very lovely young woman. Then, she arched up, sitting straighter, and Celeste could see her graceful physique.

"Is she the spirit of the wall?" Trinity whispered while peering through her hagstone.

"I don't know." Celeste let out a nervous giggle. Then, she nodded to the woman. "I'm Celeste, and this is my sister, Trinity. We're staying with Auntie Meg. Are you a ghost, or are you one of the sisters? Are you here to see Auntie Meg?"

The woman finally turned her body to align with her head and that suddenly seemed much better, a relief. The woman gave the slightest nod and closed her generous lips. Trinity's hand tightened. Celeste realized her sister was very frightened.

"Shall we go wake Meg?" Celeste asked. "Auntie is sleeping near the hearth, inside." Would Auntie Meg wish to be woken for a guest or a ghost?

"Dinna wake the auld witch." Her voice sounded like a soothing melody. "Lest ye risk the wrath of Caer Ibormieth."

"Why are you here?" Celeste asked weakly.

"A *dragoma* called," her green eyes peered intensely and untamed hair flowed in a luxurious wave in the air. "One to wrest a curse from the demon's grasp."

Celeste felt a cold tickle run up her back.

"A curse, which bids *one each for redemption*, over and over." Her melodic voice warped midsentence into a scratchy hiss, "Lest it be wrested away, it shall play out forever, over and over, into eternity."

The woman turned slowly and became tall and straight, beautifully framed by the star filled sky. How did she become so tall? A lone owl hooted in the far distance and the woman began to chuckle softly. Celeste felt Trinity's hand shake with fright. The tallness of the woman disturbed Celeste, her dimensions seemed out of bounds, too tall, too thin, too beautiful. Then, her melody emerged in discordant tones as her glowing green eyes held fast to the girls.

"Beware, wee lassie, the demon preys on one such as you."

An undertone of woe whistled through the air and Celeste realized that it came from her sister. Trinity stood wide-eyed with terror. Then, the light in Trinity's eyes fluctuated and she knew it meant the woman was moving. Celeste glanced back and nearly jumped from her own skin.

The woman shrank before their eyes. Her tall frame inched shorter and shorter, and her round shoulders began to hunch forward into the posture of a crone. That black silky hair withered into a charred grey wiry mess, and her once luminous skin dulled and wrinkled while her plump lips contracted into a parched tightness. Worst of all, her eyes lost the green glow of life and became dark orbs of blackness.

All the while, her mouth remained open in a small O as she seemed to shrivel and burn with no flame. As the woman dried and charred before their eyes, her arms reached out. Did she wish to embrace them? Celeste pulled her sister further away, but the woman's long arms kept stretching toward them, closer and closer.

Celeste could barely breathe, but managed to squeak out, "Leave us!"

Then came the thump of footsteps, fast and loud on the crunchy ground. As the mystery woman deteriorated into fine particles, Auntie Meg stepped into her spot. Sleepy eyes blinked at them. Meg, in her night dress, looked just out of a deep dream. Her soft pudges were a sight for scared eyes.

There was no longer a trace of the other woman. Meg stepped forward to catch up a teetering Trinity. As Meg held Trinity, her eyes sought out Celeste, searching for an answer.

"To whom were you speaking?" Meg asked, but anyone could see that she did not need telling.

Meg nodded. They remained a moment longer before heading for the farm house. Meg insisted they tell her everything and then add it to the big book locked away in her cabinet, the coven *Book of Happenings*, where everything worth noting was written.

Chapter 1
Rio Linda

Janine

A yellow bulldozer creeped over the hill that separated Gram's house from the river. Gram, Martha Williams Stinger, still retained hints of auburn interwoven in her silver hair. Janine adored her grandmother and ached seeing her in despair as her prized backyard was destroyed.

After a year in court battling over mineral rights, the far mound was ordered to be torn up for the removal of a rocky deposit below the top soil. Giant boulders embedded with copious amounts of rare earth minerals lay hidden on her property, and their value proved far too great to win the fight against their removal. Plus, Gram would receive a nice six figure settlement for her portion of the boulders, a quarter of their worth.

Janine watched from the back glass patio as her grandmother *tsked* each time the earth mover jolted. She didn't want to admit to Gram that the disruption of the backyard was a relief. The changing scenery made it easier to face the house again. That dirt mover erased every place Janine had seen the River Ghost.

"Are they going to cut into the green?" Janine watched the machine roll over the edge of Gram's manicured lawn. It erased the sharp edge the landscapers often labored over. The machine smudged out that border alarmingly easy.

"They are cleared to dig all the way to the chicken coop." Gram stood with her arms akimbo and shook her head. "But that TJ Grounder from the county assured me they'd stay in the rough, up on that mound. He also promised to shut down at a reasonable hour each day, but look at the time. He also said they'd cart in a truckload of dirt to reform my mound, but who knows if that'll happen?"

Gram turned her back on the destruction and pulled Janine into the kitchen.

"Come on, girl, tell me what you have planned over a nice cup of tea. Does that look like Camilla hiding in the bush over there? It is!" Camilla was a large Americana hen that dropped blue-green eggs on occasion. She was one of the older hens in Gram's free range flock.

Fresh biscuits cooled on the stovetop, all set to accent their planned picnic dinner of fried chicken. Gram's roommate and house keeper, Misty, made a batch of homemade biscuits every weekday. In the early mornings, she delivered a dozen biscuits and fresh eggs to the small care home down the street. In all the years she lived with Gram, Misty never missed a day with that delivery.

Not until the bulldozer. With the mineral removal activity, Gram said the free range hens have been spooked and flew the coop. Usually, the hens dropped so many eggs they donated dozens to the farmers market in the summer, but for the past couple of days, only a few eggs waited in the rack, and that morning, there hadn't been any.

"Those poor girls are probably terrified of the ruckus. They've all run for their lives. We'll be lucky if we ever see them again. A stressed out hen can have a heart attack you know."

"Oh, Gram, they're probably just hiding in the brush waiting for that machine to go away. They'll be back."

"I hope so." Gram pointed toward the window. "But did you see any of the girls out there, beside Camilla? Think about that. When have you ever seen that hill without a large gaggle walking about? I don't know why men like TJ Grounder think a few dollars is worth spoiling the view, destroying the environment, and obliterating the wildlife."

A few dollars? More like six hundred thousand dollars, and disrupting a gaggle of free range hens was hardly obliterating the wildlife, nor was turning over half an acre of land destroying the environment, but they certainly spoiled Gram's beautiful view with their digging. Janine knew that Gram loved her home and looked forward to spending her twilight years in the peaceful routines of her small town community.

Ever since the rare earth mineral discovery, the entire town had turned topsy-turvy with activity. *Not just rare elements, but maybe even ghostly energy too. Some believed the boulders bore an element mixture perfect for absorbing the energy from a soul.* Janine wonder if any spiritual energy hid in the rocky samples under Gram's mound.

"I'm sorry, Gram," Janine said softly.

Gram patted her hand, "Not your fault, girl, now drink your tea." Gram pushed a small cup across the table. "Me and the gals have taken up tealeaf reading. We became very interested after Kiki Mellow gave us each a personal reading that time."

Kiki Mellow happened to be a self-proclaimed witch and the popular star of a ghost hunting television show called *Spectral Analysis*. Up until several months ago, Janine had been a tech specialist and cast member on the same show. About a year before Janine decided to leave *Spectral Analysis*, they brought the ghost hunting crew to Gram's small town and filmed a very successful documentary on a spirit that haunted the river. Gram and Kiki developed a fast friendship during the documentary's research phase and they still kept in touch. Those two were birds of a feather.

"Kiki gave us a special contact to learn tea reading. Have you met Annelise Batten? Kiki insists that Annelise is the one to study the leaves with. Annie also specializes in the short tarot deck, but that's too much work, She requires students to make their own cards if they're serious about lessons. Can you imagine?" Gram exclaimed. "As you know, Leone is very in touch with technology and has attended hundreds of zoom sessions with Annelise. They drink tea, with others, in an online tea party, then screen share and read the leaves as a group. Leone says people from all over the world join the tea parties. It's very international. Apparently, an interesting older gentleman from France joins once a month. Leone believes he flirts with her, can you imagine that? I want to sit in too, if I can figure out how to use that computer. Of course, Leone shares her lessons with the rest of us. She's our local expert now." Gram tapped the teacup with a spoon. "Drink up, girl, I want to have a try without Leone looking over my shoulder."

Janine bit back the acid that welled up in her mouth. Did Gram forget Kiki's tealeaf reading the first morning *Spectral Analysis* came into her home?

Great fortune is coming your way, but the return may not be worth the investment.

Did Gram even consider that Kiki's reading may have been for both of them? Janine had sipped some of the tea that morning. Did Kiki's tea reading predict everything that happened? It certainly seemed so. Becoming friends with Kiki Mellow had proven life altering for Janine. In a couple of short years, Kiki managed to upset her whole view of the universe.

"Let's put the backyard out of our minds." Gram patted her hand. "Let's focus on what we want to know. Annelise urges a calm atmosphere while sipping our tea, with minds actively on the concerns you want addressed. So, sip your tea slowly and thoughtfully, girl." Gram demonstrated by sipping her own tea.

They clinked cups and enjoyed a biscuit with cream, yum, but the tea, yuck! Gram insisted on her bitter homemade raspberry tea. Janine would have no problem sipping that liquid slowly. She added a generous helping of honey to sweeten it up.

Gram rolled her eyes, then donned her kitchen spectacles. They had been resting on top of the Sacramento Bee. Janine noticed the crossword was barely started. Gram usually completed it before breakfast. A telling sign that Gram's mind wandered, most likely to that machine in the backyard.

"How about I get another look at your ring? I want to see the design up close again." Gram reached out to take her hand.

Janine had gotten engaged barely eight weeks ago. Her fiancé happened to be the other star of the *Spectral Analysis* show, Doctor Ian McNally. He was a professor of paranormal electromagnetic energy and very handsome. He currently ran a research lab out of Berkeley while also teaching a class at Davis, where Janine happened to be finishing her degree. Three episodes into the new season, just after she left the show, it morphed from the filming of ghost encounters to filming research and development. The next few episodes focused on the creation of sensors and devices designed to measure energy associated with ghostly encounters.

Ian and his crew were currently enroute to the haunted orchard in Rio Linda. They planned a field test of prototype instruments and to film clips for an upcoming episode.

"Oh my," Gram exclaimed. "That design is the exact little triangle symbol! I thought so."

"Triquetra," Janine told her. On either side of the beautiful one carat diamond, the white gold metal twisted into delicate Celtic knots.

They were a symbol of Ian's genetic roots. The ring had passed down from his maternal grandmother. When Janine described the ring to Kiki over the phone, she knew it well. Kiki and Ian were cousins, so, the grandmother belonged to Kiki too. Janine wondered if Kiki desired the ring for herself. If she did, she gave no hint of it.

"It's a family heirloom from his grandmother."

Gram nodded thoughtfully. "Have you gotten Ian a ring yet? Perhaps, he would like a family heirloom from you. I need to show you something." Gram sprang from her chair and dashed out of the room, her voice carried back, "You'll never believe what I've found!"

Janine could hear footsteps fly through the living room, followed by a distressed shout, then the steps moved into the study. Janine heard a distinct "Aha!" before the footsteps returned to the kitchen. Gram's bright eyes blazed with excitement.

"You may just flip your lid over this." She waved her finger in the air.

Gram settled behind her tea and took a careful sip. On the table, she placed a simple wooden box, old and weathered, the size of a very small shoebox with an ornate metal clasp system and key hole. Gram took care not to allow the clasp to seal the box when she set it down. Her beaming expression made Janine laugh.

"So, what do we have here, Gram? What's in the box? Where did it come from?"

"You'll never believe it," Gram let out a long breath. "Since all that poking around the attic last year, I've been clearing things out, sorting through the mess. After Caroline Govant left her own mess, I especially wanted to straighten things out in case something happened to me."

Caroline Govant had lived on the other side of Marysville Boulevard and owned the haunted forty acre almond orchard made famous in the *Spectral Analysis* ghost documentary. Janine felt terrible about the last time she spoke with Caroline. She practically accused Caroline of heading up a cult group that lured kids into the river. Janine will never forget Caroline's dark beady eyes and how she chuckled after that accusation.

Caroline died less than a week later. The sole beneficiary of her property went to a man named Henry Webber, the other person Janine accused of being in the cult group. The more time that passed between her initial accusations and the present, the more idiotic they seemed. Now, she regretted her rash words.

"Nothing is going to happen to you, Gram," Janine said softy.

"I know that, girl." Gram laughed at her. "I just don't want to leave a mess and wanted to find more historic clues. Henry Webber claims there are boxes of things at Caroline Govant's place. Things she wanted destroyed. She was holding out on you guys. H says there are loads of ghost diaries."

Gram pulled the wooden box closer and put it between them.

"This one was hiding in my attic, locked and tucked away in a corner, and for over a week Misty and I tried to open it with a screw driver, and failed. Misty suggested taking a hammer to it, but I couldn't destroy such a lovely old box. Look at that delicate catch."

"It's unlocked now." Janine touched the open clasp.

"It is," Gram told her. "Day before yesterday, when you and Ian asked to stay here after his thing in the orchard, I came downstairs and the box was open. Just popped open like that. Misty says she didn't do it."

Gram's wide eyes suggested a mysterious, unnatural event must have opened the box.

"Gram," Janine chuckled under her breath. "You said you've been jiggling that lock for days? And even took a tool to it?"

Gram nodded. "And nothing. Still locked tight."

"Yes, but all that activity surely loosened it up a bit." Janine noticed the clasp naturally swung down with gravity. "Most likely, you loosened it enough for it to finally to pop on its own. I doubt a ghost came wandering in and opened it for you."

Gram wrinkled her nose in disappointment with that logical explanation.

"Don't be so sure," Gram told her. "Not till you see what's inside. Just so you know, this box came off the wagon train, I'm certain of it by the few things in here. They're labeled with the names Finn and Irene, and there's a perfect ring for Ian, a real family heirloom."

The wagon train! Rio Linda was initially populated with people who survived a horrific wagon expedition over the Sierra Nevada range. Those brave ancestors built part of Gram's house and founded the town and orchard. Gram discovered an old Bible from the original group on their initial attic search. Now, Gram stumbled upon a box with some of their long lost treasure.

"Why would anything of value still be in the box?" Janine asked. "Why wouldn't someone remove it long ago? It doesn't make any sense."

"It's bits and pieces from our lost Lumens," Gram told her. "Leftovers from the family that didn't make it over the pass. Not much, just a couple of trinkets. Perhaps someone planned to deliver them to Christopher Williams someday, when they revisited his history, and then hid it all away when they couldn't tell him that he was adopted. Or, maybe they forgot these things. Or, maybe he didn't care for them. Go on, open it up."

Janine opened the box.

Several pieces of folded yellow paper tumbled out, along with an old pocketwatch. Gram impatiently fished one clump to unfold. The paper was stiff and thick and possibly homemade. A slender silver ring spun out on the table and Janine could see the name *Irene* faintly scratched on the paper. Gram chose another clump and opened it. A larger ring, with engraved Celtic knots, rolled onto the table. It was a thick man's ring with a repeating pattern of triquetra encircling the band. Gram retrieved the ring and displayed it on the tip of her pointer finger.

"Here it is." Her eyes glowed. "The designs match your ring perfectly."

She placed the band next to Janine's engagement ring to compare the Celtic knots. They could be forged from the same artistic jeweler.

"It's not silver, doesn't tarnish, and not soft. Maybe some sort of white gold alloy. Can you believe this luck?"

Janine took the ring and turned it in her hand. It really was a perfect match. Just the other day, she visited a jeweler inquiring about finding a ring with that exact knot pattern. She approved of the weight of it in her hand. She also picked up the smaller woman's ring. Not triquetra, but the twists in the pattern complimented the Celtic bends in the male ring, a matched set.

"You might use that one as well, it could be your wedding band." Gram exclaimed. "You take the rings and use them if you like, no problem if you don't. There are other nice things in here that I can give to Juju, she won't mind."

"I like them." Janine smiled. Of course, she wanted to let Ian look at them as well.

Janine reached to the other folded papers and Gram helped her open them. They each contained something special, a hair comb, a brooch, and a silver charm on a slender chain. That charm caused Janine's heart to skip a beat. When it plopped onto the table, it landed face down, but she felt certain she had seen it before. A chill ran down her spine as Gram reached over to right it.

"This one's interesting." Gram caressed the necklace. "Again, it's not silver, but something else, strong stuff, maybe the same metal as those rings. But it's a funny name for a saint, don't you think? Could it be a joke?" Gram glanced up and stopped chatting. "Jaja, what's wrong? Are you okay?"

Good question. Janine could not believe her eyes at what popped of that banged up wooden box from Gram's attic. *A Saint Comba pendant!* She gasped for oxygen just looking at it.

S, A, I, N, T, C, O, M, B, and A were stamped along the bottom, and in the center was the impression of a woman with long flowing hair. One of her wrists was shackled to a wall with an animal at her feet. It was an exact copy of the ornament a haunted college guy delivered during her last *Spectral Analysis* shoot. A very disturbed young man who popped up out of nowhere and insisted a *ghost* demanded he deliver the charm to her. A scary ghost that seemed connected to Janine through a psychopath that once tried to kill her.

But Kiki had taken the pendant and delivered it to the rightful owners, didn't she? It was a thousand of miles away. How did it end up in Gram's kitchen in California?

"Jaja?" Gram grabbed her arm. "What is it?" She sounded worried.

"Where did you get this charm? Did someone send it to you?"

"It came out of the box," Gram told her. "From the attic. It belonged to Irene Lumen, see the paper?" Gram pushed a slip of paper to her. *Irene* was scribbled in flowing script near the torn edge. "It's been in the attic for over a century."

Janine needed to think. *If Irene Lumen owned a Saint Comba charm, did that make her a witch?* Saint Comba was considered the witch's saint.

"Gram, I saw a charm exactly like this earlier this year."

Janine pulled out her phone and dialed Kiki's number, then remembered Kiki was in Scotland and the time difference was huge. She hung up immediately.

"Crap! She's probably sleeping."

She peered at Gram, then snapped a picture of the charm and sent it in a text to Kiki, typing out where they found it.

"It was an exact copy with the same exact saint. It belonged to a very scary ghost, one that helped me in the woods a long time ago. Remember, I told—"

Her phone chimed loudly, Kiki Mellow, and she answered quickly.

"Kiki! The charm, it's here. I can't explain it, but my gram has it in her kitchen, or one like it. The Saint Comba charm."

"How did she get it? Your message says she found it in a box? Did the box come in the mail? Was it addressed to you? To her?" Kiki asked. "That doesn't make any sense at all. How would the Daily's know where to send it?"

"No, no, it was in her attic. It came out of a box from the attic," Janine told her. "An old box from the wagon train."

That inspired a long silence, then Kiki's calm voice came back.

"Well then, I've got your photo side by side with the one I sent to… *that* detective. It's definitely from the same source, an exact twin, but not *the* exact charm. Look at the top left. The other charm didn't have that wee mark. This is quite a find, Janine. I'm very interested in this charm. It's very rare and I have to say, I'm dumbfounded. Two Comba charms dropped right into your hands. This is no coincidence. What does it mean? I can hardly wait to see you in November and want to fly out right now! But I have the Samhain with the sisters, and my thing that I really must do, very soon. Maybe I'll come early, right after my obligations. Can I call you tomorrow about this? I'm actually on a date right now and I'm hiding in the loo to take this call." She laughed. "You never ever call anybody and you scared me ringing so late. I almost thought something happened because of Ian's talk with his father. I about had a heart attack. Can I ring you tomorrow at a better time, or a little later? I admit it, I'm pished right now. Can you tell?"

"Sure, sure," Janine said.

There was a lot of mystery packed into Kiki's short outburst. Too many key words opening up trap doors in her mind. Ian had a *talk* with his father? When? Implying the Comba charms were *deliberately* dropped into *Janine's* hands? Kiki *hiding* in a loo on a date? Referring to Bob Anderson as *that detective*? Detective Anderson was supposed to be in Scotland, with Kiki, at the moment.

"Kiki, are you on a date with Detective Anderson?"

There was a very pregnant pause before Kiki spoke.

"Well, that particular detective got a bit skittish on me." There was a hint of sharpness in her tone. "I can't stand a skittish man, Janine, it's not attractive. Let's chat tomorrow at a more reasonable hour."

Janine pressed her lips together. She had been hoping that Kiki and Bob Anderson would work out.

She noticed Gram waiting patiently, fingering the Saint Comba charm. Her eyebrows rose at Janine. Her doe shaped brown eyes were unwavering, but sweet. Janine's own eyes were very similar.

"Kiki Mellow? She knows of a charm like this?" Gram inquired. "And what's this about the woods? Do you mean *the woods*, your woods, Thatcher Woods? And a ghost? You're not telling me something, Jaja."

Janine took a deep breath and another sip of her bitter raspberry tea. Several years ago, when she attended the University of Chicago, Janine had gotten involved with a very charming man that turned out to be a psychopath, Richard Wilkens. Quite unexpectedly, their relationship turned violent and Janine found herself running for her life in a wooded area of Chicago. She endured several knife wounds before her *boyfriend* suddenly stopped stabbing her. Janine swore that a woman appeared in the woods and scared Rick away, but no witness ever came forward. There was no trace of anyone being there except Janine and her attacker.

Then came the Comba charm, just half a year ago, and the ghost she summoned with Kiki Mellow and Gwen Murphy. That ghost led them to a set of bones hidden in the woods. Almost everyone, even Detective Anderson, believed the skeleton belonged to a prior victim of Richard Wilkens. And now, a charm matching the first one had suddenly appeared. She recapped the entire story for Gram.

"Gram, you realize that before we opened this box, everything in my world was settling down and flowing calmly for the first time in… in forever. And now, I don't know what is going on."

Gram let out a nervous laugh and patted Janine's hand reassuringly.

"That's the way of life, girl, there are no guarantees. Now give me your cup to read. I want to see what's in there. Then, we need to start frying the chicken."

"Oh, no." Janine quickly took her cup to the sink, ignoring Gram's pout. There was no way she'd have her tealeaves read, not even by a novice just fooling around, not after what had tumbled out of Gram's box a moment ago.

Chapter 2
The Orchard

Janine

They packed up a basket of homemade fried chicken, corn on the cob, potato salad, and Misty's famous biscuits with a plan to drive into the orchard and meet Doctor McNally's crew. The picnic dinner would give the crew a break between equipment set up and a long night of field tests. Afterward, Ian's crew would stay at Gram's large house and get a good night's sleep before heading back to the bay area.

As Janine steered the old truck down Marysville Boulevard, she noticed changes to the road. Four pole lamps now lined the orchard and a gravel parking area had been constructed.

Gram said a local group of spiritualists pitched in for the parking lot. They began holding séances in the old orchard by appointment. During the summer, time slots were filled every hour of the night. Henry Webber hated that arrangement, Gram laughed, but he was stuck with it. Caroline Govant signed a five year contract with the spiritual guides before she died. The lot appeared empty when they drove past, but Gram predicted that there'd be a few groups arriving later in the night.

"I hope that doesn't spoil Ian's testing," Janine said.

The *Spectral Analysis* van sat along the edge of the trees in the dirt. The back van doors were wide open, and they could see the computers and monitors. Janine stopped the truck a few feet from the back bumper. She stomped on the parking brake just as Doctor McNally stepped into view.

The sight of him put an automatic smile on her face. She was definitely addicted to Ian McNally. His bright blue eyes fixed on her and he said one last thing before slipping his phone into his pocket. He hurried to help her from the truck and pulled her into a close embrace.

"You brought my favorite truck," he whispered with an enthusiastic kiss.

Then, he smiled at Gram and paused to hug her too. Gram appeared pleased as punch with Ian McNally. The next moment, three chatting men and a young woman strolled out of the orchard.

"We've got the cream of the crop from the Berkeley lab here," Ian told Janine and Gram. "Oliver, Chet, Emma, and of course, you know Ben."

Janine gave Ben a brief hug. Ben joined *Spectral Analysis* before she left the show and they had worked on two episodes together. He was a computer expert with a bachelor's of science degree, but was not yet of legal drinking age. He wore his standard *Star Wars* T-shirt, wire rimmed glasses, and jeans. He gave her a big toothy grin. Oliver appeared to be an Asian version of Ben, and Emma was the female version with a pixie haircut. Both were extremely thin, compact, and wore comic-hero shirts. Chet, on the other hand, was boldly bald and stocky. He wore an ensemble of Cal workout clothes and looked a couple of days away from his last shave.

Janine and Gram gave each crew member an enthusiastic greeting before ferrying out the late dinner. They arranged a picnic blanket under the flood lights near the van and everyone gathered around.

"So, the big controversy right now is, who will wear the *mellow-skin*," Ben told them. "Emma doesn't think it should be a girl and Chet believes his arm hair will get in the way, so that leaves Ollie."

Bald Chet made up for his lack of head hair with curly masses on his forelimbs. Ollie did not hide his perturbed expression. He flipped his long black bangs and flashed a frown at Emma.

"I don't know why it shouldn't be a girl. Why not, are we protecting you? What happened to equal rights?" He glanced around. "Girls are more sensitive anyway, right? Maybe the skin will work better on Emma. We might get a better test. Who gets cold first in the lab? Emma does. She's already halfway more sensitive than the rest of us."

"Boom! That's exactly why I shouldn't test the skin," Emma countered. "I might not even need it. I bet I'm already sensitive enough to pick up paranormal energy, and we'd get a false positive. And you're not protecting me, I don't need protecting. I'm not the one scared of ghosts." She passed the chicken basket to Oliver. "Do you want a fork for that potato salad?"

"Oh yeah, thanks," Oliver nodded.

The doctor seemed to ignore the discussion as it vacillated between Emma and Oliver, but Janine knew he listened intently. He refrained from adding his opinion because he wanted them to work out the best solution for testing their own gadgets. Finally, they decided that Oliver would be the *mellow-skin* guinea pig.

"I'm just a little old lady," Gram smiled when the discussion came to a resolution. "I have no idea what *mellow-skin* is. I confess that I'm very confused."

The research and development crew erupted into giggles.

"No one knows what *mellow-skin* is." Emma grinned at her. "It's a brand new thing. It might not even be a thing, really. We're just experimenting with an idea."

"Yes, it's something new that we threw together this last month," Oliver told them. "A skin-like sensing device for ghosts. It's one of the main senses people use to detect ghosts, and we brainstormed how to boost sensitivity of spiritual energy."

"The doctor challenged us to review video and audio tapes of people encountering spirits." Emma sat up and pulled her knees up to hug to her chest. Her tone became more commanding than in the previous discussion. "Most mediums first sense a presence through their skin, a tingling. Kiki Mellow was our prime study subject, hence the nickname *mellow-skin*. She does a spectacular job of describing what she feels each step of the way. Well, you already know that." Emma looked a little bashful at schooling Janine on Kiki.

"But what is it?" Gram asked again.

"A thin layer of film, like plastic wrap." Chet laughed.

Oliver ignored him. "It's more like nylon. It goes over your own skin and amplifies signals to your receptors, skin receptors. Kind of like an arm sleeve. Not the temperature or actual touch receptors, but the type that detect vibrations at different frequencies. The *mellow-skin* will zone in on both types."

"Are you talking about Meissner or Pacinian corpuscles?" Janine asked.

"Yes!" Emma exclaimed. "Boom! Exactly. The *mellow-skin* amplifies in the 20-60 hertz range for the Meisser, and 90-420 hertz for the Pacinian, we went a little outside of the box just in case. The skin will take signals from the environment, normal signals that any person would feel, and amplifies them in the film before it reaches real skin. It's basically an amplifier, like wearing earbuds for skin."

The *Spectral Analysis* crew got into many discussions about the ability to see, hear, and detect ghosts. They discussed theories on why Kiki Mellow easily detected spirits when other people didn't. They hypothesized that it had to do with early development of sensory receptors. Plain and simple, people needed to develop ghost sensing talents at an early age, sometimes while still in the womb. The senses of smell and hearing began in the fetal stage, why not ghost detection too? And if the development of those senses failed to occur early enough, then those receptors might not develop at all. Many experiments provided evidence supporting that theory, at least in regards to the other senses. Consider the Harvard Pirate Cat experiment and the visual cortex, Emma challenged.

Janine recalled the cat experiment as Emma relayed it to Gram. In the 1960s, researchers Hubel and Wiesel attested that if a kitten was deprived of normal visual stimuli early in life, their ability to see would be irreversibly altered. They took a number of newborn kittens and sutured one of their eyes shut. They kept the kitten's eye sewn shut for 6 months, until they reached adulthood. At that time, the sutured eyelid was opened to finally allow visual stimuli. They found that the newly opened, perfectly normal eyes failed to send messages to their feline visual cortexes. Unfortunately for those cats, they were blind for life in the eye that had been sewn shut. Further, the experimenters conducted a similar process on an adult cat. One eye was sutured shut for a complete year. Because the adult cat had already developed normal vision, the experiment did not have a similar result. Vision in the eye that had been shut for the adult cat was just as good after the experiment as before. Hubel and Wiesel concluded that early visual stimuli proved critical for the development of vision in cats.

"How terrible for those kittens!" Gram exclaimed, distressed.

"Boom. Right, I know," Emma agreed.

Ian's crew felt certain that early paranormal encounters provided critical stimuli for the development of extrasensory abilities. Kiki experienced ghosts in her youth and likely developed the critical receptors to see, hear, and speak to them. Those Meissner and Pacinian corpuscles, sensitive skin receptors, also developed very early in life, in the very first months. Kiki certainly had many experiences, almost from birth, with paranormal situations. That could be a big factor in why Kiki Mellow was so tuned in to the spiritual world compared to most people.

"We also set up incongruent and antipode motion detectors. They detect odd motions that defy physical logic. In other words, they detect forces that don't seem to be there or don't have a detectable origin," Ben told them. "We also perfected the magnetic antennae for the big EMF box. There are now six spools that will swivel until they lock onto a signal, and then they move with the signal. Not as heavy as the spool of copper that shocked you in that tunnel."

"Oh my gosh, that was such a tight episode!" Oliver gushed at Janine and then at the doctor. "Did you guys ever find out how you took on so much charge? I watched the clip over and over and couldn't see anything supplying that electric charge."

In an episode from the second season of *Spectral Analysis*, Janine suffered a static electric shock on the magnitude of a weak bolt of lightning. It was a much talked about scene. A myriad of theories floated around the blogs speculating on how it happened and where the energy might have originated. Janine shook her head at Oliver.

"Okay, I don't want to pry, but will you settle something here for me? My friends and I have a bet going, and the doctor won't settle it."

Emma's girlish tone and bashful smile gave her age away. She was either Ben's age or less, maybe nineteen Janine guessed.

"When you fainted into the doctor's arms in that tunnel and opened your eyes, my friend Sandy swears that's when you two fell in love. I think she's wrong, I think it was earlier than that."

"At the graveyard in Savannah!" Gram exclaimed, just as excited as Emma. "In season one! All the gals think that's when it happened. Remember the look they exchanged?"

"Yes!" Emma and Gram high fived. "Savannah. Boom! *The look*. I never believed the Kiki spin."

"Oh yes, *boom* on that too." Gram high fived Emma again. "Me and my gals never believed the Kiki-doctor nonsense, either."

Janine couldn't help chuckling at them. She glanced at Ian and caught his eyes on her, smiling, ever the even-tempered professor. When *had* it all started? To Janine, it felt like she had always been in love with Ian, but it took time to trust herself with it. She couldn't really be upset with Emma and her questions, because it was certainly something the tabloids focused on.

When Ian showed up at UC Davis with Janine there as a student, it took no time at all for entertainment reporters to spot her engagement ring and figure out they shared a small apartment. That fact, added with Kiki Mellow being indisposed in Scotland, got the gossip machine rolling on why *Spectral Analysis* suddenly changed focus. When the stories spun out of control about a love triangle breaking up the *Spectral Analysis* team, the doctor agreed to an interview to clear everything up. To the great shock of their viewing audience, the doctor finally revealed that Kiki Mellow was his cousin. Though viewers fondly imagined a romance between those two, people realized the possibility never existed and it became clear why the doctor was never distressed when Kiki went out with famous athletes "behind his back." Instead of being a clueless nerd, he was a care less cousin. Many fans of the show were very relieved for him.

"Gram and I are right, right? It all started in the Savannah graveyard," Emma pressed her. She also peered at the doctor. "Come on, old man, tell us. Tunnel or Savannah?"

"Wrong and wrong." Ian grinned at Emma. He stood up and helped Janine with a hand. "It was love at first sight, the first moment I laid eyes on her. So, be careful who you look at, young lady." He pulled Janine toward the truck. "And you lot need to start tuning up and getting ready." He led her to the truck's tail gate for a little privacy. "Thanks for bringing the picnic. It was a very nice break. Sure you don't want to stay and watch the action?"

"Maybe I'll drop Gram off, help her clean up and then head back. I'll bring Gram's big coffee dispenser. I'm curious about the new gadgets." Janine chuckled. "*Mellow-skin?* Really?"

Ian nodded. "You have to admit, it's innovative. Emma and Oliver came up with that one. These kids are really imaginative. We've got ultralow and ultrahigh band audio and video, and Ben didn't mention it, but he rigged an audio receiver to automatically shift subsonic patterns into the sonic range. There's a three second delay, but it's very close to real time, so it'll be interesting. Maybe we can have an actual conversation with a spirit."

Then he told her about how they designed the thin film for the *mellow-skin*, but she got distracted watching his neck move as he spoke. He recently shaved off his thick beard, and although she had adored it, she was happy to see the lines of his jaw again. She loved how he kept his sideburns just a tad too long. But his mouth stopped moving and she realized that he stopped talking.

"Sorry, I got a little distracted."

Ian leaned in and gave her a nice kiss. "I like it when you get distracted that way."

"Speaking of distractions, did you know there might be séance seekers in the orchard tonight? Gram says they're a regular thing now."

Ian nodded. "We're kind of counting on it. I'm told they've had lots of success with the Mary ghost out here."

"They've actually had success, how? I thought the river stones held the spiritual energy from those ghosts, and the stones have been obliterated," Janine said. "And the dictum. Wasn't the dictum met? Why would the Mary ghost hang around if her purpose had been met?"

Ian shook his head. "Maybe it's an echo. Or, those boulders did not hold the energy of Mary. Perhaps her essence is in the trees, or in that little tombstone. One thing is certain, people are still reporting consistent encounters in this orchard. You remember Angie Minnihan, the redhead from Kiki's séance? Well, she's one of the local mediums. She insists there is still a very strong presence haunting the area. We're expecting her to bring two groups later tonight."

"Angie Minnihan?" Janine recalled Angie.

Angie had been very eager to participate in the *Spectral Analysis* research and production. She consented to an interview, the séance, and she even played a part in the wagon train reenactment skit at the river. She played her own direct ancestor, Ingrid Stauch, the mother of the girl who became the river ghost.

The metal charm from Gram's wooden box popped into her head. The Saint Comba charm belonged to Irene Lumen, that's what the paper scratched with Irene's name implied. In the original diary of the wagon train, it mentioned that Irene Lumen and Ingrid Stauch were related. Janine was certain she remembered that connection correctly. If Irene had been a witch, it's likely that her cousin Ingrid had also been a witch. Either way, the charm suggests there must have been a pagan in their lineage.

"What is it?" Ian noticed her unease.

"Nothing, I'm just pondering something Gram found in her attic," she said. "Old jewelry, possibly from the wagon train. There were some interesting pieces in the box. I may have found the perfect ring for you, but you should have a look at it and tell me what you think."

"You found a wedding band for me?" His eyes brightened and he kissed her deeply. She felt flooded with warmth at his spontaneous burst of emotion. "I can't wait to see it." He kissed her again.

Ian had wanted to marry right away. When he showed up on her doorstep a few weeks before the start of the fall term, he urged her to elope that very day. But Janine couldn't just marry without telling her family, and then her sister and niece vehemently insisted on being present for the vows. So, instead of an elopement, they agreed to a small ceremony at the Thanksgiving break, hopefully in Gram's back yard if it wasn't still torn up. Her sister Juliana already planned to visit Gram on that holiday and it fell well after Kiki's important pagan events Scotland.

Ian was still being quite attentive with his kisses, and they didn't notice someone had walked up until a deliberate sound interrupted them.

"Ahem."

Chet stood a few feet away holding the blanket and large picnic basket. He gave them an amused pressed-lip smile before shyly looking away. Janine could hear Gram chatting as she got closer. Janine and Ian both jumped off the tail gate so Chet could load up the picnic supplies. Gram came up behind him and added the small cooler.

"I'm going to have a small sticky note on each door with your names on them," Gram said. "And I'll put a big sign on the bathroom door as well. That door looks just like all the others and there's no way to know until you find it for the first time."

"Thank you, ma'am. It was very nice meeting you, Gram. And you too, Mrs. McNally… Miss Stinger… Miss… Janine," Chet stammered.

"You should just call me Janine," she told him.

Chet nodded shyly, then skittered off. He seemed a tad timid for a large muscle-bound man. His bulk probably made him appear older than his years, she concluded. Ian did mention that Ben was the only graduate student in the bunch. Then, Ian helped her close the tail gate and remained by the side of the road, watching them drive off.

Janine returned with a large dispenser filled with coffee and a platter of fresh baked cookies. Gram insisted on whipping out the cookies before heading to bed. She predicted the doctor's researchers would need a little sugar on their late night coffee break.

As she passed the new gravel parking area, Janine spotted a car with people sitting inside. Were they coming or going? Janine continued up the road and parked behind the van again. She spotted Ian standing with his arms crossed facing the orchard. She stepped on the parking break and dimmed the headlights. Chet appeared and waved. He trotted over to help her out of the truck and held the door open for her.

"Thank you." She passed him the large tray of cookies. Chet smiled big.

"I was hoping," he scanned the cookies. "Gram looks like the kind of grandma that always comes through."

Janine laughed, he certainly hit the nail on the head with that remark. Ian strolled over and Janine passed him the large coffee dispenser. She followed them around to the lit area and the table someone set up near the van. She could see the shadows of Emma and Oliver in the trees growing larger and more defined as they came into the light.

"Just in time," Ian kissed her. "We're taking a little break in the action right now. Angie's got a second set of ghost seekers just arriving. I need to warn you," he pulled her to the side, "Someone mentioned that you might be back and Angie became very excited. I think she's going to ask if you to join their small group. She goes by Mistress Mini, by the way."

Janine's encounter with the ghost in the orchard had been a huge highlight in the documentary film of the Rio Linda area. Angie would certainly ask Janine to at least take photos with her guests, it could only help her séance business. But it was just the sort of attention that turned Janine off about the television show, the celebrity. Janine did not enjoy being on camera, or the notoriety that came with it. Sure enough, the small group from the gravel parking area headed right toward them. Janine noticed Emma and Oliver eyeing her.

"How's the testing so far?" Janine asked them.

"We've got nothing, nothing, and nothing." Emma grumbled. She moved to the table to grab a couple of cookies.

Janine moved closer to Oliver to inspect the sleeve on his arm. It looked soft and resembled sheer tights. She could see very thin wires snaking through the seams and noticed very small dots scattered everywhere.

"It feels constantly creepy," Oliver confessed. "It's like a million worms are sliding around my arm. I'm just now getting used to it enough to ignore it."

Emma delivered a cookie to Oliver. Apparently, they had bad luck finding paranormal activity and were disappointed. Angie Minnihan's first group had consisted of two boisterous couples that laughed through their entire hour in the orchard. Even though the séance members claimed to "feel a presence" and "hear faint voices," the

Spectral Analysis gadgets didn't agree. Angie Minnihan admitted that even though her participants were happy, it was a failed outing. The tipsy California tourists basically spooked themselves with their active imaginations. Angie declared that the night might not be ripe for the orchard ghost to appear.

"Mistress Minni says the ghost only appears if descendants of the wagon train are near. She was pretty excited to hear that you might be back tonight. She felt certain the ghost would appear with the two of you here, even though there's no moon." Emma peeked hopefully at Janine. "But the doctor said you might not be into that."

The new moon affects the tides as vigorously as a full moon. It's no different for the aether of spiritual energy, Gwen once told her.

Angie Minnihan entered the halo of flood lights with a trio of middle aged women. The women each toted a large glass of wine and sipped while chatting and giggling. Angie was clad in a hooded velvet cape and carried a soft mushy bag of items. Janine shook hands with each of the ladies while Doctor McNally greeted them enthusiastically. He asked if they had any objections to having their excursion filmed, and they didn't. When he told them some of the footage might be used on an upcoming show, the women became very excited. He needed them to sign off on an agreement and they were very happy to comply.

Emma and Oliver wore skeptical expressions, probably wondering what a ghostly spirit might possibly have to say to those wine drinking women. As Ian obtained their signatures, Janine allowed Angie to lure her from the small crowd. Before Angie could say a thing, Janine pointed to her velvet bag.

"What do you have in there? Anything useful? Do you have jet or black tourmaline?"

"Yes," Angie said, suddenly alert. "I also have a rose candle."

"Do you have a stone for everyone? One for each of those ladies to hold? And something for the doctor's students?" Janine asked.

"I have five tourmaline stones, and I also have a big bag of bay leaves," Angie said.

Kiki Mellow claimed to be a witch, and all her friends claimed to be witches. Not the worship the devil, cast evil spells, and ride on broomsticks variety. Her coven of friends studied from an ancient book of pagan practices passed down from mother to daughter for generations.

The study and knowledge began before monotheism and then incorporated itself into the folds of society as the world changed into the current male dominated system. Saint Comba had been a witch as well. A witch that met and accepted Jesus as the savior of men, because men needed saving. The world would cease to exist without both the masculine and feminine aspects mixing together, and together they formed the aether of the cosmos and the Trio of Wells.

Janine ruminated on those ideas, because one of Kiki's coven friends, Gwen Murphy, began feeding the information to her little by little over the past months. Both Kiki and Gwen claimed Janine was a gifted speaker to the spirits and might even be able to command them, and Janine felt herself beginning to agree with them. So many unexplainable events contributed to her paradigm shift regarding the paranormal, especially the encounter with the ghost in the Chicago woods. She called on that ghost more than once, and that ghost had saved her life, she was sure of it. That ghost sent her a Comba charm, exactly like the one in Grams wooden box, and in some opaque way, Janine felt that she was being drawn into action for some important event.

A vital lesson Janine gathered after summoning the woods ghost was; that a spirit could be dangerous and unpredictable, like a wild animal. Both Kiki and Gwen had been vulnerable when the woods ghost appeared, so, most of Gwen's lessons revolved around minimizing the danger.

Black tourmaline proved to be an essential mineral for protection. No one knew why it worked, but like gravity, it just did. Gwen's lessons increased Janine's curiosity, and she constantly wondered if she could really do it: summon a ghost at will, whenever she wanted. She'd been itching to try again, since the encounter in Thatcher Woods, but Janine would need someone to see the ghost, a receiver to verify it. Perhaps Mistress Mini was a talented receiver.

"Caroline Govant always insisted that Mary is a kind spirit," Angie said softly.

Janine nodded. "I know, but there's nothing wrong with being a little careful."

"Does this mean you'll participate in my group?" Angie asked.

Janine nodded.

Angie was elated.

The séance participates were excited.

The doctor's research crew became hopeful.

Only Doctor McNally appeared a little apprehensive.

Mistress Mini instructed each of the research crew to place a bay leaf into their shirts, above their hearts, and gave each of her participants a sample of black tourmaline to clutch in their left hands. The research crew laughed about the bay leaves, but placed them as directed before disappearing into the orchard.

The gaggle of séance women stood at the edge of the tree line emptying a fresh bottle of wine into their glasses. Ian watched them, then strolled up next to her.

"Are you sure about this?" he asked. "We're going to be filming and may use some of the clips on the show. You don't have to do this for me, you know, you can run home and warm up the bed. I'm perfectly happy with that, even prefer imagining you there, rather than in those trees. You weren't too fond of the Mary spirit, as I recall."

"I've seen scarier," Janine said.

She told him bits and pieces of the Thatcher Woods séance, but not everything. He overheard Kiki and Gwen refer to Janine as a *dragoma*, a speaker to the spirits, but didn't know how much stock Ian put in their witching beliefs. He seemed to accept most of them, but not all of them.

"Don't you want your students to get something to record? Apparently, I'm the person to call if you want a ghost to appear, just ask Kiki and Gwen."

He kissed her, then strapped a small earpiece over her right ear. He adjusted the microphone so it wouldn't bother her. "Thank you. But at least wear one of these, and I'll come running at your slightest word. I'm going to have you on hot mic. Is there anyone you want to hear?"

"Oliver with the skin," she said.

He nodded. "Good luck, and don't faint."

Janine followed Mistress Mini and her three séance participants into the orchard. Ian lent her a flashlight, but she kept it turned off. The electric lantern Angie carried illuminated the ground plenty for their small group and

Janine didn't want to spoil the ambience of Angie's activity. Although her earbud was turned down quite low, she could hear the research crew's excited babble. Most likely, the EMF box picked up some vibes. Janine grinned at their excitement. They would learn soon enough that heavy footsteps could set off a bleep or two on that box, and those drinking women were stepping very heavily. She decided to dream up an original rhyme for the ghost of Mary Miller. What type of charm would woo that spirit out on a dark night?

Angie escorted them to a spot cleared of almond husks and fallen debris. A flat-topped stone messy with frozen wax dribbles lay in the center. The large shadows moving in the trees must belong to Ian's gang, Janine noted. She could easily pick out Chet, but Emma and Oliver were harder to distinguish until they moved. Emma walked with a bounce in her step while Oliver glided from place to place like a shadowy ninja.

Janine found her spot near the stone, sat down, and nodded at Angie to go ahead and do her thing. Angie positioned a large three-tapered candle on the flat top rock. There were rose petals of red and white mixed into the wax.

"I am going to light this slender candle and pass it to each of you," Angie informed her giggly ladies. "Remember to inhale deep breaths to clear your heads, calm yourselves, then light one of the wicks."

She took her own cleansing breaths before passing the slender taper to her left. The first woman took obvious deep breaths before setting her wick aflame. She passed the taper on and the other two mimicked her. Angie's ladies were very tipsy, Janine noticed. When Janine accepted the taper, she blew it out and set it down. Then, Angie began to sing in a soft sweet voice. Janine could not understand any of the words, but the soft tune succeeded in quieting the giggling women. They listened silently as Angie sang her eerie song, mesmerized.

"I think I'm starting to feel something brewing," one whispered huskily after Angie quieted. The others agreed, and they all proceeded to giggle again.

"Let us concentrate." Angie used an ominous voice, low and halting. "Mary, Mary of the orchard, we desire your presence. Come to us and show us your essence. We call on you to visit and reveal yourself. We come as friends and desire an audience. Come now, spirit of the orchard, come out, come out and quench our curiosity, As I command it, so shall it be." Angie peered at Janine. "Would you also address the spirit?"

Should she? Could she? Janine drew in a deep breath and let it go slowly. Why not try? Try it all by herself without Kiki or Gwen around. Did she need them to do it? Maybe yes, maybe no. Was Angie a receiver?

"May I suggest holding the gemstones between your palms like this." Janine clasped her hands together.

Gwen advised that a good way to keep a spirit from invading your core was to place your hands together in a prayer or clasping position in front of your chest. *Best done with a bit of jet, very dark amethyst, or black tourmaline between the palms. Some sisters use a Christian rosary made with those very stones.*

"Keep hold of them like that." Janine turned to Angie. "I have a little charm we can recite. It's one that Kiki Mellow would approve of."

That wasn't entirely a lie, Kiki would likely approve of any charm Janine might dream up. She actually encouraged Janine to practice developing them. Bringing up Kiki's name had the desired effect, Angie and her participants were very eager to try anything Kiki Mellow would approve of. Janine waited for them to calm down and then recited her charm made up for Mary.

"To one that spread a dictums dread, to us appear, and come you near. Meet us under this almond tree. So I command, so mote it be."

The temperature instantly dropped and the three women went stone silent. Chet's voice filtered faintly into her receiver, calling out the falling numbers on his thermal-panger. Emma and Oliver were also talking, noting swings and changes in the gadgets they carried. But Janine tuned out Ian's college students to focus around the circle. She repeated the charm.

"To one that spread a dictums dread, to us appear, and come you near. Meet us under this almond tree. So I command, so mote it be."

The facial expressions in the circle went from giddy, to confused, to slightly alarmed. The temperature drop was certainly noticeable without need of any thermal gage. A familiar charged sensation began to develop and the hairs on her arms stood on end. Angie's eyes darted around expectantly, then flew to the rising smoke from the rose candle. It swirled and collected into an unusual wispy cloud above the rock alter. It became thicker and thicker as the temperature dropped faster and faster.

Oliver, in her earbud, complained about the *mellow-skin* and Emma's dim voice noticed something on one of her cameras.

"Ian, Emma," Janine whispered into the microphone. "Is Emma getting something in the middle of the circle? Above the candle?"

"Aye. A bit of light, like last time." Ian's voice filtered over the airwaves right into her ear, soothing her. "Do you see something?"

"It's a form," Janine whispered. Then, she spoke to the spirit, *"Yes, yes, Mary. Come you near and meet us here. Meet us under this almond tree, so I command, so mote it be."*

The smoky cloud morphed and grew thicker and denser by the second. It began to resemble the body of a young girl. Janine watched arms and legs stretch out of the central mass as the ghost took shape. More smoky darkness swirled around, and a head formed. Everything but the eyes filled in on that familiar face. Then, her clothes took on a dingy, murky color.

Is that what happened the last time, when her eyes had been closed?

Angie's middle lady dropped her stone and the sound of the impact echoed to the tree tops. The ghostly girl twirled around and the woman let out a whimper. The woman's eyes grew into wide circles as she cringed from the specter.

"Pick it up," Janine gently urged. "Pick up your stone."

But the lady was frozen with fear and didn't seem able to move. All three of the séance guests seemed frozen in place. Even Angie appeared frightened as she stared toward the nearly solid smoky girl in their circle. Janine watched the spirit move a fraction closer to the woman who dropped her stone.

"No!" Janine said firmly. *"Stay away from her."*

The ghost spun round to glare at Janine. Her sockets had filled in with eyes. It was the familiar sight of Mary Miller. Her dark hair hung over her right shoulder in a single braid. Her eyes were black, and her lips and skin were red.

For a moment, she was a pleasant young child standing in the orchard, grinning, then quite suddenly, her face became a clear grimace of anger. Janine could make out a bit of Caroline Govant in that face. Her heart raced, pounding out of control, and the knavish girl let out a laugh that sounded like Caroline's when Janine had accused her of leading a cult. Janine studied plenty of photos of Caroline as a young girl, and this ghost smiled in the same manner.

Then, the ghostly girl moved out of the circle, toward the trees, her motion was both agitated and quick. Her voice carried back toward the circle, a lullaby in direct discordance with her choppy dysfunctional movements.

Heed this, her voice wavered similar to guitar strings out of tune. *One each for redemption.*

Then, the ghostly voice was replaced by a human yelp. It was Oliver. He screeched into the cold dark night. Janine could hear Emma's rapid voice wondering what was going on, what was happening to him. Oliver's soft wail echoed painfully.

"My arm, the skin!" he moaned. "Something's grabbing my arm, I think."

Janine quickly stood and peered into the trees, focusing on the area she last noted Oliver and Emma. She couldn't see a thing. Then, she remembered the flashlight and scooped it up. It had three beams, low red, regular dim, and high beam white. She flipped on the high beam white as Angie and the drunk women moved behind her. Janine scanned until she got to the right spot. One of Angie's women screamed, making her jump.

Emma stood like a deer in headlights staring back at them, while Oliver appeared startled and held his arm straight out, the one with the *mellow-skin*. They both seemed oblivious to the dark cloud of mist surrounding them.

Oh my, Janine's blood raced. *Calm, calm, calm*, she told herself. Gwen had warned her once: never let a spirit feel your fear, or they may begin to control you.

Janine forced herself to breathe easy as she watched the ghost phase in and out. The spirit had Oliver's arm in her jaw, like a dog. Then, the spirit let go and grinned at Janine with an unsavory glint in her eye. *That little shit!* She knew he would feel that bite.

"*Go! Leave us!*" Janine yelled.

And just like that the ghost disappeared, poof! No more mist.

The temperature began to readjust, and the séance ladies started moving. Both Emma and Oliver appeared stunned, backing away in confusion and she realized they thought she had been yelling at them. Ian's voice dribbled through her earpiece, but the blood thumping in her ears drowned him out. She felt woozy.

Janine reached to pull the earpiece away, she needed to control her fear. That entire experience had been so unexpected. *Mary is a kindred spirit*, Caroline Govant had insisted. *I don't think so, Caroline*, Janine thought. She didn't think so then, and certainly did not think so now. Her muscles felt completely exhausted and she just wanted to lie down.

"Not you two." Janine waved Emma and Oliver to her. "Not you two. You two come here."

Angie Minnihan couldn't stay and talk, she needed to escort her shaken up séance guests back to her parlor. One of the guests couldn't stop crying, the woman who dropped her stone and witnessed a very "evil" black mass with glowing eyes. *It wanted to grab my heart, I swear it,* she blubbered between hiccups. She had also been the screamer and watched the dark mass circling Oliver. The other two women only saw smoky fog gather above the candle and got chilled, but they each agreed *a feeling of dread* had closed into circle. Angie visualized Mary. She described a distinct girl outlined in the mist, and she heard the voice warning them to heed the dictum. She'd seen the same apparition many times before, just not as clearly.

Ian's students didn't see anything other than "needle swings" on their devices. Chet recorded temperature changes, noted odd motion on the incongruent detection device, and watched the EMF antenna lock and track activity from the circle to Emma and Oliver.

Emma filmed faint flickers of light on her ultralow IR camera, and "something" on the ultrahigh UV recorder. Emma and Oliver didn't notice anything with the naked eye and were skeptical of the woman who said a mist surrounded them. Oliver felt a terrible pressure from the *mellow-skin*. He believed it had have been caused by either the temperature drop or faulty wiring. Yet, under the thin sheath, distinct red marks stuck out on his arm in a crescent pattern, like a bite mark. Ben took several photos of the marks.

Janine didn't say much about anything, she only confirmed that the ghost of Mary Miller did indeed visit them. She didn't want to scare Angie's ladies any more than necessary. All in all, the research crew would go home with a ton of recorded data to review.

Janine sat puddled in the truck while they gathered their equipment, feeling weak. She asked Ian to drive her in the F-

150 back to Gram's house. Ben and the crew followed in the van.

That woman was not drunk enough to hallucinate, Janine told herself. *Angie witnessed almost everything with no ill effects, so she's a receiver. And I should just accept it, I can summon ghosts.*

Kiki once asked Janine how many experiences she needed before she would no longer question her paranormal abilities. Perhaps, she was finally there.

Typically, after a *Spectral Analysis* shoot, the crew would drink whisky and debrief the encounter in the comfort of Gram's den, or other comfortable gathering place. But with the crew all under drinking age, and exhausted from the excitement, they each went straight to bed.

Chapter 3
Scotland

Kiki

Kiki woke very late in the day. The previous night had spiraled into a awful disaster. Going on a date with Rory O'Hara, an old boyfriend from her school days, was a huge mistake. Why did she imagine things would be easier with Rory simply because she was familiar with him and he was a coven lad?

He had been thrilled when she called. He always knew she'd seek him out for her awakening, he just didn't think it would take so long. At one point, he laughed at her Kiki Mellow persona and said he found it very *cute*. Nice to see she had melted from the frozen girl he once knew. He always felt there was unfinished business between him and his wee Kiera Lovett.

It was her own fault for listening to Gwen and calling on Rory, but she agreed, there weren't many men that she could trust with the little experiment she needed to conduct. Perhaps it was karma that she needed to suffer through it, because she should have done it years ago when she dated Rory back in school. If she had opened up just a little bit back then, when it was normal behavior to learn the ropes, she wouldn't be so apprehensive now. But she had been completely focused on developing her Core Well, and that entailed shunning any type of physical pleasure. Having an older fellow, a coven lad like Rory to deflect away the other blokes, had been very helpful. He had been quite the gentleman with her, gambling that he'd be called on to attend her sacred ritual someday.

And now, here was Gwen at her kitchen table, fishing for the results of Kiki's experiment. There she was, sitting across the table with her wicked lemon scones and prying blue eyes.

"Come on then, let's have it. How far did you let yourself go before shutting off your base door?"

"You don't need to give me your truth scones, Gwen, I have no ego left in this situation." Kiki drank a bit of the coffee Gwen brought and took a bite of a lemon scone. "Well, Rory brought me home after a fun filled night of tomfoolery and I invited him in for more fooling around, in which I consciously allowed every ounce of energy into my base zones."

Gwen suggested Kiki prepare before her ritual by experiencing passion energy through her base aspects, to get used to it. It might help her resist diverting the energy for comfort's sake during her ritual. She didn't want to cheat herself from the truth of the experience. An awakening couldn't happen with a closed Base Well or without a true climax. Then, it would just be a physical act and not a true awakening. Gwen's colors, aura, hair, everything, ran very red, as her own passions ran deep. No woman had as healthy a Base Well as Gwen Murphy.

"I actually allowed the energy through my bosom, because he seemed pretty focused there."

"Ho ho, so Rory O'Hara finally got to second base." Gwen laughed. "Nice of you to finally give him what he always talked about. Were you able to let that passion flow freely?"

Kiki could feel the heat creep into her face and nodded. "As I said earlier, yes. It was very unexpected, titillating and uncomfortably warm. I really wanted to alter the energy to my core right away. I felt so, so…"

"Vulnerable?"

Kiki nodded. "I had no idea minor massaging up top could quickly flood a body down below."

Gwen laughed again, this time her whole body got into it.

"I could barely sit still, my private areas felt hot, I admit, nice and not nice at the same time. Soon after his ministrations, I completely shut down my base zone. Now I know why men are heavily drawn to cleavage, it gets them quick results."

"You have very nice breasts, Kiki, very eye catching. Are you telling me this is the first time you let someone go there?"

"Yes. I've never let anyone touch me that way before," Kiki admitted. "Is it the same for everybody?"

"Everybody is different, of course," Gwen said sadly. "But I certainly enjoy it."

"Oh, Gwen, I'm so sorry." Kiki came around and gave her tall friend a hug. "I'm such an idiot."

"You really are, Kiera, and a complete minx." Gwen hugged her back. "You need to stop shutting off your passion zone. Believe me, eventually, that vulnerability, the giving in, becomes power. You need to experience these sensations and not run away from them. Just go on and give it another practice or two. I admit to feeling very angry at you right now. Nobody gets to twenty-eight in this day and age, you know. Resisting and avoiding the natural flow of any type of energy is an aberration. Are you going to give Rory another go? Could he be the stag for your ritual? He's always adored you and no one would be surprised if you chose him. Or, will you try to woo that detective back?"

"That one's not interested."

Kiki wished she could woo the detective back. Her experiment would have gone differently with Bob Anderson. She would not have had the desire to alter the flow of energy with the detective. He mixed his energy in a way that she could easily accept, without fear of losing control.

"I can't ask Rory, either. I believe he actually loves me a little bit, and I won't have him chasing after me or break his heart."

"He's always loved you," Gwen nodded. "More than a little. So, a blind stag then?"

"God, no. No blind stag. And I'm afraid to see *the list* that surely awaits me at the cottage. I could never allow a stranger to touch me like that, I'd totally shut down." Kiki stared at Gwen. "I'm floating the idea of inviting Max Colliers. We have a very flirty rapport and I believe I could accept his passion adequately, and it's not like he has a heart to break, not like Rory. I'm familiar with Max and know his intent would be straightforward."

Gwen's shocked, amused face was well worth it. She wasn't expecting that name to come out of the hat. Gwen bit thoughtfully into a scone. "I can actually see that working out fairly well." She nodded, then started laughing again.

Max Colliers was the executive producer of the *Spectral Analysis* television show Kiki starred in. He happened to be a salacious rogue who sported in the seduction of women. His beguiling nature and handsome appearance actually made him very pleasant company. He might not believe in the ideas involved in a witch's ritual, but Max would certainly honor them and play the game to the best of his ability, and he would jump at the chance if she offered it, not just to couple with Kiki, but to participate in a sultry pagan event. One of his life goals seemed to revolve around having various sexual experiences. He had recently fixated on Janine Stinger when he believed her knife scars implied she enjoyed sexual cutting games. He became quite upset when she refused to share anything about those experiences with him. It would be hard for Max to pass up a scandalous sex ritual.

The thought of Janine Stinger brought that late night phone call back to mind. Kiki had been very tipsy when the call came and begged off a little quickly. She picked up her phone to find the message with the photo. There it was, the Comba charm. She checked the clock.

"What time is it in California?" Kiki asked Gwen.

"Oh goodness, that's some quick math you're asking." Gwen pulled out her own phone and tapped away. "I've got a world time app. It looks to be about six in the morning there. What's cooking in California? Ian didn't tell Janine what his arse of a father said, did he? Why does he even talk to that man anymore?"

Kiki went ahead and dialed the number. Knowing Janine, the girl wouldn't be able to sleep with thinking about the charm. Kiki shook her head at Gwen as the connection rang.

"It's not that."

After a couple of rings, she heard a commotion and then a very groggy voice. Ian grumbled through the line, probably still mostly asleep. In a hushed voice, he told her Janine was sleeping and they had gotten in very late. Did Kiki realize the time difference? He refused to wake Janine, she had a big night. She helped summon the orchard ghost in Rio Linda and needed to sleep.

Kiki passed her phone to Gwen. The Comba charm lit up the screen.

"Sounds like your protégé has summoned a spirit," Kiki told her. "Not only that, look what she found at Gram's house. It came out of a box from the attic, she said."

All of Gwen's humor altered into a very serious expression on her freckled face. Her natural reddish aura took on a more anxious orange, and she pushed red wispy strands of wavy hair from her eyes as she pulled Kiki's phone closer. She studied the photo.

"You're joking, she *found* this? Another Comba charm?" Gwen asked. "We haven't seen this one, there's a wee blemish in the corner. Every girl in the coven wanted one of these charms when we were young, how does Janine manage to have two delivered to her?"

They contemplated the photo in silence. Not counting the one in the picture, Kiki had only seen two other Comba charms in her life. The most recent one popped up less than a year ago, in Chicago of all places. It came by way of a haunted man in the service of a ghostly witch, one who had been strangled in the woods. The other charm belonged to her late Auntie Celeste, Ian's mother, and her auntie wore it sparingly, only on a special occasion. Kiki recently asked Ian's father if he knew of its location and Roger McNally claimed it was gone, lost.

"Kiki, remember my vision in the woods?" Gwen asked. "A gathering of women hand in hand?"

Kiki nodded at her.

"Well, I've been dreaming of it, often, since that night."

Gwen picked up her coffee and walked around, pacing to dissipate her anxiety. Kiki watched the orange in her aura wane ever so slightly.

"At first, I imagined it was a celebration, like part of a festival even, but now I feel that it may be a massive summoning to end something, or to start something, something big. Beyond the boundaries of just our coven of sisters. Something dark. Not a happy event."

"With ties to the charms?" Kiki asked.

"We should go see Trinity," Gwen told her. "She's keeper of the books. If something is brewing, she would know, and I should tell her of this vision, write it down in the book, just in case it has meaning. I've been waiting for you to be ready to go to the Isle. Trinity has been asking after you and expects me to bring you."

Oh, Trinity, Kiki grimaced. She needed more time before a visit to her mother. She always felt like such a little girl near her and she had a few issues to work out regarding her awakening before letting Trinity add her two cents.

Kiki made a command decision and sent Max Colliers a detailed message inviting him to participate in her awakening ritual. She didn't mince words, but sent him a link to a website that explained a ceremony similar to what the coven planned. It covered the usual: candles, drinking, singing, drumming, and dancing skyclad in a natural setting with the sexual awakening of a virgin witch. The coven always chose a nice spot near the cliffs of the Quiraing in the Trotternish area of Skye. It included a beautiful and dramatic landscape which the sisters often used at the Samhain and for awakening rituals. But an awakening event was very rare. Not every witch celebrated an end to their celibacy, only those that had taken a vow of chastity at fourteen and kept that vow for seven years, and if that witch persistently kept her vow for seven more years, then the ritual became significant on an exponential level. The tantric power that passed to the coven was a blessing to them all. But it needed to be remedied in ritual before the witch reached her twenty ninth year. If she waited too long, the ritual would lose meaning and her triad might never become balanced.

It was a three hour drive from Inverness to her mother's cottage on Skye. Kiki slept some of the way, but woke to answer her phone. Less than an hour after leaving the message, Max called with questions.

Was she joking? No. *Wasn't she still angry about the incident with Janine?* Of course. *Would everyone really be nude, outside, under a full moon?* Skyclad, and yes, though some wore hooded capes. *Did she imply that she actually planned to have sex with him?* No implications there, that's exactly why she was inviting him. *In front of people?* Only a few others, seven women. *Did she also imply that she was a virgin?* She'd let him determine that during the ritual. Max laughed, then continued, *Would he be expected to have sex with other people?* Only if he wanted. *So, it's a witch's orgy?* No, not usually, but if he inspired another girl in the ritual, and they were both willing, they could certainly do as they pleased. No one would frown upon them. Three sisters would be there to get him warmed up, so he was sure to be plenty satisfied if he was worried. *You are being perfectly serious?* Very serious. The ritual was all about animal instincts and eroticism, right up his alley. *This isn't some sort of joke they're playing? Pay back for Janine? Because he'd understand that and would fly over just for them to get it out of their systems.* Well, he'd have to take that chance then. But she assured him, she was inviting him to a serious pagan event. *And you're definitely going to participate in it?*

"Of course, it's an important pagan rite. This is a very sacred ritual for me, I'm a priestess in my coven and I want to do things right by my sisters. There are other men the Priestess of the Base Well can call on, but I have the right to bring my own male. I could invite anyone, Max, but I really think you'd appreciate it more than everyone I know. You've said it before, many times, we should do this because we understand each other and are physically suited for one another. I want you here. I'm asking you to open the door to my Base Well, my passions, and initiate me into the world of sex and pleasure. Just let me know if it's too much to ask and I'll choose someone else."

"Wow, Kiki, I don't know what to say. I really want to believe this is a real thing and not a joke on me, pay back," Max said over the line. "Let me check my calendar and get back to you."

"Of course," Kiki said. "Think it over."

Gwen glanced at her with a raised red eyebrow. The sun was setting, and they still had twenty more minutes on their drive.

"I see you're brooding about the balance of things," Gwen said. "But don't feel rushed. If you're not feeling right about the ritual, you shouldn't do it. I know the coven is super excited and this is a momentous event for the sisters, but it's also a very intimate experience. Many witches break their vow on purpose, to avoid a ritual. You could easily do the same. You can take things slow and private, call up your detective. Kiki, you have almost no experience here, the other sisters don't quite realize it because of your flirty behavior and that television show. Usually in a ritual like this, it's a young lassie in a heated state, yearning to be released from her vow as quickly as possible. That's not you."

"A high coven virginal priestess run and hide? My sexual awakening belongs to all the sisters. I'm a Core Master. I'm going to follow what's written and celebrate the aethereal energy the old fashioned way. I'm not going to cheat and I'm not going to hide, and it's going to be a true awakening, a true joining of Core, Head, and Base, in ritual." Kiki was angry again. "And the more I think about it, Max Colliers is completely right for this role, he was born for it. Perhaps that's the reason he was placed in my path in the first place. There's a reason for everything."

Her phone suddenly pinged with a message from Max. She read it quickly. Not the man she originally wanted, but she felt relieved that she could now dismiss the vetted list Trinity was compiling. She smiled at Gwen.

"Can you believe it? The bastard has cleared his schedule to frolic wantonly in the glen with me. I told you he was completely right for this role."

Chapter 4
The Coven Cottage

Kiki

Trinity Lovett resided in an old cottage near the coast of Uig Bay in a small crofting village on the island of Skye. The cottage once to belong to Trinity's Great Auntie Meg and Kiki visited every summer of her youth. There, she explored the glens and lochs with the children of other pagan sisters. When her great auntie passed, Trinity moved into the cottage and became the new keeper of the coven books. By that time, Kiki had completed academy and followed her peers to the university. Kiki flittered about with classes but never came close to completing a course of study. She bailed out early and ran off with a friend on a traveling adventure. They meandered from festivals to cultural events, dabbling in fortunes, reading auras, and gaining quite a cult following. It lasted until she decided to visit her cousin Ian in the United States, where she found her way to becoming a television star.

Kiki's mother, Trinity, ran a small bed and breakfast with her business partner, Annelise Batten, Kiki's old traveling friend. Annie had remained on Skye when Kiki left for New York. While waiting on Kiki to return, Annie expanded the business to include an online shop and school of sorts. She conducted a series of online lessons on tarot, tealeaf reading, crystal grids, and herbal magic. As herbalists, they expanded the coven garden, cultivating the weeds and old plants and expanded their drying room. They bottled and sold packets of special herbs over the internet. They also managed a website on ethnobotany and were considered a resource in pagan herbal circles.

Trinity gathered Kiki in for a hug before ushering them into her private sitting room. They arrived too late for dinner, but tea and cookies were served in front of a blazing hearth. If they had used their phones, Trinity would have saved a bit of the baked bass for them. Trinity also offered rooms if they wished to stay the night, but Gwen had a shift the next evening and they planned to drive back.

In the far corner of the room, Kiki noticed a familiar older man sipping a dram of golden fluid, likely a batch from a local homemade highlands mash. He was quite tall, with a head full of speckled salt and pepper hair and wild bushy eyebrows. It was her stand-in father figure, George MacLeod, and Kiki smiled wide at him as he winked at her.

George was one of the many men that circled around her mother all the years of her life. Even after he wed, then divorced, he kept returning as if a tether held him to Trinity Lovett. Perhaps it was because he fancied he was Kiki's real father and often acted as such. George MacLeod boomed with pleasure at the sight of Kiki and Gwen and bestowed generous hugs on them. They both knew George well. He was a local Uig Bay fisherman, and as a young man he helped around the cottage when Auntie Meg had been alive. He took the girls on outings when they were young and all the locals believed Kiki was his illegitimate love child.

"Well, the wee lassie has returned." He gave Kiki a thorough up and down before kissing her cheek. "Ye're quite an eyeful, my bonnie dove, your mother all over again. And Gwen! Ye're a pleasant sight for my weary eyes."

His accent always thickened with whisky. George made his way to the door. He knew the routine. When the witches dropped in, the men must depart.

"I'll just be gone. I dropped off a fresh batch of the MacLeod cask 345 and a bit-o-bass. I'm off, ladies. If ye'll be stayin' the night, mayhap I'll bring my young nephew, Andrew, aroond. Ye kin get a good keek at him. Young, but he's able." He chuckled at Kiki.

Trinity escorted him to the door, flirting all the while. Kiki watched her mother's emerald eyes flash at the old man teasingly. Kiki grimaced at how Trinity leaned in just barely touching him but kept a scant sliver of air between them as if she didn't notice she invaded his space. One might believe she couldn't resist him. Kiki would be happy if Trinity would act her age for one second. Did she always need to behave so openly ardent with George MacLeod and every other man who happened to drop into her presence?

Then, like a splash of cold water in the face, Kiki realized that George was correct: Kiki was the spitting image of her mother Trinity, in looks and behavior. They both had dark wavy hair, green eyes, and dramatically curvy bodies. Kiki also knew that their mannerisms, mode of movement, facial expressions, and even their auras, were alike. *Her mother all over again*, George was spot on. The only difference between them was their skin tone. Trinity's skin shone ivory white with a sprinkle of freckles, while Kiki's skin was a deep smooth olive color.

Trinity once divulged that Kiki's coloring came from her true father, a Spaniard of Moorish descent, powerfully built, with hazel eyes, a strong square jaw, and handsome beyond belief. Trinity swore his aura often took on a pinkish hue. He was her green man at the Beltane one year and they spent three days of the festival conceiving a baby, but she let him go when invited her to transplant to an eastern country with him. No way, not after the disaster her sister made by marrying a demon, abandoning the coven ways, and following Roger McNally's orders. Don't worry, Trinity purred, she had loved him a bit, and she dearly missed him after he left. But it was for the best, a man just got in the way with the raising of a daughter, and Kiki was a Beltane baby, a blessing, a true *Next*. And please don't be upset, Trinity urged, she was very sorry that she couldn't remember her green man's actual name. She had called him "mo leannan" and always thought of him with that term of endearment. He will forever be "Leannan" to Trinity, and so he was "Leannan" to Kiki.

Trinity returned with a grin and finally hugged Gwen. She gave Kiki a more careful looking over, during which Kiki rolled her eyes and reached for the bottle of MacLeod 345 to fill their tea cups. Gwen's blue eyes flew open in pleasant anticipation. Nothing ran down as smooth as home cooked highland whisky, especially after a long drive on a cold night, and George MacLeod's batch was always a fine example.

"My darling daughter, how long have you been back? Nearly a month? And you're only now payin' your poor old mum a visit?"

Trinity's green eyes flashed briefly before she spun round to poked up the fire. Then, she accepted a cup of the whisky.

"Really, Kiera! You have Annelise and Gwen, and every girl buzzing about your awakening ritual, are you *truly* still chaste? Is that why you've been hiding from me? I have seen the gossip, and I finally watched a couple of those shows and that documentary movie. If you have broken your vow of chastity, just admit it. Nobody would be upset or think less of you. Well, a few might think a little less, but truth be told, some believe that vow has already been goosed."

"Ugh! Mother, you are impossible."

"Dinna take that tone with me, lass. You've been known to cover your missteps with me, Kiera Lovett. This is nae the time to hide from a broken vow of chastity."

Trinity pulled a magazine from her side chair holder.

"What am I to think, when all these reports are, Kiki Mellow tames this bloke, then succumbs to that one, and look over here, she's hooked the playboy. Dinna get me wrong, lassie, I admit to being a wee proud of this reputation of yours. If you have goosed your vow, at least you've done it in grand style, some of these fellows are nothing to sneeze at."

Trinity flipped to a page with a photo of Kiki and a certain NBA athlete.

"But keep this in mind, lass, an awakening is a sacred ceremony, and I'll not have you make light of it to cover your arse with the sisters. Tisn't unheard of, to hide a broken vow."

"How could you even suggest such a thing," Kiki fumed. "I would never make light of a sacred ceremony!"

"You seem to be making light of quite a lot of our practices that show. You have no qualms about brandishing untenable tea or tarot readings, and that comical, sultry, witch persona you're pushing? What am I supposed to think?

I have seen your behavior on camera, flirting shamelessly with every male in the vicinity, even your own cousin!"

Kiki's arms crossed over her chest and she narrowed her eyes.

Gwen calmly stepped between the mother and daughter to gaze at the magazine. She nodded to Trinity.

"That's a very nice sample of a male in that picture, I don't see how anyone could resist that."

After a pause, they both chuckled.

"Trinity," Gwen added gently, "Kiki has kept her vow beyond a shadow of a doubt. *You know that*. Besides, it's quite clear that this fellow doesn't fancy girls, why do you think she ran around with him so often?"

Trinity pressed her lips together and conceded. She moved to Kiki and administered another hug, a proper embrace, and patted her hair down in her annoying motherly way.

"I'm sorry, my wee yin," she said softly. "You leaving so suddenly upset me. Then, staying away so long got me afraid you lost our ways. You haven't attended one coven event in three years and with the magazines spinning gossip with these odd stories, it got me questioning things. It is not uncommon for girls to fly off and do their own thing, rebel it up a bit, grow up and out of the practice. That's what your grandmother did. I'd understand it."

Trinity took the chair between them and placed her magical green eyes on Kiki. When they looked on her like that, Kiki always felt a surge of love and wanted to please her mother all over again. Why did she need this crazy woman's approval all the time?

"And spending all your time with Ian, I love him, but his father *is* a demon. Never forget that. How do I know what influence the man has on the boy?"

Kiki shook her head. "Ian is a gem, Mother."

"I can't help my bias. Lots of times the apple doesn't fall far from the tree." Trinity turned toward Gwen. "I'm sorry, lass, but I'm not happy with how he left you after all that business, either."

"Trinity," Gwen rolled her eyes. "I'm the one who broke it off. How many times do I need to tell everyone that?"

They gossiped about Ian's upcoming wedding at the end of November. Both Gwen and Kiki planned a trip to California to witness Ian exchange vows with Janine, who was the other girl on the ghost hunting television show. Kiki pointed to a magazine picture of Janine. Trinity believed she resembled a princess, big doe eyes, long auburn hair, long and legs with just the right curves to be quite attractive. Intelligent looking. Trinity wondered out loud if Janine might be a little reserved perhaps, even judgmental? Gwen and Kiki both assured Trinity that Janine was very level headed, nice, and loyal. After Gwen, Ian certainly deserved a loyal girl.

"We've actually come in regards to Janine Stinger," Kiki told Trinity.

"A coincidence then," Trinity said. "Because I've been patiently waiting to ask you about her."

Trinity went to her den console and opened the top drawer. She pulled out a large book, one of Great Auntie Meg's chronicles by the look of it. Auntie Meg always kept a hand written loose leafed collection of important events she often called the *Book of Happenings.* Kiki remembered Meg carefully adding a page to the book after an outing near the Pass of Odall. They had spotted an unidentifiable beast eyeing them. Meg called that animal a demon, one that lost its human shape. She swore it was a man she once knew.

Beware, Auntie Meg warned a very young Kiera Lovett, *a man may become a demon if his core slips away.*

"I dinna watch many of your shows, only a few in the first season," Trinity said. "Then Annelise put on the movie, the documentary you won a prize for, that's when I noticed her, your Janine."

Trinity placed the book on the table in front of Kiki. The old leather cover was cut with a spiral Celtic triskelion.

"Now tell me, daughter, have you seen this book before? Peeked deep into it perhaps? Do you know things that are in it? Used something written in here, maybe, to add spice to that movie of yours?"

"Well," Kiki snapped defensively. "This is one of Great Auntie Meg's book of happenings and I recall one incident she added to those pages, but other than that, I don't know anything in there. I would never use a witches diary without invitation."

"I'm not accusing you of anything, Kiki, I only need to hear you confirm that," Trinity added gently. "That you dinna use words found in here in that movie."

Kiki threw her arms up in vexation. "What's in the book?"

"One each for redemption." Trinity's glowing eyes stared at her. "Those words are written in this book, *One each for redemption*. The same curse in your movie, the one that clings to your friend Janine is recorded in these pages, several times, and I remembered it from my youth. Auntie Meg wrote them here," Trinity paused to drain her cup of whisky.

"The ghost of the wall, a hag of a witch, appeared to myself and Celeste on one of our nightly romps to the Faerie Glen. The hag said those exact words to us." Trinity's eyes shone with emotion. "It made my skin crawl hearing it in your movie and I'm afraid of what it might mean. So, if you say you read it here first, I'll be quite happy."

Kiki moved closer to the book and placed her hand on the smooth leather cover. She asked Trinity if they could see the entry. Trinity had marked the spot with a purple silk ribbon and quickly opened to the correct page.

"I dinna remember everything at first," Trinity admitted, "because I was terrified and then fainted. I was a very young girl at the time."

In giant loose script, Meg had written a short paragraph. An inked oblong circle hovered at the top right hand corner indicating a waning gibbous moon, a witch's knot on the left was drawn to protect against evil. Near the bottom of the page, Meg had sketched a beautiful figure of a woman in the left margin and an old hag in the right. The paragraph read,

The ghost of the wall did appear to young Celeste and Trinity Lovett. Celeste did give a summoning call. She claims to have said, "Come wise soul, to us appear. Show yourself as we come near. Draw us in to make us three, so I command, so mote it be." To which, the spirit answered. She appeared old and hunched, then young and beautiful. Green eyes and smooth skin. But she grew tall and moved in unusual ways and eventually became a hag with black eyes. She gave a warning. To the best of her recollection, Celeste heard, "One each for redemption, forever, unless the curse be washed away." The wall ghost also claimed that, "A **dragoma** *called, one to take the curse from the demon's grasp." And she did warn Celeste that the "demon comes for one such as you,"* *meaning Celeste. I did catch sight of a shadow of the spirit when I heard the girls talking at the wall.*

"There hasn't been another entry for the wall ghost since this one," Trinity told them. "But there are many entries further back in the pages. Look here, an entry from over eighty years ago."

She flipped the pages to a spot marked with a different silk ribbon. This time the moon symbol indicated a waxing crescent and the only other picture was a beautiful unclothed woman sitting on the wall. The short paragraph read,

The spirit of the wall appeared before a séance of six. Present were Abigail, Sara, Meghan, Sissy, Gillian, and Katelyn. Not all saw the young woman on the wall, and only young Sara could give a full description, smooth alabaster skin, deep green eyes, nary a stitch of cloth. Her beautiful body curved into the shape of the moon under which she sat. Everyone heard something akin to whispers, then clear words. All agreed on their content and relayed the speaking to the best of their ability. "Tae wear the saint beware. One each for redemption, must feed the dark soul, 'til such a one wrests this curse from his hands."

"So you see," Trinity sighed, moving nervously around the room. "It's the same curse, one each for redemption, to feed a demon. Every wall entry repeats it, *one each for redemption*, these are not ordinary spirits relaying this curse. The wall ghost, and that one from your movie, not ghosts, but spirits compelled by a demon." Trinity pointed to the names in the older entry. "You see here, that's Great Auntie Meg. Meg always reminisced on her old friends. Gillian MacDonald was killed, strangled. Meg says that Gillian's lover did it because she was leaving him. Abigail Kirkpatrick also met a violent end, and my dear sister Celeste was strangled too, *I know it.* Don't worry, I won't be pointing fingers, but everyone knew she was finally leaving Roger McNally. I bring it up because all these women heard that warning, the curse, from the demon's mouth, before they met a violent end from someone they loved."

"But Meg heard it too," Gwen said gently. "And you and the others. I knew Sissy and Katelyn, they were very old ladies who passed on naturally. Sara was Diana's great grandmother, Cara's mother. I'm missing your point."

"Aye, my dear, tis true. We heard it as well and live on," Trinity said. "But these three that died had something else in common that the rest of us lacked, and I wonder how the same demon haunts your friend's folks half a world away. If there's more to it than what you think, perhaps—"

The den door flew open, and a burst of vivacious energy entered to break up their serious conversation. A woman taller than Kiki, but shorter than Gwen, flashed a mouth full of white teeth at them. Her golden hair had grown longer and curled wilder, and her laughing hazel eyes seemed brighter. Kiki noticed that Annelise Batten put on a few pounds and changed from a twig of a girl to one with a womanly figure. She seemed very happy and healthy, blossoming. Kiki and Gwen both jumped up to greet their old friend.

"So then, Kiera, shall I call you Kiki Mellow?" Annie asked, "Are you going by Kiki or Kiera here in Scotland?"

"Kiki."

Annelise just finished an online tarot lesson and set her prized cards on the side table. The three chatted a bit and laughed as Trinity brewed more tea. Annelise told them of her online lessons and the herb shop. She thanked Kiki very much for recommending folks seek her council, they've gained quite a following from *Spectral Analysis* fans in their online school. Everyone wanted to glean a bit of the ancient ways these days. Then, Annie came round to see what they were looking at.

"Trinity is asking about the curse," Annie noticed. "I thought she was having a heart attack when we heard it in the movie. She hoped you read it in the book and made it all up." Annelise glanced at Trinity, "But we knew deep down something strange was brewing."

Trinity poured everyone a nice cup of tea and passed the honey around. Kiki had gone back to flip through the pages of Auntie Meg's book. Annie vocally admired Meg's skilled and artistic entries, pointing out the perfect symmetry and bold lines in dark ink. Every page pleased the eye. The paper felt thick and the edges were slightly jagged. Small shapes and colors were sprinkled prettily across the pages. Auntie Meg must have made all of the paper using stem cuttings from unwanted herbs and weeds.

As a very young girl, Kiki often watched Meg cook plant matter in lye and then beat the fibers by hand. Auntie Meg often tasked the summer kids to have at the pulpy mess in that big mortar of hers. It was loads of fun for kids, whacking the mess. Some of those thick sheets might contain the energy of their youth beaten into the pulp. Kiki flipped the pages back to the older ghost entry and viewed the warning again. One line caught Kiki's eye and seemed to jump off the page in an ominous way.

Tae wear the saint beware, Kiki placed her finger on it. Gwen and Annie both nodded their heads at the line she pointed out.

"This must be a reference to Saint Comba." Gwen exchanged a look with Kiki.

"Aye," Annie said. "We figured it out because of the charm necklaces."

"Celeste, Gillian, and Abigail," Trinity named them. "They all wore an heirloom necklace with the Saint Comba charm, passed down from mother to daughter. Each wore one when they died, and the charms emit a faint feeling of their death. It makes procuring all of the charms worth a bother, if we hope to solve more of the puzzle. There are many old diaries in Meg's library, most are written poorly, or writ in the old way, but many tell of the curse. I mean to have them translated better. Cara says she'll have a look and help with the old Gaelic and Latin, but some of it is just gibberish."

Gwen sank heavily into a chair and set her teacup on a saucer. Her red brow furrowed and she shook her red head. Trinity stopped talking and waited.

"I have something for the *Book of Happenings*, a distinct vision recently crowded into my subconscious," Gwen told them. "A gathering is coming, an important one, a gathering involving the charms." Gwen recounted her vision for them.

Kiki came round to sit next to Gwen and pulled out her phone. She called up the photo Janine sent of the most recent charm and held it for Annie's round eyes to see, then passed it to Trinity.

"We found a Comba charm for you, Mother," Kiki said very softly.

The magnitude of that coincidence weighed on the very air itself. Kiki continued in a subdued tone.

"Ian's fiancé found it in an old box in her grandmother's attic. There's your demon's connection to

California and perhaps our pagan connection to Janine. Perhaps her distant lineage traces back to this very cottage."

Trinity and Annelise were stunned to see the silver charm in the photo.

"That's incredible!" Annie said to Kiki and Gwen. "Do you know how difficult a time we've had tracking down any of the charms?"

"I can imagine." Kiki glanced at her. "I actually called Roger McNally about Auntie's charm, but he said it was long lost."

"I have it," Trinity told her.

She returned to the console and bent to a lower drawer. Very carefully, she fetched out a carved wooden box and set it atop the leather bound book.

"I have your auntie's Saint Comba necklace in here. Actually, Meg had it. All this time she's kept a collection of them in this box. She may have suspected the unsavory death curse before she died. But she didn't share what she knew, didn't write it down anywhere that I can find. And Meg became a recluse in her old age, shunning people more and more in her paranoia. Maybe she was afraid of what she surmised, afraid to share it, and perhaps she was afraid of the curse herself."

Trinity used a large ornate key on the wooden box. When it popped open, all four women tilted forward to peer inside. Small, sheer, drawstring bags in different colors lay on the bottom of the box. Six bags, Kiki counted, and silver charms could be seen in each of them. Trinity reached inside and fished out a pearl colored bag. She handed it to Kiki.

"Here's your auntie's charm," she said.

Kiki opened the small bag and the Comba necklace spilled into her palm. At the touch of the metal, Kiki got a shock to her heart. A lingering echo of Celeste vibrated in that metal triggering a sudden emotion to well up behind her eyes. Kiki fingered the chain that slithered around the charm. She remembered how she studied the intricate pattern as her auntie tucked her in on a summer night. Kiki drew in a breath and then passed the charm to Gwen.

Gwen had always been very close with Celeste, because her mother had been dear friends with Celeste and passed away too young. Then, young Ian always insisted he'd marry Gwen someday, and when Gwen broke her vow of chastity with Ian at sixteen, Celeste treated Gwen like her own true daughter. Kiki could see Gwen's brilliant blue eyes sparkling with emotion.

"I can sense her." Gwen's ginger lashes fluttered.

Kiki nodded and hugged her friend.

Gwen gave the charm back to Trinity and she held it quietly for a moment before pouring it back into the shear little bag. Then, she returned the bag to the box and stared at the treasure.

"Auntie Meg collected six of these Comba charms. She kept them a secret from everyone. I stumbled on them accidently behind the drying racks in the kitchen herb room. Annie and I were rearranging things. Meg must have suspected their connection to the curse after Celeste was murdered," Trinity said softly. "I'm pretty certain twelve of these charms were made, one for each moon priestess in a traditional pagan coven. With the one in your picture, there are only five to be found. We need to find them before your gathering occurs."

Trinity peered at Gwen. She continued,

"The high sisters believe it'll take all of the charms to obliterate this curse, that was why Meg gathered them. And we'll need a *dragoma*. A real *dragoma* to command the demon. Those writings did advise that it'll take a *dragoma* to *wrest the curse from the demon's grasp*," Trinity added.

She'd found the cask of whisky and poured herself another sample. Trinity's glowing green eyes bore into Kiki's again.

"Have you become a *dragoma*, my dear daughter? It certainly appeared so to me. With the cultivation of your core aspect these fourteen years, did your skills evolve to such an interesting level? Both of us, Annie and I, we recognized your increasing successes on that television show. Is it true?"

Kiki exchanged a long look with Gwen.

A mysterious vortex of aethereal energy revolved around that little cottage near Uig Bay, on the island of Skye. Certainly, it was the nexus of the curse. It had been in that very room when Kiki discovered Ian went to New York, and she became obsessed with visiting him. Kiki ignored the council of every person in her inner circle when she flew off on that trip, a trip that led her to a real *dragoma*, a witch who spoke to spirits and demons. Unusual and rare, and just what they needed.

That *dragoma* led to more charms and might be linked to the coven in ways no one could have imagined. A cosmic energy guided Kiki to find what she hadn't even known she sought. Kiki stared back at Trinity.

"Well, Mother, I'm going to have to disappoint you there," Kiki said.

"It's Ian's girl, then, isn't it," Trinity interrupted. "She's the *dragoma*. Does she even know it?"

Kiki nodded. "She does now."

Gwen added. "She's a powerful caller, even as a novice, but there's something else. There's also another charm. We've seen it."

"One was delivered to Janine in Chicago this past spring," Kiki said. "At the request of a ghost, a witch's spirit. In the woods where the witch was murdered, strangled, Janine summoned her. Gwen and I are witnesses."

"She used one of Celeste's summoning charms," Gwen confessed. "It came from her grimoire, the one she placed in my care. Celeste wrote a special summons for calling out a sister, and though this *dragoma* had no concept of her power, it was a wonderful success. I actually visualized the spirit and she gave me the initial vision of the gathering. All three of us were able to visualize the spirit, just like the testimonies given in Celeste's circles of the past."

"That spirit's murderer also tried to kill Janine Stinger, but failed. We hoped to find the victim's body or bones to prove the murderer's guilt."

Kiki reached to the bottle of highland whisky and charged her cup, sipped, then continued.

"The spirit showed me a vision of her death. She was leaving him, after discovering he was a demon, and running from an intimate situation with someone she had loved. She was strangled. Sound familiar?"

"Like Gillian and Celeste. You're grandmother, Gwen. Perhaps even Abigail would tell something similar, and who knows who else. Does she have both charms? Please tell me the *dragoma* did not wear one, you must call her immediately and warn her not to wear them, to put them aside and then bring them here. She should come too. I wish she could come for the Samhain, we could take all the charms to the castle rock and see what happens. I would very much like to meet her."

Trinity lounged back in her seat, contemplating this new information. The light from the fire flickered over her features. Trinity was still a very beautiful woman, with intense green eyes and dark hair only lightly speckled with grey. Kiki watched her mother's eyes come round to return her gaze, they were hypnotic.

Gwen sighed. "The wood's spirit also spoke out loud, not just in visions. She said that an empty place needed to be filled. What do you think that means?"

Kiki stood up. She needed fresh air, and to warn Janine Stinger not to wear the charm. She also resisted confessing to Trinity that the other charm was gone, slipped through her grasp when she returned it to the Daily family. It was likely somewhere lost in transit, trying to find its way back to Miranda, who most likely died years ago in Thatcher Woods. Kiki shot Gwen an urgent eye, and thankfully, Gwen got the message. She'd take on the task of explaining the blunder to Trinity.

Kiki left voice messages because no one was answering a phone, then slunk back into the cottage and found the three women laughing as they flipped through the entertainment rags. Kiki could see her own image posing at a party. They glanced up with amused eyes.

"Gwen says none of these men are the detective fellow you've mentioned. That he's a bit messy and has quite a slender build and he's not so glamorous at all," Trinity said.

Gwen shrugged her shoulders, what could she do? As High Priestess of the Base Well, Trinity would be very interested in the selection of the male for the awakening ritual.

"Gwen says this is the fellow you've selected."

Trinity pointed to a photo of the *Spectral Analysis* team. Max Colliers's hand was under Kiki's arm in a possessive manner. He had pulled her very close for that group shot, and they definitely appeared to be a couple.

"He's quite handsome. Annelise perked up at the sight of your choice."

Annie nodded, "He is very handsome, and looks refined. I truly like the look of him. But are you positive he knows what an awakening ritual entails? He won't be too prim and proper, or too shy, will he? He looks very proper. It'll be an embarrassing disaster if he's too shy to perform. Is he your love interest?"

Both Gwen and Kiki laughed at all that, answering her questions with their amused chuckles.

"You know," Trinity's voice took on a more sensual tone, and she fluttered the lids above her glowing green eyes, "George MacLeod has suggested his cousin's son, Andrew, for your awakening ritual. He's a couple of years younger than you, but he's a very well made man and knows the way of things. He's popular with the lassies here. A sure success for an awakening. We can bring him around and you can get a good look at him. He's at the top of my short list and he's bound to be as capable as George was at my awakening. He may seem like a simple headed fisherman to you, but the MacLeod men are gifted with an orgiastic pleasing of women and blessed with a fine tool for it. From my own experience, I can tell you…"

Kiki threw her hands over her ears.

"I can't listen to this, you're my mother. I don't want to hear the details of your experiences, especially not with George MacLeod. And I don't know how, or why, George is privy to the details of my awakening. I can only guess who's been bending his ear there."

Kiki watched Trinity's lips continue moving and glared until they stopped, then she slowly removed her hands. Both Annie and Gwen could barely contain their giggles.

"Are you sure?" Trinity asked softly. "A blind stag ensures he'll no follow you for life."

She made a good a point. Trinity picked a friend, George MacLeod, and he has hovered near her hearth since the night Trinity lost her virginity nearly thirty years ago. Sisters often advised girls to choose a blind stag, or they might be choosing their future husband. Then, Annie grabbed up her tarot cards and began shuffling the deck.

"Shall we ask the cards their opinion?" Annie winked at Kiki. "We'll keep it simple. Pull a card for your Max Colliers, and another for our Andrew MacLeod."

Annie Batten's tarot deck was a *one of a kind* treasure. At the university, Annie had been an art major and each of her cards was a miniature original water color with an ink outline.

She created other decks for reproduction, the Kiki Mellow cards for example, but the cards in her hand were for her own personal use. They were sacred to her. Kiki knew the deck well. It had gone with them on their travels and Annie claimed that the images revealed themselves in dreams. There would never be another deck like the one she presented to Kiki. Annie would never give them out to be copied and always replaced a worn card by creating a new original artwork. Annie once tore up a beautiful rendering of her High Priestess card and created a different image, just because the original vision had altered slightly in her dreams. *She has a hint of a smile now*, Annie had said.

"Max first," Annie ordered.

To placate the laughing women, Kiki drew a card and placed it face down.

"Now one for Andrew," she urged. Again, Kiki drew a card and placed it next to the other.

A funny feeling descended on Kiki. That familiar feeling she often garnered from Annie's beautiful cards, that they contained a subliminal message meant to be obeyed. Gwen, Kiki, and Trinity all watched as Annie simultaneously flipped both cards over.

Ace of wands for Max. Three of swords for Andrew.

"Ho ho, that closes that discussion." Gwen giggled at Annie. "Fine tool or no, your Andrew is off the list."

Then, they recapped a general plan for the upcoming awakening ritual, which would be followed a few days later by a special Samhain in the Faerie Glen. Kiki promised to make a final decision on the seven witches she desired for her awakening, and Trinity delivered a small list of the sisters that vied for a spot.

It was very late, past midnight, when they finally strolled out to Gwen's car. Gwen was scheduled to work the next evening and wanted to get back to the city to sleep in her own bed. She worked the night shift on the children's oncology floor and never liked to call in sick and have someone work a double shift for her.

Chapter 5
Rugby

Janine

Janine aroused lazily in the midmorning to find Ian spying at her through a small scope of some type. She shifted and pulled the sheet to cover her body better, wondering at his strange behavior.

"What are you doing?"

Ian removed the device from his eye and grinned at her. "Just admiring you through this little toy Ben designed." He passed it to her. "He calls it an ocular prism spectrometer. It's fun. Needs a bit of white light to work, but not full direct sunlight or it washes out. This filtered morning light works nice."

Janine examined the tubular device. It appeared similar to a small monocular telescope, except both sides had similar sized lenses. A little lip on one end identified it as the eyepiece. Janine pointed the scope toward Ian and was startled to see iridescent rainbows surrounding him. She twisted the end ring to bring the light into better focus and watched the rainbows become more distinct. Ian appeared to radiate energy in colorful radiating waves that shot outward in every direction. Certain areas of his body, the top of the head, thorax area, and the groin area, projected brighter patterns that extended the furthest. The rippling rainbow effect waxed and waned in intensity when he moved and she heard herself giggling.

"Aye, right." Ian laughed with her. "It's an infrared signature."

"It's a rainbow," she said, transfixed. The pulsing colorful array outlining him was a bit erotic, and she quite enjoyed the effect.

"A little converter takes each infrared frequency and multiplies it, then expands the scale for the full visible range. Similar to what Ben did with the subsonic audio," Ian told her.

"It's fun, and colorful, but why do all this work for a fancy heat display?" She realized that she was ogling him quite blatantly and handed the scope back.

"He thinks it might be what Kiki sees when she talks about auras. He's fascinated with Kiki, obsessed with her."

Ian aimed the scope back on Janine and tugged the blanket away.

"This blanket is interfering with my assessment," he said. "This is very enlightening, lass, you're radiating lots of heat energy from a very interesting location. Bonnie rainbows, very sweet. After last night, I'm pleasantly surprised to see that you're very warmed and ready."

"I don't think so." she protested, pulling the thick covers over herself.

All this talk of Kiki reminded her of that phone conversation the night before. Kiki might call at any minute, and she wanted to hear her thoughts about the charm, then there was that disturbing comment about Ian's father. Ian remained focused on his little scope and she nudged his arm, but he kept the scope pointed at her and tugged the covers off again.

"I'm still looking, it's very stimulating. I don't think this is what Kiki sees, but there may be a good use for this little scope." Ian grinned slyly at her. "A wee look through this piece and there'll be no confusing if a lass is warmed up, and I'd say you're very warmed up, Janine, eagerly warmed up in fact. That is a very bright rainbow leading to your pot of gold."

"Put that thing down. You don't know what you're talking about."

He set it aside and then rolled over to pull her into a full embrace, tugging the covers out from between them as he kissed her. She put up a feeble fight, but got overwhelmed with the feel of him and ended up wrapping her legs around him instead. His earthy smell, and the sweet taste of his kisses, were intoxicating. The way his hands drifted down her body stirred her blood into a nice state of excitement. Living together for the past several weeks had been the most sensual time of her life. She couldn't get enough of her fiancé, and his closeness had a euphoric effect on her.

"See there, I knew you were hot for me, that scope doesn't lie," he whispered, as he nuzzled her ear.

A loud bang startled them. A door shut somewhere near. Then, another thump sounded followed by the footfalls of someone walking down the hall. That much mass had to be Chet. Low murmuring voices sounded right outside their door. Janine scooted away from Ian, embarrassed that his students may have heard the bed squeaking with their wrestling. Maybe they actually woke his crew up with their activity. Ian glanced toward the door, then back at her.

"Sorry lass," he whispered. "Maybe you'll get lucky after the rugby match."

"Not another rugby match."

Janine detested the rugby matches. Ian enjoyed a very rough game, and she always feared he'd come out of it with a broken bone or something. He got the wind knocked out of him often, and once he lay on the ground unmoving for several minutes before jumping up and running back into play. Rugby was more violent than regular football and often resembled a crazy group of men wrestling in the mud.

"Ian, what if you get seriously hurt or something? I want you intact for our honeymoon."

He just grinned at her.

"Isn't your team a man short? Don't tell me you're playing with a man short again." That'd be just like his mates.

Ian laughed. "No, no, settle down. I've recruited some of the Berkeley kids to fill in."

"You mean Ben and Oliver?" Janine sat up, alarmed. "Tell me you didn't bully those guys into playing rugby. They'll get creamed." Did they realize rugby was a full contact sport?

Ian was laughing, motioning her to quiet down a bit.

"No, no. But Chet. And another young bloke named Andy. He played the line in lots of American football. And Emma. Emma's coming out too."

"Emma! You mean boom Emma in the hall? What is wrong with you? That little girl is going to get hurt."

"She insisted." Ian nodded at her. "Really, she'll be fine. I think she's going to zip around the big blokes quite nicely. We don't discriminate in rugby, if a girl wants to play, that's fine with us, and I'm confident Emma will make a right brilliant scrum half. She's played before too, on a team back home, she says."

Janine stared at him. He never asked her to play on the team. They were short in the last game, and he didn't even consider asking her to fill in, and Janine was a very serious athlete. She played varsity soccer at the University of Chicago for two years and played on a club team at Davis. She could run circles around some of his rugby mates, and she certainly knew how to handle a ball. All this time, she thought his team was a men's only group and now she felt a little rejected.

"Why don't you ask me to play?" she asked. "Maybe I can help too."

"Oh no, you don't like rugby," he shook his head. "Besides, you've already got an important job in the match."

"Really, and what is that?"

"You know, being my sexy cheering section. Watching me show off." He smiled at her. "I always play better when I think you might be impressed with my moves. I enjoy you on the sideline, rooting for me, ready with a cool cup of water and a nice fresh kiss between phases."

She didn't expect that. Rugby always drew out his baser side, but this was outright patronizing.

"You want me to be some sort of sideline, nitwit treat?"

"Crikes, Janine, I didn't mean it like that. I'm your cheering section at your soccer matches, right? Don't you love it when I run cool water to you when you come out of play? Don't you enjoy showing off a bit for me? I certainly enjoy watching you show off."

He took her hand.

"Total truth, I wouldn't be able to play right if you were on the field. What if you got ruffed up? I'd bloody get ejected dealing with the idiot, even if it was an accident. I know you're tough, I just don't like the idea of some bloke knocking you down. And the other players would sense it on me, me watching over you. You'd be a liability. I'm sorry, I know it's a little old fashioned, but girls don't play rugby," he said firmly.

She frowned at him.

"Well, I mean, *my girl* doesn't play rugby."

He just called her a liability. Somehow, she found the conversation both sweet and irritating at the same time. Should she punch him or hug him? Ian sidled up next to her, still a little amused but cautious.

In a clear attempt to change the subject, he asked, "So, are you going to show me the ring you found?"

That reminded Janine of her conversation with Kiki, and she pulled the covers tightly around herself thinking about it. Kiki let it slip that something was said between Ian and his father, *something bad* by the sound of it. Kiki sounded worried that the conversation may have caused *something to happen* in California.

Janine didn't know how to bring it up. Ian was very tight lipped about his father. It was not an amiable relationship, that was clear. *But Ian must have discussed it with Kiki already.* Why didn't he discuss it with Janine? Would it cause *something to happen* if she knew what was said? Janine finally decided to wait and give Ian time to bring it up on his own. Maybe he was waiting for the right moment or when they got home. Or maybe it was nothing at all.

Ian loved the Celtic ring Gram found in the box. Finn's ring fit him perfectly and he wanted to begin wearing it right away. He wanted to wear it to his rugby match, which was silly, because he wasn't supposed to wear jewelry during the game. They rushed out of Rio Linda and barely made the start of the match. The *Spectral Analysis* students had outraced them to the field and Chet and Emma were already warming up.

Janine watched from the sidelines as Ian got knocked around that afternoon. She sat in the rooting section with the other girlfriends, drinking white wine and discussing both the gluteus and cerebral assets of their respective partners. At the half, she gave him a nice steamy kiss like the other sideline treats. After a quick dinner with the team, they went home to finally be alone. Ian had just excused himself to a shower, and Janine lounged on the sofa waiting for the after match luck he promised her. That's when her cell phone pinged with a call from Scotland.

"So, this charm you found is just an unbelievable thing," Kiki said. "Beware, though, clues point to it being attached to an ancient curse. Don't wear it and try not to touch it. If possible, I'd like to buy it from you, or Gram, or whoever it belongs to."

"Nonsense," Janine told her. "I have it here. It's yours, just like the last one. And don't worry about me wearing it, I have no desire to even touch it. I can send it to you."

"Thank you, Janine," Kiki said. "But don't send it in the mail. Hold on to it, and I'll fetch it. I'm going to come early for your nuptials, by at least a week or more. Maybe we can go out and celebrate before the big day, like a little hen."

"You mean a bridal shower or something? My soccer team is throwing something next week, I'm covered."

"I want to do something too, and I bet Gwen wants to participate as well. You're one of us now, a sister. Maybe a spa day for the three of us," Kiki said. "And there are things we can discuss, the charms, the curse, the Mary spirit you summoned. Can you tell me what happened? I spoke with Ian and he said you conjured her again."

"It was very unpleasant," Janine confessed. "I told everyone the last time that the spirit was angry. This time it was obviously so. One lady thought the spirit wanted to grab her heart and I'm sure the spirit bit one of Ian's students, because he felt it. Caroline Govant claimed that Mary was a kind spirit, but I think she knew better. Gram says Caroline was holding out on us, that Henry Webber found a pile of old history stuffed in her attic."

"Really?" Kiki sounded surprised. "How do you know she bit this person? It could have been something else."

"Angie Minnihan and I both saw it," Janine said. "When she ran into the trees, she clamped her jaws on Oliver, one of the techies, because she knew that he would feel it. He was wearing a device called…" Janine couldn't say *mellow-skin* to Kiki. "A device that makes the skin receptors heightened, more sensitive. I got the distinct feeling that she chose to attack him because he would feel her and she could hurt him, to make a point."

"Interesting," Kiki said. "Maybe I can sweet talk Henry Webber into letting us ransack Caroline's pile of papers. Maybe others have reported her sinister ways too."

"Whatever you think is best," Janine said.

"I hope you and Ian are still coming to Scotland, no matter what happened," Kiki said. "Make it a point to come to the Isle too, my mum would love to meet you. You can visit the coven cottage and the Faerie Glen. I know you have the end of your term, and then your honeymoon, but promise to come at the start of the year, please. Are you still waiting for next fall to think about grad school, is that still your plan? I don't want to keep you too long, I'm supposed to call that detective about the other charm and I'm not sure that I want to talk to him."

Janine blinked. What did Kiki mean? *No matter what happened?* What was she talking about? What had happened? The *talk* that Ian had with his father? Is that what she meant? Were they not planning to see Ian's father at the start of the year any longer?

"Yes," Janine said. "Yes. That's the plan. You guys will be on location somewhere and I might come along to watch. But, Kiki, what did you just say? What did you mean by that? What happened? Can you tell me what happened?"

There was a long pause.

"It's my awakening ritual, Janine. I've kept my vow of chastity for two cycles of seven years. That's a lot of mystical power to the coven, but weakened if I break my vow on a whim. There needs to be a ritual, a purification of sorts, because sex can be very spiritual to the coven. And that detective promised he would participate in any pagan ceremony I asked, remember? You're a witness."

Kiki's voice was rising and cracking.

"He broke his promise. It was too much to ask of him. Sure, he'd have no problem bedding me in private, on his terms, but ask him to participate in this very important sacred ritual and it's too much for him to bear! He broke a promise, Janine, a promise!" Kiki sounded very upset. Did Janine hear an actual sob? "He left. He's out of the picture now."

"Kiki," Janine said. "I'm so sorry."

"No, no." Kiki's voice pulled back together. "That was a stupid outburst. Don't listen to a word of it. I'm just pouting because I had it planned so nicely, everything is good. Things are going grand, who needs that detective anyway."

"Kiki."

"No, no. I'm just a little stretched over these charms. Do not wear the charm. Put it somewhere safe. I've got to find a way to get the other one back, and, Janine…" Kiki's voice was calm again. "We're going to need a *dragoma* over here, to break a curse, a curse that seems to bring a violent death to certain women, like what happened to Miranda. I really, really, really don't want to ask you to do it, so just think on it. When we see each other, you can tell me how you feel about it, and don't be afraid to say no," she said. "Anyone in their right mind would say no, Janine. No, to getting involved in a curse. But we don't know another living *dragoma*, so we'll need you to say yes, but don't let that sway you."

Kiki rung off.

Of course she would say yes, Kiki knew that. There were too many omens for Janine to turn around now, and in reality, saying yes would not be Janine helping Kiki, it would be Kiki helping Janine. Those charms found Janine. Janine was the one who barely escaped a violent death like Miranda's, and Janine was meant to participate in whatever was going to happen, she knew it. She could feel it. Whether she truly believed any of it or not, she was mixed up in it.

Ian poked his head into the room with an amorous expression on his face. He was fresh and clean and only wore a towel from the shower, but that phone call dashed any hope of an ardent tryst.

"Are you ready for anything special?" he teased. She nodded.

"I'm ready to hear about the conversation you had with your father."

She had not seen those blinking eyes in a very long time. Ian McNally's eyelids always went out of whack when he felt nervous or stressed about something, and now they were revving up to a nice speed.

Chapter 6
Balance

Kiki

Kiki shuffled through her notes on the haunting of Rio Linda. According to the wagon diary, Irene Lumen and Ingrid Stauch had been cousins. More, the river spirit had been Ingrid's daughter and the charm had belonged to Irene. They probably shared a grandmother who had been a witch of the coven. Wedding bands with triquetra knots were found with the charm, confirming the Celtic origins of Janine's ancestors. It would not be presumptuous to assume those two women practiced pagan teachings. Janine didn't remember it, but under hypnosis, she said the river spirit mentioned a necklace. *Had she meant the Comba Charm?*

Kiki sipped an Irish Coffee in the Blue Pilot, watching for Gwen. The nurses of the cancer ward often frequented the pub in the morning after a night shift and Gwen promised to meet her there. She'd solicit Gwen to make the phone call, because she didn't want to do it herself, not after breaking down when she mentioned the detective to Janine. How embarrassing was that? At least she warned Janine about the charm and asked about the recent summoning. It sounded very unsettling. The orchard spirit actually sounded sinister.

Gwen poked her shoulder making her jump. Kiki stood and greeted the nurses behind Gwen before they disappeared to their usual spot in the back of the bar. Gwen wriggled into the booth looking very professional in her nurse scrubs. With her long red hair tied neatly in an elegant low bun and her speckled face free of make-up, she looked quite youthful and pretty. None of her colleagues suspected Gwen's practices in the coven community, except Bridget Murphy, the pediatric oncologist Gwen was currently attached to.

"Did you give a mind to your seven awakening angels? Katie Walsh rang me today and is dying to know if she's on the list. That lassie is truly enamored with your media persona and she'll be discussing it for years if she's in the mix. But everyone knows she can't keep a steady beat and the drumming will be all out of whack. You'll want a steady beat to help you along."

"Yikes." Kiki sipped her drink. "She's on my list. What do you think of Katie, Annelise, Diana, Roxy, Liz, Ginger and then you?"

"Poor Trinity, she'll be heartbroken, and not a single one of the older sisters, very unbalanced," Gwen observed. "And only Ginger and Diana in that mix suffered an awakening of their own, kept their sacred vow, those two are great choices, but the others, myself included… Maybe drop a couple of us vow breakers for a mother or a crone. Please, seriously consider Trinity, she'll be pleased as punch, and Diana's mum Kate and her grandmother Cara are lovely women that would be grand at such a ritual, all vow keepers. That old lady is still a stunner and could actually be an initiator if you wanted. Each generation should be represented, Kiki, for the best balance."

"God, Gwen, I can't choose another mother if I don't ask the High Priestess of the Base Well. This way I can claim a maiden centered circle of sisters, only those who haven't conceived. Truthfully, I'd rather have five hundred other witches witness my ritual than one Trinity Lovett. I've so failed her by being so happily asexual," Kiki said. "Did you see her eyes? She was very excited when she imagined I broke my vow. Now, she worries I won't be able to fully open up. I know it. She expects to be disappointed and I can't say I'm not worried about it too."

Gwen chuckled and wave her hand. "She expects no such thing, Kiki. That's your wee lassie taking. Dinna forget, Trinity is often asked to such rituals as High Priestess. You don't like to think on these things, but your mother is a very wise woman when it comes to the passions. She's a proper choice for any awakening ritual. You're a sister who's held her vow for seven and seven, to feed your core, that's a first in her lifetime. You're likely the only Core Master she'll ever know, and your awakening is significant on many spiritual levels. Kiki, she'll want be there to send you some supporting energy."

Kiki rolled her eyes at that. Gwen spoke a truth she didn't want to hear.

"At least invite a couple of the older sisters, so she can gossip with them on it. It'll keep your ritual a mite more respectable with a couple of mothers there. I'd wager Roxy and Liz will cozy up to Max the moment you're done and not let the stag get away without a taste of him. A proper initiator should only look to light the flame, but those two will hope to quench part of the fire as well."

Kiki smiled slyly, "Maybe that's why they're on the list. Why should I be the only one in the hot spot in this awakening? Our roguish hero fancies himself quite the adventurer, right? Let's see how he keeps up with Roxy or Liz. I'd love to see Max squirm his way around those two."

Gwen gave her a stern eye. "Always enticing trouble. Do you really want your ritual to end up in debauchery? Please, include a mother in there, maybe two. You can leave in Liz, if you must, but definitely take out Roxy, she never even made a vow. And take me out too. You'll not want any imagery that might spoil his appetite, not during your ritual. He'll be looking around, that one. Include Diana's mum for sure, she's absolutely beautiful, and Trinity if you dare…"

Well then, Gwen never liked it to show, but she was still coming to terms with it all. Most people never suspected, because she was tall and slender, athletic looking, and had a confident air about her. She kept quite fit and most believed she was naturally flat chested. But that wasn't always so.

Gwen went through a very tough time at the end of her teens, breast cancer that led to a double mastectomy, treatment that required harvesting and freezing her eggs, just in case. Her coarse straight hair had come back very curly, and years later, it was still quite wavy with a deeper shade of red, softer. There was no reconstructive surgery for Gwen, and she'd never be able to naturally feed a baby, even if she opted for the reconstruction. Although Gwen quickly accepted her altered body, she claimed it startled new lovers, especially men, and it was the main reason she left Ian. Kiki could still remember Gwen fuming with anger after a weekend with him.

Ian is a liar, she said. *He lied when he said it dinna matter to him. He closed his eyes, Kiki*, she spat. *Every time we faced each other, in the heat of passion, when his eyes fell to my chest, he faltered and I could feel him soften. He needed to look away to get hard again. I'm never going to fuck him again.*

"Don't give me that look, Kiki."

"I'm not giving you a look, my dear," Kiki said. "I'm preparing to ask for favors."

Kiki pulled out her phone, scrolled to Detective Anderson's number, and wrote it down on a sheet of paper.

"I can't talk to him. You have to call and see if he'll give us his man's contact. A member of the Daily family carried the charm to Turkey, to find Miranda and return it. The detective sent a private investigator to follow along and confirm when, and if, they found her. No news means she hasn't been found yet. We need to get that charm back. Maybe the PI can do that for us."

Kiki slid the number to Gwen.

"Better use your phone, he hasn't been accepting my calls."

Everyone except the Daily family assumed the skeleton that turned up in Thatcher Pond was Miranda, strangled and abandoned in the woods, killed by the same man, Richard Wilkens, who brutally knifed Janine Stinger. When Janine summoned the woods ghost, all indications pointed to the spirit being Miranda, who else could it have been? Even Richard's own sister believed her brother murdered Miranda. They sought proof of Richard's dark deeds when they called out the spirit, proof that might help keep him behind bars.

Gwen dialed the detective and he picked up on the third ring. They exchanged pleasantries and she put him on speaker phone so Kiki could hear the conversation. The detective last heard from his private investigator that morning. The PI tailed the family member into the hills around Mount Palandoken. It was rough country and the cell service was sketchy at best, so it might be a few days until the next message came. The detective agreed to give the PI their request to buy the charm. He'd also send the PI Gwen's number.

"So, I guess that necklace is pretty important to your… your group," Detective Anderson said. "I remember Miss Mellow already tried to purchase it from the family. What makes you think anyone will change their mind?"

"No harm in asking again," Gwen said. "But I get your point. We'll probably need to speak to someone else as well."

"Do you have the number for the family?" he asked, "I can send it to you in a text."

"Thank you, detective, as always, you've been very helpful." Gwen's eyes went to Kiki, flustered about what to say next, then shook her red head. "I'm sure you heard the news about Janine and Ian," Gwen spoke toward the phone. "They're making it official the weekend after Thanksgiving."

"It's wonderful news. I could tell the first time I saw them together, those two are meant for each other."

In her mind's eye, Kiki envisioned the detective smiling with his pink aura flaring. Bob Anderson had a soft spot for Janine. As the detective on site when she turned up a bloody mess, he took a personal interest in her case and always kept in touch with her.

"I agree," Gwen said. "I'll be flying to California for the small ceremony."

"I may attend as well, if I can break free. We'll see." He hesitated a moment. "Please give my regards to—Look, I'm aware that Kiki is probably sitting right there, likely listening in," his voice turned soft. "She is, isn't she? Listening."

Gwen's blue eyes glanced toward Kiki, "You're a very good detective," Gwen said.

That got a small chuckle out of him. "I like to think so. So, hello, Kiki. I want to apologize to you, for avoiding your phone calls." He paused. "I admit to behaving a little childish lately. I guess that's why you needed Gwen to make this call. It's unprofessional of me and I hope I haven't burned a bridge. You should know, I have nothing but fond thoughts of our times together and… well, I do miss you."

Kiki snatched up the phone and turned off the speaker. "I miss you too," she said quietly. "Does this mean you might reconsider and come out here next week, and participate in my awakening? It's not the wild affair you imagine it is. We can —"

"I can't," he cut her off. "You know how I feel about it. What you're asking is something that should be a private affair between two people in love, following a wedding. At least for me, it has to be…"

Kiki thrust the phone back at Gwen, shaking her head. "I can't talk to him."

She could feel the tears threatening to flow and wiped her eyes just in case. For one bleeping moment, she thought he was going to throw his conservative, romantic ideas aside and come back to Scotland. She didn't need to hear his excuses. *Why did he get to decide what was right,* Kiki steamed silently?

With deaf ears, she watched Gwen complete the phone conversation and she got her emotions under control. Kiki never met a man that didn't follow the script she wrote out for him, and she never felt the sting of rejection before Detective Anderson. She took a small swallow of the Irish Coffee in front of her, wishing it was something stiffer. With the detective, she was guaranteed a true awakening, but with anyone else, she might divert the energy out of unease. She didn't want to disappoint the High Priestess of the Base Well, or herself.

Gwen took a sip of her own drink and shot her a tender smile.

"What else I can do for you?" Gwen asked gently.

"Come with me early to California and help look through Caroline Govant's things, possibly meet the orchard ghost. We should give Janine a little bit of a hen, don't you think?"

Gwen nodded. "Without question, a girls' night. Anything else?"

"Yes. Be the one to fetch Max from the airport and be in charge of him. Annie wants to do it, but I'd rather it was you. Give him a good talk about everything, spell it all out for him. Take him to Trinity, if you must, and to the pastor, he'll need to confess."

Kiki wouldn't interact with anyone for a full day and night before her awakening, and someone needed to manage Max for the time before and after her part in the ritual. Max was an outsider and knew nothing.

"Of course," Gwen said. "Any other favors?"

"Yes," Kiki said. "Please participate in this awakening ritual. I'll invite Annelise, Diana, Diana's mum Kate and grandmother Cara, then Ginger, then you, and… and Trinity. You're right about the balance. So, I'll have them all; a dear friend, a maiden, mother and a crone of one family, a coven witch who's recently had an awakening of her own, the High Priestess of the Base Well, and also, the sister I love the most." Kiki took Gwen's hand. "The most beautiful woman I know. I want you there."

Gwen nodded.

"A perfect list then." Her eyes suddenly opened wide. She sat up straight, alert and amused. She smirked. "Ho, ho, here comes your second baseman. Were you planning to meet him?"

Kiki turned just in time to see Rory O'Hara reach their table.

"Kiera Lovett! I've been trying to get a hold of you. You're back from you mum's! Hey there, Gwen." He grinned at them.

Gwen was giving no more favors that day. To Kiki's horror, Gwen swiftly stood and offered Rory her empty seat. She winked at Kiki and suggested waiting for her blood alcohol level to drop considerably before setting out to practice anything. Then, she begged off to join her lovely nurses group in the back, chuckling wickedly the whole way.

The full moon shines for only a moment in time. It occurs at the instant the satellite passes in orbit 180 degrees from the new moon stage and the entire lunar surface facing earth is illuminated. Yet, to the naked eye, the moon appears in the full stage throughout the night before and the night after that singular moment. Those two nights are called the first and last cusps of the full moon, respectively. During the awakening of the Base Well, a coven virgin will enter into a secluded meditation on the first cusp and will not reenter society until the last cusp completely passes, with the ritual event occurring as close to conjunction of sun, earth, and moon as possible.

Annie drove Kiki into the hills on the Quiraing, in the Trotternish area of northern Skye, and dropped her in a carpark at the end of a single track of road. Kiki disappeared into the hills toward a special secret valley, to a little known cave carved into the jagged stones where a girl could spend her meditation before an awakening. She needed to return to the elements, stripped bare of the fabric of society and the unnatural comforts of a human designed world, to prepare her inner Wells. Her singular goal in seclusion was to redirect her flow of energy into opening her animal instincts and preparing her passion center.

Their pagan ethos specified that energy was focused in three infinite wells called the Head, the Core, and the Base, or the Triquetra of Wells. Each well contained characteristics that pointed in either a masculine or feminine direction and formed a trio that snapped together to make a whole. For her entire life, Kiki focused on her Core Well, the spiritual center, so intensely that her Base, the passions that included her sexual appetites, became tenuous. She was practically asexual. But now her time was up and she needed to acknowledge her primal aspects. It was unnatural and unhealthy to shun part of one's Triquetra of Wells, and Kiki's Base needed to be explored. Her soul might become crippled if her wells remained unbalanced, and Coven teaching only allowed for celibacy until the night before her twenty-ninth year. At that age, a maiden needed to transition into becoming a mother if she hadn't already taken that step. As a coven virginal priestess, the transition occurred with an awakening ritual to initiate her into the physical drives and pleasures that led to motherhood.

The man she initially sought for her ritual didn't understand it. Her Base Well had naturally opened to him and she believed the cosmos sent him to share in her initial sexual encounter and to father her child. But when she described the events of an awakening ritual to him, he refused to participate. It never occurred to her, that her ideal man might not be the one to awaken her. That he'd be wrong for it and another might be better suited for the job.

Annie's tarot never lied. The Ace of Wands pointed to a powerful creative rebirth of her Wells, and Max Colliers's name pulled that card. He was very confident, and naughty enough to jump at the chance of participating in what most might consider a risqué exhibitionist escapade. She knew exactly what she'd be getting with Max, and she had been sexually drawn to Max on several occasions. His Base Well overflowed with passion energy and perhaps he was her perfect opposite.

Kiki slipped into the rocky cave with a special tea and candles. She would cleanse her system with fasting and pray for the next twenty-four hours, at which time, her entire balance of energy would be altered completely. She was nervous, excited, and scared. She knelt down and placed a single candle on the floor of the cave. Then, she began an ancient pagan meditation prayer to pry open her base door.

Hidden further in the cliffs lay a small protected flat area which the coven often used for awakening rituals. Porous basaltic rocks lined the outer edge of the clearing providing perfect fire bowls. As the moon climbed higher into the night, Kiki detected the fragrance of smoke from those bowls. *They were waiting.* She emerged from her cave hungry and sore, feeling every cell in her body. Her eyes beheld a cloudless night and she took in the cool air. It was a short walk to the protected clearing and the rhythmic drumming drew her to their call. The drums set a steady pace for her beating heart, keeping her calm but alert, knowing he was waiting for her.

For centuries, the women of the cottage respected the lunar effects on a woman's cycle and an awakening ceremony would only occurred during a full moon, because a full moon increased a woman's sexual desire. She rounded the top of the mound and spied into the small valley. She watched her seven angels drumming in a circle, corralling her stag.

Max felt her and looked her way. She watched his red passionate aura flair and practically flood the entire clearing. Yes, she chose the perfect awakening stag. The moon hung directly overhead and the drummers increased their tempo. The time had come. The small valley radiated warmth and her stag stood ablaze and ready, watching her. She could see that Max still didn't quite believe she was coming for him, but he was ready for anything. Well, then, Max was in for a nice surprise. Kiki drew one last breath as a coven virgin, then obliterated any lingering barrier to her base aspects. She was finally ready to jump into the fire.

Chapter 7
Jane Doe

Janine

One last set of final exams and her Bachelors of Science in Biology from UC Davis will be complete. Not the fancy University of Chicago degree in Biochemistry she once dreamed of, but who cared? What did the exact title on her undergraduate degree matter? What mattered was that she finally completed something. A miracle, especially after the major detours she took along the way: recovering from a near fatal knife attack, being cross-examined in a courtroom, having her sanity questioned, losing herself in a psychiatric ward, battling a crippling depression, months of weaning on and off mentally foggy medication, *losing Sammy*, and two years of *Spectral Analysis* where she was reborn. But reborn into what? A witch? A medium? A *dragoma*? Janine returned the metal charm necklace to the folded paper. She didn't understand her to urge to study it, but lately, she often felt compelled to look at it.

Janine didn't quite accept any of Kiki's labels, she wanted the regular B.S. in Biology instead. It sounded normal, and half a semester away. Afterwards, she'd be free to run off on a honeymoon to the South Pacific with her incredibly attractive fiancé, a man she completely adored. He was sweet, sexy, smart, and loved her. They fit so perfectly together and after finals, she'd be carefree and able to focus solely on him. Carefree, except for wondering what would happen in Scotland.

It took major pulling to get the details out of Ian and his fluttering eyelids, but the gist of it entailed his father's total rejection of their planned marriage. Roger McNally decided that Janine was not the right stock after what he witnessed through the lens of the *Spectral Analysis* film. He noticed Janine *bending* to the influence of Ian's cousin, Kiera Lovett, aka Kiki Mellow. Janine stepped into forbidden territory, according to Ian's father. Roger McNally refused to allow the pagan community to darken his door ever again and wouldn't accept a witch into the family, or any woman who remotely accepted their pagan ways.

Hang him, Ian had said. There was a time his father enjoyed his mother's folks on the isle and begged to be included in their world. But once he got his woman and tied her down with a child, Roger set about cutting her off from her coven background. Ian watched his father control his mother in oppressive ways, cutting off her friends, her funds, her automobile, and hiring help that *discouraged* her from leaving the estate, all in the guise of her own protection.

The final straw came when teenaged Ian and Gwen became romantically involved one summer. Neither Ian nor his mother were allowed back to Skye, and Roger had Celeste *watched* and followed. He questioned her motherly instincts and the faulty parenting of their teenaged son. That's when Celeste finally decided to leave Roger. Ian's father first institutionalized her, and when that didn't work, Ian actually believed…

"You aren't serious," Janine said. "You think he had a hand in her accident?"

"I did at fir-first. Sometimes, I still do, somewhere inside." Ian began stuttering as well as blinking. "I accused him outright of ki-killing her with no proof at all. I know, I know, it was a terrible thing to do. Cost him friends, and clients, and a scandal to live down."

Ian got his nerves under control with deep breathing, and his stuttering disappeared.

"All because of my gut feelings and bad dreams, which came from grief. It can make a person believe crazy things, grief. You know about that. He couldn't have done anything near what I had accused him of, because he was out of the country when everything happened. And he was heartbroken too, but I didn't care and kept blaming him. It's idiotic. I was just s-so angry at him for the rest of it too. I'm older now, and realize that a sixteen-year-old boy probably shouldn't carry on with girls the way my mother encouraged me on Skye."

Janine hugged him. She pulled him close and kissed him gently. That was the most he ever talked about the bad blood between him and his father, and she understood him better. She now understood why he had been so harsh about her wild accusations when Sammy was lost.

She wanted to help him mend his relationship with his father, if he'd let her. Janine missed her own father terribly and didn't want that for Ian. She had been locked away in a hospital refusing to see anyone when her father suddenly passed, and she deeply regretted it. Ian wanted to be forgiven, she could tell by the way his blinking and stuttering came and went. He was upset at himself for believing such terrible things about his own father.

"I think I should meet him." Janine climbed into his lap and cuddled him. "Even if you think he is an ass, he's your father and I should meet him and at least try to win him over. You don't have to protect me from him, you know. I'd like to meet your aunt too, Kiki's mother, I'd love to see what she's like."

Ian agreed to take her to Scotland on the return from their honeymoon, but not before, as originally planned. He didn't want his father spoiling the romance. If she wanted, they could drive onto Skye and meet his Auntie Trinity too, Kiki's mother. But when that happened, she should remember that she had asked for it. If she thought Kiki was a bit colorful, just wait until she met Trinity.

After Ian departed to teach his night class, Janine flipped on the television for background noise as she organized her notes. The Comba charm and the conversation with Kiki crowded her thoughts. Kiki's special ritual must have already occurred, because the full moon had just passed. Janine wondered who Kiki invited and felt disappointed that Detective Anderson let her down. He seemed positively in love with Kiki when they met in Chicago. Whatever happened in Scotland, whatever was said, really hurt Kiki's feelings, she had been very upset during that phone call. Then, Janine's phone pinged, and the caller ID told her it was the detective.

"Detective Bob Anderson," Janine said. "I was just thinking about you."

"I'll bet," he said. "I'm so sorry, Janine. I didn't expect it."

My goodness, Janine thought. Did he have ESP?

"Well, you know, sometimes Kiki comes up with some surprising ideas. It's not your fault for hesitating. It took me a while to take some of her pagan rituals seriously. Not your fault for being put off by it. She's just used to getting her way with people…" Janine heard him take in a breath and paused.

"No, no. It's not about any of that. It's about the commuting of his sentence. The dental results on that skeleton came back and it was not Miranda Daily in the pond. We don't know who the skeleton belongs to, not yet, and the governor decided to immediately commute Richard Wilkens's sentence. He's signing the papers next week. The governor believes the department was out to get him, set him up unfairly due to an ongoing squabble between law enforcement and his family. They've been pushing that narrative for quite some time."

"What?" She was stunned.

"I'm sorry, Janine. Wilkens has been working the governor since before his parole hearing. And I have to warn you, that's just the tip of the iceberg here. Maybe you'd better turn on the news, national news, they caught me outside a moment ago. I believe it's just starting to break."

She switched channels to the national news and the picture on the screen startled her. A reporter stood outside the house on Thatcher Road and a mug shot of Richard Wilkens popped up in the top righthand corner of the screen. He wore a sweet smile with his angelic face, and they actually used a photo of him in a choir robe.

Then came a picture of Janine. It was a promo shot from *Spectral Analysis* in that racy outfit Max Colliers insisted on. *Good grief!* The reporter babbled on, but Janine didn't hear a word. She always knew her secret would get out, being the girl left for dead in the woods who actually survived. In the distant background, she recognized Detective Anderson's voice calling her name and retrieved her cell phone.

"What does this mean? Is this worse than parole?" she asked softly.

"I'm afraid it is," the detective said. "He's still a convicted felon, of course, but his punishment has been erased. We won't be able to tie him down when he gets out. The governor doesn't believe he's guilty and nearly pardoned him."

Janine forgot to say goodbye when she hung up, then muted her phone because call after call after call kept coming in. Her sister, Lauren, Gram, girls on the soccer team, unidentified numbers, Gwen, Misha from her study group, her sister again, Carlos, Doctor Crisper, Max, an old friend from her University of Chicago days, and several unidentified numbers. She muted the chime for texts too, because when people couldn't get through, most sent a message instead. Janine set the phone down. She pushed it away and focused on the news. They stretched the story out, it was their highlight, so the reporter decided to recap the entire Coed Captive case of sex, blood, and deceit.

It was a black Labrador that led Hank Jones to a gruesome scene in a secluded area of Thatcher Woods where a brutal attack had occurred. Mr. Jones feared they had stumbled upon a dead body, until his dog Sparky insistently began licking the face and neck of Jane Doe from Chicago and he realized that she was still breathing, but just barely. The victim was a young student from the University of Chicago, and for years, the court ordered her identity be kept confidential, but today we learn her true identity. Jane Doe from Chicago is none other than Janine Stinger from the hit ghost hunting television program Spectral Analysis. *Janine Stinger went mysteriously missing for ten days before*

Mr. Jones and his dog Sparky found her. Evidence indicates that she had been shackled by the wrist, beaten, and sexually assaulted before taking multiple knife blows to her torso. She very nearly died. The big shocker for folks following the story occurred when she finally named her attacker. After nearly two weeks of recovery, she finally opted to tell the police that Richard Wilkens, the man keeping vigil by her hospital bedside, was the man who stabbed her. Miss Stinger claimed that Wilkens held her captive in a house across the street from Thatcher Woods, chased her down, and tried to kill her after she escaped. Many people wondered why she didn't name him sooner? Some believe it was to protect the baby she carried. Perhaps she did not want to send the father of her child to prison. Others believed she suffered from hysterical delusions, or perhaps she wanted revenge following a lover's quarrel. Others suggested she stabbed herself in an attempt to abort the baby. What followed next was a long and sensational trial in which the defense claimed Miss Stinger suffered from traumatic delusions and was mistaken in her claims. Many believed Richard Wilkens had been unfairly accused and convicted, and today those people are celebrating. Richard Wilkens will be set free by noon on...

The reporter continued with speculations about the baby, where was it, who had it, what gender was it and why did Janine Stinger give it up for adoption? Did Richard Wilkens now have the right to demand meeting his child? They showed a few clips from the *Spectral Analysis* television show and reminded the country that Janine Stinger recently announced her engagement to Ian McNally.

Detective Anderson popped up on the split screen speaking to a different reporter, followed by Doctor Crisper from the psychiatric hospital. He nervously patted down his crazy hair while smiling self-consciously. As usual, his buttons were misaligned. Janine turned the volume down and picked up her phone.

She called Gram to let her know she was fine. Then, she called her sister, Juliana. She tried Kiki, but there was no answer, so she called Gwen. Gwen sounded very concerned.

"Will he try to contact you, do you think?"

"I don't know," Janine said. "Maybe."

The real answer was *yes*. Even though he would be told to stay away from her, she knew he wouldn't. When would he show up? Next week, when he emerged from incarceration, or next month? Or would he wait until she became relaxed and unwary? That's probably what he'd do, wait and surprise her when she least expected it. Janine didn't want to think about that yet.

"It's the skeleton I'm calling about, Gwen. They didn't mention it on the news, but Detective Anderson told me a little while ago that it isn't Miranda Daily, the skeleton from the pond. It's somebody else. Is Kiki around? She's not answering her phone. Is she okay? Did her ritual go well?"

"Kiki's in a solitary meditation," Gwen said. "Her awakening was a glorious success, but she's still in seclusion. Sometimes a witch will stay secluded far into a waning gibbous. I'm not expecting to see Kiki until the Samhain in a couple of days. None of this news has touched her ears yet."

"Well, it's not really an emergency, is it?" Janine said. "The notoriety will just be an annoyance for a few days, and Rick doesn't scare me anymore, well, not too much. It's the skeleton I'm confused about."

"I agree, it's very confusing. We'll figure it out. I'm worried about you, lass. You're bound to get a lot of unwanted attention. Shocked folks might try calling you. Do you have a preference there?"

Janine sighed. "I'm going to handle it by ignoring the calls. I mean, it is what it is. I can't stop people from talking, but I don't have to participate in it, right? About that skeleton, do you think it belongs to the spirit? Was it her own death vision, or Miranda's, that she gave to Kiki? Where do think Miranda is? Do you think there's another body in those woods?"

"I truly believe the spirit would only give her own death vision," Gwen said. "And the charm necklace must have been hers as well. At first, Kiki claimed the vision appeared to be two visions woven into one. Perhaps the skeleton is a girl who died after Miranda, or before, another victim he passed the charm to. As for Miranda, there's a private investigator in Turkey right now. If she's still alive, we'll hear of it soon enough. Don't worry about these things, Janine, just focus on your wedding and all the happy events going on around you. Let us worry about the charms and such. I'll make sure to keep you informed of important news. For now, put this stuff behind you, if you can. Move forward."

"Thanks, Gwen."

Then, Ian burst through the door, he cut his class short when someone mentioned the Coed Captive case. She spotted a news van outside, on the curb, before he closed the door. Now it was his turn to comfort her. Janine couldn't help blaming the charm in the bottom drawer of her jewelry box for bringing the negative luck. She never should have taken it out of its wrapper.

Chapter 8
The Samhain

Kiki

Trinity invited Max Colliers to stay through the harvest holiday, but he declined as business called. He lingered around the cottage for two days, hoping to see Kiki, but she stayed in seclusion and his time ran out. Gwen ferried him to the small Isle airstrip where he caught his private jet. Annelise went along for the ride, practically drooling over the fact that Max owned a private jet, and she answered all his questions about Kiki and their college days, telling him anything he wanted to know. When they returned to the cottage, Kiki had emerged from her post awakening seclusion, ready to rest in luxury before the Wiccan festivities began.

"Well then," Gwen meandered around her room. "Were you waiting for Max Colliers to depart, or did you really need a prolonged seclusion to recover from that very nice awakening ritual?"

Kiki smirked at her, relaxing with a sample of George MacLeod's homemade whisky. She sat atop the bedsheets scribbling in her notebook. Her phone lay charging off to the side with all the alerts still flashing. She hadn't checked a message yet. She noticed Gwen acting a tad uneasy, the sparking green in her aura gave her away.

"Aye, I was waiting for Max to leave," Kiki confessed. "But mostly for Trinity to get busy with Samhain doings. Do you think the ritual went well? I certainly felt a surge of cosmic energy flooding the small valley. How did the sisters take it?"

"Trinity raved that it was the most passionate and powerful awakening she's ever seen. Then again, she's your mother and has always bragged about you. She was very lit up about the way you came in and took charge of the stag, then just let go like that." Gwen chuckled. "It was a highly energized event, and you very nearly shocked me, my wee yin. I've never witnessed an awakening before, but I can't imagine anything to top that business. I hid my eyes most of the time, concentrating on my job as drum leader. Dinna worry, I spied your mother hiding her eyes too, you made the High Priestess of the Base Well quite bashful and proud!" Gwen laughed hard enough to turn her whole face red.

"I very much enjoyed making her proud," Kiki said, and they both fell over in a giggling fit. "I hope Trinity doesn't sit me down to discuss it," Kiki got herself under control. "What did Max do after my departure? Did he dally? I could see Ginger get googly eyed on him out there, hard to imagine he'd resist that toothsome lass."

"Not just Ginger. Annie and Diana got pretty stirred up after that display of yours, but they each had a man nearby to settle them up. Max may be a player, but he's first string from what I saw, and funnily, Max wasn't having any of it when you left." Gwen nodded at her surprise. "When we got back here, Ginger hung about, plying him with drink, but he was waiting on you, acting like a perfect gentleman at the queen's dinner, charming and refined. Your mother approves of him, I must warn you. He charmed the socks off her."

Kiki hooted at that, "Is that so? Maybe I should have come back sooner. I felt an interesting desire to revisit some of his finer points during my seclusion."

It was true. The next morning, she found herself fanaticizing about Max Colliers with very erotic images, which completely surprised her.

Gwen picked up Kiki's phone.

"A natural reaction. You dinna check your messages yet? Shall I tell you what's transpired while you were out hiking the hills?" Gwen poured more whisky into Kiki's copper cup and took a sip for herself. "The results are back on the skeleton in the pond. Not Miranda Daily."

Kiki blinked.

"They dinna know who it is yet. And then I got a message from the private investigator. There's a woman in Turkey, and everyone says the woman is Miranda, even the family member positively identifies her as Miranda. Miranda is alive and well, not dead at all, and definitely not the spirit from the woods."

"How did we get it wrong?" Kiki's eyes were wide. "Who was that spirit, if not Miranda Daily? Do you think she will give up her Comba necklace? Did the investigator ask about that?"

Gwen giggled almost uncontrollably. The very freckles on her face darkened, and her eyes were watering.

"Oh, Kiki," Gwen caught her breath. She took another deep sip out of Kiki's whisky cup. "That girl in Turkey says the charm isn't hers. She never lost her charm." Gwen's blue eyes reflected her unease. "She says she'd like to keep it but knows it isn't hers to keep." Gwen nodded and paced, skin growing redder by the second. "She's planning to come here and bring the charm, to discuss where it really belongs. She actually asked about our Comba charms. Apparently, someone else is attempting to procure them."

"Good god, when is she coming? I don't want to miss it."

"Not till after the winter solstice. The cabal she lives in is very bound to the Samhain and Yule seasons and cannot leave their homeland until after the new year. We'll need to be patient," Gwen told her. "Of course, Trinity is beside herself with the whole affair. She's adamantly looking for a translator for those books. Cara has been a bit of help but doesn't know the language used in some of it. She says it's an old code, long forgotten and they're looking for the cypher. Those ladies have been very busy flushing out the elements of the charm curse."

Kiki suddenly realized something of personal significance. She regained her copper cup, drained it, and smiled at Gwen.

"Do you know what this means?" she asked. "It means that he didn't break his promise to me after all, Bob Anderson. He only promised to participate in a pagan ritual if they found Miranda Daily in that pond. So then, maybe I'll forgive him for standing me up and allow him to sire my baby at the Beltane. Perhaps I'll meet him halfway with that, private and proper."

Kiki stretched out on the bed.

"That spirit, even if the bones weren't Miranda, she's still a victim of that demon in the jail. The spirit affirmed her murderer as Richard Wilkens, remember? And I saw him in my vision. Maybe there's some way to link him to her murder."

"Oh, and that." Gwen closed her eyes. "Apparently, he's not dangerous enough to keep locked up. Some governor decided to let him go."

"So, he got his parole." Kiki grabbed her phone. Should she call Janine?

"Something like that. But they dinna call it parole. And now everyone knows the lass in that story is Janine. It was all over the news. Don't call right away. Give her a breather. Leave a text message, maybe. She's dealing with it in her own way." Gwen gave Kiki a hug. "You'll need to get a bit of sleep yerself, for the Samhain. We're planning something with the charms in Trinity's cabinet."

Back in the wild hills, a large bonfire blazed in an open glen close to the small valley of her awakening. Fast moving clouds swirled in the upper atmosphere and the air felt cool and crisp. Sharp igneous stones poked defiantly from the emerald grasses. She had never seen anything more beautiful, or erotic, as that expanse of highland hills. Kiki inhaled sea salt intwined with oak smoke, an aroma that stirred the life between her legs, bringing back memories of Max and his engorged male appendage. *Shut it off, close the door*, she ordered herself, shocked that her energy drained so easily into lust.

Several small fires littered the landscape, which, along with a waning gibbous moon, cast dramatic shadows over the festivities. Tourist and locals dressed for the occasion with painted faces in red or white, or with adornments that hinted at sacred animals. Children bobbed for apples, scurrying about dressed as ghouls. The coven purposely mixed with the outsiders at the harvest bonfire, the bigger the party, the better. Festive events provided the perfect lure to keep prying eyes from the more sacred aspects of the Samhain. Later, select sisters of the coven would quietly gather in the Faerie Glen to make an offering to the fae, then, at the witching hour, coven members would climb atop Castle Ewen to pray and attempt a summoning. This year, they hoped to summon victims of the charms. Often, they would meditate until dawn on that rocky spire.

Annelise, Gwen, and Kiki carried cups of warm mead and wore long flowing capes. Besides having a bit of fun, the main goal of attending the bonfire festival was to absorb positive energy into their cores. They would need it later, at Castle Ewen when they prayed for the new year and summoned the spirits. After her awakening, Kiki's energy wells felt very out of whack and her entire focus now dropped to her Base Well, distracting her. She dearly needed to refill her core.

Kiki spotted Trinity in the center of the music, surrounded by her usual collection of male admirers, dancing quite vigorously in a jig some might define as Irish line dancing. Her mother's green eyes flash wickedly at everyone they encountered.

A bit further from the main crowd, a small group prepared for a fire dancing show. Attractive men and women in dark leather clothing placed cans of water in a semicircle, clearing an area for their act. Annie pulled Gwen and Kiki closer to get a good spot.

The fire dancing ritual had become more and more elaborate in recent years. Unlike a Polynesian show with staff torches, the dancers in this pagan arena used fire poi, which consisted of a wick at the end of a long chain. It resembled a medieval weapon. The dancers swung the glowing wicks in elaborate patterns while dancing to drum heavy music.

Kiki's eyes kept falling on a particular fellow with thick black hair and taunt bulging muscles under his leather vest. His black eyes fixed on her, holding her captive. At one point, he poured a flammable liquid across his leather covered chest and lit it aflame before tossing his fire poi about. He glared intensely as he performed, sending a cascade of hot sexual energy at her. Kiki was surprised at how easily her passion well flooded while watching his gyrating movements.

Normally, she'd divert that energy right into her core, but somehow, she had problems closing that door again. The sea aromas, the bonfires, the tight pants on that man, and the night air were doing a number on her senses. She glanced to Annie and Gwen as they dissolved into giggles.

"Your mouth is hanging open, Kiera, and you too, Annie. I take it those fire gods have bewitched the both of you." Gwen laughed at them, but she was quite flushed herself.

"It's my Base Well door. I find now that I've opened it, I cannot seem to close it again," Kiki observed.

Annie giggled and pushed her blond rings aside.

"He's hot, right? Shall we talk to him? That fine fellow happens to be Andrew MacLeod. He might be a bit put off with you, Kiki. He dearly wanted to participate in your ritual awakening and you crossed him off the list pretty quickly. The other man is Sam Welks, he's my fellow. He's pretty exciting, right?"

"Very exciting," Kiki agreed.

Kiki gave Andrew MacLeod another long look. Red blaring passion emanated from his halo as he stared across the short distance. Her mouth watered and she realized that she desperately wanted him in a venereal way. She was flooded with an erotic vision of his thick thighs between her legs. Kiki grimaced at herself and consciously bent his energy toward her core. She shook her head at Annie and they broke off in different directions. She needed to escape from that fire god before she jumped right on top of him.

While Annie skipped over to chat with the fire dancers, Kiki and Gwen slunk off to find a quiet spot away from the main throng of the crowd. Her eyes flitted from one man to another, imagining how each might have behaved in her ritual. Perhaps she should have stayed in seclusion a bit longer, she felt as if the entire cosmos had turned upside down. Here she sat, lusting after everything in trousers when just a few days ago she couldn't have cared less. Kiki stewed a bit, drinking her mead while actually daydreaming about Max Colliers. *How ridiculous.* Gwen's eyes were amused as they passed in her direction.

"Maybe you need to run loose a little," Gwen chuckled. "It happens after an awakening, they say, girls will enter a very lustful stage. I mean, hello, you've been awakened. No worries, I'll keep an eye on Trinity and let you know when we're moving to the glen. Go on and get it out of your system. I hear Andrew MacLeod has a very nice tool for such things."

Kiki set her mead down hard and glared at Gwen.

"I don't have anything in my system, Gwen, at least nothing I can't control," Kiki snapped, but suddenly stopped. She glanced around the hundreds of faces walking in the crowd, something was wrong. "Where's Bridget, the oncologist?" Kiki asked. "I thought she was coming to Skye? I didn't even notice she wasn't here." Kiki studied Gwen.

Gwen might be chuckling, but she wasn't happy.

"I am such an *eejit*, Gwen. A totally self-absorbed *eejit*."

"A flooding of the Base Well can make one a bit self-absorbed, my wee lass." Gwen patted her back. "Bridget is a tad upset at me and decided not to come."

Kiki sidled next to Gwen and put a comforting arm around her, worried. She hoped Bridget hadn't gotten a false idea about Kiki. It's happened before. Kiki and Gwen's friendship was deep and everlasting, coven sisters that bonded since before their memories could recall, but Kiki was not one of the many lovers from Gwen's past. Even so, whenever Gwen chose a girlfriend, they often became suspicious of Kiki because Gwen was not the most faithful partner in a relationship and often succumbed to her spontaneous desires, fouling things up.

Gwen sighed. "My fault again, I had a bit of a snogging session with Max before your awakening and tried to explain it to her. She found my reasoning extremely weak."

"Gwen!"

"It needed doing," Gwen defended herself. "It's the only way I could ease into the situation of showing him my chest, or lack thereof. I dinna want his first glance to be during your ritual. It's the sort of thing that needs to be seen and absorbed over time. You dinna understand, Kiki, the initial sight can turn a person quite solidly cold. I've plenty of experience with this."

Kiki didn't know Bridget as well as she'd like because they only just met when Kiki returned to Scotland. Bridget had a very sweet and serious aura, all blue and golden highlights. Kiki realized that, in her egocentric pursuits, she had been monopolizing Gwen's life, getting Gwen into all kinds of situations and asking for favors as if they were still young girls. Grown up Gwen moved in circles that didn't include the coven, or Kiki.

"Dinna worry yerself over Bridget, she'll come around or she won't." Gwen wrinkled her speckled nose as her ginger eyelashes fluttered. "She knows I couldn't possibly be interested in one such as Max Colliers."

"I bet she's getting tired of me too," Kiki said. "If you need to run off right now, you should do it, and if you really shouldn't fly out to California, especially early, it's okay. I'm starting to realize I might be mucking things up for you, dropping back onto your life like this."

Gwen smiled at her with the familiar expression she always used when she thought Kiki was being stubborn or silly. Gwen took her hand and squeezed it.

"I need to go to the castle at three and see what's to be known when Trinity takes out those charms. You don't have to be sorry, or thinking it's always you dragging me into these things. Celeste was dear to me too, you know, and I want to know the history of those charms. I'm well invested in what's to do about it."

Gwen eyes were quite serious.

"And nothing could keep me from being at Ian's wedding, I've been waiting for it, praying for it. I need to be there. Bridget will be patient with me, or no, and she could come to California if she wants. I invited her. I just need to wait on her forgiveness, and she does make a good a point. I've messed up in the past, and so it wasn't a singular event, fooling around with Max. I can't help it if sometimes I itch for a lad. She's usually very understanding about a lad."

Kiki nodded, "I hope Max wasn't an arse about it. He can be a world class arse."

"He was a wee shocked at first, but recovered in a grand way. He asked a lot of questions, like he was trying to understand things, and he wasn't an arse, he really wasn't. I was delighted and surprised with Max. He wondered why I opted away from a reconstruction and said my reasoning was spot on." Gwen laughed. "I like Max, Kiki."

"That's because you two are very alike in your rooted aspects."

Gwen laughed at that. Then, she stood up and looked to the far side of the clearing toward the bonfire. Kiki could see what got her attention. Trinity was on the move. Kiki watched her mother's head turn, and their eyes met. Time to head to the Faerie Glen, Trinity eyes conveyed, and then to the castle with the charms.

Chapter 9
Castle Ewen

Kiki

Trinity sent Annelise into the Faerie Glen with several of the younger sisters to make offerings to *them* that reside between the cottage and Castle Ewen. They prepared gemstone bowls with a portion of thick milk, butter, and the dried petals of wild flowers and herbs. Trinity also baked sweet cakes. The offering needed to be made, if they planned to stir the aether on the top of Castle Ewen, and gifts were always placed in the glen on the night of their pagan new year. The tradition went back centuries. After the younger girls left, Trinity gathered the small collection of Saint Comba charms and ten of their twelve coven priestesses converged in her den. Two missing priestesses would put a blemish on their ritual, but a couple of other sisters were thrilled to fill in.

Each moon priestess represented one of the twelve lunar cycles, as well as a Sacred Well. Coven Priestesses of the Base Well included Gwen, Ginger, a mother named Rebecca, and Trinity as the High Priestess. The maiden, mother, and crone from Kiki's awakening, Diana, Kate, and Cara, were all Priestesses of the Head Well, along with another woman named Lisa. Kiki belonged to the Core Well, along with two very old women, and a young mother, Rebecca. Other witches in the coven included virginal priestesses keeping a vow of chastity and those waiting to become a moon priestess someday. They were mostly young girls learning the pagan arts or late joiners to the coven, like Annie. They rarely attended a meeting in the private den, but were always invited to rituals in the glen. The two missing witches, Rebecca and Lisa, were in the midst of motherhood and could not attend the celebration on Skye that year.

Each priestess silently filed out carrying a portion of the alter to be built, while Trinity ferried the box of charms. At the witching hour on the Samhain, the veil between worlds stretched so thin that it was possible to communicate to loved ones long passed. Whispers in prayer resulted in answers. Mostly in the form of a silent touch of a rekindled memory, but sometimes in a full vision. Never, in all her years of ritual on Castle Ewen, had Kiki actually seen, or heard, a ghost. Although the hill vibrated with cosmic energy, it was not the same as a soul stamped with enough essence to form a true entity. But this year was different. This Samhain, they planned a summoning ritual along with the prayer. They hoped the residual energy in each Saint Comba charm would coax out their lost sisters.

Castle Ewen emerged at the end of a narrow dirt trail, which required a single file line for the hike. The castle stood above the brilliant green of the Faerie Glen and rose strikingly into the night sky. Castle Ewen wasn't a castle at all, but a natural tubular rock formation that appeared to be the hardened stone tower of ancient ruins. On top of the rocky hill, there was only enough room for the alter and the twelve lunar priestesses. Any other witch would have to stay in the glen and take their chances among the fae. When the last coven priestess reached the summit of the rocky hill, they began to build an alter on the small plateau.

They built a small fire and placed a cauldron over the flames. Old Cara added water, herbs, and spice to the pot to make a special tea. Next to the cauldron, a small oak plank was balanced on the ground until it lay flat, then a three wick candle was placed in the center. Circling the candle, Kiki and Gwen built a crystal grid of gemstones in the shape of a hexagram, leaving the six points of the star open for each of the Comba charms in Trinity's box. Larger stones, with the Celtic carvings, were placed at opposite the edges of the plank and incense sticks were placed on top of them. A two handled metallic cup sat on the plank while a basket of odd shaped black candles lay at the other end. Trinity slowly pulled the charms from her pockets and named the owner of each charm as she placed them at the tips of the crystal grid.

"Sister Lillias Blair, sister Holly MacLeod, sister Freya Tod, sister Gillian MacDonald, sister Abigail Kirkpatrick, and sister Celeste McNally." She kissed the last charm before placing it, then lit one wick of the thick candle before stepping back with the others.

Cara ignited the second wick before returning to her cauldron to stir the contents. Her granddaughter Diana sat very close to her, at the ready to assist as needed.

From the back of the group, another old woman stepped forward. This woman radiated a brilliant aura, even in the darkened night. Kiki watched swirls of blue intertwined with purple radiate from Eva's core. Her energy was surprisingly thick, even though she was a stooped, wizened woman with silver white hair and a face carved with age. Eva was the oldest living sister in their coven. She neared the century mark but refused to slow down or step aside for a younger witch to step up. Aside from being the High Priestess of the Core Well, she was also Priestess of the Blood Moon, sometimes called the Hunter's Moon, and she ruled the Samhain. She stepped forward and lit the last wick with a shaky hand, then set the sticks of incense aflame releasing a sweet spicy odor which permeated the air.

"Ring in here, ring in clear, all ring in our new year. Night will fall, night will laugh, we welcome in our darker half. Burn the veil, till shriveled and curled, met us from the other world. Come sisters hear, come sisters see, so I command, so mote it be."

Eva's voice came so loud and strong that in Kiki's mind, Eva appeared a giant.

"Sisters Lillias, Holly, Freya, Gillian, Abigail Celeste."

Each witch knelt on the top of Castle Ewen to pray for the six sisters named. They prayed for them to find peace and to bring them word of what must be done. Breathing in the fragrance of incense, each searched and cleansed their own hearts of foul feelings. They each prayed to be worthy of a vision. Eva repeated the names.

"Lillias, Holly, Freya, Gillian, Abigail, Celeste."

Eva kept reciting the names and composed it into a song and the others collectively joined in. From down in the glen, Kiki could hear the music of younger voices echoing the chant. From behind her on the path a few younger girls had climbed the hill to watch, beautiful maidens with bright eyes on high alert, hoping for a vision. The air rang with the melody of those names.

The name chant continued softly as Diana fetched the metallic two handled Quaich and held it while Cara spooned in liquid from the cauldron. Then, she raised the cup high and recited a common oath.

"We share this drink and every breath, to seal our bonds in life and death."

Cara carefully swallowed a sample of the tea, then she passed the cup to Diana. Diana also recited the oath before drinking, then passed the silver cup to Eva, who passed it to Trinity. After her sip and oath, Trinity reached into the basket of black candle stubs and lit one with the flame of the alter candle, then found a spot to settle.

Soon, each moon priestesses moved to the alter and recited the oath, *we share this drink and every breath, to seal our bonds in life and death.* Each took a mouthful of the bitter sweet potion and ignited a small candle. Each carefully cradled the flame back to their place of prayer, forming a tight circle around the center alter.

Kiki sipped the tea after Gwen and felt the warm spice run fast in her veins. Kiki sheltered her candle, thinking of her Auntie Celeste. When the final priestess joined the circle of light, the High Priestess Eva raised her hands and the chanting ceased. Eva bent to the alter and whispered something softly before blowing out the alter candle. Then, she closed her eyes to see what she would see.

"My heart summons you, my auntie," Kiki whispered, then blew out her own candle and closed her eyes. Kiki could already feel the tea coloring the visions in her head.

The air over Castle Ewen grew cold, and the stillness grew tense with concentrated energy. Kiki watched an image of her Auntie Celeste grow very distinct behind her eyes. Celeste's own eyes were the same blue as Ian's, and they shared a similar smile. Kiki felt the warmth of Celeste's embrace. She calmed as the essence flooded her core. She could hear the melody of Celeste's lullaby whispering in her ear. The sound lulled her breathing into an slow rhythm as a vision took form.

Her auntie tending the herbs in Meg's garden in the summer, while sunlight magnified the red highlights in her dark hair. Then, the images cascaded rapidly; her auntie crushing herbs in a mortar, swimming in lochs, spying faeries, designing gemstone grids, brewing tea, braiding hair, walking the hills, holding hands, and on and on they went. But mostly, she saw that beaming smile for Kiera Lovett, her favorite wee lassie. *Kiki*, Celeste called her, whenever Kiera ran from Trinity in a huff. *Oh, dear Kiki, mellow out, my wee yin,* that's how Celeste always began her consolations, even as Kiki grew older. *Kiki, be mellow, your green eyed monster is just yourself, looking back to smooth your path.* Then, her auntie would speak to her green eyed mother and Kiki knew everything would be better, because her auntie was the big sister and Trinity had to listen.

But listen to me carefully, my wee yin. The voice turned very quiet and hard. *You wore the charm and now you are marked. Complete the curse, expel the demon, to erase your mark.*

Then, there were more images of her auntie in the glen, and the cottage, and on the McNally Manor. The Comba charm hung around her auntie's neck glinting in the moonlight, calling for attention. A distorted image reflected in the metal as someone closed in. But who? Surely someone Celeste knew. Kiki watched a large hand reach out to grab Celeste's long slender neck, then another hand reached up to help the first, and Kiki could see the fat ring that might be the one on her Uncle Roger McNally. She could feel her auntie strain with the task of trying to breath and not succeeding. As the life left her eyes, Kiki could see Celeste's recognition of her murderer reflected clearly in those bulging blue pools, and even with the life being squeezed out of her, Kiki knew that her auntie still loved him.

Dawn broke and woke her. The cauldron fire had gone out. Kiki felt the caps of her knees aching and the beginnings of a headache behind her eyes. She came to a sitting position, drained. Around her, every priestess wore a tired and worn face. Gwen stirred, wiping the tears from her lovely freckled cheeks. Gwen and Kiki grasped hands.

"Kiera," Gwen whispered. "Celeste spoke to me. She was indeed strangled by someone she knew. I got the sense that it was Roger."

Kiki nodded. "I saw it too." But it was something they always suspected.

"Celeste urged me to search the grimoire." Gwen's eyes were rimmed with red. "*Her grimoire.* There is a charm that can be used to expel a demon and it *must be recited to the demon to release the death marks*, she said. I'm not certain what that means. She wrote hundreds of charms in her book, how will I know which it is?"

As the sisters began to chat, they discovered that nearly all of them had a vision or heard something in an episode of clairaudience. They began to share stories of what transpired in their encounters.

Eva reported seeing Freya Tod, a lovely young woman from generations past. Freya insisted that *who'll be the last one, must be. And she who can speak the words, must speak. Otherwise the demon will live forever, feasting on the sins of the chosen.*

Diana heard from Holly MacLeod, who warned that those who follow Comba are cursed. There must be an offering, *one each for redemption*, before the curse can be broken. *There is still a missing piece.*

Trinity witnessed the murder of all six of the sisters. Each knew their murderer intimately with love, and lust, and passion.

Kate, Diana's mother, was given a vision from one who may have been Gillian. That spirit warned that the demon will try to weasel away from accepting an agreed payment and will seek to mark more and more. The demon must witness the testimony while in the presence of a strong ring of energy. It will take a collective effort to move the fae.

The lovely crone, Cara, heard from Lillias Blair. Lillias once lived in the cottage and built the stone wall. Her ashes lay scattered under the oak tree near the wall. She had been strangled and burned at the stake. She chose the lustful seed of the wrong man, and her predicament put her sisters in danger. Lillias did say, *do you th' evil deed 'n it wull come back on ye twelvefold. One each fer redemption shall hurl th' curse.* At least, that's what old Cara believed was said.

The others reported similar visions, with similar warnings. Trinity invited the sisters to the cottage, to write their accounts into the book of happenings and to enjoy a hearty breakfast. It had been a long time since such visons touched each of them so equally.

Gwen drove back to the city hoping to patch things up with Bridget before the trip to California, while Kiki decided to stay extra days at the cottage at her mother's request. Most of the coven sisters spent the day in and out of Trinity's house, excited and nervous at the same time. Everyone could feel something brewing in the air. Even the small non-pagan community reeled from the aftereffects of the Samhain Fire Festival.

Trinity organize a small feast and bonfire in the rear yard to settle their agitation, but Kiki opted to stay hidden inside. She hadn't divulged everything about her vision to Trinity, because she didn't want an interrogation from her mother. No one knew that she was warned that she had been marked. Kiki only reported the part where Celeste said, *complete the curse, expel the demon, erase the marks.* Kiki didn't want to admit to her mother that she had worn one of the charms in the spring. *Trinity was right again, Kiki was hiding her missteps from her mother.* She knew her lingering childish pride was a stupid thing, but she couldn't help it.

Kiki lounged in the front parlor drinking more of George MacLeod's smooth whisky. She felt a strong desire to deliver some to California for the wedding, along with an engraved Quaich cup. Ian would love drinking a communal pinch with Janine to seal their union.

Kiki was enjoying her moment of solitude when the door burst open and two fellows carrying flowers stumbled in. Right behind them, Annelise was laughing. Already two sheets to the wind, Annie enjoyed her festival days.

"Ho there, Kiera," Annie giggled under her halo of yellow curls. "Looks like your stag sent bunches of pretty blooms. I think he meant them to come on different days, but with the goings on, nothing's been delivered. They were sitting in the post, as pretty as a garden."

One of the men chuckled with Annie, but the other man stood stiffly, staring at Kiki with dark intense eyes, Andrew MacLeod. He no longer wore his tight leather pants, but his denim was just as form fitting. Kiki spotted the curve of that tool everyone kept talking about. He noticed her interest and gave her a thorough looking over. She felt volumes of passion sent her way, exactly what she needed to recharge her weakened core.

Kiki sat up and smiled sweetly at Andrew, soaking in the testosterone powered surge of energy. It was an old trick some of the witches used, taking in one type of energy and changing it to another. Kiki was very good at funneling any type of energy into her psychic core. Spiritual communication required core energy and the previous night had drained her into a limp mess. She imagined the other sisters were out recharging their own batteries with festive merrymaking.

"We meant to deliver these to your room and surprise you. Surprise!" Annie's big blue eyes blazed with humor. "Come join us outside? There's a nice fire and a cookout commencing in the back. There's a fiddler and a handsome singer with a guitar. Maybe we can dance slow with these fellows."

"Oh, no, just go on without me. Maybe I'll come later, maybe not."

Kiki stood up and took the flowers from Annie and her chuckling friend, who Kiki realized was Annie's fellow Sam. Andrew held fast to his bunches of blooms and she met his unwavering eye. He didn't blink.

"Are you going to give those flowers to me, or would you like to keep them for yourself?"

"I'm going to carry them upstairs for you." He gave her a devilish little grin. "I wouldn't want you to drop them with being so overburdened."

"Come along then."

Kiki started up the stairs, feeling him follow very close behind. The energy felt good filling into her core, and she believed she may have gotten control over that base door again.

"We haven't met yet," he said. "I'm Andrew MacLeod. George is my uncle, or great uncle. Something like that. I used to live on Islay, but I live here now."

"I'm Kiki," she said simply.

She kicked her room door open and set both vases of flowers on the dresser. Andrew strolled right in like he owned the place and set his vase on the bedside table. He looked around, taking in her messy habits, before turning his dark eyes back to her. He sent a gust of that passion again and she took as much of it into her core as possible.

She felt ten times better than she did before he arrived. It unsettled her that some of his energy seeped into her base, and she felt a wee stirring of actual desire. She could not completely seal off that particular door since the awakening and it caused a measure of uneasiness she wasn't used to in the presence of an admiring man.

"Thank you for the delivery. You're very nice."

"No problem, I usually make the deliveries here, I work on the farm." He moved around slowly. "Trinity often talks about you. You should visit your mother more often."

Kiki stood on one side of the room, studying him. He moved like a giant cat, stalking about in a circle. Andrew was aware that he was a fine looking man, and he had a charming way about him. He cleverly allowed her to get a good look at all his best angles and knew he had her attention.

"The sender is very enamored with you."

Andrew glanced at the flowers. Then, he reached into the bunch by the bed and pulled out the card. The nerve of him! Kiki couldn't help chuckling at his boldness. She loved a rebel.

"Well, he thanks you for the best night of his life." Andrew's playful grin grew wide and even. "Just what did he do to get those exquisite green eyes to notice him? What do you suggest I do? I already set myself on fire. So then, love, are you going to come downstairs and dance slow with me?"

That got her laughing.

"Men and their honey talk. Look here, Andrew. I can see what you're thinking, but if George MacLeod is your uncle, then that means we're very likely cousins. You are aware that George MacLeod may well be my father. So, I must regretfully say *no thank you*, and you shouldn't take it as a big brush off. My tune might be different if there wasn't a chance we were cousins."

She didn't expect Andrew MacLeod to let out such a guffaw. He pushed aside the dark bangs falling in his black eyes and preened up like a rooster. He exuded power and sent a surge of it right at her. Kiki felt her mouth water at the sight of the taunt bulge in his breeches. He stepped a little closer and Kiki watched his aura flare up an even deeper crimson. His other energy, head and core, ebbed significantly to feed his base.

This man is all about sex, she mused, breathing harder, startled at her own physical responses. Every part of her body felt his presence in that small room. Her eyes kept drifting to stared at his large hands.

"Come now, lass," he grinned confidently. "You and George both know he's not your father. Don't get me wrong, he loves you dearly, but knows you're not truly his daughter. He only says such things to keep hanging around Trinity Lovett without causing a stir. He actually reaps lots of respect for tending to the mother of his love child." His volume dropped. "I was completely crushed when they told me you chose someone else." He certainly didn't look crushed.

Three of swords. That was Andrew's card.

Kiki could see it now. If a man like Andrew MacLeod, all heat and fire and passion, wasn't a demon already, he might easily become one. Could she accidently push him into it, if she fed his ardor haphazardly? Could she destroy his fragile core?

Especially now that she was marked, and the demon hunted her? Was some dark energy pushing him toward her? Was that how it happened?

Kiki needed to be watchful and seal her passion door tight. She needed someone else to feed her Base Well. Someone like the detective, a man whose passion mixed with his emotions. One who would only act from love. Or she should accept no one at all, especially not one so mired in his physical plane. She reached up and pushed Andrew MacLeod away. She pushed him right to her door and his face turned startled.

"Whoa there," he stepped back so as not to stumble. "I'm sorry. I thought you were interested. You seemed to be very interested. I can tell that you're interested."

She was relieved to see his aura change. A bit of brown tamped down his red mess, and energy returned to radiate from his core and head. Andrew was no demon, and she felt bad for thinking he could become one.

That was ludicrous, *wasn't it?*

She continued to shoo him out the door and sent him away to the party. Then, she shut herself up in her room.

Kiki needed to be careful with her newly awakened Base Well of passion. She couldn't let herself spin out of control with the wrong person, *she was marked.* The wrong intimate partner could become her murderer. She wouldn't be safe until they *completed the curse, expelled the demon, and erased her mark.* Her Auntie Celeste would not steer her wrong in such things. It was just so hard to push him out that door, because now that she's had sex, she desperately wanted it again.

Chapter 10
The Hen

Janine

Kiki and Gwen landed in Sacramento one week prior to Janine's scheduled wedding in Gram's backyard. They spent their first two days at Henry Webber's house, the old Miller estate, rummaging through Caroline's old boxes. On Wednesday morning, Kiki sent a limousine into Davis to fetch her and insisted on a full day pampering session at the Isba Spa and Baths.

It'll be our little hen for you, Kiki had said.

Steam room, hot springs, massages, body wraps, facials and nails, then a fancy dinner before conducting a séance to summon a local ghost. Janine hoped the outing in Sacramento would help her decompress from the hoopla surrounding the media. Although the attention died down considerably, people still wanted to hear Jane Doe from Chicago's reaction to the recent release of Richard Wilkens.

"You keep calling him a demon." Janine gifted them Irene's Saint Comba Charm necklace and watched Kiki stow it in her bag. "You use that term a lot. You've called Ian's father a demon too. Do you mean someone possessed, or a person from hell? What exactly do you mean by demon?"

"It's an ancient pagan term," Gwen told her. "In modern times, people don't say demon. They say sociopath or psychopath instead. But a true demon is something worse than a person with just antisocial personality disorder, they have zero conscience and they completely lack empathy. What they're really lacking is a functioning Core Well, and we've always called them demons. The spiritual center is in the core, it's the center of the soul. Having an odd Core Well is crippling in many ways, but it's not always obvious to most people." Gwen crinkled her freckled nose and winked at her. "Of course, a demon might also be an evil spirit from hell."

"True demons don't emanate an aura from their Core, they've got nothing. No soul," Kiki said. "You'd be surprised at the number of near demons running around the world. It's a fair amount. It's mostly those that avoid developing their cores, but an actual demon is rare and scary, and doesn't have a core to develop in the first place."

"Remember the Trio of Wells," Gwen said. "Head, Core, Base. The lack of an aspect, or a very weak aspect, makes for an incomplete person. Sometimes their other wells are stronger, to make up for that lack of energy, and a demon can be very charming and alluring. Most are highly sexed and very smart. Demons are often hard to spot unless you can see an aura, like Kiki, but most people can't see an aura, and demons blend in very well. They often live perfectly normal, productive lives and can be very nice, especially if they're lucky enough to pair with a person with a strong core aspect and that person sticks it out with them. But demons eventually devour the cores of the people around them. They constantly seek that part of the soul they are missing, and their partners suffer the consequences."

"Do you have special vocabulary for people who lack one of the other wells?" Janine asked.

"Idiots and anhedonics," Gwen told her. "Idiot is misused a lot, and a true anhedonic will rarely last into adulthood."

As they entered the Isba dressing room to don robes, Janine gushed about the wedding plans. Ian asked Carlos to be his best man, she asked her niece Ashly to be maid of honor, and her brother-in-law would walk her down the aisle. Her dress might be demure, but Kiki would approve of it. Gram recently dropped an expanded the guest list on them, and there would be an outdoor meal and a live band now.

Ian and Janine planned to escape to Tahoe for only three days because they'd needed to return to Davis to finish the school term. Over the winter break, they reserved a secluded bungalow in Tahiti for a real honeymoon, and then they would detour to Scotland on the way home. Ian didn't need to be anywhere until the *Spectral Analysis* shoot was scheduled, and Janine was completely free until she made further plans.

"Oh good," Kiki said. "My mother is dying to meet you."

After the attendant left them to get undressed, Janine hesitated. Gwen had never seen her knife wounds before. Her back and stomach scars were both very deep and scary. Why hadn't she thought about that when she agreed to a spa day? Did she imagine she would get a full body massage wearing a T-shirt? Gwen and Kiki didn't notice her unease as they continued to chat and get undressed, then Janine saw Gwen's chest and the two long marks where her breasts should be. Janine realized that she was staring and looked away, embarrassed at herself for gapping.

"I'm sorry," she said. "I had no idea."

"Don't worry about it," Gwen told her. "Come on, let's see yours then."

Janine showed them the jagged scars from the knife attack, all seven of the gash marks. Janine lifted her shirt to show them the stomach marks first. Then, she exposed the two large scars on her back to include the deep shoulder gash and the uneven wound down her lower back, near her kidney, the near fatal one. All the rest were basically lighter cuts. Dramatic but survivable lines drawn onto her skin, like the X carved into her cleavage close to her left breast, over her heart.

"Well," Gwen pressed her lips together. "Those are very angry marks. You know, I made up my mind a long time ago to accept that my chest was gone and to stop worrying about it. Most people barely notice after the first look. There's no way I'm going to hide from a nice massage and body wrap over something like a couple of missing breasts."

Throughout their spa treatment, Kiki and Gwen relayed stories of their Celtic Halloween and the six victims who wore a charm from Trinity's box. Then, they discussed Caroline's old house and her stuffed attic. After hours of hunting through useless documents, they barely found any extra information about the local ghosts, just diaries with simple accounts of the orchard ghost over the years. Most entries were limited to a date with the name of a witness. Very few included a few short description lines or ghostly a quote. Only Caroline described the spirit as *kindred*, all the others found Mary quite sinister.

The oldest ledger was filled with math sums regarding the almonds and contained dated entries from the 1840s. It was created when Mary Miller was still alive. Someone kept an account of the trees, how many survived and how many were transplanted each year. In the back of those pages, they found a very dramatic entry scrawled with a heavy hand. Kiki snapped a photo of it.

Not a blessing, but a devil that fed from unholy flesh while in the womb. She's drawn to watch bodies stuck in the river rocks. Some think it brave, but I spy a curious pleasure in her eye. I fear, for as she grows older, her face becomes his.

"We believe the writer is referring to Mary Miller. The girl would have been six or seven at the time of that writing, right before she died," Kiki said. "I wager it's the mother who wrote it. Apparently, Mary was a morbid girl."

"Kiki, you wore a charm," Janine said bluntly because they kept changing the subject.

It'd bothered her since that phone call, when Kiki warned her not to touch the Comba charm. It bothered her to imagine it folded inside the crinkled paper in Kiki's purse, waiting to be worn again, and Janine knew Kiki gravitated toward those charms. She kept flashing on Kiki in the Chicago graveyard with one between her breasts, caressing it. She had insisted on wearing it with her gothic outfit and now Gwen and Kiki just claimed that six women wore a charm and were murdered. They believed wearing the charm cursed those women.

"You wore it on the last day of the Chicago shoot."

"Is that right? I dinna know that." Gwen glanced at Kiki. They were in the hot bath soaking in the mineral water, faces pink. "But maybe it's okay. Not every lassie who's worn a charm has been murdered, only women who bound themselves to a demon and then tried to leave him."

"Exactly. They were killed by a spurned lover." Kiki chuckled. "It's not like I have a long list of lovers to avoid, right?"

"What about the man from your awakening?" Janine asked. "If he wasn't Detective Anderson, who was it? Can you be certain he isn't dangerous, a demon feeling spurned? Do you know him very well? Can he be trusted?"

Kiki and Gwen exchanged guilty looks as they divulged who it was. She couldn't believe it. Kiki invited that deceitful asshole deviant who tried to coerce her into a sexual relationship by making it hard to get out of her *Spectral Analysis* contract. That's the man Kiki selected for her *important* ritual. Why Max Colliers of all people? He was the last person Janine would have guessed.

"If I couldn't have my triquetra connection, I needed someone with a very strong base aspect who would be open to a pagan sex ritual," Kiki defended herself.

But Max Colliers? "If anyone could be a demon, Max Colliers could be one," Janine spat.

"Well, he's not a demon. He has a strong yellowish core aura," Kiki said firmly, rising from the bath to wrap into a towel. "He's just a very naughty boy. If he had known the real source of your scars, he never would have chased you so ardently. He became fixated on the risky things he hoped you'd show him, Janine. I know that doesn't excuse his behavior, and he'll always be an unsavory arse, but he's exactly the type of arse I needed for that particular ritual."

"When your story broke, Max was devastated," Gwen added softly, also toweling off. "He wanted to ring you and apologize. Remember when we spoke on the phone? He was still on Skye and stewing about what to do. I believe he was truly upset with himself, if that's a consolation."

Janine already knew Max was sorry, he sent her flowers and a letter. She threw the flowers away and only opened the letter because he sent it via a currier to be delivered into her hand. She initially believed Max found some way to reinstate her contract. She opened the letter, expecting to see some type of legal document, instead she found a simple apology drawn in Max's bold artistic handwriting.

My behavior was monstrous, and I apologize. My lawyers are investigating the legality of that governor's actions at this writing. Max.

But she still harbored angry feelings toward Max and was now a little miffed at Kiki.

They decided to drop the subject during the massage and body wraps and focus on relaxing. Gwen relayed stories about growing up with Ian and their adventures on Skye. She described swimming in small lochs, the dangerous faerie niches in the green glens, and fishing off the dock in Uig Bay. Ian always had good luck with the fishes in Uig. He'd still be able to feed her if he ever lost his job, Gwen joked. Then, she recalled the lopsided distilling apparatus Ian and another boy built in Auntie Meg's shed when they were twelve. He wanted to make his own highland whisky and Gwen helped with the mash. They were lucky they didn't burn down the whole farm after making their undrinkable poison. Of course, that one was all Ian's idea.

Kiki said she brought a small cask of highland spirits and a special engraved Quaich for the wedding. The whisky was homemade from the isle, and Ian knew the maker, George MacLeod. George taught the boys secrets of whisky production during the summers when the girls were inside studying the ancient arts.

"What's a Quaich?" Janine asked.

"It's a two handled cup for sharing the whisky," Gwen told her. "It's a Scottish tradition to drink together from the same cup, to seal your bond, and then pass it to your clan."

After their seaweed and mineral body wraps, they headed to the massage room and rounded out their spa day with manicures and pedicures. Their driver suggested a fancy French eatery for dinner, where they made plans for the summoning later that night.

Instead of the orchard, they decided to visit the Old Rio Linda Graveyard and would attempt to summon Susan Miller, the mother of Mary, the orchard ghost. Kiki and Gwen worked out questions to ask Susan regarding the pre-ghost child.

From the wagon train documents, they knew that Susan had been pregnant with Mary during her months in the Sierra, Nevada. He group had gotten stuck on the mountaintop during a blizzard and people froze and starved to death. While isolated during the winter, some members of the Hansen Wagon Train resorted to cannibalism to survive. For roughly one month of her pregnancy, Susan nourished her fetus with human flesh from dead companions, flesh that provided the elements that formed the early cells of Mary Miller. After the end of that nightmare, Susan Miller and the survivors descended into the valley where she gave birth to Mary, and the town was born.

"If the spirit in the orchard actually attacked a person, tried to hurt them, then it's not a normal spirit," Kiki said. "It's an evil spirit and it will do us no good to call on a such a spirit. That spirit only repeats the dictum anyway, and little else, according to the recorded sightings."

Gwen nodded. "Aye. Twill only give the spirit a better view of our hearts and it can learn ways to trick our thinking. Best to leave that one alone. We dinna want a demon's false intentions to muddy our minds."

The Miller family gravesite loomed on a small hill in the graveyard. An ominous monument for John and Susan Miller towered over the other markers. A wall of granite six feet high, dark and menacing. One side of the placard was carved with a tree of life symbol, possibly meant to be an almond tree, and both John and Susan shared a gravestone. By the look of things, they lay side by side.

The placard was etched with a short blurb honoring John Miller for founding the orchard and town. Janine noticed they died within a month of each other in 1865. She didn't bother searching for Mary Miller's grave. It was hidden far away in the orchard, a small river stone flush with the ground. Mary had committed suicide in the at the tender age of seven and her body had probably been banned from the consecrated grounds of the church graveyard.

Janine set out a rough cobble and placed Gwen's dark candle in the center of it. Along the edge of the rock, she placed crystal gemstones of jet, amethyst, black tourmaline, and selenite. Then, she pulled out her smart phone and activated the electromagnetic field analyzer app she downloaded earlier. She propped it against a rock. Why not try to get some rough data? If they were summoning a ghost, Ian might be interested in seeing the readouts. Gwen pulled out sachets of protective herbs to place over their hearts and they arranged themselves into a small circle. Kiki lit the candle.

"I'm not sure what type of summoning to use," Janine confessed.

"We don't know much about Susan Miller," Kiki said. "Maybe just a generic summoning charm then?"

"How about the one you always use? We seek yon souls of near to there, we call on you to us appear, reveal yourself for us to see, so I command, so mote it be?" Janine offered. They each nodded. Janine settled herself to recite it.

"Dinna forget tap into your heart." Gwen put a hand on her knee. "Just pause, and take a cleansing breath, and find yerself. Slow down and consciously seek your core. Reach into your well of love, lassie. When you're ready, go on. We'll be ready with you."

Janine drew a few deep breaths and tried to clear her head, but the summoning several months ago in Thatcher Woods kept returning to her mind. The deep dark eyes and long hair of that ghost had been frightening. Who had she been, if not Miranda Daily? *Doesn't matter here, get her out of your head,* Janine told herself. She needed to relax and find her core.

Janine focused her thoughts on Ian and the Celtic rings waiting for them. She recalled Ian's eagerness to wear the thick metallic band right away. She set her mind on how he often cuddled her through the night, breathing softly into her ear after making love. Then, she reached for Kiki and Gwen's hands. They formed a connected ring around the candle, because joining hands allowed witches to share gifts with one another. Holding Kiki's hand meant she'd have a better chance of seeing and hearing something.

"*We seek yon souls of near to there, we call on you to us appear, reveal yourself for us to see, so I command, so mote it be,*" Janine said softly. Then, she repeated it more firmly, "*We seek yon souls of near to there, we call on you to us appear, reveal yourself for us to see, so I command, so mote it be.*"

They remained quiet for several long minutes as the sounds of the night emerged; the lonely song of a cricket, the rustle of a branch in the breeze, the hoot of an owl, a train lolling on the tracks several blocks away. Janine opened her eyes and glanced at Kiki and Gwen, both sat perfectly still with closed eyes. Then, Janine felt Kiki's grip loosen and watched those green eyes pop open.

"Nothing here," Kiki sighed.

Gwen also opened her eyes and relaxed.

It was a little disappointing. Susan Miller did not leave any ghostly energy in the graveyard. Kiki suddenly twisted around, stood up, and searched across the dark night. Janine was very familiar with that pursed lip look on Kiki's face, and her heart began to beat faster.

"I feel something out there," Kiki stared into the darkness. "I believe someone has heard your summons and is interested in us." Kiki knelt down to retrieve the candle and stones. She glanced at Gwen. "You have the electric torch? Let's go see who's buried over there."

Janine and Gwen followed her. They each carried a flashlight and used them to illuminate the ground. The moon was well past the first quarter, but a thin sheath of low level stratus clouds shielded most of the lunar light and the night was dark. The Rio Linda graveyard emitted a wet musty odor that intensified with their footsteps. Elaborate trees loomed creepily and cast dark shadows across the old burial grounds. Kiki led them toward a series of graves with similar markers, thick crosses with a circle around the center, Celtic crosses. The whiteness of the stones glowed luminous in the meager light.

"Have you noticed these names?" Gwen whispered. "We've left the Miller section and crossed over a variety zone and now these here are mostly Stauch."

She was right, Janine could see Stauch carved on several of the markers. Her heart tightened when she spotted three small stones that indicated children were buried side by side.

Were they victims of the river ghost?

Kiki paused in front of an old weathered Celtic cross. The white stone reflected brightly in the dark night, like an ominous beacon. Kiki knelt down to place the candle in front of the grave and lay the gemstones beside it.

"Look at this. Ingrid Stauch has beckoned us." Kiki smiled and her eyes flashed in the darkness. "This was Linda's mother, mother of the River Ghost. Ingrid may have been a witch, you know."

"That's right," Janine added. "The charm in your purse belonged to Irene Lumen, and Irene and Ingrid were related."

Gwen gave the rock to Janine to rebuild the alter. Janine transferred the candle and gemstones to the top of the stone.

The dragoma *is supposed to build the alter*, they always told her. Gwen reached over to briefly clutch Janine's hand.

"If she's a sister, maybe summon her with a joining charm like the one you used in Thatcher Woods," Gwen said softly. "We'll open our circle for her. Do you remember the words?"

Janine nodded. How could she forget them?

"Remember what happened last time, Janine." Kiki reached into her shirt to adjust her sachet. "Don't release our hands, no matter what. We need to stay connected and share our gifts. It's likely Gwen and I may both go cold again and only be able to see, hear, or have a vision. Those are our talents, audience and prophesy. So, you should ask the questions. Don't expect us to say anything."

"And remember to speak from your core, dinna waver or show weakness," Gwen added rapidly. "Be commanding, but loving. She won't come or participate if she thinks your heart is closed off to her. If you're speaking to a sister, she may be able to feel your intent."

"Okay, okay." Janine nodded. "But what am I going to ask her? We only worked out questions for Susan Miller."

Gwen and Kiki exchanged looks.

"Well," Gwen said. "Ask if she's a pagan sister. What she knows of the Comba charms. If she is aware of a curse and what it entails. What she knows about young Mary."

"Ask her who the demon is," Kiki said. "And who might be marked. What Mary means when she says, *one each for redemption*." Kiki must have seen Janine's agitated face. "Don't worry if you miss something, let's just see what she does. I can already feel her here, or someone, just hovering here. She wants to speak but needs help."

Then, Gwen passed the lighter to Janine. "Cleansing breaths," she coached gently. "Find your core."

Okay then, Janine tried relaxing. *This is Linda's mother here. Mother of the river ghost. Did the spirit of her daughter lure Sammy, my birth daughter, into the river? Good grief, Janine, let's not get into a mom fight with this spirit! Focus!*

Janine drew in deep breaths and let the air escape slowly. She mused about Ian again and their upcoming vows. She concentrated on her sister Juliana and how her sister always stood by her, even when she was upset with Janine. She recalled how Juliana swooped in, adopted Sammy, and cared for her. Then, Juliana shared Sammy with Janine, without a qualm, when Janine was finally ready to wake up.

Ingrid Stauch also lost a little girl, at that very same spot in that river. She could surely open her heart in commiseration with Ingrid on that point. Janine reached out and took Kiki and Gwen's hands all over again. Then, she focused on the candle flame and recited the charm.

"Sister come complete our ring, it's assist and ease we bring. Meet us now, and reap your meed. A sister's oath we do concede. Accept our vow to set you free. So I command. So mote it be."

Janine felt the air change, but couldn't describe it. Not colder, not warmer, just stale air. Like the molecules stopped moving and hung suspended in space. Was that why it often felt cold? She noticed a tingling, just very light touches on her face, similar to soap bubbles alighting and popping on her skin. It was an unsettling, unnatural sensation. She glanced at Kiki and Gwen, and they seemed fine. Then, she looked to the empty spot in their circle and saw nothing unusual.

But someone or something filled that void, Janine sensed it, and her heart rate began to pick up. She felt eyes bearing down on her, eyes from the empty spot in their circle. She repeated the summons in a soft commanding voice.

"Sister come complete our ring, it's assist and ease we bring. Meet us now, and reap your meed. A sister's oath we do concede. Accept our vow to set you free. So I command. So mote it be."

Kiki turned slightly to face the empty spot in their circle. *Did Kiki see something?* Janine glanced at Gwen. Gwen's eyes fluttered between open and closed, and her head tilted downward. Janine examined the empty spot. What did Kiki see? Janine strained to distinguish something, anything, and noticed the air become a little out of focus over there, a little evanescent. Or was it only the dim light and the moist night playing tricks on her vision?

"Are you Ingrid Stauch?" Kiki asked quietly. "Can you hear me?"

After a moment, Kiki squeezed Janine's hand.

"I don't think she can hear me," Kiki whispered to Janine. "You try asking."

"Are you Ingrid Stauch?" Janine asked the empty spot.

Kiki's reaction indicated that her invisible friend had answered. On the *Spectral Analysis* television show, Janine and Kiki attempted something similar. Janine spoke to a ghost while Kiki listened and watched for it. If Janine or Kiki exerted an extreme amount of psychic effort, they could do it all, speak, see, and hear a ghost, especially if they held hands and shared their gifts.

But then, how had she managed to see the Mary ghost so easily when Kiki wasn't there?

"Do you know of the Saint Comba charms?" Kiki inquired.

"Do you know of the Saint Comba charms?" Janine repeated.

Kiki posed, "What do you know of the curse? Who is the demon?"

Everything Kiki asked, Janine repeated, and while she parroted Kiki's questions, she kept one eye on the empty space and one eye on Gwen. Gwen appeared to be sleeping and dreaming. Her eyes fluttered beneath her lids in a REM like pattern. The empty space became more and more unfocused. The air took on a wave-like quality, as if atmospheric gasses were turning to liquid or being heated over a very hot surface. Janine could see an outline begin to emerge in the wavering molecules.

"Are you a student of the pagan ways?"

It was a womanly shape, quivering through the surface of a mysterious fluid. Janine could just detect the edges of her body. She could make out the curve of a long slender neck, rolling with the rhythm of her trembling visage. It began to reflect the candlelight and called to mind those female silhouettes on the mud flaps of big trucks, bouncing along the highway at night.

"What does *one each for redemption* mean?"

An oval face filled in with large eyes and a wide mouth. As she became more vivid, Janine could see that her skin was smooth and creamy. Very pleasing. Her hair was shiny, lush, with a bright buttery color. Her entire image oscillated continuously, as if she stood behind a flowing wall of water. Very disturbing. She gave the impression of a young and vibrant woman, but her face was aged and her expression uncomfortable. The image generated sadness which Janine felt it in her own heart, effusive sorrow.

"Who is marked?"

Her agitated movements were odd and inspired fear. Her eyes fluctuated from Kiki to Janine in stop action motion, like a strobe light. It made Janine nervous, and the beat of her heart drummed faster. The ghost moved in such disharmony with her beautiful flowing image. While her likeness rippled steadily in that unknown liquid, her gestures were jerky and harsh. Her hand was here, then there. Her head faced right, then left. There was no way to predict her movements, and Janine felt a surge of acid build in the pit of her stomach. Her own limbs became heavy. Core energy began draining from Janine's chest as the sadness overtook her, she could feel her core empty out. Feelings of abandonment, grief, and hopelessness dominated her heart and soul.

"What did Linda die of?" Kiki asked.

"Did Linda lure Sammy into the river?" Janine asked quickly, instead.

The woman's mouth opened, then closed without a sound. The wavering head faced right, then left, then right again. The womanly image began fading from sight because Janine's eyes were blurring and clouding over. Janine felt herself moving further and further away from the situation as her eyes tunneled. Her pulse raced. She knew she should not have tried so hard to see this spirit. Janine lost focus and she couldn't decipher the next question Kiki asked.

"Why can I see the ghost of Mary Miller?" Janine gasped in a whisper.

Then, she heard the old woman's voice, soft, choppy and distinct, one word at a time.

"You. Can. Be. The. Last. One."

Then, the world contracted dramatically and pulsed once before expiring, and Janine passed out.

Chapter 11

Vows

Janine

When they returned from the graveyard, they found the bar in their Old Town Sacramento hotel pulsing with activity. Gwen and Kiki insisted on finding a back table to discuss the séance. They might be able absorb some ambient energy into their drained cores, Kiki whispered. She didn't fool Janine, Kiki planned to absorb more than ambient energy, she was outright trying to attract attention as they worked their way to a back table. At one point, Kiki glided into a random fellow and gave him a very slow appraisal. Then, she smiled sweetly at him, flashed her bright green eyes and drew in an exaggerated breath.

"Well, aren't you a stimulating sight," Kiki purred in her silky, seductive voice. Then, she hugged Janine with one arm as the man and his friends quickly gathered around. "My friend is getting married this weekend. So, please excuse us for appraising you fellows a little blatantly, we mean no harm. She'll be mourning all the fine blokes she'll be giving up… but that's not till this weekend. I hope we've come to the right place to celebrate."

Kiki winked at them, then she pulled Janine along. Gwen hung back to order the drinks.

"Good grief, Kiki, really?" She still felt weak and irritated from her encounter in the graveyard, and Kiki's remedy of attracting male attention to recharge her psychic batteries was not high on Janine's to do list.

"You're the one that fainted out there," Kiki whispered. "Now you've got a ton of testosterone fueled energy focused right on your ass. Stop deflecting it. Just divert it into your core and thank me later."

Gwen caught up to them as they sat down. She brought three tumblers of neat whisky and scooted into the booth across from Kiki and Janine. She brushed her long red hair aside and grinned at them.

"Well, that wee group is now convinced our lassie is looking for a final fling. I'd wager they're a little drunk." Gwen's pink cheeks glowed as she glanced around. "I asked them to hang back and allow you to decide from afar. I hinted that we may bring over a key with terms of engagement in a wee bit. So then, Janine, they'll be vying for your attention. Soak it up, lass."

"Not you too!" She tried to hide and slid further into the booth. She could see the group of men glancing over, checking her out, starting to strut a bit. "Didn't you advise me not to try this sort of thing without a lot of practice? I'm not soaking up anything from anyone that isn't Ian McNally."

"Oh, calm yerself. No harm in letting those nice lads flood you with admiring energy," Gwen said. "Just try to redirect it to your core. You can practice right now." Gwen glanced over her shoulder. "As long as they stay over there, you'll be grand, no pressure. Ho ho, look at this."

The waiter delivered three new drinks from that small group of five men. He said the group sent them a message.

Congratulations, and they'd be happy to help celebrate as needed.

"I'm going to leave." But Janine was boxed in and Kiki gave her a stern look.

"No, you're not. It's your hen, and you're staying," Kiki insisted. "Those fellows are just flirting. They just want to see who you'd pick. They probably got a bet going by the way they're standing like that. It's just harmless fun. Just try to absorb some of their energy and then we'll forget about them. They'll lose interest after a while."

"I don't understand why I'm the one who fainted," Janine said miserably. "I didn't faint in the orchard. I got weak, but I didn't faint. And I didn't need to hold your hand to see the ghost in the orchard."

"Did you hear the ghost at all? Ingrid's spirit?" Kiki asked them.

"Not me, I was in a trance. I had another vision," Gwen said.

"Only what she said right before I fainted, when she said *you can be the last one*," Janine grumbled. "She said that to me, didn't she? She meant that *I* can be the last one. Last one for what? To drown in the river? I thought that was part of the river curse and Sammy had been the last one! So, what did she mean then? Is there another curse? Did we get it all wrong?"

Gwen stared at Janine, then glanced at Kiki. Kiki shook her head.

"No, no, you didn't hear everything. It wasn't quite like that," Kiki said.

"I asked her why I could see the ghost of Mary, and she responded with, *you can be the last one.*" Janine felt like Kiki and Gwen had both come to a similar conclusion but weren't sharing it with her. Kiki continued shaking her head.

"That's not what she meant."

"What's wrong?" Janine asked. "What do you think it means?" Janine asked Gwen.

Gwen settled comfortably in her seat and played with a stray loop of her red hair.

"It could mean many things, we're still piecing the puzzle together and it'll do us no good to be jumping to conclusions at this early stage. One thing is clear, that dictum was never about your river." Then, her blue eyes settled on Janine a little more tenderly. "Besides, lass, you never wore a Comba charm. The ghost can't mean *you* when she said you. Maybe she meant a generic *you*."

"That's exactly what it was. The Mary ghost has been making that same statement for decades. It's a generic warning. She could have meant me, just as much as Janine, or anyone." Kiki stared at Gwen with her intense green eyes.

Who was she trying to convince, Janine thought.

"Look here. Let's just share what we saw and heard," Gwen proposed. "We'll gather all the information and sit on it for a wee bit of time before drawing any conclusions."

She reached into her purse and pulled out a little notebook.

"We'll jot it down separately, so as not influence each other, and then share it out. We'll draw no conclusions, not tonight. Not until we've sorted through those old tomes back home and discussed it with the other sisters. Not until we gather as much information as we can."

Janine wrote her description of the spirit of Ingrid Stauch, the very beautiful ghost that appeared to be underwater. She also angrily wrote out the one patchy sentence about her being the last one. She also noted that her EMF app didn't pick up anything in that graveyard, probably because the phone app didn't make a very good receiver.

Gwen wrote a narrative of her vision, which was quite disturbing to Janine. A large gathering was on the horizon, with twelve Saint Comba charms brought before a demon spirit to bear witness to everything. Gwen could not identify anyone present, because everyone came shrouded in capes, but it appeared to be their coven sisters in a dark gathering. She saw a witch's dagger and indications of a blood ritual, not something they'd done before.

"Not every charm had a story of redemption," Gwen said of her vision. "At least one pendant was still in need of a redeemer, and it allows the demon to continue marking people who come near any of the charms. Several sisters at the gathering were marked already, we'll see it on them. So, in front of the demon's spirit, a pledge is made to complete the curse before anyone else is tagged for death. I could not see anything past that gathering and I could not see the faces of anyone there."

"Holy crap," Janine cursed.

"A vision isn't always a premonition," Kiki added forcefully. "Sometimes nothing comes of it."

Gwen nodded. "She's right. Remember, we make no conclusions here. Who knows, we may discover something else that'll bend the meaning in that vision. It's likely we've got things wrong. Come now, Kiki, your turn. What did Ingrid have to say about things?"

Kiki wrote a description similar to Janine's, except the spirit appeared crystal clear and not wavy in the least for her. Ingrid's hair was a gorgeous blonde cascade, and her eyes were big round balls of sky blue. She had a dainty nose and pink rosy lips, beautiful. She seemed a little on the shy side, eyes pointed down and away, and Kiki felt that made her slightly shifty, perhaps untrustworthy. But her movements flowed, no stop action for Kiki, and she wasn't scary in the least. The ghost confirmed that she was once Ingrid Stauch, and that Saint Comba was the patron saint of her birth family. The spirit believed a curse followed the women in her family, a curse that bestowed physical beauty on them but drew evil intentions.

"She was marked," Kiki said. "When we asked her who was marked by the demon, she said that every woman in her family was marked, even Linda, the girl. They fled the big city because of the marks. She said that Linda died of being baptized in the river."

"Did she answer my question?" Janine asked. "Did the ghost of Linda lure Sammy into the river, or was it something else?"

"She didn't say anything about that," Kiki told her.

"Did she identify the demon?" Gwen asked.

"She named Hansen as a demon, and his father, but never suspected either of them until the wagon train. Hansen marked others too," Kiki told them. "She said he continues to leave marks, as his child leaves a mark."

"His child? What child?" Janine asked.

"I don't want to speculate, but I got a gut feeling during that whole episode," Kiki said. "I feel like this ghost implied that Mary Miller was the demon's daughter. That Mary became the demon, *in flesh*, when she was born. It makes sense. Remember the scribbling that said, *as she grows older, her face becomes his*. That's got to be a reference to Hansen. You read the wagon train diary. Stanley Hansen was a predator, chasing every woman in that group. The ghost said he marked others. We can be the last to deal with Mary, if the curse is broken. Perhaps that's what she meant with the words, *you can be the last one.*"

That was a much nicer interpretation than the one formed in Janine's head. Both Gwen and Kiki didn't want to say it, but clearly, the ghost believed Janine could be the last one to die wearing a Comba charm. She was slated to be the last redeemer of the curse, *wasn't it obvious?* It didn't take rocket science to figure it out. Those charms fell into Janine's lap, both of them, and she successfully attracted a psychopath in her past. She was probably marked already. Holy crap, and her psychopath was out freely roaming the country.

"Hey, ladies."

Two of the flirty men were standing next to the table carrying more drinks. They each wore a mischievous smile. The taller man grinned quite handsomely with an attractive tilt to his lips, but his brow suddenly furrowed in a concerned way.

"Hope we're not interrupting. It looked like a serious discussion going on, so we thought we'd come over and lighten your mood. You're supposed to be celebrating we're told."

"We're happy to help you ladies celebrate." The other one grinned. "Any final decisions over here?"

"Good grief!" Janine slapped her hand on the table. "Do you really think I'm looking for a final fling three days before I get married?"

By the look on their faces, she might have just slapped them on the face instead. They visibly shrank a tiny bit, preparing to bolt, but Kiki quickly jumped up and fluttered her eyes at them, smiling. She leaned in a little close, so they were doubly confused. Gwen also started to rise but stopped about halfway and chuckled. She retrieved one of the whiskies from their hands and flicked her red hair.

"Oh, don't listen to her," Gwen said. "She's a wee vexed because she really wanted to misbehave but is chickening out. She's way too attached and loyal to her man, you understand. And I see you must have guessed, that's why you came over, it was you that caught her eye before losing her nerve." Gwen smiled sweetly at the taller man, the one with the handsome smile.

He didn't appear to quite believe that, but chuckled anyway. The shorter man stared at Kiki with owl eyes.

"Aren't you Kiki Mellow?"

"I am." Kiki maneuvered between the two men and slipped a hand on each of their arms. She began walking them back to their little crowd and appeared very interested in both of them. "Why don't you introduce me to your friends?"

When they had gotten out of earshot, Gwen slipped back down to a sitting position and gave Janine a small smile.

"The task is not yours to be a sacrifice. I can see you're thinking it. Just because we might guess a curse's meaning does not mean we need to follow it. Besides, you never wore a Comba charm, and as long as you don't wear one, you can never be the last redeemer." Gwen split up the rest of the drinks between them. "You shunned those charms instinctively and must have felt the curse. You realize that we are nae letting you anywhere near the charms. There'll be no wearing a Saint Comba charm for you, ever. The spirits and ghosts dinna know all that, you know, and visions do not make a fixed future. So, please relax, it's probably wedding jitters that got you spinning your doomsday scenario." Gwen glanced toward Kiki and the group of five men. "I'm getting a wee bit drowsy and Kiki's stilling running off at the mouth. Is she over there getting her energy reset, or do you wager she fancies one of them?"

"Sorry about snapping. You think I was a little harsh on that guy?"

Gwen shook her heard. "Not too bad, but a good rule of thumb, Janine. Treat nicely the ones replenishing your core energy. It's the least we can do to repay that kind deed."

Gram's backyard was back to normal. After the excavation of large boulders from the hill, truckloads of dirt and soil were carted in to rebuild the mound. At first, the workmen didn't follow Mother Nature's lead and the mound took the shape of a small angular levy wall, but Gram personally redirected the spread of earth to flatten the landscape in a more pleasing way. Afterwards, a landscaper arrived and seeded the soil for grasses and wildflowers. Gram was delighted, because the seeds attracted the hens back to the hill. Their clucking and strutting calmed Gram tremendously. So, she managed to save the wildlife, the environment, and the view from the evil bulldozers.

Gram's five acre manicured lawn had further been transformed for the outdoor wedding and reception with a large tented area. A false floor lay under a canopy of high spires, and the sides of the giant tent were tied open to allow a cool breeze to flow over the diners. Chandeliers decorated the high areas while round tables with tall floral centerpieces were scattered over two thirds of the false floor. The last third was cleared for dancing. Gram solicited a bluegrass rock band, *Joe Craven and The Sometimers*, with a double bass player, drummer, guitarist, and mandolin/fiddler to provide the entertainment. The small wedding Janine and Ian initially planned morphed into something larger than anticipated. Besides Janine's immediate family, and Ian's cousin, Ian's research students, rugby team, as well as Janine's soccer team were all invited. Then, Gram added her own personal friends and local relatives. Close to seventy plus people socialized in Gram's backyard. Not the handful of people they first imagined when they agreed not to elope.

Near the glass back patio, an area with rows of foldout wooden chairs had been arranged to face the elevated wooden deck. A beautiful floral arch of white roses, peonies, and hydrangeas in eucalyptus greens framed the steps off the deck. That was the spot Janine and Ian exchanged vows with the pretty Lutheran minister from Gram's church officiating the ceremony. Gram bragged proudly that her own wedding had taken place in that same backyard in a very similar setup.

Most of the day had gone by in a blur for Janine. Her soccer teammates helped her get ready, along with her young niece, who appeared very grown up in her pinkish bridesmaid dress. Her sister Juliana teared up at the sight of them, while her brother-in-law Adam laughed, looking very smart in his tuxedo. He whispered that it wasn't too late to run away if she wasn't completely sure. Then, Adam escorted her down the aisle, beaming proudly.

Janine felt wobbly as she followed the confident steps of teenaged Ashley. She walked between the rows of chairs with every eye on her and wished that they had eloped instead. The undivided attention was nerve racking. She calmed down when spotted Gram and Juliana weeping together and fidgeting Carlos next to Ian. Carlos, with his deep cheek dimples, seemed to be biting back a witty remark. Ian appeared absolutely in love. When his soft blue eyes met hers, she melted all over again, and everyone else become a blur. It no longer mattered whether the others were there or not, all that mattered was the starry-eyed guy staring back at her.

It was getting late and Janine hadn't really chatted with anyone. She'd been tasked to dance with old relatives and rugby players and Ian in between. When she saw Ian dancing with Gwen, Carlos came round to claim her.

"Oh my god, this dress! At first, I was wondering, who is that gorgeous woman the doctor's marrying, whatever happened to Janine? I'm not kidding, every jaw dropped. We all wondered where and when you finally escaped." He finally got his wisecrack out. "I totally expected you to be in clumpy boots and a T-shirt. I'm very disappointed."

"You look nice too, Carlos," Janine said, and they both laughed. "How's being a weatherman?"

Carlos scowled, then smiled. "Early mornings. But I'm home every day. Maria is actually getting annoyed with me. Me, annoying? Tell me you find that unbelievable?" *Not at all.*

They searched the crowd and spotted Maria chatting with Kiki Mellow and a few older women. It appeared to be a nice tea party around that table. Janine spied Leone sitting next to Kiki, peering into a coffee cup. No doubt they were exchanging readings. Janine and Carlos strolled in that direction when Ben rushed up to greet them. Emma and Oliver were close behind. Janine hugged each of the research crew before introducing Carlos them.

"You guys are the tech experts developing new gadgets?" Carlos asked.

"Boom. Yes." Emma nodded and started speaking rapidly. "We actually field tested a few of our tools recently, on a real ghost. Very successful. It was eerie. If you're staying around for a while, we can show you some of the equipment. In fact, we've brought the *mellow-skin* and UV cams and other stuff out here for another try in the orchard tonight. Why not, since we're in Sacramento again, right? Boom! If you like, you can come along. It wouldn't be a problem, and it might be fun. I think you'd like what we've come up with."

Then, Emma gave a quick nod and bee-lined away. She pulled Oliver with her and they disappeared to the dance floor.

"What was that?" Carlos was all dimples, chuckling.

"Oh, just Emma," Ben told him. "She's your biggest fan and has a major crush on you. Are you guys heading to Kiki Mellow? I've been waiting to say hello, but she seems a little busy."

"Come on," Janine grabbed Bens arm and they continued to Kiki's table. Everyone stood up to hug Janine. The small group chatted about the online tea-reading lessons from Annelise Batten. Janine finally gave Kiki a proper hug. They hadn't seen each other since the hotel in Old Town and Janine wished she hadn't gotten so upset that night. Now that the wedding was winding down, and the media had disappeared, her stress lifted and she felt a little silly about everything.

"Hello there, cousin." Kiki engulfed her and then also hugged Carlos. "Hello, you." Then, she smiled at Ben, who had turned a slight shade of red. "And hello to you, you handsome fellow. I was wondering when you'd find the time to come and say hello to me. I was getting very jealous of those girls in your group."

Someone brought over bubbling wine, and they toasted Janine again. Then, Carlos started bragging about his twins' soccer successes. The twins, Milo and Mimi, were off playing in the grassy area with the other children, kicking a ball around. Janine watched the kids for a bit. Her nephew Jack, the oldest of the lot, dominated the action. Two of her soccer teammates played with them, keeping things even. They had kicked off their heels and played in pretty dresses with bare feet. For a brief moment, Janine felt sad.

Sammy should be out there kicking the soccer ball.

She shook that out of her head and pretended to listen to the chatter surrounding her. She searched around and spotted her sister Juliana watching the band, then she watched her niece Ashley dancing with Oliver and Emma in a circle with other young people. Ian still danced with Gwen.

"So, I was thinking," Ben stammered at Kiki, "would you consider coming out with us?"

"Well, it sounds like fun," Kiki said, "but Gwen and I are actually flying to Chicago on the red eye. As soon as the newlyweds drive off to Tahoe, we've got to pack up and run to the airport."

Chicago? Janine finally noticed that Detective Anderson was not at her wedding. Janine glanced around the crowd for him and settled on Gwen and Ian instead. Those two were speaking intimately as they slowly made their way toward Janine. Gwen's face appeared redder than usual and... *Were Ian's eyes blinking? Did he look upset?*

Gram ran up to their little group.

"The limo's out front," she practically squealed. "I have it all planned out! Jaja, I want you and *your groom* to walk out the front door toward the limo. There are bubbles in a basket on the porch, and everyone is going to line up along the walk and blow them at you. The photographer is standing ready and says that the light is perfect right now, perfect! It's going to look magical."

"You want us to head around and gather in the front yard, right now?" Carlos asked.

"Boom!" Gram winked at him before running off to prompt another group to move to the front.

Carlos watched Gram run off with a confused expression on his face. "Did she just say boom?"

"She's convinced it's the new slang for *yes*." Janine giggled. "Gram refuses to give it up because she thinks she sounds very hip saying it. She's got all of her girls saying it now. Right, Leone?"

The tall, thin old lady smiled up from her tea cup. "Oh yes, boom," she agreed.

Ian and Gwen finally reached them. If he had been blinking earlier, he wasn't anymore. To everyone's pleasure, he gave Janine a nice deep kiss. Then, he whispered that the car was waiting out front to take them to Donner Lake and that hotel they once stayed in.

Chapter 12
Chicago

Kiki

iki and Gwen lounged in the rooftop bar of the London House Hotel enjoying the sunset. They were waiting for Detective Anderson and a woman named Mary Kline. They scheduled a dinner meeting in the restaurant and went up for an early cocktail to cool their nerves. Or, at least, Kiki needed to cool her nerves. She hadn't seen Bob Anderson since he bailed on their budding romance and she was nervous about the dinner.

She noticed Gwen admiring three very pretty professional looking women at the end of the bar. Gwen gravitated toward confident, feminine women, as she was quite graceful herself. Feminine, but with an *Annie Hall* type of flair. Gwen preferred flowing slacks and blouses to dainty dresses. She detested an overtly sexy look and loved a classic, professional, ladylike style. She never tired of chiding Kiki for dressing in silly racy outfits with high hems, sheer material, and revealing necklines.

"Dream on, those girls are as straight as arrows." Kiki laughed. "And shouldn't you mind your eyes anyway?"

"Don't be so sure, my wee yin. You may be the master of the Core Well, but I am the tutor of the Base Well. I'd wager that pretty lass on the left leans my way," Gwen confided. "Besides, I'm a free agent now. I can do whatever I want, without the guilt."

"Tell the truth, Gwen, this new Comba pendant Janine found. Did you feel anything in it? A death? Or do you think it's one that needs a redeemer?" She asked. "Do you think the redeemer can be anyone, or do you think the charm will select a specific soul? Perhaps someone is already marked by that charm. Are we going to say it out loud?"

"No conclusions. Not until we go over everything. Not until we relay everything. There must be another meaning in it all. Janine *shunned* those charms, how could it be her if she was repelled by them? It would have to be someone who is attracted to them." Gwen sighed, "She looked beautiful in that gown, didn't she? A very refined and modest choice. It cut a nice silhouette, don't you think? And Ian. The way he gazed at her. I'm very proud of him. I just want to declare it… that I deserve a little credit for molding him so well."

Kiki started laughing at that.

"Ho ho, I absolutely molded him, you little witch."

"What is it you were talking about at the end there? I saw his colors turn the wrong shade of brown."

Gwen's eyelids fluttered and she wrinkled her freckled nose at Kiki. Definitely something personal. Since Gwen started dating women, she kept her personal business closer to the chest. She freely discussed coven friends, boyfriends, other friends, other couples, but never deeply discussed her *girl*friends with Kiki. This last girlfriend had been serious, and Kiki knew that waves started rocking that boat when Gwen visited back in the spring for Ian's birthday. It's likely that Bridget was jealous of Ian. He had been Gwen's longest relationship to date, and first love, but Gwen rarely discussed those details with Kiki anymore.

"If you must know, my embryos," Gwen said. "Back at his birthday, I told Ian that I finally planned to use the embryos, and he was happy about it. Bridget begged to carry the baby, to make it ours, my egg and her womb. But that's all moot now. Doesn't matter anyway, because he hasn't even discussed it with Janine. After they got engaged so suddenly, I wanted her to know those embryos existed before proceeding, but he's a blockhead and didn't know why she would care about my embryos and I had to explain it to him. Oh no, Kiki, here you are making your face. This is why I don't like discussing things with you." Gwen finished her drink. "You're making things worse with that face of yours."

"Is it really over with Bridget, Gwen? You don't think she'll come around?"

"It's the coven," Gwen told her. "It kills a lot of relationships, not just mine. Look at how your Detective Anderson ran away. Most people fancy dating a witch as cute, but then they delve deeper into things, and they dinna understand it. Best to find someone from a coven family. Annie is the smart one, fixing herself on Sam Welks. He's one of old Cara's grandsons, you know. It's a rare outsider that can truly accept the pagan ways."

Perhaps Gwen was right, but Kiki was still going to give it another try with the detective. His deep, rich aura pointed to a highly spiritual person who she wanted to learn more about. The detective had just gotten a shock at the magnitude of her pagan practices. His conventional religious background made it difficult for him to accept the things she asked of him, and Kiki had dropped too many bombs too fast. They completely connected in their core wells. They just needed to find some sort of compromise between his conventional belief system and her pagan one. Then, maybe, they could conceive a child. Kiki definitely felt that Bob Anderson was the correct man for that task. A powerful core, that's what she wanted for her daughter.

Gwen knocked her arm to get her attention.

"Ho, ho, look who just walked in. Your rare outsider."

His eyes locked right onto her, Max Colliers. She should have known. That'll teach her to use Cheryl from the *Spectral Analysis* office to book all her travel and hotel plans. He pushed his designer glasses back into position and walked toward her with a big smile under his bright happy eyes. He hugged both of them warmly.

"Kiki and Gwen, so nice to see you." He signaled the bartender with a flick of his hand. "Before you say anything, this is my week in Chicago, board meetings every day downstairs. I'm not stalking you, I promise. I was delighted to hear you would be here during our Chicago summit, a little bird told me. I'm going to call it fate, unless you admit that you were actually trying to bump into me."

Max loosened his dot patterned silk luxury tie and unbuttoned his collar. He insisted on treating them to drinks and dinner. They told him they were waiting for the detective and would have to decline the dinner, but they would never say no to free drinks. He didn't mention the texts and phone calls Kiki never returned. They told him a little about the Samhain bonfire festival that he missed, and also about the wedding in Sacramento.

"I'm sorry I missed it, but you couldn't get me to step foot in that cow town again," he meant Sacramento. Kiki knew that he would have gone, if he had been invited. "Did you meet the new tech crew? Ian has some interesting kids in that lab."

The Colliers company was funding the entire grant for *Spectral Analysis* research and development, and Max happened to be the top active executive. Half the kids in Ian's lab received scholarships from his parent company, and Max Colliers was basically paying for Ben's doctorate degree. No one could accuse Max of being tight with his money, but Kiki knew there were lots of thick strings attached to all those investments.

Gwen excused herself to go chat with the three women she had been eyeing earlier, she wanted to give Kiki and Max a private moment. She knew it was their first face to face meeting after the ritual on Skye. Max kept his eyes on Kiki as Gwen walked away.

"I stayed as long as I could, to see you at the cottage, but Gwen said you might be gone another day or another week, no one knew. I already rearranged my schedule and then there were—"

"I wasn't expecting you to hang around," Kiki cut him off.

She found it hard to meet Max's eye, his expression was so happy and earnest. All of his usual Max Colliers flirty sparring was replaced with a bit of maudlin adoration, and it was hard to take. She felt herself being drawn in by his good humor. If her aura had taken on a new red tinge in places, his had developed a bit of soft blue around his yellow core, and she found it quite attractive. Maybe the whole experience had just brought the blue out from hiding. That awakening may have been a good growth experiment for both of them.

His proximity stimulated a sudden flash of the ritual to mind, and the memory tingled all over her. She actually felt a little embarrassed and slightly stirred up. If she felt that way, it was likely he did too.

"Look, Max, I want to thank you for flying to Scotland at the drop of a hat," Kiki said. "There aren't very many men I could have asked…"

"Are you kidding?" He shook his head in disagreement.

"There aren't many men I could have asked that I would have opened with like that. And I needed to open up for a successful awakening," she insisted to his shaking head. "Listen up, I need to say this clearly. Although I opened my passion center to you, and it was an amazing experience, that's all it was. You must know that it had nothing to do with love, or relationships, or anything near that vicinity. That's why I chose you. I knew you could meet me with the passion and not get it mixed up with the other stuff. It was just a fun…experience. Okay? You did me a big favor, and I appreciate it."

"It can be whatever you want it to be." He grinned at her. "I promise to never mix anything up. You can decide what everything means. I love that you believe I did you a big favor. Any time you need a favor…"

He took her hand and kissed it before she knew what he was doing. Then, he paused and kissed her knuckles slowly, more sensually, to remind her of that passion he opened up. She felt her blood bubbling and her breath come quicker. Sitting across from her first erotic partner and inhaling the scent of him caused an automatic response to develop inside of her. She pulled her hand away and slammed her Base Well door shut on him. It was something Kiki had always been able to do, better than anyone else. He didn't seem to notice and stuck his hand in a pocket to pull something out.

"I admit you have an effect on me, Max," she uttered, avoiding his eyes. "But I'm actually interested in someone else quite seriously. I'm talking about love with him. He's going to be showing up pretty soon and I'd like to gather my wits before he gets here, and not have any added complications."

Max nodded, still smiling. "I understand. So, it's a love thing with him? Of course." He set a velvet box on the bar. "But you'll allow me to give you a little gift first? No, don't worry, I promise to get promptly out of your way after you accept my gift nicely."

His boyish eyes danced with amusement.

"That event was a big one for me, the coolest experience ever. And it was especially big for you, I didn't realize that when you said you were breaking a virginal vow of chastity that you weren't kidding. I was floored. First, that it was a true witch's ritual and not some joke, then that you were just… just… You're the sexiest woman ever, Kiki, I've always thought so. And you were really a virgin, I couldn't believe it. But I need to fix something. I didn't bring you a gift, like an offering. Your mother, Trinity, told me that traditionally the man might bring the virgin a little gift. You didn't mention that part to me. I should have thought of it, but it all happened so quickly."

"Usually, it's just a little food and whisky," Kiki told him. "You brought that, remember?"

"That wasn't my gift," Max said. "Your friends, Gwen, Annie, and your mother put that together, it was their gift. I didn't gather those things. Besides, if I'm going to give you a gift, I want my gift to be more permanent and everlasting, a true Max Colliers gift." He slid the velvet box across the bar to her. "I had it specially made, right when I got home."

Max opened the box and she saw a bracelet of diamonds and emeralds glittering in the dim light. The elongated cut emeralds were set in pairs and the seven princess cut diamonds split up the pairs as they lay in a simple line. The gems sparkled beautifully and she held her breath for a second. Max discovered her weakness: gemstones.

"One diamond for each of those lovely ladies you invited, and the emeralds remind me of you, Kiki. That's your exact eye color when you're angry… or aroused." He glanced shyly into her eyes. "Now, accept it nicely and I promise to get out of your way."

Kiki admitted to herself that the bracelet was a stunner, and she wanted it. It was bad luck to refuse an awakening gift, she reasoned, so she held out her hand and allowed him to clasp it onto her wrist. He gazed into her eyes again and Kiki felt an odd warmth. She expected Max to be gung-ho and a little sentimental, but she didn't expect that she'd develop tender feelings for him in return. But there they were, and underneath those feelings, there was still a bit of simmering lust running through her system. She closed it all down as she watched those jewels slide down her arm.

"If things go south with the love guy, you know where to find me. I'm always available if you need any little favors." He smiled at her.

Gwen came around to look at her new bracelet and two of the women professionals followed her over. Apparently, they had been in the same board meetings with Max earlier, and they all knew each other well. Kiki showed off her wrist as they oohed and aahed. Max told them it was a present, and they assumed it was for her recent birthday. They chatted about the *Spectral Analysis* show until Kiki spotted the detective at the lounge entrance, then Kiki and Gwen begged off for their dinner meeting.

Detective Robert Anderson stood about five foot six, not tall by male standards, but still taller than Kiki. She knew most women preferred fellows like Max Colliers, but she loved that the detective appeared large without taking up so much space. He had wiry curly hair and a bit of a receding chin. His huge white teeth were very bright against his dark skin, and his clothes always seemed perpetually wrinkled. Most people would not classify the detective as a handsome man, but Kiki saw something different when she looked at him. She saw the energy that pulsed around him. His aura was very bright and pulsed pinkish in a thick cloud around his core. It extended about three feet from his center and people visibly calmed when they passed close enough to touch it.

When the detective fixed his eyes on a person, he had a keen way of focusing on them. The few times he sent Kiki passion energy, he had mixed it with his pink core tones, and it made her swoon with feelings of love. It had been a knee buckling experience and very unexpected. Kiki watched him for a full minute before he turned his big brown eyes in her direction. He couldn't help himself and smiled widely. He was happy to see her too.

"Wow, she's cute," Gwen said. "Looks like her brother."

The woman standing next to the detective was an inch taller than the detective and better groomed. Her shoulder length dirty blond hair framed an oval face with eyes that might be light blue but appeared grey in the distance. Her body still looked in good shape, but her hips had clearly let loose a baby or two in the past. Her attention landed right on Kiki and she started walking toward them before the detective moved. The detective hurried after her.

"Miss Mellow, Miss Murphy." The detective gave them each a warm smile.

He introduced Mary Kline and they all exchanged greetings. They were escorted to a table on the outside patio near one of the heat lamps. It afforded a spectacular view of the buildings and river along Chicago's River Walk. The detective pointed out the clock tower at the Wrigley Building, a historic landmark visible from their table. Like Big Ben, it had a clock face on every side and was startlingly white against the blue sky.

The detective retrieved an eight by ten picture of one of the Saint Comba charms. The charm had an imprint of a woman with her left hand chained to a wall and a large animal at her feet. Kiki sent him that photo because she thought the charm might belong to Miranda Daily. A college guy found the necklace in Thatcher Woods and insisted on delivering it to Janine Stinger at the urgings of a scary ghost.

Kiki wore it on one of their ghost hunting nights and it gave her a death vision. The original vision had been confusing, like two versions of the same death, or perhaps two different deaths. Later, Janine, Kiki, and Gwen took the charm back to Thatcher Woods and used it to call up a ghost who led them to some bones. Up until a few weeks ago, they had been convinced that the ghost and bones belonged to Miranda Daily, a girl that dated the man who once tried to kill Janine Stinger. A man Kiki believed was a true demon, a person without a core. Now, they sat across from that man's sister.

"I'll come right out with it," Mary Kline said. "That necklace belonged to my mother. She wore it every day of her life and now it belongs to me. I'd like to have it back."

Her mother?

The Comba charm necklace belonged to Richard Wilkens's mother? Kiki searched Gwen's big blue eyes and she appeared just as stunned as Kiki. Mary Kline waited patiently. She was an attractive woman who came across as tired and worried. Her hands fidgeted around her cup. Her grey eyes darted from person to person.

"Detective Anderson tells me a private investigator contacted the people you gave the necklace to and they know it doesn't belong to them, but they refuse to send it to me because they got it from you. They plan to deliver it to you somewhere in Scotland." Mary Kline leaned forward. "I want it back. You must understand my feelings. It's my mother's necklace and she always wore it." A fat tear rolled down her cheek.

Kiki and Gwen both nodded their heads, of course they understood. If it had belonged to their mother, they'd want it returned as well. Such objects bore an imprint of a person's soul, which made the object invaluable. Kiki detected high levels of energy in that particular charm, powerful and positive energy along with the death vision.

Gwen reached across the table to gently pat Mary's hand. "There, there, lassie."

"I thought Rick gave it away, to that girl, Miranda Daily. I accused him of giving her my mother's jewelry." Mary wiped her tears away. "Miranda was wearing it when I met her and I became livid when she refused to give it back. But the detective says that she has one of her own. I never knew there was more than one of those necklaces. Believe me, I tried to find one for years."

Several months before her father's heart attack, Mary and Rick's mother left with no forwarding address. Mary wasn't worried about her mother, because she always planned to leave someday and said if she ever did, she would need to stay hidden until the senior Richard Wilkens accepted that she was gone. Mary had believed her mother was alive somewhere with no knowledge that the senior Wilkens suffered a heart attack.

So, when her father had that heart attack, Mary returned to the Thatcher house to act as guardian of the junior Richard Wilkens. Mary recently graduated from the University of Chicago and gladly took on the task of managing her teen brother. She always expected her mother to pop up again and wanted to make sure everything was taken care of.

Then, Miranda Daily showed up wearing a Comba charm. That necklace was the only thing her mother never would have left at the house. If that necklace was still in Chicago three years later, it meant something terrible happened to her. Her brother must have known how she disappeared, Mary deduced, if he hid the charm and then gave it to a girl.

"You believe your mother was killed?" Kiki asked. "And that your brother gave the Saint Comba charm to his girlfriend."

Mary nodded, "I looked everywhere in the house for that charm. Not finding it meant she was still alive. Then, unexpectedly, to see it around that girl's neck, I imagined Rick stashed it somewhere the entire time. He hid other things too, and I already suspected him of killing my father.

It wasn't a stretch to imagine he killed my mother as well. Why else would he hide that necklace? My mother always worried that Rick might be worse than my father." Mary closed her eyes. "But the private investigator reported that Miranda has her own Comba necklace, so I might have been wrong about my brother."

"Your brother may have given it to someone else then. Whoever those bones belong to…"

Gwen stopped and glanced at Kiki as it finally caught up to her. She turned back to Mary.

"Those bones belonged to your mother?"

The detective confirmed the identity of the victim found at the bottom of Thatcher Pond, Alice Wilkens, wife of Richard Wilkens and mother of Mary and Richard Junior. The DNA report made it certain. How Alice ended up at the bottom of the pond is another mystery. The broken hyoid bone and kettle bell weights pointed to a definite murder. Based on the fact that Alice Wilkens was never reported missing, her husband would've been the prime suspect.

"I know what I said to you on the phone." Mary drummed her knuckles on the table. "And what I said to that girl, Janine Stinger, but I may have been wrong about my brother. I never understood him because he was disturbing as a kid, but that doesn't make him a mass murderer. He obviously did not kill Miranda Daily, and he did not give away my mother's charm. He told the truth about Miranda running off to Turkey, and my father probably really did die from a heart attack and not because my brother poisoned him as I always suspected."

Mary shot a glance at the detective, "And that girl, Janine Stinger, maybe she really was suffering from post-traumatic delusions and remember her attack wrong. Rick has always maintained his innocence, even though an admission would have gotten him a lighter sentence. The governor always believed him. And he admitted the other stuff, just not the woods attack."

Mary Kline rung her hands.

"What if Janine Stinger's delusions were my fault because of the notes I sent her? Maybe I planted the idea in her head, that Rick was violent, and I broke them up." Mary teared up again and used a knuckle to wipe the moisture away. "All I wanted was my mother's necklace back."

"We'll try to return it to you, if possible," Kiki said. "But can we ask you some questions?"

They discussed several people during their lengthy dinner, Mary's mother, her father, her brother, Miranda, and Janine. One thing was clear, Mary still feared her own brother. Kiki could see in her colors when she spoke about him, deep in her gut, she didn't trust him. Her descriptions of their father indicated a sociopathic personality. The home she described was practically a prison for her mother, and she revealed that both her brothers had been the spitting image of her late father, all identical. *Obviously, Kiki mistook the father for the son in that death vision. It hadn't been Janine's Richard, but the senior Richard she'd seen.*

"Yes, Rick locked Janine Stinger in the house before the attack, but that was how my father dealt with my mother, locking her in when they disagreed."

Mary tried to explain her brother's motivation.

"Our father always said that a woman might flee, from weak resolve, unless she was anchored against her whims. Locking the door was one way, but he also said a baby made an anchor that rarely failed. Better than a marriage license. My mother disliked when he said such things, but we could see that it worked on her. Rick may have wanted Janine pregnant, so that she wouldn't leave him. She called it rape, but they were already in an intimate relationship and maybe he thought of things differently. We grew up in a different sort of home and I'm certain he didn't mean to hurt her."

That was a twisted justification for some of what happened, Kiki observed.

Mary also supposed that Janine may have been unbalanced and erratic to begin with, didn't she end up in a mental ward? And Janine admitted to snatching up the knife herself, why? Why would she pick up a knife?

For years Mary believed the worse of her own brother, just because he had similar traits as her father. But some of his actions, the ones he admitted, like keeping Janine in the house, was because he didn't know better. She felt guilty for her presumptions and for adding to the confusion.

But she still fears him, Kiki observed.

The detective leaned in and gently added,

"It's understandable, feeling the way you do. Even the guilt. But listen to your gut feelings, Mary." He gathered up the papers and photographs. "Being wrong on one point does not negate the rest of it. Often, the apple doesn't fall far from the tree."

The apple doesn't fall far from the tree! Kiki stared at the detective.

"There's no family reunion planned," Mary said. "I don't even know where he is."

The detective nodded, "Another red flag, Mary. He disappeared after leaving the penitentiary and hasn't checked in once. That doesn't bode well for his character or intent."

Richard Wilkens had gone directly into hiding. The media speculated that he was afraid of being incarcerated again, due to the efforts of a legal team paid for by the *Spectral Analysis* executives. Janine's former bosses were suing the state and governor for dereliction of duty and a miscarriage of justice.

Chapter 13
Séance

Kiki

Kiki enticed the detective to have a private drink after Mary Kline left. Gwen disappeared to join a small group hidden in the back of the lounge that included the professional women interested in the séance. Kiki ordered a coffee, like the detective, and they sat at the end of the bar sipping quietly.

Bob Anderson drinks coffee like a Scot drinks whisky, Kiki noticed.

He gave her a nice smile and settled into gazing into her eyes. Detective Anderson was blessed with light brown, almost golden eyes that always appeared wide and clear. It appeared clear to Kiki that he was bothered by something.

"I hoped to attend Janine's wedding," He shook his head. "But things were breaking around here pretty quickly and I needed to hear it all first hand. I'm sorry, because I wanted to see her happy event, and, I hoped to see you as well. In a better situation than talking about skeletons with Mary Kline." He smiled again. "I have to say, you light up a room."

"It was a beautiful afternoon wedding," Kiki told him. "And I'm sure Janine understands. Does she know about Rick Wilkens being unaccounted for?"

He nodded. "That was a hard call to make."

He took her hand in his and she could feel the positive feelings he sent her way. Nothing like when Max held that hand earlier and generated a flash of uncomfortable passion energy. The detective's vibe was softer and sweeter, easier to absorb, *balanced*. She wondered if her body would react similarly with him, as it did with Max, when he finally decided to focus his undivided base energy at her. He noticed the emerald bracelet, then glanced to where Gwen had gone off to flirt with those professional women.

"Your boyfriend is doing a good thing with those lawyers of his." He gently released her hand to hold his coffee cup instead. "There's actually a petition of recall slated to hit the judge's desk in two days. I think he might actually be successful, so I can't be too upset with him."

"Are you talking about Max Colliers? He isn't my boyfriend," Kiki retorted sharply.

"You forget, I'm a detective," Bob Anderson told her gently. He didn't look upset, he looked reconciled. "I find out a lot of things very easily. It didn't take much to find out Mr. Colliers took his jet to Scotland for four days. Right around the time of the full moon."

"That doesn't make him my boyfriend." Kiki sat back feeling a little burned. "You made it quite clear you would not participate in that particular ritual, and I was running out of full moons before my birthday. I explained everything to you and I invited you first. It would have been a very different experience with you, Bob, more balanced and tempered, and that's what I wanted. But I couldn't wait any longer, and it needed doing. Max is a fine friend who came through for me. It was just a raw passion ritual and nothing else. So don't judge."

Bob Anderson chuckled humorlessly and turned his head away. "Wow."

"I grew up with some very firm spiritual beliefs and practices, Bob. Different from yours, but very important to me. That ritual was a celebration of my personal growth and self-enlightenment. I kept a vow for fourteen years in order to develop my spiritual center, my core aspects. Priests and nuns try it for life, but we consider that unnatural. That ritual was the celebratory release of my vow, and a pledge to finally develop my Base Well, my passions. That event marked a formal transition to my next stage of life, from maiden to mother. Tell me you'd refuse a rite of passage, like a confirmation or some other important spiritual ceremony," Kiki said. "Would you refused it, if someone casually asked you to? If I asked you? Would you stop taking communion if I thought it was a terrible or ridiculous ritual?"

"That's not exactly the same thing," Bob said gently. "You're comparing apples to oranges again. A confirmation is a widely common and socially acceptable event. So is communion. It's not shrouded in intimate activities that should be kept private."

"You mean like the wedding I just attended? That was shrouded in quite a bit of ceremony and intimacy, and though we didn't witness anything beyond that kiss, we definitely expect Ian and Janine to consummate their union. In some parts of the world, even that part of the event is witnessed. Let's just compromise here. You didn't want to participate in one of my spiritual rituals, and I don't want to participate in one of yours. That's fine. Why don't we leave all the rituals off the table, and go on from here?"

"You realize that your religion leaves little room for men. It's hard for me to get behind it."

"I might say something similar of yours," Kiki said. "But to clarify, the coven is a practice, not a religion. And I do get behind yours, your religion. We all belong to the Kirk, to support our men. I'm just not a fan of the male dominated sexism in some of it."

"I don't mean to argue with you." He shook his head.

"I don't want to argue, either. Let's just forget all of that," she said softly. "I'm ready to meet you in private now. My vow has been released, and there's nothing to stop us from picking up where we left off. I've entered a very lustful stage in my development, and I'd like to explore that with you."

Detective Anderson stood up and drained the last of his coffee.

"Balanced and tempered?" He nodded to her, and she knew she had lost him. "That's not part of a lustful stage." He sounded angry. "As always, it's been a pleasure, Miss Mellow."

Kiki fumed as she watched him leave. Her pulse raced a mile a minute. How did that little cup of coffee go so wrong? Why did Bob Anderson feel so justified with his own opinion? She was well aware that the detective was no saint in the area of relationships. He admitted to having lovers in his past, and he didn't need to marry those women before taking them to bed. In fact, when he first met her, he assumed she had an elaborate past as well. Back then, it hadn't bothered him in the least that she might have plenty of experience, and had been eager to jump right in. So, why did he act so upset now? It exasperated her, because on top of it all, Kiki had residual simmering energy in her Base Well, passion energy that she had been saving for that particular detective.

She made her way toward Gwen and saw him, Max Colliers cozy between two beautiful women. He lounged at the same table as Gwen, and Gwen appeared to have made a connection with the female executive. Max jumped up when Kiki joined their group. He strained his neck around, searching for the detective. He maneuvered to get closer to her and his eyes were hopeful. He had been patiently waiting for her to seek him out.

"Where'd Detective Anderson go?" Gwen finally noticed that Kiki joined them.

"He went south," Kiki snapped, then glanced at Max. "But I'm not looking for any favors," she added and steered clear of the arc of Max's red hot aura.

The next day, Gwen and Kiki arranged for a small séance in the Congress Plaza Hotel. During the last *Spectral Analysis* investigation, Kiki hosted a very successful séance in the Plaza, thanks to Janine Stinger. Having a *dragoma* entice spirits to the room proved overwhelming. One spirit didn't need a *dragoma* and had desperately wanted to communicate with her.

Having more participants would extract the cosmic energy better, so Gwen solicited folks in the bar the previous night and they lucked out with Max Colliers's colleagues. The women lawyers were intrigued by the idea of a séance and Max was interested in spending time with Kiki. They scheduled an event for right after noon, because the conjunction of the earth, new moon, and sun always affected the aether in significant ways.

Max Colliers invented an excuse to cancel his afternoon sessions for the day and all three women lawyers agreed to attend, Olivia, Michelle, and Theresa-May. They were all employed by the Colliers Empire. Michelle and Theresa-May worked out of the Chicago office and were on a team suing the governor among other things, while Olivia had traveled from Austin with Max.

Up close, Kiki recognized Olivia. She was a common sight in the Austin office building and had even attended Ian's birthday party with Max. She was the stereotypical blueblood; polished, elegant, blonde, and very thin. Rumors revealed that her family had close ties to the Colliers clan and that Max and Olivia had an on-again, off-again, relationship that had gone on for years. At the moment, they were off-again, but all the gossip speculated that one day they'd be on-again for life, after the wild oats were all sowed.

Kiki and Gwen reserved a suite on the third floor of the plaza. They maneuvered the small round table to the center of the room and began placing minerals in a pattern on the surface. Michelle, a dark-eyed woman with wavy short hair, arrived early with Max.

Kiki quickly tasked Max with arranging placing candles around. At the table, Gwen explained mineral order in the crystal grid to Michelle, constantly giggling about something, and Max followed Kiki around, administering a constant dribble of blandishments.

"I was sorry to miss the other séance," Max said. He had gotten very intoxicated and couldn't participate the night of the *Spectral Analysis* shoot. "The playback looked very spooky. You're irresistible dressed like a gypsy. I love it when you wear this type of sheer flowy material." He moved very close and admired her gossamer blouse.

"You know that's not working on me right now," Kiki told him. "All your efforts are being sent to my spiritual center. You're having no physical effects on me at this moment."

"Really, you can just turn it off like that?" Max asked.

"That's right," Kiki smiled at him, realizing she was lying a little. "It's the natural state of my Base Well. My passion center, it's closed. I would have to open that door on purpose to feel any of this heat you're sending me. But keep that attention coming, I can use the energy elsewhere."

Olivia and Theresa-May finally arrived, and just in time, the exact moment of syzygy was at hand. Max closed the blackout curtains and everyone helped light the rest of the candles. Kiki admired the cubic grid of jaspers, quartz crystals, and dark amethyst pyramids that Gwen and Michelle created. Kiki noticed Janine's Saint Comba charm in the center of those minerals.

Olivia, on the other hand, chuckled at the sight of the grid. She had been the least interested in a séance and clearly considered Kiki a silly woman. She obviously considered Kiki another itch Max needed to satisfy before finally settling down. Kiki could feel the animosity hit her in the face and felt a bit of hostility in return. *Never blame another woman for the behavior of a man.*

Everyone gathered at the table and Gwen directed each to a different spot. She led them in breathing exercises to relax their bodies, then proceeded to explain the paper and pens in front of them.

"Many mediums call it automatic writing," Gwen told them. "Nae like what you may have seen in a scary film, your minds won't be possessed when you write, only your hand. The crystal grid is arranged to keep disengaged spirits on the table. Notice the placement of the paper, just under the wee pyramid. Keep it there. If your hand moves too far from the grid, it may drift out of the sphere of influence and not feel the spirit."

"Just how big is the *sphere of influence?*" Olivia smirked and glanced at Max.

"Come on, Ollie, keep an open mind." Max grinned at her.

"Almost the size of this table." Gwen smiled at Olivia. "So, only allow your writing hand on the table. I might warn everyone not to lean over the table, you dinna want your heart to drift into that sphere of influence."

Everyone chuckled, thinking Gwen was teasing, but Kiki knew she wasn't. Cracking open the aethereal veil into the darkness could be risky business. Participating in a summoning opened wide one's core door, where a disembodied spirit might easily sneak into a warm body. The core, or heart, was where an essence could stick. Hands were safe, hearts were not. Gwen chuckled and gave Kiki a brief glance.

"Allow your hand to hover over the paper while holding the pen. When I give you the signal, allow your hand to write whatever it desires. Dinna think about what you're writing, just allow your hand to flow freely," Gwen told them. "You won't get more than a word, or two, before your brains take over. The moment you begin thinking about what you're doing, just stop. It'll nae be the spirit writing, if you're thinking about it."

"What spirit are we trying to reach?" Theresa-May asked.

"It's a spirit I met in this hotel before," Kiki told them. "It'll be on the Chicago episode, I believe it airs next week."

"Yes." Max openly admired her. "Next week."

Kiki returned his boyish grin. She could feel him sending his testosterone fueled passion at her and she just fed it into her core. His determination must be hard to resist for most girls. Janine actually hid from Max when he turned his attentions to her the last time they were in Chicago.

"It's a spirit that felt eager to speak to us," Kiki told them. "Keep this in mind, we are calling on one who feels ignored, misunderstood and disregarded, and possibly seeks vengeance for something. We hope the spirit will tell us about a curse mentioned in our last séance and elaborate on the name Irene that was mentioned." Kiki pointed to the center of the table. "See that silver pendant? If you need to focus on something, focus on that."

Gwen coached them through deep cleansing breaths using soothing, lilting words. Her voice resembled a lullaby. Gwen never wrote a summoning charm of her own, she claimed to be a dunce with words and always chose the written charms in Celeste's grimoire. Kiki could hear her auntie's voice whenever Gwen quoted her.

"As the aether flows and opens wide, enter from that great divide, earth, moon, and sun point the way, to ears to hear what you might say, feed us now your potpourri, so I command, so mote it be."

Gwen paused and the room became very quiet. Kiki felt an electric tingling in the air. Max began to speak, but Gwen hushed him with a wave of her hand.

Gwen continued, "We are seeking one who spoke here before. We desire to learn of Irene and the curse, and the vengeance mentioned. *As the aether flows and opens wide, enter from that great divide, earth, moon, and sun point the way, to ears to hear what you might say, feed us now your potpourri, so I command, so mote it be."*

Kiki felt the spirit. A wisp of air flowed into her fingertips from the crystal grid, intense and strong, and moved very slowly over her knuckles. This spirit felt connected to someone close, or perhaps, it was *attached to that charm!* Kiki noticed Theresa-May's face change into an expression of someone straining to hear something. She felt it too.

"Write!" Gwen ordered.

Everyone scribbled.

"Flip your papers over," Gwen ordered. "Now, inhale for a wee count of three and exhale slowly. Dinna think about anything that just occurred and don't speak, not yet. Keep that writing hand over the table."

Then, Gwen repeated the charm.

"As the aether flows and opens wide, enter from that great divide, earth, moon, and sun point the way, to ears to hear what you might say, feed us now your potpourri, so I command, so mote it be. Spirit, tell us what we need to know."

Kiki could feel the energy circling the grid. Did Gwen also detect a minor glow off the Comba charm, or the static charge building in her hand?

"Write!" Gwen ordered again.

Everyone scribbled again.

"I don't want to do this anymore," Theresa-May whispered. She tossed her pen to the table and pulled her hand into her lap.

"Of course," Gwen nodded. "You can drop your pens and move from the table. Just sit quietly for a moment and collect yourselves. I'm going to lean forward a wee bit. Dinna anyone else lean in. Just try to relax." Then, her voice came stronger as she spoke to the spirit. "Come now, whisper into my ear."

Gwen leaned ever so slightly toward the table and Kiki could hear a soft growl trickling from the center of the grid. It sounded like a low growl of a dog, and the density of the air grew heavy. Gwen closed her eyes to focus better.

Be careful, Kiki sent Gwen the silent message.

Theresa-May wore a concerned expression and Michelle fidgeted as she quietly watched. Max glanced around, totally unaware of the changes in the air and stared at their quiet, serious eyes. He exchanged an amused look with Olivia.

Olivia chuckled softly and leaned her thin frame toward the table with her ear pointed to the grid, mirroring Gwen. She tucked her hand behind an ear and Kiki watched her amused smirk suddenly freeze and change.

"I hear something," Olivia whispered and leaned in further.

"Stay back," Kiki said sharply.

But it was too late. Olivia's body contracted and she shot to a rigid stance over the table. *That spirit is at least six inches beyond the grid,* Kiki noticed. Olivia's hands gripped the table and every muscle in her body appeared to contract. Her arms began to shake. Her eyes rolled into her head so that the whites showed large. She appeared to be having a standing seizure. Max jumped up, but Kiki grabbed his arm and pulled him away before he could touch her.

"Don't!" Kiki warned. "It's like electricity and can transfer to you if you make a connection."

Kiki glanced around for something to use and tried to pick up the chair but it was very cumbersome. Max took it from her, but before he could use it to push Olivia from the table she let out a loud long tone that startled them all.

"Ahhhhhhhhhhhhhhhhh." Olivia's mouth hung wide open as the sound emerged. A single note, B flat. Then, she said quite clearly, in a high pitched voice, "One of each for redemption shall atone for your deed."

Max pushed her away from the table with the chair. She stumbled two steps but didn't fall. Her eyes instantly snapped back to normal. She stared at them with the amusement back on her face. She began chuckling at them, especially at Max standing there holding a chair. He set the chair down and stepped closer to rub her arm but Olivia pulled away and gave him a cutting look.

"Spirit depart, spirit go home. I command you, go away!" Gwen said harshly and repeated it.

That made Olivia chuckle again. Everyone stood up and moved away from the table. Theresa-May went quickly to one of the lamps and flipped it on while Max moved to open the blackout curtains. Michelle blew out a few candles. Everyone glanced periodically at Olivia.

"Are you okay?" Michelle ventured with a meek voice.

"What do you mean?" Olivia chuckled. "Of course I'm okay. Are you okay? Why is everybody staring at me?"

Typical, Kiki thought. Many times the one possessed won't have a clue about it.

"What did you mean with that squeaky voice?" Michelle asked her.

"What are you talking about?" Olivia stopped chuckling.

"It's no matter," Gwen smiled reassuringly, yet her skin was very red. Her big blue eyes turned to Olivia. "The spirit gave a wee bit of a message through you. It can happen."

It took several minutes to calm their nerves. All the while, Olivia refused to believe she had said anything in a high pitched voice. She rolled her eyes and refused to fall for any of their jokes. She admitted to hearing a whispering sound, like a harsh voice or the bark of a dog. Gwen heard the same sound, but the others hadn't heard a thing. Kiki heard a voice rapidly repeat *beware the mark*, but would wait to share that with Gwen later, in private. Then, they shared their automatic writings.

In the first round Gwen had written *lured*, Michelle wrote *diverted*, Theresa-May wrote *outwitted*, Kiki wrote *avoided*, Max wrote *served*, and Olivia wrote *the demon*. In the second round, they had written *life, eye, nose, ear, tooth, and wound*, respectively. Max had stashed a few bottles of wine in the cooler and he dispensed the liquid as they discussed the automatic writings.

"Isn't it obvious," Theresa-May's eyes darkened. "The second round of words refer to the idiom, an eye for an eye, a tooth for a tooth, from the holy texts. We're being told that justice must be served. We're all lawyers here, we're familiar with that sentiment. Maybe that was a special message, just for us, because we're lawyers."

"What about ear, nose, and wound?" Olivia chuckled, enjoying her wine. "I don't remember those being in the Bible quote."

"It's in the Quran." Theresa-May appeared unsettled as she realized something strange had happened in that room. "How did we come up with those exact words, in the correct order?"

"What about the first round," Michelle's dark eyes searched out Gwen. "Sounds like someone was tricked, or lured by a… demon?"

"Irene." Gwen nodded at her, then stared directly at Kiki. Even her neck had gone pink, it wasn't the wine. Gwen pulled her long red tresses into a pony tail, and Kiki noticed Michelle's dark eyes drawn to Gwen's long white neck. "Irene lured the demon away. She outwitted and avoided a him by diverting his attention and serving him. That's the image I saw. What do you think, Kiki? That is Irene's charm in the middle of the table, she wore it last, as far as we know."

"Thinking back on the wagon train entries, it would fit," Kiki said. "This spirit felt different than what I felt before, maybe it wasn't the one we were hoping for. It could have been a voice from the charm."

"What is on the back of your neck? You have a tiny tattoo!" Michelle reached over to brush Gwen's curls aside. "It's so cute. I didn't notice it before. Just below your hairline"

"It's a trinity knot," Gwen showed her. "Kiki has one too."

Michelle becoming chummy with Gwen got Theresa-May and Olivia a bit fidgety and they began moving to leave. Then, everyone started moving at once.

"Why don't you ladies all go and I'll help Kiki clean up." Max nodded at the three lawyers. He smiled at Gwen. "You too, you look like you could use a nap. They tell me Kiki gets very taxed after she hosts a séance."

He glanced at Kiki and everyone in the room knew that he was trying to get her alone. Theresa-May and Olivia moved to the door, ready to leave. Olivia openly glared at Kiki and only paused to wait for Michelle. When she realized Michelle was going to wait on Gwen, she left abruptly with Theresa-May.

Max kept their wine glasses full and the conversation rolling as they tidied up. Gwen gathered the minerals and the charm while Kiki gathered up the candles. Kiki accidently smudged soot on her silky shirt and ducked into the bathroom to wash up. When Kiki emerged, she found that Max had successfully shooed Gwen and Michelle out the door. There he stood, with two recharged glasses of wine and the top two buttons of his shirt undone. She felt a sudden surge of his passion energy hit her.

"How about we do a little exploring of your Base Well?" Max smiled confidently.

"Max, we are not going to become a thing," Kiki purred at him. "Just so you know, you are not having an effect on me. That door is closed."

He nodded. "I blame Gwen for reminding me of that little tattoo on the back of your neck. I'm dying to see it again."

He offered her the wine glass and she took it. As always, Max had expensive taste in wine. It went down smoothly. He had provided her so much energy during the séance that she felt terrific. She took another look around the room and spotted a few places where the wax had solidified to the table. Before she could get to it, Max came around with the hotel room keycard and scraped it up. He stood very close to her and she realized that her sexual center easily sensed him. It made her curious. She noticed a force deep inside compelling her to move toward him. She pointed out a couple more spots and he scraped those up too.

"Am I still having zero effect on you?" Max grinned at her. "Because you're having a major effect on me." He reached out and took her hand. He bent down to kiss her knuckles again. "Why don't you do me the favor this time? Brave enough to do a little dare?"

"What kind of dare?" He just said the magic words, she rarely passed up a good dare.

"Open your door, you know the one I mean, just for one minute, and let me in." He stared into her eyes, he was tenacious. "If you can still brush me off, I lose, and I'll back off for good. I'll never bother you again, I promise. And you can ask me to do whatever favor you want. I'll be happy to comply."

"Anything? Such as, lend me your private jet to fly home?"

"Oh."

He laughed, taken back. He looked up and away, he clearly did not want to lend out his private jet. Max Colliers loved his private jet. He shook his head and groaned.

"I don't know, that trip will take a while and the crew couldn't fly back right away. They'd have to crew-rest a night in Scotland. They'd be tied up for three days, minimum. I'd have to fly back to Austin commercial."

"Well, I guess that's that." Kiki sipped her wine with a grin. "Perhaps, you're not as sure about us as you think."

He took in her grinning lips and let out a long breath.

"No, no, sure, okay, my jet will be at your disposal, if I lose. But you have to promise you'll open your door as wide as you did back in October, out in that wilderness, no cheating. And we should up the time. Two minutes."

Confidence was an attractive quality, and Max had plenty of that.

"Let's get this straight. I open my passion well for two full minutes and if I can resist you in the end, I win. I get to use your jet for a trip back to Scotland and you will never proposition me again. I like that. You truly believe I can't resist you? You're going to lose, Max."

"Who knows?" He grinned. "It's really a win-win for me. I get a couple of minutes to jump into your passion well and have another look at that tattoo, I'm dying to kiss you behind the ears. I get to do that in the dare, right, kiss you? God Kiki, I just want to touch you. I'll be happy if I just get a little reaction from you and see your eyes turn that dark green," his eyes bore into hers, "You know, like they did when you were screaming my name."

His glance shifted to her lips and he licked his own.

"That would be a minor win for me, right? Knowing that somewhere in there, you want me, even if you make yourself walk away."

His eyes drifted down to her sheer shirt and her open cleavage.

"I believe I have a good chance of winning it all, I know where your buttons are. At that ritual, it wasn't normal stuff. Tell me you haven't been thinking about it every minute since it happened. You're going to find out soon enough, we generate something that's very hard to resist."

She would have to take his word for that, and Kiki wanted to see how hard it would be to resist him. Opening her Base Well was new territory for her. How difficult would it be to push Max aside when her desire was fully inflamed? She should find out, for future situations, so she agreed to the bet. Two minutes shouldn't be too much trouble. Kiki pulled out her cell phone and set the timer for one hundred and twenty seconds. She set it on the table and smiled sweetly at him.

"When you're ready, just hit that button and say go. I promise not to block you out. Good luck."

Max suddenly appeared nervous. He drained the rest of his wine and then removed his shirt. He had a beautifully fit physique, smooth, well-shaped muscles, ripples over his stomach. He worked hard at being attractive, at least on the outside. He rubbed his arms and jumped like he was warming up for a boxing match. He grinned at her and shook his head of hair. She couldn't help giggling at his antics and felt a little of his energy already seeping into interesting places, warming her up. She actually itched to touch him. Then, he pressed the button and said "go." Kiki consciously unblocked her Base Well and the feeling was instantaneous.

Every nerve in her body was back on the cliffs of the Quiraing. All of his red hot energy flooded into her system and rippled through her veins like a fire. The scent of him caused a heady sensation that made her feel unsteady. His eyes drifted to her neck and she realized he hadn't even touched her, but she felt him everywhere. She was doomed.

Then, his hand came up to gently moved her hair aside as he stepped behind her. Just the one hand, and then his lips made contact as he slowly kissed the back of her neck. A spark shot all the down her spine, right to a spot between her legs, and she melted. She sank into his body, craving the contact. She sensed his hands hover over her hips, then slowly move to her waist before finally grabbing her, claiming her, and she let out a raspy breath. His large hand massaged her and she was disappointed that he did not move them further down, into that fire. But she stayed quiet, statue still, trying to withstand the passion he fanned.

She heard him groan as his hand explored her fully clothed breasts and she felt her nipples pulse in response, aching for attention as they recalled his ministrations at her awakening. The sounds he made were animal erotic to her, wooing the cells of her body into submission. His hand moved back to her neck and he moved around as if he prepared to kiss her. She definitely wanted it, tilted her head for him, slightly opened her mouth in anticipation. Her own hands slid eagerly up to caress his smooth sculpted chest, taking in the shape and hardness of his muscles. Her mouth watered and she resisted allowing her hands to wander further. She was beginning to get impatient and wondered why he did not kiss her. If he would just kiss her, she could calm down. She moved her lips closer, to invite him, but he moved excruciatingly slow, breathing into her ear instead, whispering.

"I want to— "

The alarm suddenly went off startling them both so much that they jumped apart. He watched her, breathing hard, eyes flickering everywhere, and he let out a long breath.

"That went too fast," he chuckled softly. "I guess you win then, but at least I can see it in your eyes. That's a small victory for me, right? That's a beautiful color, Kiki."

She didn't want to feed his cocky attitude and tell him that he had won in the first ten seconds. There was no way she could shut the door on that unbridled heat now. He made a move to retrieve his shirt and she grabbed his wrist.

"Just where the hell do you think you're going?" she snapped and pushed him onto the bed.

Chapter 14
Making a Demon

Kiki

Waking in the Congress Plaza suite disoriented her. Her cell phone kept beeping and she noticed several missed messages and calls. Kiki grabbed her device from the side table and saw that they were all from Gwen. She turned and Max stirred beside her. She was astonished to see his aura so bright and blue. Sure, his red base was still intact, but the blue pulse he developed around his core had grown. *Oh no, was Max feeling love?* Was it temporary or permanent? Did she fill him with her core energy the way he filled her with his lust? That was not her intent. If she could fill his core, could she empty it too? What was going on here? *Was she falling into a demon's trap?* The phone pinged again and she answered it quickly.

"Kiki, where are you?" Gwen asked. "It's after eight o'clock in the morning. The detective is coming around at nine and then we have to catch our flight. The plane takes off before noon!"

"It's morning?" Kiki spun around to the clock. *She had been holed up with Max Colliers the entire night.* That was impossible! No wonder she was starving. "What, why is the detective coming? I don't want to see him."

"Rick Wilkens popped up in California," Gwen said. "Apparently, your cousin beat him pretty badly. Detective Anderson has the full clip of a video and offered to fill us in on the details. I certainly want to hear what happened, without the media spin."

"Can he come a little later? I don't know if I can get there by nine."

"He actually has to leave by ten, unless we can meet at one, over lunch. He sounds pretty booked. Court in the morning and afternoon. Should I try to change our tickets? Where are you?"

Max sat up with his glasses back on, took the phone, and greeted Gwen. His free hand stroked Kiki in a comforting way, but she slapped it away because she still felt a tincture of the heat between them and that annoyed her. One would think multiple sessions in a row would have sated their desires. Carnal memories flashed through her brain and she had to tamp down an urge to roll up and straddle him. She couldn't believe the crazy night they'd shared, or that her blood was pumping up for more. Her base instincts had a mind of their own and her foolish body yearned for Max Colliers.

"Tell him to meet you at one. I promised Kiki I'd let her use my private jet to get home. If I call right now, they can be set to take off as soon as five. You can be late and they won't take off without you." Max chatted a little longer, then hung up and returned the phone to Kiki.

He reached for his own cell phone and made a few calls. He scheduled the jet and then called to push his board meetings back till the afternoon, apologizing profusely into the phone. Clearly, a room full of people were waiting for him back at the London House. Kiki tried to get out of bed but he held fast to her wrist and pulled her closer, making her blood race off the charts. He made another short business call, then used the hotel phone to order room service. When he finally set his phone down, he grinned and pulled her into a tight embrace. She couldn't understand why her body desired to mold into his, it made no sense at all, but her skin craved his and she pressed herself into him, savoring the feel of his muscular torso. She ached to have him between her legs but keeping them pressed tightly together instead.

"You're a bad influence on me, Kiki," he whispered into her ear. "I've never missed a board meeting at a summit. I'm going to catch a lot of flak back home because of you."

"Max, you know this isn't going to last. I might never agree to a rendezvous like this again, it's an aberration. It's just lust, pure lust. I'm in a lustful state right now, after that awakening. I'm going to get over it. That's all this is. This is going to end very soon."

"Of course. It's whatever you want it to be." He chuckled softly. "It's a lust thing for me too. I find you X rated, Kiki, that's what I've always loved about you. I realize it won't last forever, but it can last another few hours, right?" But his core pulsed light blue while he babbled on and he became incredibly attractive to her on different level. She felt herself opening up to him, head, heart, legs, and she realized that now her own core was getting mixed up in it.

Was this how the demon spirit worked? Was she being used to morph a regular man into something else? Was she creating her own demon? Who could she talk to about it? Trinity, maybe? *Terrific, she would have to discuss all her personal business with her mother.*

Gwen shot her a raised eyebrow when she finally returned to pack, but Kiki just ignored her. She picked out a pretty dress to wear for lunch with the detective, then she carefully applied just enough eye shadow to accentuate her green eyes, and just enough gloss to draw attention to her lips. She finished by rubbing lotion, with a sexy floral scent, all over her arms and legs. Gwen patiently watched her with an eyebrow still raised.

"What is going on here?" Gwen mused. "This looks like Kiki Mellow preparing to yank someone's chain."

"Don't judge me, I'm a bit of a woman scorned," Kiki told her. "I just want that detective to realize he's made a terrible mistake, and his mistake is causing me to make mistakes. I want him to rue the day he led me to this ruin. I am so furious with myself."

"You're a self-absorbed teenager," Gwen said and stood up.

Kiki followed Gwen into the elevator. Of course Gwen was right, just what was she hoping to accomplish by trying to tease a reaction from the detective? He made his decision. Their preplanned ideas of what a relationship should look like were just too different. She would never consent to moving to Chicago and playing a detective's wife, and he would never father a child out of wedlock. In a way, Kiki respected the detective more for refusing it, but she blamed his rejection for leading her right back into Max Colliers's bed. When the doors of the elevator opened on the top floor, Detective Anderson was waiting for them.

He smiled as usual, then shook their hands. *He shook her hand.* Then, they were escorted to a table. He didn't seem to notice her dress, but when his eyes touched hers, she sensed it. The little flare up of his core aura. Protest all he wanted,

Detective Anderson felt love for her. This was the man she wanted, a respectable man in touch with his soul, not a shallow rogue with a flash of fire. She detested her weakness with Max, he was not what she wanted.

"Rick Wilkens attended a night class at UC Davis." he told them. "If you followed the cyber story, then you know he snuck into Doctor McNally's lecture. The news isn't reporting his identity yet, just the fact that the doctor beat someone pretty badly."

Kiki hadn't seen the story at all. She had been too occupied at the Congress Plaza with Max. Gwen could see that she hadn't heard anything and quickly took out a phone. She found the news story.

Kiki read the headline. *UC Davis Professor's harsh reprimand for speaking out of turn.* She scanned the story quickly. An unidentified man crashed Ian's class. When the professor asked the man to identify himself, the man teased the professor with personal questions. That's when the professor punched him and began beating him down. Three students stepped in to pull their teacher back. When authorities arrived, the professor was taken into custody and the unidentified man was taken to UC Davis Medical Center in a state of unconsciousness. Kiki peered at Gwen.

"I already spoke to him, he's fine, he doesn't want to talk about it," Gwen told her.

"He's not facing any charges," Detective Anderson told them. "From the local authorities, that is, but the university might take a different tactic in regards to his standing."

"I don't understand," Kiki said.

"Rick Wilkens left a note," the detective told them. "He doesn't want to press charges."

"Where is he? Is he being sent back here?" Kiki asked.

"He's gone," the detective told them. "No one knew who he was at first. He miraculously woke up and dragged himself out of the hospital before being identified. All he left was a note that said he didn't want to press charges. To answer your next question, if Rick spied on Janine, she didn't notice him. As far as we know, he only dropped in on the doctor. Due to the nature of his incarceration, Janine and Ian are now under police protection until Wilkens can be picked up, or until they depart on their trip. I understand they are leaving the country in soon."

Detective Anderson placed his phone on the table between Gwen and Kiki. He hit the play button and they watched a clip of Ian standing in front of a white board with waves and formula's written all over it. He held a gadget with multicolored lights and chuckled at something that just happened. Then, someone on the side of the room got his attention. Ian glanced over, smiled, and ask that person to repeat the question. A murmuring voice, calm but unclear, wiped the grin off Ian's face. Ian stepped toward the speaker with his eyelids blinking rapidly.

"You're not registered for this class. Who are you?"

Just the top of a head poked into the corner of the screen. Even though his voice was muffled, they could hear the man distinctly.

"You know who I am," the man said. "You think you're married to her, but you're not. Not really. I'm the one to…"

Ian jumped at the man with fists flying, and they both fell from the screen. They could hear a crash, and shouting, and different people moving about. Loud words interrupted the sickening smacks and Kiki knew it was Ian cursing as he hit Richard Wilkens over and over again. Then, three fellows pulled Ian toward the front of the class. Kiki barely recognized Ian's furious, murderous face at the end of the clip.

"Only the last bit, starting with the first punch, is being shown on the net," Detective Anderson told them. "The media is in the dark regarding the man's identity and we hope to keep it that way. It might help the story go away if the media doesn't find out it was Wilkens. But, they're already speculating."

"Do you know what he said at the beginning?" Gwen asked. "It was muffled."

The detective nodded. "Several people said that he mentioned a baby, that he claimed a connection through their baby, and that Janine was his soulmate."

They rewatched the clip. Fortunate that the three fellows stepped in before Ian regretted going too far. Kiki had seen Ian in a few fights and he always stopped when the other fellow hit the ground. This time he didn't stop, and Ian's expression had been frightening. He would have a tough time living down that video in the faculty lounge.

Kiki abruptly stood and hurried to the far end of the outdoor restaurant where she could see the Wrigley Clock Tower and the river below. It was a windy day and the air whistled around her. She dialed Ian's number. He picked up on the first ring.

"I'm fine." He sounded dejected.

"You're not fine, Ian," she said quickly, loudly, and instantly wished she hadn't because it sounded very harsh. She shook her head and continued in a softer tone, "You lifted your hip on that first punch, it just screws with your balance and doesn't add a bit of power. I bet you rolled to your toes as well. How many times do you need to be reminded to keep a firm footing? What would George say?"

She heard him let out a breath.

"Did I tell you, I met up with Rory in Inverness? You were punching like a Rory, Ian."

Now he let out a little chuckle. "Oh now, lass, be nice. Actually, Rory called me a few weeks ago, when you first went home. But thanks for calling, I really am fine. Don't worry yourself."

"Is Janine fine too? Should I call her?"

"Maybe in a day or so. Give her a little break from answering all the questions," he said. "Truly, Kiki, I'm fine. The only part I'm upset about is that he's still out there… and for scaring those kids. I think a few are fair terrified of me now. They didn't need to see that."

"They'll come round, if they're smart. Smart kids in that class, right?" Kiki said. "They know you by now, Ian. The media is going to find out, sooner or later, who that guy is, and then you'll be a hero. A hero with a lame ass punch, but a hero. Someone will see him and they'll pick him up."

"You're probably right," Ian said.

They chatted a while longer before Kiki hung up. He sounded upset, but okay. She made her way back to the table and found Gwen sitting alone with an open file of papers. Gwen glanced up from her tuna melt sandwich.

"The detective left a copy of the skeleton report."

"He left?" Kiki couldn't believe it. "Without saying goodbye? He knows we're leaving today. He couldn't step over there and let me know he was going and say goodbye?"

"He only just left. He's probably at the elevator now. He has somewhere else to be, court. I tried to stall him."

Kiki ran to the elevator, but he wasn't there. She pushed the buttons in vexation, then he was standing right next to her as the doors opened. He had come out of the men's room. They entered the elevator car together. Another couple followed them in.

"Were you going to leave without saying goodbye?" she asked quietly.

"I was going back and forth on it," he answered softly. "I didn't want to, but I'm due in court. I can't be late."

The elevator stopped and the other couple disembarked. It was a relief to have a moment alone with him. Kiki stood on one side of the elevator car, staring at him. The only other person she had ever known with a large pink core aura had been her Auntie Celeste, and his was the same exact color. She loved that aura, and the feeling it generated in her, and Kiki knew that he felt something for her too. She could see it in the way he gazed at her. Kiki felt angry and sad at the same time.

"I didn't say it earlier, because I know you're very aware of it." He smiled softly. "You look lovely today. Radiant." *He had noticed.*

"You look lovely too," she said.

"I'm not quite sure what you and Miss Murphy are chasing, but I hope you two are careful. Richard Wilkens is a dangerous man, as his father was before him. The senior Wilkens had been on our radar for a very long time."

Kiki nodded and glanced at the numbers. The elevator moved very close to the lobby floor.

"I guess this is goodbye then," she said, and he nodded.

Detective Anderson's hand went out, and he pushed the *Emergency Stop* button on the elevator. The car came to sudden halt. Then, he took the two steps over to her side of the car and she felt his soothing core as his aura engulfed hers. She felt that leg buckling reaction set in. But he didn't let her fall. The detective gathered her into his arms and slowly kissed her. All his soothing, creamy core energy streamed everywhere, covering her like a warm blanket. Completely different from the red hot passion Max pushed through her Base Well. This feeling was balanced, and tempered, and bound to last a lifetime. Then, he stepped back and put his hands into his pockets.

"I couldn't help myself." He shrugged at her. "I guess that was your intent."

"Detective Anderson, you realize that this is a love connection," Kiki told him. "That I feel love for you."

He reached out and pushed the *Emergency Stop* button again, and the car jolted into motion. His eyes had turned serious.

"I believe it, Miss Mellow," he said. "And I feel love for you too. If I didn't feel this way, I certainly would have met you alone the other day. But I'm in a self-preservation state, you realize. There is a lot of variable, unusual activity in your life and I'm not sure I fit in with the scheme of things. I don't envision a role for me in your life, and I don't believe you would be satisfied following a normal life path in mine. So, I'd rather remember you fondly as the one that got away rather than risk what I'm sure will be a bitter broken heart for one of us."

The elevator doors slid open and they were on the lobby floor. He pressed the button for the roof top dining room before stepping out. He motioned for her stay in the elevator. He reminded her that she still needed to finish her lunch upstairs and he needed to hurry away. He enjoyed seeing her and hoped she would remember to be careful doing whatever it was they were doing. As the doors closed again, he kept his steady eyes on her.

Max Colliers's private jet was a Gulfstream G550. It bragged two Rolls Royce BR710 engines and had a range of 6700 nautical miles, which translated into flying from Chicago to Inverness in one hop. Kiki and Gwen were not the only passengers. Max Colliers often allowed people in his business empire to jump on flights if space was available. Eight others were waiting in the airplane when they arrived, all lounging in the forward two sections, chatting and laughing. The two aft sections were Max Colliers's personal area of the airplane and were separated from the rest of the plane by a private screen. One of the two pilots greeted and escorted them to their seats.

"That phone is a direct line to the cockpit." The pilot pointed to a beige telephone attached to the table. "In case you have a concern or want to change anything about the flight plan, or need one of us back here, I'm happy to be of service." He glanced at each of them. "I set our flight plan for Inverness, Scotland. To call on Kathy, the flight helper, just hit that red button." He smiled at Gwen. "If you'd like to visit the cockpit at any time, the door is always open. Just give us a ring and I'll come to escort you up."

He patted the seat with his hand to indicate they should sit down.

"Let me show you how to use these buckles."

He gave Gwen another handsome smile and moved around to adjust the seat belt for the right length. He knelt down and gazed up at her.

"Just like regular airplanes," he demonstrated. He stopped for a moment to consider Gwen. "Can I just say something? You have very beautiful hair, just an incredible color. I bet people tell you that all the time."

Then, he stood. He was very tall. He nodded to Kiki.

"Whenever you're ready, Miss Mellow, we'll get going. We can start up now or standby until you give us the go. Mr. Colliers said that it's your airplane for the next twenty-four hours."

"Well then, let's get going," Kiki said.

"Good plan," he agreed. "I'll send Kathy to get you set up with refreshments. It might take few minutes to get us into the lineup." He gave Gwen another pleasing smile.

Gwen watched him leave with big, blue, amused eyes. Gwen attracted her fair share of men, but not usually when she was standing next to vivacious Kiki. Kiki was so curvy, and exuded so much energy, that most male eyes couldn't resist her. It was unusual for a man to flirt openly with Gwen and barely glance at Kiki.

"You might try a lad this time," Kiki said. "He certainly preferred you."

"Ho ho, isn't it obvious," Gwen chuckled. "He's scared to look at you. God forbid he sends the wrong message to Max Colliers's woman. He probably thinks he'd lose his job if you thought he was hitting on you. Safest thing for him would be to hit hard on your friend instead."

"You think that pilot believes I'm Max Colliers's woman? Well, I would be one of many."

"I don't think many have borrowed his private jet." Gwen smirked.

Kathy, the helper, popped her head in and delivered cold bottled water. She rattled off a list of refreshments and asked what they'd like. Then, she left an inflight menu and said she'd be back to turn down the beds when they reached flight level. Kathy also pointed out a wet bar in the back, in case they preferred mixing their own drinks. Gwen went off to do just that.

Gwen's assessment worried Kiki. If other people saw her as Max Colliers's woman, then Max very likely thought of her that way too, even though he adamantly denied it. He was a terrible skirt chaser, and his aura never deviated from basic yellows and reds around most of those skirts. She had detected softness in his core aura that morning, which unsettled her and made her wonder just how far a person could change. Kiki wondered if the demon's mark attracted questionable people to close in on her, people that could be used to meet the needs of the curse. Max never presented a particularly strong core signature, then he insisted they use his private jet even though she had lost that bet. What did it mean?

Kiki finally confessed her worries to Gwen. She told Gwen about Celeste's warning, that she was marked for death, and about hearing a voice bark *beware the mark*, over and over again at the séance table.

Kiki declared her concerns about the alternate death vision she had in Chicago, how the landscape changed from green heather on a rocky hill to cattails in a meadow. The evergreen heather in her vision was the same as the winter plants along the outer edges of the Faerie Glen on Skye.

She also professed her new theory to Gwen, that she might be making her own demon with her actions regarding Max. Perhaps the dark part of the aether was working toward a resolution to the curse by molding victims and murderers, and the ghost meant either Janine or Kiki could be the last one.

"The apple doesn't fall far from the tree," Kiki said. "Didn't you find that eerie? Trinity saying it about Ian and then the detective saying it about Wilkens. Both of Janine's men were described with the same words. I'm afraid to think what it could mean."

"Just stop right there." Gwen's face flamed red hot angry. "I'm about ready to slap you, Kiki. You cannot turn someone into a demon with your actions. A person either does or doesn't have a core, a soul. Don't start blaming the *victim* for creating their own attackers. You really think Janine caused that guy to stab her seven times? Just because she loved him and then didn't? Even if some mystic energy is pushing people around, it could never force a hand to act in such an evil way. Do you actually believe Ian could be pushed to do such a thing?"

"No!" Kiki said. "I just wondered if dark energy is maneuvering people into position. I was marked, and suddenly, I'm attracted to the wrong type of man. Don't you think Max, and also Andrew MacLeod, are risky men? They're full of physical energy and have very weak spiritual centers. Both are the perfect type of person for a crime of passion, skirt chasers like Stanley Hansen, and Hansen was a demon. Could one of them become my demon if I push them too far? Both those guys crossed directly into my path after I wore that charm and I find myself extremely attracted to both of them."

"They crossed into your path because they are the exact type of man needed in an awakening ritual, guys that are all yang. The type you really need, lots of yang because you're practically all yin. Opposites attract, Kiki. You are the exact opposite of each of them. Don't forget you pulled the Ace of Wands for Max Colliers, that card wasn't just meant for you, it was also meant for him. You both needed to balance your Base-Core aspects. Whatever growth he makes to his core is not going to disappear just because you leave him. His base is just learning to chase his core better, and he's developing what he already has. It's not possible for you to change Max, or anyone else, into a demon. And there is no way in hell Ian could be changed into a murderer!"

"That video didn't scare you?" Kiki said. "I've never seen Ian so angry. I don't think he'd murder anyone, but something dark has been working on him, wouldn't you say?"

"That something dark is named Richard Wilkens," Gwen steamed at her. "He tried to kill Ian's wife! *He made all those marks on her body.* And did you hear what he said to Ian? He bragged about fathering a child with Janine, and you know how that happened."

Gwen took a deep breath and settled her anger down.

"This is really not your business, but it may help give you more context. The main reason Bridget was so upset at me was because I balked on using the embryos. When Ian suddenly got engaged, I needed him to tell Janine first, but he was having a problem telling her about it. Apparently, he pushed hard to try for a baby right away, but said she wasn't sure about ever trying for a baby." Gwen said. "Then, that guy went and said those things to Ian. Of course it would make him angry. I wasn't surprised at his response at all."

Kathy popped her head in. A call waited on the tan phone for Kiki Mellow, it was Max on the line. Kathy inquired if they were quite comfortable. Did they want a snack or dinner? Anything else to drink?

"Hi, Kiki, I hope everything is going smoothly," Max said. "Dave said that you guys got settled in okay. He found Gwen very captivating. Also, what do you think about *Spectral Analysis* doing a feature on Skye instead of the main island? I hear there's a phantom fiddler in one of the castles out there. We need a location and you haven't put in your thoughts. Ian's crew thinks it's a splendid idea, and so do I."

"It's a phantom piper," Kiki corrected. "Your airplane is a wonderful treat by the way. Thank you for lending it out."

He laughed. "My pleasure. Hey, since McNally is planning to be in Scotland next month, maybe I'll have the *Spectral Analysis* crew fly out to meet you two. I might come along too."

Gwen reclined her chair while watching with annoying raised eyebrows and a smirk on her freckled face. When Kiki finally hung up, Gwen shook her head.

"He's coming up with reasons to see you, and he gave you *emeralds*, Kiki," Gwen said. "Even if he doesn't realized the significance, there it is. It is definitely serious. Just what were you thinking, carrying on with him like that in Chicago? I thought you were all about that detective."

"The detective is looking for a proper wife," Kiki frowned at her. "And I'm in deep trouble here. This Base Well of mine is either on or off. I feel bipolar. I used to have total control and now I have absolutely no control, especially with Max. Once that door opens a crack, the lust quickly becomes overpowering and I cave in to my base urges. I don't want to admit what hearing his voice did to me just now. So, what am I going to do? "

Gwen was laughing. "You're going to have to talk to your mother, my wee lassie. This might be a genetic problem."

Chapter 15
The Manor

Janine

Janine and Ian both glowed a golden brown. They spent ten days in a beach bungalow on a small semi-secluded Pacific island below the equator. Only one other couple had slept on the island, on the opposite side about half a mile away, but they never crossed paths with them. They spent each day swimming and snorkeling in the ocean, lazing in a large hammock, and making love before falling asleep and upon waking. On three occasions a speed boat came around and took them scuba diving. One afternoon, Ian built a fish trap and caught their dinner. On another night, they pretended to be stranded on a deserted island and camped on the beach next to a small fire sleeping naked under the stars. Ian sparked the fire with a frictional hand drill. He insisted on showing off his survival skills. They wouldn't have matches on a deserted island, he said, and she should know that he could take care of her anywhere. Ian stopped shaving, and she loved how rough he looked after all the sun, and sand, and swimming. Janine barely thought about her scars, and for the first time in several years, her tan covered ninety percent of her body.

Janine lapsed into a sense of perpetual pleasure and joyful feelings in the presence of her new husband. She found him absolutely magnetic. Ian completely mesmerized her with his survival instincts, and she found his efforts to impress her extremely attractive. She giggled at how he wanted to pretend they were the last people on earth and needed to repopulate the world. Really, a deserted island would not have a fully stocked wine cellar to accent the fish on skewers. She couldn't imagine being more blissful. She loved the South Pacific.

Their transition to Scotland was a shocker. They suddenly went from barely dressed to fully covered in winter wear. Good thing they packed an overlarge suitcase of coats and sweaters. Ian insisted on wool and now she knew why, the itchy weave trapped the heat nicely. Even the landscape was dramatically different, rolling hills and startling rock formations broke up the view. Instead of the warm serenity of a flat blue horizon stretching into infinity, her eyes were flooded with contrasting shapes in an agitated skyline.

They landed in Inverness and drove toward Dornoch to meet Ian's father and visit for a couple of days, then they'd stay with Kiki one night in the city before driving onto Skye to visit Ian's aunt. Apparently, the *Spectral Analysis* team would meet them on Skye to film at one of the castles. Ian thought she might enjoy hanging out at his auntie's cottage while that was going on. The coven women were very fun and the local landscape provided nice hiking trails.

McNally Manor included both horse pastures and woodland hills, and it lay near the east coast on the main landmass. The drive from the main road to the front door consisted of a half mile of winding driveway, which Ian seemed determined to attack at top speed. The entire drive to Dornoch had Janine scared out of her wits. If the warm Pacific island had calmed Ian, the cold Atlantic one irritated him. Ian's blinking eyes told her that he was nervous about seeing his father again and his driving had become very reckless. She tried not to snap at him, but the jet lag, cold, and fast driving unnerved her. It made her a little nauseous, and his blinking eyes were causing her to panic. He was not calm, good natured Ian McNally in Scotland.

"We're late," Ian said. "He doesn't like late."

Her hands were on the dash holding on for dear life. He glanced at her tight grip and then into her eyes. He was upset at her for being upset. He flew through another turn and their tires just skimmed the edge of the road.

"Ian!"

"Relax," he said. "I've driven this a thousand of times."

He brought the car speeding into the large driveway and screeched to halt. It took all of her strength not to fling forward too dramatically. She felt her seat belt lock, protecting her from smashing into the dashboard, and she gave him a good glare.

"Can you just calm down? It's not going to be that bad," she snapped.

"I'm sorry." Ian let out a long breath. He glanced past her. "Crikes, here he comes."

Janine glanced around to see three people emerge from the front door. Two men headed down the steps, and a woman hung behind in the doorway. Anyone could tell which man was Ian's father, the resemblance was spot on, and it made her smile. Janine popped open the door and jumped out before anyone arrived at the car to help. The elder McNally walked right up and appraised her with Ian-shaped grey eyes and had a strong Ian-shaped jawline. He only glanced fleetingly at his son before returning those strange eyes to study her.

"Hello there, lassie, you must be Janine. I'm Roger McNally. That laddie failed to tell us how captivating you are in person." He smiled at her. "Can I get a hug from my new daughter?"

He was just shy of Ian's height and seemed very friendly. She couldn't understand why Ian had been so nervous. His father seemed positively happy to see them. After a brief hug, he pointed out the other man and introduced him as Stan, the manager of the stable. Roger gave Ian a brief hug and survey, then he tucked Janine's hand into his arm and walked her up the front steps asking about their trip. The woman who had been in the doorway had disappeared and Roger McNally turned his head back toward Ian.

"You might have time to clean up before dinner," he said. "You look rough."

Ian shaved off his rough face and she sadly watched it all go down the drain. She got a lot of enjoyment from his whiskers. She asked him not to shave, but he said his father practically ordered him to shave with that *clean up* comment. Ian glared at himself in the mirror. Was he still feeling nervous? His father had been pleasant so far. She didn't know why Ian was still so grouchy. She tried to hug him, but he felt so rigid.

"Ian, I think it's going to be okay. He seems to have gotten over the shock of you marrying someone he's never met."

"I can't help it," he turned around and kissed her. "I'm sorry. I'll try to loosen up."

"Who was the woman in the door?" Janine asked.

"That's a good question," Ian said. "I didn't recognize her at all. I guess we'll find out soon enough. Are you ready to go downstairs?"

The McNally house was actually a small mansion. Ian said that they were staying in his old room and the rugby trophies along the wall were his, but besides those relics, there was nothing else of Ian's on display. It had been redecorated since the last time he visited back when he had been in college. He did find a few of his old things in the drawers and closet. Would she like one of his old rugby jerseys? *Yes!*

Ian led her down the generous staircase, through a large sitting room, and into a formal dining room. His father and a middle aged woman were waiting for them. Roger McNally introduced his good friend, Chloe Kirby, who happened to live on McNally Manor. She helped keep the grounds and the house up, and exercised the horses. Janine wondered at their relationship. He called her a friend but acted very familiar with her. Were they platonic or romantic? It was hard to tell. She admired Janine's ring and asked to see Ian's while Roger delivered cocktails. They waited for the groundskeeper, Stan, then they sat down for dinner.

Janine relayed details about their wedding in California, and also their living arrangements in Davis. Ian answered questions about the research he was conducting, and his father told him about the horses and the drainage problems in some sector of the manor. After polite small talk, Ian's father began asking Janine about her family. He asked detailed questions about her sister and grandmother. Ian got a little perturbed with the interrogation, but she didn't mind. This was Ian's father and he'd want to know about his daughter-in-law's family. All in all, it was a very pleasant evening. By the time they retired to bed, she fell right into a deep sleep, exhausted from traveling.

Sleeping in a new place always brought odd dreams. Unlike the tropical island where her night visions had been sweet and erotic, the cold Scottish winter revealed unsettling images lurking in her subconscious. A familiar nightmare crept its way back into her dreams, spoiling her peace of mind.

She ran in the dark of night, stumbling through the foliage. She was cold and shivering, and knew *he* followed directly behind. If she turned left instead of right, things might end differently, but she always chose wrong and ended up in the same little copse of trees. Perhaps she could hide better. As she sunk into the ground, trying to blend into the foliage, she knew it was no use and the trees receded rapidly, exposing her, the ground spitting her out. Then, he stood in front of her, staring down, ready to strike with the knife she dropped. She needed to remember not to bring the knife next time. She looked up and saw him clearly. It wasn't Rick, it was Ian. He had that look in his eyes and she was relieved. Or was it his father? His eyes had turned grey and she was terrified again.

Janine awoke disturbed. Letting her past nightmare sneak into her present relationship almost doomed them before and she vowed never to let it happen again. She needed to clear those images from her head and decided to sneak out for a run. Running always helped clear out the dreams. It had been two weeks since she last ran, and her legs needed a good workout. She didn't wake Ian because he snored soundly, finally peaceful. She crept out the door, down the stairs, and quietly slipped into the cold dark air. She'd be warm once she stared moving, she knew, and took off in a trot down the drive. She decided on an out and back, down the winding drive and a bit of the road.

It was cold and a little foggy. She couldn't see much of the landscape or the manor. She had no idea how far she had gone, but by the amount of time, she could make a good guess. She decided to limit herself to two miles because the cold air made it hard to breath. She had been spoiled by the warm, dry, California climate. When she turned back down the drive, the porch lights had broken through the fog and she could see the outline of the house. *Was that Chloe in the distance, near the end of the drive?* No, it had been a trick of the fog, no one was there.

Janine jogged up the steps and welcomed the warmth as she entered into the foyer. She pulled off layers in the heat to get down to her full body spandex. When she turned, she noticed Roger McNally standing in the doorway to the sitting room. For one brief moment, she thought he was staring at her body, then he wasn't. She found herself slipping back into her hot hoody, but not the sweat pants, that would be too obvious. What was wrong with her? She must have been mistaken.

"Nice to see you're an athletic girl," he said. "But it's very cold this time of morning. Come and get something warm inside o' ye."

"I think I'll just run upstairs to…"

"I insist." He waved her over. "Have a cuppa coffee or tea, or I can call Cookie to warm up some milk. You don't want to catch a cold. Maybe warm porridge or oatmeal. You can go up in a minute, but first, you need something warm to coat your throat. Come along, Janine."

What could she do? She followed him toward the dining room where he poured her a warm cup of tea and added loads of honey to it. He stirred it, then handed it over. He waited to watch her drink it down and smiled at her. He was right, the warm fluid felt good on her cold throat. He added more tea to her cup.

"The honey will coat your throat well." He nodded, pleased with her compliance.

Janine sipped the tea feeling a little uncomfortable with his scrutiny. Usually, she never gave a thought to her spandex running attire but the dream, and that look at the door, unsettled her. Her idea of personal space was probably wider American rather than closer European. She thanked him for the tea and tried to excuse herself to get cleaned up.

"Let me show you something first."

He reached down and took her hand with an exact replica of Ian's hand. He lightly pulled her through the house, moving from room to room, chatting as they walked. He regaled her with Ian's antics as a small boy and the speech therapist Ian terrorized when he was working on his stutter. He seemed to be sharing simple, humorous anecdotes, but Janine didn't appreciate how he spoke about Ian. He seemed to be mocking his son. They finally ended up in the library where Roger presented a large painting of Ian's late mother. She wore a Comba charm necklace in the portrait and was very pretty with a hint of Kiki in her face and form.

"She was a beauty, don't you think?" He gazed at the portrait. "A little flighty, like Ian, and given to imaginative fanciful yarn." He turned his grey eyes on Janine. "Not unlike his cousin Kiera and the women that hang about that cottage on the isle. I hear it's great fun spinning the tales they do, but more than one woman has confused herself out there." He pointed to the painting of Ian's mother. "Celeste for one. She actually suffered from delusions and needed to be hospitalized. She took her own life. Ian blames me for that. He wasn't quite a fully grown man, in the storm of adolescence, rebellious and wild. Ian's likely told you a bit of it. He was a little hard headed to remember everything, but the doctors believe she drank hallucinogenic teas. Those women at that cottage encouraged Celeste that way. I'm only telling you this because I know that you're planning a trip to the isle soon. *Don't drink the homemade tea.*"

He noticed that she finished her own tea and took the cup to carefully set it down on a desk. Janine found it hard to continually meet his eye. Her skin crawled because his eyes were exactly like Ian's but they weren't the same color. He squinted and moved his head similar to Ian, which further unsettled her. Janine took a step back. She was wary of Roger McNally. Although he appeared to be an older version of Ian, there was something missing in him, something she couldn't see. *Kiki and Gwen both called him a demon.* Maybe it was his Core Well she couldn't sense. Then, his expression became cautious. His eyes bore right into hers, locking her into place. His voice dropped very low as he leaned in.

"Ian would be upset at me for asking, so please don't share this, but I would like to see something before you go upstairs. I'm afraid I must insist."

"What?" She was shocked. What did he need to see? Janine tensed, ready to spring from the room.

"The back of your neck," he said quietly. "It's where they place their witch's mark. Ian assured me that you weren't involved in their nonsense. His cousin, and her friends, and her mother, are a terrible influence. Easy to get caught up with them. I know you're friendly with Kiera. I just need to confirm that you're not part of that cult."

Janine took a shaky breath. He just wanted to see if she had that tattoo. What was wrong with her thinking? It must be some of Ian's nervousness rubbing off on her. She pulled her hair up and turned around to give him a good look at her neck, then became suddenly upset at her own easy obedience. She dropped her hair and turned back around.

"Thank you. Thank you." He was visibly relieved and extremely happy. "Forgive me, lass, but for many years, I feared he would marry into that cult and meet the same misfortunes I have. You may not know this, but Ian was bewitched by one of them, as a young lad. Very wild behavior with those girls, especially with that one. Fortunately, God saved him. She was disfigured. You've made me very happy. Very happy. When you go see his auntie, just remember, they often spike the tea."

Disfigured? Was he referring to Gwen? His tone almost sounded like he blamed Gwen for her own misfortune. *Would he consider Janine disfigured if he saw her scars?*

"I'll remember that." She gave him her best try at a smile. "Now, I think I'd better run upstairs and get cleaned up."

Roger and Chloe took them on a driving tour of the local landscape and sights, then they went into town for lunch. Ian seemed considerably more relaxed in the glow of his father's good humor. As time separated her from that disturbing dream, Janine chastised herself for getting so uncomfortable with Ian's father that morning. Her father-in-law came across very likeable in the light of day. She could clearly see that

Chloe was more than a friend and they were being modest to spare Ian's sensitivities. Although, Janine didn't think Ian would mind at all if his father had a companion.

That afternoon, Roger urged Ian to go on a walking pheasant and partridge hunt over the north end of the grounds. There were flocks of birdies and they could get in a good chat. Chloe offered to take Janine on a horse ride if she liked, or perhaps she'd like to nap after all the traveling. Janine opted for the riding. It would get dark soon enough and then they'd be cooped up in the house.

The barn was large and Roger owned four horses. Chloe exercised each of them at least two days a week. That meant two rides a day for four days. She missed a morning ride, so Janine was helping her make up for that session by coming along. Chloe even lent her a pair of breeches, but she didn't have the right sized boots. Janine just threw on her tennis shoes and said that she wasn't planning anything fancy. No jumps or gallops, just walk, trot, and canter if that was okay. Chloe nodded and smiled, then asked if she was familiar with an English saddle.

Unlike a western saddle, the English saddle was very small and lacked a horn to grab. Although Janine had ridden in an English seat as a kid, she was nowhere near as proficient as her sister Juliana. She was confident that she could still sit well enough not to fall off.

The barn manager saddled up two Cleveland mares when they arrived. He helped Janine mount and adjusted the stirrup straps for her. He raised an eyebrow at her sneakers.

"Mind you don't go past the red marked fence posts," he said. "These here have a chip in the ear. It'll sound the alarm if you take her out of bounds."

Janine chuckled. "Horse thieves a problem out here?"

"I think it's more to keep us girls corralled in." Chloe chuckled in a matter of fact way before trotting away.

Chloe and Janine spent the next two hours trotting around the grounds, mostly over very green pasture lands, but there was a nice section of trees within the horse boundaries that they zig zagged through. Riding in nature was much more fun than strutting about in mock shows in a ring. Chloe didn't talk much and that was okay with Janine, they were both just enjoying the quiet exercise. Janine fantasized about living on McNally Manor with Ian someday. Her sister Juliana would love visiting. Better yet, maybe they could reproduce a McNally Manor somewhere back home.

Ian and his father each bagged a couple of pheasants and they put them on the menu for the following day. *Ugh, the menu in Scotland was not agreeing with her.* Everyone went off to clean up and change for dinner. She was happy to see Ian calm and peaceful. Maybe he'd get his South Pacific mojo back. He grabbed her when she came out of the shower and snuggled with her on the bed for several minutes.

"Thank you for making us come here," Ian said. "I think he's forgiven my wild accusations and he's actually behaving himself, right? He's been very nice and polite to you, right? No funny stuff. He seems so normal with Chloe, it's not how I imagined it'd be at all. Finally getting on with him is just… just brilliant."

"He's very nice." Janine didn't want to mention the neck incident, or the dig about Gwen. "The bottom line is he loves you, and is just worried about you. He wants to make sure I'm right for his son. Do you think he approves?"

"Absolutely." He kissed her. "He'd be an idiot not to. He can clearly see you're very intelligent and well grounded. Not to mention a stunner. I think you've given me a little clout with my old man. I think maybe he was expecting a frivolous airhead or something. He's got to be amazed at the brilliant bird I managed to capture." Ian looked so happy she decided to try to get over her uneasiness around his father.

Janine couldn't sleep again. She either felt someone stirring in the house, or the heavy air kept her from sleeping. Plus, she had another disturbing dream. She dreamt that she was riding horses with Ian's mother, Celeste. But they couldn't talk on the manor grounds, they needed to find a place right outside the perimeter, out of earshot of the grounds. Apparently, Roger McNally's ears could pick up anything said within the red markers of McNally Manor. They needed to find someplace outside the red posts that wouldn't set off those alarms. There was a spot near the perimeter fence and they rode the horses there. It looked just like the entrance to the main arena at Gold Country back in Rio Linda. Then, Celeste whispered and Janine needed to lean very close to hear, almost slipping off the English saddle.

He'll bend you to his will, she said.

Janine didn't know who she was talking about. She couldn't ask for clarification because the mare's ear went just outside of the red posts and they were caught.

It was four o'clock in the morning and pitch black outside. After laying wide awake for more than thirty minutes, Janine decided to go for another jog. Why not, no one would miss her. After that horse ride, she knew the grounds pretty well and she had a small flashlight she could take. It wouldn't be totally crazy to jog so early in the morning. All the traveling had likely gotten her internal clock out of whack, so she decided to go. She had been feeling blah lately and knew it must be from of lack of exercise. Janine slipped into her warm jogging gear and tiptoed down the stairs.

A layer of low level clouds trapped the earth's heat so it did not feel as cold as the previous morning. She decided to jog past the stables and toward the little gathering of trees, then she'd turn around and run along the fence back toward the house. That would be between two and three miles.

She set out at a nice even pace. She always found it a good time to think things over on a private run. She didn't know what to make of Roger McNally. She wanted to feel comfortable around him, was happy Ian was getting on with him, but deep down, she had reservations about him.

His comment about Gwen upset her. Was that because of the word he used, *disfigured,* or was it something else? Janine didn't want to process the thought, but there she was, on her private morning jog and she had to. Roger implied that Ian left Gwen because of the double mastectomy. Was it just too much for Ian to accept? Did Gwen push him away because of it? Ian and Gwen were certainly very bonded and something was being said between them at the wedding.

Janine wondered if Ian would still desire her if she was as altered as Gwen? *Damn! Why would she even think that,* she chastised herself. Ian had not even blinked the first time he saw her knife wounds. *But Ian did enjoy all of her womanly parts,* she admitted. Would he feel differently if one of her womanly parts was missing?

Janine reached the small woods and paused to drink the water in her flat flask. It had been tucked into her belt and her body heat kept it warm. She took a few slow sips and looked around. It was very quiet in the highland hills at night. She tucked the flask back into her belt and started jogging again.

The portrait in the library popped into her mind. Roger still displayed that overlarge portrait. In fact, Janine noticed Celeste's image in several rooms of the house. Janine wondered how Chloe felt about that. Celeste appeared intelligent in that portrait, not fragile in the least, as Roger claimed. Every story Gwen or Kiki told of Ian's mother painted her as a strong caring woman, and she actually wrote a book full of summoning spells. Gwen promised to give Janine that book soon, because Celeste hoped to pass the book to her granddaughter.

But was that even possible, with only one ovary and a damaged womb? Janine found herself wishing she could have met Ian's mother.

When she reached the perimeter fence, she turned toward the house. The jog was going to be a good three miles. Either that, or she was out of shape. She spotted a dim light in the barn house. Someone must have left it on. Then, she saw a woman standing along the fence again. Was it Chloe? No chance of calling out, the crisp air was too cold and her vocal cords felt stiff. Janine would catch up soon enough. Maybe Chloe enjoyed an early morning walk.

In the pitch black?

Janine glanced up again, but no one was there. The woman suddenly disappeared as Janine drew closer to the house. Janine glanced around. Had she been mistaken two nights in a row? *Could it be a ghost? Celeste?* More likely, the bent pole with the flag fooled her at a distance. Janine just shook it off and went inside to warm up.

Roger stood waiting in the foyer. He already poured the tea and urged her to sit with him in the den. He hoped to catch her alone again. He actually had a tray of steaming hot oatmeal waiting for her. He noticed her odd appetite the night before and predicted that she would be hungry.

"I thought I saw Chloe out there," Janine told him. "But it must have been a trick of the light and shadows. The past two mornings, I could have sworn she was standing right at the end of the fence when I was at a distance. But then no one was there when I got closer. Maybe it was that pole with the flag on it."

Roger chuckled. "You don't think it was a ghost? After your adventures on that show, I'd guess your first reaction to be that you saw a ghost. Nice to know you steer clear of the fanciful. Must be hard to take Ian seriously sometimes, eh? Just so you know, lots of folks have mistaken that post for a woman when it's dark. The wood bends similar to a lass."

He handed her a small bowl of steaming hot cereal sprinkled with fresh berries. Once again he put a large helping of honey in her tea.

"Do you often have problems sleeping?"

"I think it's the time change." She felt uneasy again. "The traveling."

"Worried on something?"

"Well, no. Not anything to keep me from sleeping," she said. "What about you? You rise pretty early. Are you worried about something?"

"Aye." He locked his grey, Ian-shaped eyes on her.

Janine considered him.

"What are you worried about?"

"Neither of you have mentioned it," he said. "The man my son beat in California. I'm aware of who he was to you. Your story broke everywhere. Anyone can google anything these days. I reviewed all the news articles and brushed up on your secret scandal. I'm trying to understand it."

Janine let out a long breath and said softly, "I'm still trying to understand it too." *How awkward.*

"Did you know that you were pregnant when you ran away from him?"

"What? No." *Oh good lord, was he going to interrogate her about it?*

"Was finding out about the pregnancy what made you finally blame him?"

"I blamed him because he tried to kill me." *Did he mean to be insensitive?*

"Then, why did it take you ten days to point him out? You let him sit next to you and feed you in the hospital for ten days before saying anything. That's unusual. Isn't that when you found out about the baby?"

"I was scared. Not fully lucid at first, and then, I didn't want to believe it happened." *He doesn't believe me,* she could see it in his eyes.

"Is it possible that he's innocent? That governor thinks so."

"No, he's guilty." *He thinks I made it up.* She felt her anger bubbling up.

"What did you do to him, to inspire that kind of violence?"

"Nothing." *He thinks it was my fault.* She was fuming, *couldn't he see her reaction?*

"Would you like more tea?" He picked up the pot with a benign expression. "You look a little low there."

"No, thank you," she said sharply. *Was this just a social talk over tea for him? Was he oblivious to her reaction?*

"Where did the baby go?" he asked softly.

Janine couldn't speak. She just stared at Roger McNally, completely stunned that he had asked that question.

"That man was very angry, lassie. I saw the clip of Ian punching him down, you've got my laddie wound nice." He chuckled. "But that little brawl is not going to stop that man. He has not let you go." Roger poured himself more tea. "He's going to hound you for years to come. It's okay if you tell me what you did to him. You're my daughter now and I'm on your side no matter what it was. I'm just curious."

"Are you trying to scare me?" she asked softly.

Roger chuckled again, and he sounded strangely like Ian when he chuckled.

"I'm trying to reassure you. As long as you stay here on the manor, he won't get within an inch of you, I can guarantee you that. My men are good at keeping out the strays. They chased a fellow off the hill the day you two got here. Not to worry, probably just a laddie hiking around. Ian tells me that you finished your degree and you're between plans. Perhaps you should consider making this home part of your plan. Stay here and relax as long as you like. Why go to Skye and mix with those crazy women? Nothing good can come of it."

Janine stood up quickly and backed away. She set the bowl down and could see those grey eyes studying her. He stood with her.

"Need to get cleaned up?" He nodded at her. "Let's just keep this conversation between us. Ian gets oversensitive about things, he's always been an emotional lad. Another good reason he shouldn't go hanging around that cottage on the isle."

They were bickering on the drive to Inverness. Ian suggested she might stay at McNally Manor for several more days, but Janine insisted on sticking to the plan. Staying with Kiki one night and then going to Skye to stay at the cottage, but Ian didn't want to disappoint his father. He requested that Ian's wife stay at the Manor and skip Skye. Everyone was getting along so brilliantly, Ian said, they should ride that wave as long as possible. Plus, she could completely avoid the *Spectral Analysis* business that way. Max Colliers would be on Skye, and she detested Max. It might be better for everyone if she stayed near Dornoch instead of at Uig Bay. Ian believed she had the right touch with his father, he had warmed up to her nicely.

"As long as your wife does exactly what he wants her to do."

"What does he want you to do?" Ian asked. "Relax, ride horses in the meadow, get to know him better, it doesn't sound like too much to ask. I've never seen him so polite and nice. I think he really wants to make amends and be a part of my family. It would only be for a few days and I'll come back in the middle. Are you sure you won't change your mind about it?"

"I just want to stay with you and visit when you see everyone," Janine said softly. "I feel like you mean to hide me away up there in Dornoch. Are you hoping for a private meeting with someone? Like, with Gwen, perhaps?"

Oh goodness, why did she say that? She didn't mean it, not really. She just didn't know how to tell him that she wasn't wild about his father. She actually disliked Roger McNally.

Ian glanced at her, a bit angry. "What are you saying?"

"What were you two talking about at our wedding? I saw your eyes blinking, Ian, so it must not have been good. What was going on? What did Gwen say to you?"

He started blinking all over again. He was going to get them into a car accident with his fast driving.

"Slow down!" she snapped.

"She just wanted to wish us well," he said. "Why would you ask that? Did my father say something to you about Gwen?"

He had such a crushed looked on his face that she felt she must have hit a nerve. Maybe it was true, that he still loved Gwen and Gwen loved him. Maybe their chances were damaged by her cancer. Ian must feel like Gwen would never take him back, and she must feel like Ian still desired a woman with an undamaged chest.

Good grief, she thought, *married barely a month, and it's already over!*

"What is this, are you crying?" He sounded exasperated. "Oh, Janine, this is ridiculous. What in the world are you thinking? My father doesn't know anything about anything. I barely even talked to him back then. What did he say?" He glanced at her. "Gwen and I were just kids, experimenting too soon, that's all it was. We've been friends for as long as I can remember and we were just trying to figure it all out. And my mother, she encouraged us."

"I don't want to talk about it," she was sobbing. Why was she sobbing so uncontrollably?

"You're scaring me here," Ian said. "It was just youthful nonsense, that's all. We crossed some lines when we were young, but that wasn't really us. I… Please don't be upset with what happened with me and Gwen. What exactly did my father say?"

"I don't want to talk about it!" she snapped.

"Janine…"

"And slow down!"

He yelled back, a terrible curse word, but he did slow down for a several minutes. But his knuckles turned white as he gripped the steering wheel, and the speed inched up again. His jaw stayed clenched, and his eyes were blinking, and she really just wanted to apologize, ask him to pull over, and have a kissing session. She didn't really believe he still loved Gwen, not in a romantic way, did she? A minute ago, she had, and now that her tears were winding down, she didn't anymore. It suddenly seemed like a ridiculous idea. What was wrong with her?

Chapter 16
Unexpected News

Janine

Kiki, Gwen, and a tall, handsome fellow with a receding hair line and hazel eyes greeted them at Kiki's apartment door. They were all smiles, until they noticed Janine and Ian were miserable. Ian fought his way into Kiki's apartment with some of their luggage and tossed them haphazardly to the side. Then, he smiled big at the tall handsome fellow and high fived him.

"Rory O'Hare!" Ian yelled.

"Ian McNally!" Rory roared back.

The two fellows gave each other a boisterous hug. Ian introduced Rory to Janine, and then gave Kiki and Gwen quick brutal clutches before grabbing Rory's shirt collar. Ian practically dragged Rory to the door. He glanced back at Kiki and Gwen, avoiding Janine's eyes.

"We're going to the pub!" he announced. "We've got some catching up to do. It'll give you three some time to get your sass out and get ready for dinner. Get out there, Rory." Ian pushed his old friend out the door and then followed him, letting the door slam shut at their departure.

Kiki and Gwen stood shocked with their eyes on the door and their mouths hanging open. They turned to gaze at

Janine. *Oh ,sure, leave her with the fallout,* Janine fumed. Neither Kiki nor Gwen moved a muscle.

"Trouble in paradise?" Kiki asked softly.

Janine had to resist throwing her purse at the smirk under Kiki's beautiful eyes.

"We got into a huge fight in the car. He wanted me to stay at the manor, but I can't help it, his father creeps me out, and I can't tell him that, because they were getting along so famously. Then, Ian has to drive like a lunatic and it just drives me crazy. What is wrong with going the speed limit and staying in your own frigging lane?" Janine stomped.

"He's always been a terrible driver," Gwen agreed.

"Just tell me one thing, Gwen, because I need to know, and don't sugar coat anything." Janine let out a long breath. "Just very plainly, tell me. Did Ian leave you because of the cancer, the surgery, because of what happened to you? Is that what happened? Because, deep down, I think he might regret it. So, if you're still in love with him, I want to know about it right now. What did—"

"Janine—" Kiki interrupted.

"No, no, let her go on and get it out." Gwen stopped Kiki and nodded to Janine. "Go on."

"I saw you two talking at my wedding, and I've seen you and Ian many times before, and you cannot tell me that there isn't something there. I just want you to be up front about it, okay, be honest. Because this has been bugging me, and right now, all I can do is snap at him, and I don't want to snap at him about stupid things. If I'm going to snap at him, and cry uncontrollably, I want it to be something worth getting upset about. Half the time, I am absolutely certain he completely loves me, then I start thinking about his blinking eyes while you two were dancing at my wedding."

She felt herself crying again, tears streaming down her face.

"And what is this! I can't stop crying. This is ridiculous, I don't even feel like crying right now, so why am I crying like this! Let's be absolutely clear here, these are angry tears, not crying tears, okay? So, don't try to be all sensitive with me, just tell me the truth."

Gwen and Kiki exchanged looks. Gwen reached down and handed her purse to Kiki.

"I've got a box in there," Gwen said, then turned to Janine. "The first answer is *no*. Ian did not leave me because of the cancer and my mastectomy. And *yes*, I do love Ian, dearly, but I'm not *in love* with him and he certainly isn't in love with me. He is totally in love with you."

Gwen moved closer and put an arm around Janine. She started leading her to the bathroom and handed her the pregnancy test stick Kiki had retrieved.

"Okay, lass, I want you to go in there and pee on this little thing, then bring it out to us," Gwen told her. "While we wait, I'll tell you everything Ian and I discussed at your wedding. He obviously didn't know how to broach it with you."

Gwen pushed her into the bathroom, and Janine heard them tittering on the other side of the door. She sat down. They thought she was pregnant. That was ludicrous, it took people months, years, to get pregnant, and Ian and Janine had only started trying since their wedding night. But, it would explain her mood swings. It would even explain her recent nausea, *not a travel tummy, but a baby tummy?* She felt like a complete idiot. But in only two months, was it even possible? She peed on the stick, then washed her hands and emerged from the bathroom calm and rational again. Kiki took the test stick and placed it on the bathroom counter.

"A watched pot never boils," Kiki said stupidly.

They went to the sofa to wait.

"We've only been trying since the wedding," Janine confessed. "So, it's a long shot."

"I think it's quite obvious," Kiki told her. "Even though you're crying, you're absolutely beautiful. I've never seen your colors so bright."

Gwen leaned over and took Janine's hands.

"At the wedding, Ian and I were discussing my zygotes. They told me that zygotes had a better chance of surviving the freezing process than eggs. So, Ian donated his sperm and I had zygotes frozen just in case. Last spring, I finally decided to use those zygotes and Ian was fine with it, but then you two suddenly got engaged and I thought you should know about it first. Maybe you might not like the idea. It's okay if you don't. I might not use them after all, and I might have them destroyed, to take away the tease. I never should have asked him to speak with you again, especially after you got married, but I panicked. I'm sorry about that. I suppose he was afraid to tell you."

She did not expect that, but it made total sense.

"No, don't, don't destroy them," Janine said slowly. "If you're infertile, and they're your only chance…"

"They might not be my only chance," Gwen said. "The doctors say I might have a few good eggs lingering in there, so there's a slight possibility that I dinna absolutely need those zygotes to have my own child. I could find another donor to fertilize an egg."

"Like your pediatric oncologist, right?" Janine said. "Isn't that better? Or is he infertile, is that why you wanted to use the zygotes?"

"She," Gwen said. "She's plenty fertile. I thought you may have caught on by now. Ian and I were doomed from the start. We were always just best friends, really. I've always preferred a bonnie lass to a lad. If I try hard, I can certainly fall for a fellow, it's just so much easier for me to love a woman."

Gwen leaned back, a little perturbed at having to explain herself, and Janine felt like an idiot for being so dense.

"I'm going to go get that stick."

Kiki grabbed Janine's hand after Gwen went off.

"Gwen's girl Bridget was supposed to carry the baby. Gwen's egg and Bridget's womb. Almost as easy as a simple fertilization because the zygotes were already waiting. The big bonus was that the baby could be both of theirs, in a way."

Kiki told Janine that the whole episode broke them up for a spell. Bridget felt like Gwen betrayed their relationship by halting the use of her zygotes.

Gwen emerged from the bathroom and brought the test stick with her. She placed it on the coffee table.

"What do you think about that?" She smiled.

Double positive. What did that mean? Was that a yes or a no? The box said yes, but was it a definite yes? Her blood started racing and she wasn't sure what she should do. Panic set in. Holy crap, she had been drinking wine off and on for days, and when was the last time she took a vitamin? Kiki and Gwen were both chattering, but she couldn't hear a word they were saying. She put her hands on her belly and realized that Ian's little child was in there, and she had just been yelling at its' father. She began to hyperventilate.

Kiki sat beside her and rubbed her back. Janine didn't realize how desperately she wanted to be pregnant until that very moment. When she told Ian they should wait, she had been frightened that it would take a very long time to conceive. Her sister Juliana and Alan tried for five years, both times. Or worse, Janine feared that she might never conceive because one of her ovaries had been stabbed to death in Thatcher Woods several years ago and part of her womb had been wounded.

"Breathe easy, Janine," Kiki said. "Here, are you okay?"

Kiki dabbed Janine's eyes dry with a tissue, then Gwen gave her a wine glass of ice water while Kiki and Gwen had the real stuff, because they could. They toasted her good news and then laughed together. After a while, Gwen grabbed her purse and pulled out a small book. Gwen handed it to Janine and urged her to open it. It was a diary.

"It's perfect timing," Gwen said. "She always wanted her granddaughter to have her grimoire and now she has it right away. But there is something written in there we need to find. I'm hoping you can help me find it. A charm Celeste wrote. Maybe, as a *dragoma*, you can figure out the one we need, kind of sense it out."

Janine's phone buzzed. She could see it was Ian and snatched it up. What would she say? She should wait to tell him in person. Goodness, what if he was calling to say he wasn't coming back right away because he was fed up with her? She had been horrible to him on the recent drive.

"Ian?"

"Janine."

"Ian, we need to talk. Where are you?"

"I'm downstairs," he said. "Before you say anything, I want to apologize and…"

"No need for that, just come right up so we can talk," Janine said. "I need to tell you something."

Then, she hung up. She picked up the book and gave it back to Gwen.

"Don't destroy your zygotes. It's okay with me if you use them, then maybe you'll have the girl for the grimoire. I imagine that's what Ian's mother wanted."

"We'll see," Gwen said.

There was a knock on the door. Kiki picked up her bag and pulled Gwen along.

"We'll come back to cook supper in say, an hour?" Kiki opened the door.

Kiki pushed Rory back into the hall and stepped aside for Ian. Both Gwen and Kiki gave him a pat on the rear as they giggled and ran off. Ian stood there looking sorry and sad and very worried. Janine picked up the test stick and walked over to him.

"I'm so sorry about snapping at you. I know why I've been so irritable."

"Is it because I've been acting like an idiot?" He noticed the test stick in her hand. He kept glancing down at it, confused and blinking. "Gwen told you about the fertilized eggs? Is that? What is that?"

"It's mine," she told him. "It's mine and yours. We're going to have a baby."

Ian, Janine, and Kiki drove together onto Skye for a visit with Trinity. They received word that the *Spectral Analysis* team was on schedule to show up the next day and booked rooms at the hotel in Uig Bay. That establishment was located roughly between the two castles they meant to investigate, Duntulm Castle ruins on the northern tip of the isle and Dunvegan Castle, a tourist attraction about midway down the island. They would easily find folks to interview regarding the specters in those two places. Skye was riddled with MacDonalds and MacLeods, all privy to the spooky old tales regarding each location.

If the main island of Scotland was beautiful, it had a rival in the island of Skye. The rolling green hills were speckled with sharp boulders cutting into the skyline. The granite peaks were dramatic and pleasing to the eye, and salt water saturated the air. Scattered along the hillsides, fancy fluffy-haired cows grazed the emerald grasses comically shaking overly long bangs, very different than the cows they had in Texas.

Ian gushed that the roads were not as crowded and lacked the erratic touristy drivers in the winter, so the trip should go smoothly. Janine bit back any comments about his driving. She knew her hormones were making her crazy, because she was just as annoyed with his slowed down overly cautious driving as she had been with his speeding.

Kiki's mother lived in a cottage on the outskirts of a fishing village. They veered off the main road prior to the town and went into the hills. Ian steered down a small single lane road that seemed squeezed between two green mounds. A small farm magically emerged from between those hills. A cottage that might be a giant replica of a gingerbread house with a round topped front door, generous eaves, and lavender painted shutters over the windows sat at the end of a long drive.

Trinity ran a bed and breakfast at times, Kiki said, but she was very selective regarding who might stay in the main cottage. There were two other dwellings close to the main house and a very large garden area between them. The surrounding land consisted of gentle rolling mounds. A wood fence cut through the hill on the right, while a mossy stone wall meandered over the hill on the left.

"Wow, you're mother lives here? It's so pretty." Janine felt like they just drove into a fairy tale.

"Keeper of the coven cottage and books." Kiki pointed to the two fences. "Follow the wood fence to Uig Bay, the closest pub, shop, and post is nary quarter of a mile at the end of that fence. Follow the stone wall to the Faerie Glen, it's about half a mile away, but be sure to take a little milk and honey the first time you venture in that direction, you don't want to offend *them that live in the glen.*"

Janine glanced at Kiki. "Are you serious?"

Kiki smiled at her, "I'm always serious, Janine."

People emerged from the rounded door, two men and two women.

Kiki was a near carbon copy her mother. The only difference, besides age, was the older woman had pale skin and cheeks speckled with freckles instead of Kiki's smooth bronze color. They both shared deep green eyes, oval shaped faces, generous bosoms, and curvy hips. Trinity and Kiki even stood the same way and wore a similar expression of suppressed humor.

Next to Trinity, a woman with long blonde curls and a big smile waved enthusiastically. The two men were both tall and well built. One had very dark piercing eyes that seemed to invade her space, even at a distance. He flashed a handsome grin before turning his undivided attention to Kiki.

Ian knew everyone except the dark eyed one. He introduced Janine to his Auntie Trinity, then Kiki's old friend from the university, Annie, and then Sam Welks. Ian used to go fishing with Sam in the summers when their mothers brought them to Uig Bay. Annie told them that Sam was the Postmaster and lived just over the hill. Apparently, Annie and Kiki were college roommates and had gone hitchhiking through Europe at one point in their lives. Now, Annie helped Trinity run the Inn, an online herb store, and taught online classes in tarot and tea reading. She knew Leone from Rio Linda and had met Gram in one of her zoom sessions. Annie insisted that the ladies from Rio Linda were very serious students and quite funny.

"This is Andrew MacLeod, George's nephew from Islay. He's the cottage groundskeeper now that George has retired," Sam introduced the dark eyed man. Andrew shook their hands.

The small group remained on the drive, chatting. Between the thickening accents and the inside stories, Janine couldn't follow much of the conversation, but she did enjoy watching their animated face. Then, she noticed Kiki's mother holding up a small stone, peering at her right through a hole in the center. *Strange.*

"Mother!" Kiki also noticed.

"You've got a bonnie air, my dear," Trinity called over, then slipped the stone into a pocket on her dress. "Why don't we all go in for a spot of tea?" Trinity opened the round topped door and disappeared inside.

"That was only a hagstone, Janine," Kiki whispered to her, sounding very annoyed. "It's how my mother can get a glimpse of your aura."

It reminded Janine of Ian's rainbow infrared scope. She wondered if the *Spectral Analysis* team had packed that little gadget? It might be a fun device to share. Everyone meandered into the house as Sam and Andrew helped carry bags. Janine noticed Andrew insisting on taking Kiki's bag out of her hand as he whispered to her.

Trinity offered tea and small cakes in her large kitchen. The room was an interesting mix of modern appliances and cast iron pots stacked along the wall. A large window gave them a view of the backyard and patio area.

Off to the side, a smaller room, which might have been a breakfast nook for a different resident, was open for inspection. Many different plants hung on twine and closed topped jars lined the wall shelves. It resembled an herb and potions room from medieval times.

Trinity came round to personally deliver a special cup of tea to Janine. She chatted about the herb business Annelise expanded online. At the moment, Annie was in the process of taking photos of each herb from the picking stage to the dried stage and then the powdered stage for the eighty-two herbs and plants they grew. She was building an online photo catalogue. She dubbed it *Herbs, from Ground to Ground,* Trinity laughed at the pun. Janine noticed a couple of beautiful drawings of flowering herbs on the wall.

"Is the tea too hot? Need more honey? Maybe milk?" Trinity asked.

Trinity noticed her reluctance to drink the tea and Janine felt awful. Roger planted the idea in her head and that herb room didn't help. *Did they really spike the tea at the cottage?* People spiked tea and coffee all the time with a bit of alcohol, so it was possible that Kiki's mother might believe it normal to add an *extra spice* to the tea. Janine wouldn't put something like that past Kiki, and Ian did say that Kiki was a toned down version of Trinity. If there was any possibility of an odd chemical in the tea, Janine didn't want to chance it going to the baby. She glanced at everyone else enjoying the tea and cakes.

"I'm just hesitant because…"

Janine noticed Ian watching her. This wasn't going to make a very good first impression, being suspicious of the tea. She moved closer, speaking very softly to Trinity, so that the others wouldn't hear.

"Roger McNally said that you might spike the tea sometimes. I just wanted to make sure it's not spiked with the wrong stuff for… Because I'm… We're expecting a baby, and I need to watch what I drink."

Trinity laughed with eyes that flashed similar to Kiki's.

"Roger McNally, you say." She shot Ian a raised eyebrow. "I wouldn't listen to that old goat, but at least this time he's a wee accurate. Aye, the tea is certainly spiked, lassie, with a little ginger and mint. Someone revealed that you were feeling a wee whoosie in your pregnancy and this will settle you down nicely and mayhap brighten your dark colors. Dinna worry, we only drink the interesting stuff in ritual, and we never waste it on the men." She patted Janine on the back reassuringly.

Ian and Kiki departed on a *Spectral Analysis* errand. They drove to the Castle Duntulm ruins to scope it out and speak with possible subjects for the upcoming shoot. They planned to spend the day rounding up witnesses before the *Spectral Analysis* crew arrived. While they were gone, Annie offered to take Janine on a hike around the hills and show her the

Faerie Glen. She wanted to point out Castle Ewen, because it was a beautiful and sacred monument in that glen.

Annie regaled her with stories of hitchhiking through Europe with Kiki. They earned money fortune telling and reading auras at fairs and festivals, and lived a wild life. Annie said Kiki adopted the stage name Kiki Mellow for the first time back then, it came from a nickname her auntie gave her. Annie never met the famous Auntie Celeste, Ian's mother, and didn't have a pagan education like the others in the coven. Her sketchy interest in the tarot was fueled into a full obsession with the encouragement of her college roommate, Kiera Lovett. Their first year, the housing lottery paired them up and they have been tight friends ever since. Annie's father had been the son of a highland witch, so the ways came natural to Annie, and many of the older coven women had known her grandmother.

It was an easy hike to the glen. They followed along the low stone wall up and over a gentle mound. The dramatic rise and fall of the land, sprinkled with stones and lochs, gave the area a magical appearance.

Annie carried a bowl carved from polished wood. It was an offering bowl for the faeries in the glen. They used a smooth shelf in a large boulder to leave a milk and cake treat for the faeries. Annie passed the items to Janine and she arranged the present. By dawn the next morning, the cakes should be eaten and the milk bowl drained, Annie said, and if the faeries were pleased with her, they might leave a shiny trinket near the bowl as a thank you, but that didn't often happen. Annie's tone came off completely serious, without any hint of humor. Janine planned to jog out early the next morning and check it out for herself.

"In a week, or so, these hills may be covered in snow," Annie told her. "A light little flutter, and it becomes magical in a different way. Then, in a couple of more months, the full green returns. Then, the winter heather will be replaced with summer colors. It can get quite purple along this mound. In the summer, the aroma becomes heady and earthy, the air muggy."

"It's beautiful out here," Janine said.

"Did you feel her at all?" Annie asked. "The spirit of the wall? As we walked by?"

Janine glanced back down the hill to the low stone wall stretching toward the cottage. She hadn't felt a thing.

"The tale goes that the remains of a witch is buried down there," Annie told her. "Aboot halfway down by that old tree. She was burned at the stake and her ashes and bones were scattered there, near the wall. She was keeper of the cottage in her day."

"Really. How long ago was that? The cottage doesn't seem extremely old."

Annie laughed.

"I suppose it's been redone a few times and added to, but something has been in that spot for hundreds of years, persevered through weather and war. During the early witch hunts, the Isle avoided most of the ruckus, except for this one area here. A wee scandal occurred with the ladies of Saint Comba when someone accused them of witchcraft. The original group had to be broken up. We discovered that a woman named Lillias Blair was burned in the heart of this Faerie Glen, probably where the tourists always lay the rocks in spiraling circles."

"Ladies of Saint Comba?"

They continued walking slowly into the glen. Annie pointed out the rock formation they called Castle Ewen. There were a few hikers on the top taking photos.

"The pendant necklace you gave Kiki belonged to one of those ladies, they all wore one. We've been researching and translating cryptic writings. The ladies of Saint Comba were a close knit group of women who followed pagan healing and the sciences of the stars, among other things. They're our coven ancestors. They left writings deeply rooted in the Celtic traditions. Having a female saint who accepted both Christ and the ancient teachings was important to them, as, the times were changing. Unfortunately, the coven women didn't change fast enough. They became targets in the witch hunts and had to disperse to save their own lives."

Janine asked to hike to the top of Castle Ewen, so Annie took her around back to the narrow trail. As they tramped up the path, they could see people along the edge of distant trees and around a little loch. Janine didn't feel the wall spirit, but she did feel something in the Faerie Glen. It could be the beauty of the place, or the cold crisp air, but something was there.

The winter heather crunched under her feet and a few birds fluttered into the sky. The Gulf Stream current must keep the island warmer than normal for such a northern latitude, she wasn't nearly as chilled as she had been on McNally Manor. She suddenly wondered if Annie had been given the task of bringing her up to speed on the curse of the charms. The thought of Gwen's vision clouded her mind.

"Have they figured it all out?" Janine asked when they reached the summit of the small rocky castle. "About the charm curse, how to break it, what needs to be done? I've had two ghosts tell me that I can be the last one. Another ghost told me to fill an empty spot. Do the women in the coven talk about that?"

Annie shook her head.

"I didn't know that. I'm not privy to everything said in Trinity's den, just what I manage to eavesdrop on. All I've heard about you is, that you're a real *dragoma*. That's a rare thing."

Annie's eyes were wide.

"And I know there's a debate on whether to ask you to speak in a summoning. I admit, I have been running around it out here myself, but would it be too farfetched to ask you to whisper to the spirit of Lillias as we pass by her tree on the way home? Not a real summoning, just a little whisper?" She shrugged nervously. "I've never seen an actual ghost, you know."

Janine smiled back.

"I'm not sure if should. Isn't there some sort of protocol or something? Trinity advised me not to summon spirits while I'm pregnant. Of course, she said it was only taboo in my second trimester. Would you tell me everything you know about those charms?"

Annie didn't take part in the discussions, but she listened in on the translations of the old books and the gossip from the older ladies. From the records written by Lillias Blair in old Gaelic and Latin, there existed a tight net coven of women from all over the isles, the *Ladies of Saint Comba*, who studied together and met every full moon.

The group consisted of twelve unmarried women who took a vow of chastity, yet they were responsible for producing and training their own replacement, a *Next*. The wording was very confusing, but most believed those women were only chaste until they decided to produce a single daughter to replace them, then they would pass the ancient knowledge and the Saint Comba charm, from mother to daughter.

"No one ever gave birth to a son to pass on the knowledge?" Janine asked.

"There wasn't one mentioned in the translations, as far as I know," Annie said. "Lillias Blair became very concerned with witch hunters because the world seemed to be in a fever to root out and eliminate evil devil worshipers. The worldly devil was a new invention, spawned by male oriented religions. Foul men bred fear of the devil to amass wealth through the hunting of witches. Lots of people, women especially, were strangled and burned at the stake. Unmarried women were highly suspicious, because a male dominated world doesn't like an independent woman. The high social status of the Saint Comba Ladies made them prime targets. With their ancient knowledge and pagan ways, their lives were at stake if a witch hunter targeted them. Lillias felt it was inevitable that one of them would be accused, and she realized, if one fell accused of devil worship, then sooner or later, they all would be accused of it."

"Guilt by association," Janine said.

"Exactly," Annie said. "That's exactly what Lillias wrote in the book, so they hatched a plan to save themselves in case a witch hunter came for a sister of their circle. It's in the book. They made a pact to eliminate any threat and to safeguard the ancient teachings."

Annie paused and glanced over the glen.

"Then, they did it, right down there. They murdered four witch hunters who came to the isle. They got blood on their hands. Lillias believed their actions spawned a curse on the group. They disturbed *them of the glen*, and the *fae* granted a demon's last wish for revenge."

An emerald green stretched over the valley floor and grey stones were placed at the spot Annie had pointed out. A stone spiral radiated from the center. Hikers appeared. They nodded a greeting before starting a climb down the rocky spire. They strolled silently back to the low rock wall. Janine could see the tree in the far distance, stretching into the sky. She did not want to whisper to Lillias Blair, a murderer. They sat on the rocks to rest and enjoy the view.

"In her last entry, Lillias wrote that the coven broke up and the women ran for their lives. They dispersed because new witch hunters were on the way. The locals were also privy to sins of the glen and wanted it covered up. The magic of the glen had been spoiled and highlanders are very careful of the faeries, more so back then, than now. People were truly afraid."

"I'm surprised they didn't burn the house down, with that book and all," Janine said.

"Who can say exactly why, but the locals helped her," Annie said. "Her books were carefully tucked away in the house with other writings and her Saint Comba necklace was preserved. Someone added a few stray sentences to her book, a short tale of her death. A less educated writer by the look of it. They wrote that Lillias was strangled by her lover in the heart of the glen and burned, then laid to rest on the stone trail. An Oak sapling was planted to mark her grave, which is now that large tree. So, are you going to call on her, Lillias Blair?"

Annie searched her face with big bright eyes. Janine thought about the orchard ghost, and the woods ghost, and the ghost of Ingrid Stauch. She wasn't quite ready to see another unnerving spirit.

"Maybe we should do it another day," she told Annie.

Annie laughed in a good humored way. "That's what I thought you'd say."

Chapter 17
1649

Lillias Blair

Eric Lyndae, the avid apprentice of Mathew Hopkins, lay trussed up in the Faerie Glen along with three holy men. That small commission hoped to kill Lillias Blair, for nothing more that birthing a baby boy and passing the lad to his father. Lillias sat cross-legged in a circle with her moon sisters, Iona, Gavina, Anice, Lyndsey, Elspeth, Aileen, Fiona, Inghinn, Caroline, Robina, and Muira. Their names were each scribbled on a decree in the witch hunter's sack, along with those of their daughters. Each one of them was slated for death.

Other decrees lay folded in the sack as well. A few bore the names of cranky old mothers and one unruly wife, each accused of evil, but Lillias knew them well. They were only lonely women whose sole crime was being bitter at the many losses life bestowed on them. The sack also contained two books, a Bible and the book *Daemonologie*, along with a box filled with pins, three needles, a jar of sulfur sticks, and two small daggers.

The sisters circled the sleeping men, waiting patiently for so they might plead their case, but they knew their hope was folly. Still, if even a dim chance of a peaceful resolution remained, they needed to try for it. Perhaps the magic in the glen would open the eyes of those dark men.

Not far away, inside her cottage, Feandan MacDonald's wife waited with his bastard son, tending the baby. Feandan MacDonald himself had scampered off quite suddenly, upset that folks in the surrounding area now held him in such low esteem.

"I brewed too heavy a tea." Anice squirmed in her seat, she often struggled with patience. "We must settled this before the veil thins and the Fae awake."

In the beginning, her voice stood alone against their present action, but when she witnessed all their names on the warrant, including her own Next, her mind turned. The writ list was not title *suspected*, it was titled *confirmed*, with a death sentence plotted out for each of them. It made little sense, as Anice's daughter was only a babe barely weened. On the back of the warrant a long list of evidence gave witness against each sister. It began with Feandan MacDonald and the accusation which lured the witch finders to the isle in the first place.

Feandan MacDonald accuses Lillias Blair of bearing the devil's child and trying to pass it as his own, smearing his good name and enticing him in salacious ways.

Seeing those words drawn on paper tore at her heart. Lillias had trusted Feandan and believed that his actions had contained love. He easily consented to father her daughter and agreed to the ways of the coven ladies. Lillias would not take him to marry, only to father her Next. If something went amiss, and the baby was male, then as the father he was obligated to take the child into his own home and care for him there. Many men had wives who understood and accepted that fate, because the Saint Comba Ladies were an integral part of the land. Coven women often became chaste after a daughter was made, refusing to settle with anyone. Their unions were temporary, only agreed to last until the conception of a girl child. The Comba ladies were healers, and seers, and helpers to all. They kept the peace between the world of men, the faeries, and from the energy that seeped into the world through the cosmic veil.

Unfortunately, Feandan MacDonald persistently laid claim to Lillias Blair and desired to keep her bound to him for life. He feared that Lillias might seek her Next with another man after birthing the boy. He wished to abide in her cottage, abandon his barren wife, and bind Lillias to him. He was heartless in the matter. He commanded that Lillias raise their son and act according to his wishes.

All of those things went against their compact, and she told him *no*.

That's when Feandan accused her of bewitching him, of casting a spell and being in league with the devil. He carried on and on about it until an official of the commission overheard his rantings and wrote down his statement. The commission collected several stories about the Saint Comba women and a warrant was signed ordering each of them to death.

When Lillias informed Feandon that those men sat in the glen awaiting a correction to his accusations, he fled and hid. It didn't worry him that twelve women and their daughters were slated for death galvanized on his word. He only wished to conserve his reputation. A false accusation would cost him his title and land, and he would never admit a lie in front of *them that live in the glen*, that was bad luck. He became livid because the coven's rash actions brought danger to him. As a man with prospects, he ranted, he had more at stake than twelve pagan hags.

That's the moment Lillias Blair realized that Feandon MacDonald was bereft of a soul.

Dusk settled into night and the stars lit one by one as the four men began to stir. Disoriented, the three clergy men wormed their way to a sitting position, staring out of wide fearful eyes. The witch finder attempted to stand, but the tea Anice feed him still affected his limbs. His face burned with a hateful glare as he growled at them in a terrible voice. The ladies waited patiently for him to exhaust himself.

"No one can hear you except the faeries, and they pass their own judgement," Iona said softly. She had lived long enough for her hair to become infused with silver, and her Next had recently produced a Next, but Iona still wore her Comba charm. "You are not in mortal danger, as long as we are not in mortal danger."

"You've bound us and fed us a potion," one of the men squeaked.

"Only because you've passed judgement before introducing yourselves," Sister Aileen told them. "We seek to discuss this matter and expose the weakness in your warrant."

"You must pay for your evil deeds," the witch finder, Lyndae, spat out. "Dallying with the devil, you made your choice. Abjure your ways! Give way to what you've reaped. These actions against our holy decree prove your evil intentions."

"You've never exchanged a word with a one of us," Iona continued softly. "Yet, our names fill that decree written *confirmed of witchcraft* and acting as the devil's concubines, reeking of evil, with a recommendation for each of us to be strangled and burned to dust."

Iona gripped the paper in her hand, crushing it.

"We do not *reek of evil*. You realize that there is no devil here, not unless he comes with you. How many people met their fate in a similar way as this? From the weak testimony of strangers?"

"Did you murder every person on your list?" Sister Caroline asked. Caroline was a mother, and both herself and her teen daughter were accused together. "Did you not find any of them innocent? Did you speak with any of them before passing sentence?"

"Repent," one of the men said weakly.

"Your group is an abomination," another added. "Repent your unnatural lifestyle. A proper path is to follow the spiritual leaders placed before you by the church. By refusing a husbandly guide, you've wed yourselves to an evil influence. You poor women know not how your weak constitution draws you down a wicked path into ways that are unnatural. The evidence lies in how you bring unblessed fruit into the world, dark fruit that must be eliminated. Repent for your own souls and give yourselves to God and be saved."

"Look at this." Lillias held up her Saint Comba pendant. "This woman met Christ on the road and accepted His word as we accept His word. Our two sides can merge as one. We are not followers of a devil, we are healers and students of nature and our paths are interconnected."

Stubbornly, the witch hunter and the clergymen were deaf to the women of the coven. They refused to back down the accusations and were willing to die in the name of their god rather than admit they might be wrong. The holy men declared the witch finder a divine guide and they felt justified in their actions. They followed their leader blindly, fooled easily by Lyndae's unwavering confidence and steadfast declarations. His brazen confidence reassured them.

Lyndae showed no fear, and sensed their desperation. He believed he possessed the upper hand. He counted on their woman's weak resolve and forgiving nature to release him. With a little patience, he assumed he would gather them up, torture, strangle, and burn them to ashes for the bounty it would bring… And now, also for the vengeance. His eyes could not hide his intent from Lillias.

"How dare you claim a witch met Christ," he yelled at her, "Release us now, you evil woman. You hold a royal commission unlawfully and dare to question the word of the king!"

He hopped manically up, working his way to looser bonds. Soon, he'd be free. As time drifted deeper into the night, the women realized it was a pointless discussion. Feandan ran away instead of testifying in front of the holy commission, and these men were deaf to a woman's voice.

The sisters nodded to each other, accepting the time had come. They gave the commission a chance to walk back their warrant and now had little choice but to kill them instead. Each elder sister would contribute, because members of a coven shared their sins and guilt together. Each carried a dagger for the sacrifice of herbs and they already prepared the blades with traces of *hemlock and nightshade and snakeroot and caster bean.* All twelve of the moon sisters drew their blades with their left hands, to avoid committing a foul deed with the offering hand.

As Lyndae finally realize his mistake and he went still. He definitely deserved his fate. He murdered the innocent knowingly and darkness engulfed him. He journeyed to the isle hoping to torture them in evil ways, to feed his pleasures, and then kill them when he was done, to erase all possibility of reprove.

"I curse you!" he growled, spinning round to glare at each of them. "I curse you all! I call on all the forces of divine rage to curse your outrageous ambition! How dare you hold a dagger to me? How dare you! I act for the good of the community. I act in the name of a higher order than your dark lord. I have a royal order and I speak for God!"

The women closed in, humming softy to cover the sound of their pounding hearts and the pleading liar. They swayed to give each other courage. Each sister pledged to mark each man with a groove deep enough to draw blood. If they failed to bleed to death, then the poisons would close their air pipes and halt their hearts quickly. If they still clung to life, then they would reach their conclusion when their bodies were consumed by flames in a similar sentence as the one drawn out in the warrant.

"Heed this warning. I, Eric Lyndae will haunt you into eternity lest you release me! I warn you. If you proceed any further, each of you will meet me on this very road you walk and I will prevail again and again until you and yours are all dead!" His eyes were wild, desperate, angry.

The coven moved slowly, dancing in a delicate circle, singing softly to each other. Each Saint Comba sister, all twelve, did their deed and the glen floor slowly drank in the poisoned blood. The holy men whimpered as they flailed and gasped, but the witch finder continued to curse. He called on his god. Then, he called on his devil. Then, he called on *those that live in the glen.* In a stricken voice, he cursed the coven women again and again as the spittle flew from his lips. His vile energy flooded their circle with a blackness that tasted bitter in their mouths and with an air that parched their skin. As the poison constricted his air pipes, the witch finder used his last raspy breath to beg a favor from the fae, *a curse…* and they answered.

An eerie sound cried from the hills.

Stunned eyes watched as blue-green lights fluttered angrily around their victims. In that moment, each woman realized they saved their own lives, but lost their souls in the process. They were no better than the men they snuffed out. They lingered in the glen with the poisoned bodies, unsure of what they wrought.

Unsettled images manifested in their minds and they shared a similar vision. Their path to redemption would require an eye for an eye, a tooth for a tooth, a life for a life. With the first atonement, a script would be written and must be repeated twelvefold, one for each blood soaked Saint Comba charm. The demon would be granted his revenge because the fae were angry.

The following morning, the coven women burned the dead men and then made hasty plans to disperse. As long as one member of the coven lived, the ancient knowledge could be passed on. The link between worlds was already tenuous, and reaching across the void a delicate endeavor. They would not let the pagan teachings and the ancient learning disappear. Someday, they would meet to right their transgression in the glen and attempt to balance their foul deed.

Lillias remained at the cottage, vowing to divert any new witch seekers from the rest of the coven. She informed Feandan MacDonald's wife that when the new commission came for her, the cottage would belong to the boy. So, if

Feandan MacDonald's wife promised to care for the boy, then the cottage would be hers. She could move in right away and no longer be dependent upon a man, or go her own way.

The king sent a new commission the following year. They arrived specifically for Lillias and she lied to them. Lillias testified that she was the lone woman left of the Comba Coven. She swore on a Bible and told them Lyndae successfully murdered her sister as writ in their decree, then Lillias killed him and the others in retribution, because they acted on false testimony. She swore that she alone burned those men in the glen.

The new commission summoned Feandan MacDonald to face her. He writhed in anger that she made him a fool once again and that his word was being questioned. To prove his truth against hers, the commission insisted he be the one to strangle her. If she spoke truth and they had been lovers, he would not be able to do that deed, in which case, they would not burn her as a witch, but only hang her as a murderer.

No need to fear the noose, Feandon easily stared into her eyes as his hands encircled her neck. When he tightened his hold and closed off her air pipes, he insisted their fates were wrought by her own actions, not his. Lillias drove him to this low state when she betrayed his love for her. Why couldn't she do as he asked and be an obedient woman?

When she finally lay dead, they burned her body in the center of the glen and scattered her ashes on the trail to the cottage. Her death redeemed the first of the twelve Saint Comba sinners and ignited the redemption sequence of the demon's curse.

Chapter 18
Dark Energy

Kiki

Ian and Kiki returned late from their excursion to the north. Most everyone had gone to bed and Ian eagerly ran upstairs to check on his pregnant wife. Kiki decided to take a stroll to the pub for a quiet drink away from the cottage. So much had happened in just a short time and she fancied a nice drink without thinking about curses or babies or Roger McNally.

On the outing, Ian tried to convince Kiki that his father had changed. He insisted that Roger had been very nice, accommodating, and normal. He couldn't recall his father mentioning Skye, so wasn't sure when Roger warned Janine about spiked tea. Ian insisted that Roger never cornered Janine for a private chat.

Kiki countered by saying that Roger has always been clever at cornering people alone and then warning them to keep mum about it.

A couple of familiar old men were in the pub. Kiki waved at them before heading to the opposite side of the bar. The pub was just an old wooden room filled with fishing plaques, dart boards, and little else besides the long bar and stools. Kiki could finally check her messages in peace. The bartender nodded at her.

"Were you supposed to meet that American fellow here? You're too late. He asked if you might be coming around but I didn't think you'd be in tonight. He ran off a little while ago. Quite a handsome bloke you got there, lassie." The barkeep winked as he brought her a pint of dark ale and a dram of whisky, the usual in Uig Bay.

Kiki shook her head. Who was he referring to? Was Max Colliers already on Skye looking for her? He should know they would be busy checking locations and speaking with people.

"Or maybe you're looking for Annie, she's next door with Sam. I don't think they'll be back tonight."

Kiki leaned up to the bar and purred at the bartender, "I'm just here to see you, James, you know how I love your special blend. I hope this dram is from that old batch."

"Aye, lassie. She's a sweet one." He grinned at her.

She deleted a ton of messages, mostly from different men, some from media people, and a few from friends wanting to meet in either Austin or Inverness. None from the detective. She deleted every message from Max, unread. He absolutely irked her with his annoying confidence. His texts might be show related, but if they were, he'd message Ian as well. The last thing she wanted was to encourage Max Colliers. An interesting sensation flared between her legs when she imaged Max might be nearby searching for her and she grimaced at her own weakness.

She also deleted the messages from Rory. Rory had taken to hanging out in the pub near her apartment and had the temerity to invite himself over when he discovered Ian was on the way. Hopefully, he finally got the message that Kiki was not interested in another romantic encounter.

There was one message from an unknown number. She hesitated over the delete button. It was a couple of days old and she decided to open it.

Janine is a nice girl, and I don't like your influence on her. Stop confusing her.

She got shivers. She tapped in a response.

Who is this? She waited, but whoever it was didn't respond.

What should she do? She could call the number. She tried, but there was no answer, just a generic message response, so she hung up. She could trace the text, but how would she do that? It was a Scottish number, so that narrowed it down. Could it be her uncle? Who else could it be? He always called the coven a *bad influence*, but why would he use a random number and not sign the message?

"What are you doing there, love?"

Kiki nearly fell off the stool she was so surprised. She hadn't notice him approach and sit down. She had been too focused on that little screen. Andrew MacLeod sat next to her, having a pint of his own. He raised his glass to the two old men and they grinned at him. They probably thought she had been waiting on Andrew by the salute they gave him.

"Checking my *private* messages." She smiled sweetly at him and put her phone down. Andrew MacLeod might be good for a little energy boost.

"Whoever he is, he seems to have gotten your ire." He gave her that devilish grin of his and let his eyes drift to her lips.

"You think you're pretty charming, don't you?" Kiki made sure to lick her lips to draw in his interest.

"You're the charming one, love."

Andrew shifted to fully face her and stretched himself out to remind her of just how tall and broad a physique he had. Why did she find arrogance so attractive? He was nearly as annoying as Max. His dark eyes stared at her lips intensely.

"I'd be willing to kiss you," he offered softly. "It could help erase some of that ire."

"We've been over this, Andrew," she purred. "I've said no thank you, remember?"

His eyes never left her lips as she spoke, and so she took a sip of her ale to give him something to watch. His intensity became a little unnerving. Kiki set her glass down, suddenly worried that her Base Well door might crack open. She didn't want to dissolve into unbridled lust like she did in Chicago.

"I should probably go," she said.

He reached out and took a hold of her wrist, keeping her seated.

"I know what you're doing," he said. "You're going to run away because I'm getting in, ain't I? Having an effect on you."

"You're very handsome, but I must say *no thank you*."

"You think what you're doing is okay because nobody gets hurt. Just a little flirty fun, right? But you've used me, I know it. You used me to power up your ego, your core. I know all your tricks, I've been around you pagan lasses long enough. I see how Trinity keeps George and the others on a leash. Well, I'm no George." He let go of her wrist and then stood up. "You say no thank you, but your face belies your true meaning. You're scared of losing control to me." He took a step away. "Go on and finish your pint. I'll get out of your hair now."

He gave a short wave to the bartender, then left. The two old men gave her confused looks. It was probably the first time they'd seen Andrew MacLeod strike out. What a complete arse. How many times does a girl need to say no thank you? Perhaps if she shouted it with an explicative he'd get the hint. There were probably twenty girls in Uig Bay that'd take him in a second, why waste time with her?

Because it's the demon's curse placing people into position, the thought popped into her head.

Both Gwen and Trinity insisted she couldn't forge her own demon. However, Trinity and Gwen were not always correct and *they were not marked*. They didn't felt a constant urge to wear one of those Comba charms.

Kiki finished her pint and decided to head back over the hill before it got too cold. She popped out the door and admired a waxing moon in the star filled sky. Home again, the isle air calmed her. She only got about four steps before a large man grabbed her and pushed her against the building. He had a hand over her mouth and she could feel his warm breath in her ear. She was more incensed than frightened and she struggled. His grip became so tight she could barely move.

"Listen here, love," Andrew MacLeod whispered into her ear. "I'm inviting you over to that door there. That's my place. It's warm in there and I've got some nice whisky. I can assure you a very pleasant time. Now, whatever you do, don't say *no thank you* again, it's upsetting to me."

He maneuvered around so that his entire body pressed against hers. She could feel his red intensity and his famous MacLeod tool. She tried to worm away from him.

"Settle down, we're just playing here. You played your game, now I get to play mine. You will nae say no thank you again."

Then, Andrew MacLeod kissed her and her entire body flamed up. He had a hand on her head, so she couldn't get away and held her firmly in place with his body. She squirmed, but it was no use. It was outright assault. His lips hovered near hers and she tried to bite him, but he moved away chuckling. He lay tickling kisses along her neck and behind her ear, then gently trailed his nose just under her jaw. Kiki considered screaming but she was suddenly out of breath. She felt her mutinous limbs melting.

Her neck! That was her weak place.

Then, his mouth found hers again and his kiss became more stimulating, and sensual, and she flashed on Max Colliers of all people, and she actually started kissing him back. But he wasn't quite as potent as Max and she stopped. He loosened his grip a bit and turned his dark intense eyes on hers. He wore a smirk. He was devilishly handsome.

"You're eyes are lovely deep pools, Kiera Lovett. And your lips are like the soft petals of a rose," he said softly. "I suppose fate would have us…"

Kiki sent a swift knee into his groin, hard, and he yelped.

"Idiot arse! Let me go. You think you're going to get away with raping me?"

"Rape? This isn't rape! This is a seduction!" He let go of her abruptly and backed away. His dark eyes were alert and upset, and he stood slightly crouched over. "I'm sorry if that's what you think. Don't worry about it, I've changed my mind." Then, he turned and walked away very quickly.

"That son of a bitch!" She cursed under her breath, debating if she should chase him down and kick him again.

The next morning, Kiki found Gwen and Annie sitting on the stone wall close to the old oak tree. She could hear Annie dribbling on about the arrangement of her new herb garden and how certain plants should not be grown in the same soil as others. Kiki could see the new greenhouse in the lower field. It was the work of Andrew MacLeod, Trinity had bragged, Andrew was a very handy young man. The sky was clear and it was a beautiful crisp day. Annie and Gwen seemed surprised to see her.

"I thought you were going with Janine and Ian to Castle Dunvegan," Gwen said. "What happened?"

"I want to be here when Miranda and her group arrive." Kiki sat on the wall beside them. "Ian can work out a good guide for Dunvegan. I was just too tired, and frankly, I don't really care about making contact with the phantom piper. I don't want anything to do with the family MacLeod for a spell."

When they were small girls, George MacLeod took them to Dunvegan Castle where they browsed many artifacts from the clan MacLeod.

George told them stories on that trip, and one tale revolved around the Faerie Flag, a yellow silken scrap. According to George, the sidhe in their Faerie Glen wove that flag to grant the MacLeods three wishes. *Kiki recalled seeing the flag glow*, it had an aura of its' own, and no one but Kiki saw it. *Maybe they could use the Faerie Flag to help with the curse.* Kiki's pulse began to quicken.

"Ooch," Annie giggled. "Sounds like Andrew made his move then. He's been planning a seduction for quite some time. Says George knows how to slip into Trinity's Base Well and so he's going to figure how to slip into yours. I guess he bombed royally then, I warned him."

Gwen was laughing. "Ho ho, I hope you spoke with your mother about this."

"This is no laughing matter," Kiki told them. "Andrew MacLeod basically assaulted me last night, right outside the pub. I can't believe that bastard's nerve."

Gwen and Annie jumped off the wall, both surprised and concerned. Annie started talking,

"Are you okay? Oh my goodness, Kiki, did he hurt you? I'm so sorry, I never thought Andrew would do any such thing. Should I go find Sam to question him? Do you want to report him? I can't believe Andrew would attack a woman. I'm so incredibly upset at this."

"No, no, no," Kiki said. "I'm fine. He just held me up for a minute and kissed me without permission. There's no need to report him, it wasn't a terrible assault, and he backed off easily enough. I just wanted to point out that he assaulted me outside the pub, and it's not a laughing matter."

Both Gwen and Annie seemed very confused and concerned.

Kiki pulled out her phone to find the messages from the mystery phone number. She didn't want to discuss Andrew anymore, especially with Gwen. She wasn't sure why she brought it up in the first place. Instead, she showed them the text thread from the mystery number.

"Take a look at this message sent to my phone. I don't know the number, but my first guess is that it's from Roger McNally. But it seems odd, because I have his number, and he always signs it Uncle M. The only other 'R' I can think of is Rory… or Richard Wilkens."

Janine is a nice girl, and I don't like your influence on her. Stop confusing her. The mystery number.

Who is this? Kiki's message.

I'll give you one hint. R. The mystery number.

"Can you take a screen shot of that message thread and send it to me?" Gwen pulled out her own phone and began clicking away. She glanced at Kiki. "You should have sent it to Detective Anderson right away, I bet he can have it traced. See what other numbers are linked to it and figure out who it's from. The police can uncover digital tracks all over the world these days. Are we going to show this to Janine, or Ian? I think we have to, don't you think?"

They were interrupted by the sound of Trinity's alert bell. That could only mean one thing. The guests they've been expecting have finally arrived.

The coven High Priestesses met in the cottage sitting room along with Diana, Gwen, Kiki, and Annie. They welcomed a small group from the near east, two women and a man. The man appeared Middle Eastern with dark skin, thick dark eyebrows, and short dark hair. His eyes were a pretty hazel, and although he seemed fairly older, he kept strong and fit. He introduced himself as Dominique Diaz and Kiki felt something familiar in his manner.

The two women, although dressed modestly in the style of Turkish women, were easily Caucasian. By their accents, one might be from Germany and the other American, Bertha and Miranda. Miranda Daily was tall, thin, and angular. Her dainty wrists stretched out of her sleeves as she reached out to touch hands with each of them. Miranda gave Kiki a slight nod when they were introduced and Kiki could see that she was nothing like the specter in Thatcher Woods. Her eyes were calm and serene.

Dominique Diaz placed a Saint Comba charm on the small table. A tincture of energy seeped from the charm and Kiki knew it was the one that gave her a vision of death back in Chicago. The three visitors delivered it to Scotland, personally, for a reason. They were seeking information regarding the charm coven.

Their cabal in the Turkish mountains had been founded by a women of the Comba coven, Dominique conveyed. Their doyenne always wore one of the charms and taught the sciences of nature and other spiritual theories. Her charm passed from leader to leader, mother to daughter, and the education went almost exclusively to girls, but there were a few males as well. Their retreat provided a safe haven for women who had been marked by darkness in some way.

"My grandmother described the retreat when I was a young girl," Miranda spoke. "She warned me that demons followed our lineage and that I might meet one someday. Then, I would have a choice, either become his slave or run as far away as possible and hide."

"So, you ran and hid?" Cara the crone asked.

"Yes," Miranda said. "When his sister recognized my Saint Comba charm, I knew for certain what he was, because I already had my suspicions. My demon is the same one your Janine Stinger has encountered. I was told she might be here." Miranda glanced around but settled her gentle eyes on Kiki instead.

Trinity answered, "She'll be along later, please continue."

"I fled to the retreat. I always planned to go because that's where my great grandmother was born and I've heard tales of it. Tucked away in a faraway land, a magical kingdom dedicated to female wisdom. Much more than a nunnery or monastery, it is a place of true mystic science and a true safe haven for women like us. As long as we remain mindful that a demon spirit stalks us, we can be safe. All of us at the retreat remain reclusive and cautious."

Kiki exchanged glances with Gwen.

"There is a question of ownership," Dominique said, pointing to the charm on the table. "This one belongs to a woman, the question is… who, which woman? We would like to keep it, to safeguard it, but it must be given in good faith." He turned to Kiki. "Miranda's brother says that you delivered it to him and that you desired it's return."

"Someone gave Janine Stinger that particular charm." Kiki glanced at Miranda. She resembled Janine a little bit, tall, long hair, big eyes. "It once belonged to Richard Wilkens's mother."

Miranda nodded, "His sister accused me of stealing it from his house."

"Mary Kline claims the charm is hers. It did belong to her mother," Kiki nodded.

"But the last owner gave it to Janine Stinger?" Dominique asked.

"In a way. So, perhaps it belongs to Janine now. Only, Janine never wanted it. She refused to accept it and she gave it to me," Kiki said.

"Never wanted it? She has very good instincts. Then, that makes it yours." Dominique smiled at her and Kiki couldn't resist smiling back.

She wasn't sure if she'd like him, but she did, and that pleased her. His expression grew slightly concerned.

"I can see that it has already touched you, which means that it is definitely yours. Yours to keep, or yours to give. We are seeking these Saint Comba pendants, if you would agree to part with it."

The other woman, Bertha, gave him a signal, and he became quiet. Kiki realized that Bertha must be the leader of their small group. When she uncovered her head, they could see that she was a very old woman, maybe as old as Cara, Diana's grandmother, and yet her aura appeared vitally young and strong. Bertha slowly nodded to each woman in the room. Her thin lips bent into a smile.

She can see energy, our auras, just like me, Kiki realized.

"It's a puzzle that has been pieced together over many decades." Her voice was soft and unassuming. "You have obviously fit the pieces together well and sensed that each pendant carries a small portion of a strong curse. A curse that begins with intense carnal love, followed by a violent death. Long ago, our group discovered that only young women in the bloom of fertility are marked and the mark will follow them women for life in the guise of a dark shadow urging the curse to be fulfilled. A mark can only be erased by death and the longer it takes to fulfill the curse, the more marks each charm bestows. We also discovered the phrase, *one each for redemption*, and know it to mean this: a blood sacrifice must occur in proximity to each Saint Comba charm."

Bertha locked eyes with each sister, one after the other.

"Our groups are tributaries feeding energy into the same stream, and our groups share the burden of damming the flow of this curse. We need each other to end this."

Everyone agreed. Bertha explained the two sure ways to protect against the curse. Avoid intimate relationships or stay in a single committed relationship with a trusted partner.

Bertha also conveyed that the Saint Comba charms were interconnected in energy. They seemed to reach out to each other and were able to form a lattice pattern covering a vast area.

Many in their group believed the dark net of energy could be significantly shrunk by keeping the charms condensed in a singular location. Until a way to expunge the curse is found, they hoped to keep them in the mountains at their retreat.

"Buried?" Gwen asked.

"Oh no," Bertha said. "That was once done, and the effect was like a pressure explosion, seeming to work at first, until the day an entire community woke with the demon's mark. It is written in our history. It is better to handle the Comba charms every so often. This allows the dark energy to move through the aether of life and believe it is getting somewhere. Worn by an elder woman who is well past the phases of her moon cycles, or one already marked, is best. It minimizes the proliferation of marks. We personally came to you because we know you have other charms," Bertha said. "We are interested in them and hope to eliminate the net of darkness by keeping them closer together."

Dominique added, "Or perhaps the curse can be purged. We would need to gather all the charms for that. History indicates there were a dozen women in the original coven, so there must be a dozen charms. Your collection might bring us closer to that number."

"If we can break this curse, then the mark these girls bear might be erased." Bertha glanced momentarily at Kiki and then Miranda. "Fulfilling the curse would mean a death for any charm that still needs a blood sacrifice. I have a fear that the curse may never be fulfilled. The dark energy has grown greedy and may desire to hunt for victims into eternity."

"Do you believe you can do such a thing? Cleanse the curse from the charms if we acquire all twelve?" Trinity leaned forward.

"We can certainly make an attempt." Bertha nodded. "It would require a strong speaker. Without a *dragoma*, I could try, but I would need a powerful circle to aid me. And even then a demon spirit may not listen. There is tale that at one time your coven had a speaker to the spirits, we heard stories about her. Dominique was sent to recruit her many years ago, but said that she had already been marked and was in the hands of her demon. She refused to leave. Perhaps she left an apprentice."

"That's what you were looking for, my sister." Trinity's eyes were on Dominique. Kiki felt the energy between them, major conflict. "And Comba charms."

He nodded. "I was desperate to help end the curse. My dear mother fell victim and so did my sister. Our elders have always known the coven originated on this isle, and so there must be more charms close by. We have collected five, including the one here on this table. Would you be willing to give your Comba charms to lessen their lattice of energy? We would keep them safe and far from the general population. Or, you could safeguard them here, near their original home. We will trust you."

With the five he mentioned, all twelve charms were accounted for, Kiki realized. If Bertha knew of a way to cleanse the curse, then they had a chance of ending it instead of letting it play out. *Maybe no one need be the last one.*

Both groups shared everything they discovered about the curse. Trinity brought out her small box from Auntie

Meg's collection, and Bertha and Dominique added all the charms in their possession to Trinity's box for safe keeping. They planned an immediate summoning in the glen. Every moon priestess would be called and every member who wanted a hand in breaking the curse would be invited. They would need all the positive magic they could muster.

Later that night, Kiki, Ian, and Janine drove the short distance to the Uig Hotel. The *Spectral Analysis* tech team arrived that afternoon and a welcome dinner was planned in the hotel restaurant. Ian assured Kiki that the plan was firm for the next day. The tech crew would head out in the morning to set up sensing devices at Castle Dunvegan, rest in the afternoon, then at nightfall, *Spectral Analysis* would head north to the ruins of Castle Duntulm to attempt contact with the MacDonald ghostly family. Donald, his nephew Hugh, and his first wife Margaret were all said to haunt the ruined remains.

The previous day, they filmed locals retelling the story of how the castle became haunted. The nephew, Hugh, betrayed the Chief of Clan MacDonald in an assassination plot gone stupidly wrong and was chained and tortured in the dungeon, so, his spirit haunted the dungeon area. His uncle, Donald, also haunted the grounds, likely from being such an arse all his life. One person told a terrible tale of how Donald abandoned his first wife, Margaret, after she did not bear a son their handfasted year. In her own defense, she revealed that his impotence was to blame and he knocked out her eye in angry retaliation. He then sent her home to the MacLeod lands with only one eye, riding a one eyed horse, with a one eyed servant, and a one eyed dog. So, she returned to Castle Duntulm after passing away and haunted him the rest of his days. On the ruins of Castle Duntulm, they could expect one big family ghostly spat.

As for the Castle Dunvegan, Ian and his team would set up devices to attempt a recording of the phantom piper and the eerie music said to emanate from the Faerie Flag. They would monitor for music over a three day span and then follow up with a visit to conduct interviews with the castle staff.

Ian and Janine enjoyed their outing to Dunvegan and stayed so long they missed the cottage visitors. When Ian caught wind of the coven's planned summoning, he asked the elder women if he could bring some of his gadgets into the glen during their ritual. So, there was that to think about as well.

Chapter 19
Calling a MacLeod

Kiki

Before joining the dinner, Kiki shared the phone messages from the unknown number with Ian and Janine. Ian called his father right away and Roger adamantly claimed innocence. Janine said she wasn't going to worry about it because Kiki often got messages from mysterious senders. It was probably a rogue fan upset that Janine dropped out of the show. Kiki noticed that Janine had transitioned from the *easily sad and mad* stage to the *nothing can bother me* stage in her pregnancy. At least the hormones were good for that.

Ian's new crew included Ben, Emma, Oliver, and Chet. Emma and Oliver were replacing Janine and Carlos as the tech assistants on camera, and Chet became the new cameraman. Kiki noticed that Lauren, the hair stylist, Sally, the costume designer, and Guy, the makeup artist, had also come, plus two extra helpers and Max Colliers. When Kiki spotted him, she glanced around to see how Janine would respond, and Janine did a very good job of acting like she didn't notice Max at all.

But if looks could kill, Max would be dead by the glance Janine shot him when he rushed over and tried to take her hand in greeting. He instantly diverted his hands to his pockets and paused a safe distance away. He then nodded and offered his congratulations on their recent wedding before moving to the other end of the table to sit between Lauren and Sally. Always between two pretty girls, that was where to find Max Colliers.

After dinner, they retreated to the bar where Kiki found herself between Ben and Emma. Ben asked Kiki her opinion on setting up remote cameras in the Faerie Glen. Lots of folks in the immediate area relayed stories of faerie encounters and Ben thought it might be worth a bother. Janine divulged her own experience with making offerings to the faeries in the glen. She offered cakes and milk one day and found them gone when she checked the next morning.

"Every crumb and all the milk consumed. Plus, there was a shiny coin left in the hollowed rock." Janine nodded to Emma's wide eyes. "I suspect it may have been the work of a woman named Annie."

"Oh no," Kiki interjected. "It's bad luck to take a faerie offering. Annie would not have done anything of the sort."

"Then maybe it was the birds," Janine said. "Do you think they'd leave a coin?"

"Only if they like you." Kiki turned to Ben and caught him admiring her again. "The answer is no, Ben. Nobody should plant a camera or any other sensing device in the glen. The Faerie Glen is populated by real faeries and they'll be angry if they're spied upon," Kiki told him. "You'll just raise their ire, and we would not want that. Did you know the flag at Castle Dunvegan was given a special magic by the faeries in that glen?"

"Boom!" Emma said with energy. "I read up on it. Three wishes, right? The first wish was used to increase the MacLeod numbers, to aid them in a battle against the MacDonald clan after some church fire or something. The second wish restored their livestock after a plague. Rumor has it, the MacLeods have one more wish. I wonder why no one has ever used that last wish. What are they waiting for?"

Boom, Kiki thought. *The Faerie Flag has one last wish. What are they waiting for?* Was the flag real or just another tall tale? She had certainly seen an aura coming off that flag more than once. All they needed was a MacLeod to make the wish for them. She knew two MacLeods that might be able do it. As if the faeries themselves agreed, he came strutting into the hotel bar searching for her, Andrew MacLeod. *You've got to be kidding me*, Kiki fumed.

"Who *is* that?" Emma perked up and her eyes grew wide at the sight of Andrew.

Everyone watched him make his way to Kiki. He gave every woman in their group an appraising look. He paused on Emma, taking in her very short pixie haircut, and he winked at her. Then, he set his eyes on Kiki.

"Hello there, love. I've been looking all over for you," Andrew said.

Before she could respond, Max came around and gave Andrew a discriminating eye. Andrew smiled nicely at Max and nodded. Kiki took a moment to introduce Andrew to Emma, Ben, and Max. Kiki could see the two men sizing each other up. Max had not been concerned in the least about the detective, but he seemed very concerned about Andrew. *Was it because they were basically the same man, full of passionate base energy and little else?* What did Andrew think showing up uninvited? He had a lot of nerve smiling at her like that, especially after his assault the previous night.

"Your mother asked if I could persuade you to come home soon," Andrew told her.

"Really, is it such an emergency that I need to leave right now? Is everything okay? I thought she was visiting with George."

Andrew smiled at her. "I'm not sure what's going on, but it didn't look like anyone was falling down dyin'. A few minutes more won't hurt. Go on and finish your drink. I'll drive you home when you're ready."

Max did not like Andrew, Kiki could see it in his face and in his energy. All evening he had been sending her waves of passion from across the room. Max definitely came to Skye looking for another illicit rendezvous, and in a way, Andrew showing up was her perfect escape. Her only hesitation was wondering if Andrew really came at the bidding of her mother. He seemed like the type to invent a reason to get her to leave quietly. Max pulled her aside while Andrew chatted up Emma, Lauren, and Sally.

"Kiki, you're not really going to run off, are you?" Max glared toward Andrew. "Did you get that kid to come in here to prove something to me? Trying to make me jealous?" He grinned at her.

"Is it working?" Kiki laughed. "Because it better not be. I told you not to expect anything from me. There's nothing here, Max. We're not a thing, remember? What did you need to talk about? If it's just another little dare, I can't. We already know I can't resist you, and I won't get caught up like that ever again."

Kiki turned and waved Andrew over, better to avoid Max as much as possible, he could be her demon. Maybe she could go back to flirty avoidance, and hopefully he'll get bored with that.

"What if I told you that there might be something here? Would that change your mind?" Max whispered in her ear.

"Did you say something like that in the pub when you went looking for me? I don't appreciate it, Max, you could start a rumor. This is my home, people know me here," she whispered back.

"What pub? I don't know what you're talking about," he said innocently. She just rolled her eyes at him. Then, Max stared down Andrew, "Her mother needs to see her, you say? I can take Kiki home in a few minutes. I need to drop in and say hello anyway, no need for you to hang around."

Andrew stood about an arm length away, watching them. His dark eyes flittered back and forth and he wore a simple smile. Then, Andrew nodded at Kiki and turned to go as if it didn't matter to him one way or the other. Kiki did not want to let her "out" get away. She knew Max would stay glued to her side if she let him drive her home. Resisting him would be very difficult and she didn't want to chance it. She could not be alone with Max Colliers.

"Wait a minute, Andrew." Kiki reached out and pulled Andrew back. "I'm going with you."

Kiki pulled Andrew along to fetch her coat and held his hand as if he was her boyfriend. Max needed to get the hint that she was a free agent, like always. Kiki made sure to give Max a stern gaze to keep him away, and she could clearly see that he was bristling, even though he kept a very pleasant face. Andrew followed along, knowing exactly what she was up to. Outside, she saw that he had driven over in George MacLeod's old truck. He helped her up, then went around to climb in himself.

"Are you sure you want to offend Mister Moneybags in there?" Andrew glanced at her. "He seems very determined. It could be a good match."

Kiki laughed, "He's only interested in one thing. He's an arse in real life and is a very bad match for anyone. Did my mother really send you to fetch me, or will I be kneeing you again?"

Andrew laughed in a way that hurt her feelings a little.

"Yes, she did. There's a little storm brewing at the cottage, and she wants to see you before it gets out of hand. Don't worry, did you think I meant to bother you again?" he asked. "I'm sorry for grabbing you last night, I've never done anything like that before. Something made me imagine that you wanted me to be forceful. You may not believe me, but something strange has gotten hold of me in regards to you, controlling me like. So, maybe I better stay away from you."

Now, that got Kiki's attention. Andrew felt like something was controlling him? *Like a demon spirit?* Annie mentioned that Andrew's obsession with Kiki began before they even met. His initial interest began around March. *Right after she wore that Saint Comba charm.* He pushed to be considered for her awakening and when that fell through, he began plotting a seduction instead. Regardless of Gwen and Trinity's beliefs, the demon spirit seemed to constantly twist people into doing its bidding. Could that negative energy actually make someone murder her? Andrew came from a coven connected family and seemed very in tune with the pagan beliefs.

"Do you believe an evil spirit induced you to seduce me? You probably had little control over your actions then. Do you feel like it's pushing your hand right now?" Kiki asked him. "I've been marked, you know. I'll likely be murdered by a lover before long, unless the curse is broken," she said it half joking, but he wasn't amused.

"Well, it won't be by me," Andrew said quickly. He looked worried. "Do you think you'll be able to break this curse? Annie told us everything. It's what all the to-do is about, isn't it, breaking this curse? Annie told me the sequence the other day. Love, betrayal, death."

Kiki nodded.

"Do you know why I'm here, living with my Uncle George instead of back home?" he asked. "My own cousin was almost strangled to death on Islay by a man I'd never expect it from. Then, I almost killed the man in revenge. Nobody knows it was me that beat him so bad. I'm actually in hiding." He nodded to her. "Everyone believes that I came to learn the family mash from George, but I really came to hide. They say she was marked by a curse. It's supposed to be a secret, my violent past."

"Then, why are you telling me?"

"So that you know what I am and what I'm capable of," he said. "I don't want an evil spirit working through me. So, we can both make sure of it. No love for us, love. Keep your green eyes off of me, okay?"

"I'm not the one sending out erotic energy." Kiki glared at him.

"Don't be so sure about that." Andrew laughed. "That's about all you send out. Do you think I could help in some way with this curse before it gets the better of me? I saw that other fellow, the Turk. He's at the cottage right now and Trinity will let him help, but not George, or me, or Sam. Why? Do the old women think the demon might work through us because our mothers belong to the coven? I don't like that. I want to break that curse too. What do you think I can do?"

The Turk? Why would Trinity let any man help? Was it because the Turk could see the marks, or because Trinity had a special past with that man?

"Do you believe in the Faerie Flag? Ian is going down there tomorrow morning and will be placing sensors behind the big glass barrier," Kiki said. "I'm sure Ian would let you tag along. As a MacLeod, you can make a wish on the Faerie Flag, if you think it's important enough to use the flag wish, that is. If you can believe in this curse, maybe you can believe in the flag as well."

Andrew stared at her. She was happy to see that he was not amused.

"I've always believed in that flag," he said softly.

George, Trinity, and Dominique conversed in the sitting room, drinking. The tension in the room foretold a storm lurking on Kiki's horizon. Dominique did not drink whisky with Trinity and George, he sipped tea from a small mug, and they were patiently waiting for her. Andrew did not go into the room with her.

"Kiera, come in here." Trinity sounded tipsy. Something must be amiss, her mother usually only accepted a dram or two, unless it was a festival. Kiki noticed that George appeared tense and upset, while Dominique seemed calm and happy. Dominique rose and beamed at her when she came in.

Were they really going to do this, Kiki thought.

"Good evening, Miss Kiera Lovett," Dominique gushed.

Kiki nodded at him, then gave her mother and George a hug, she always did. For all intents and purposes, they were her parents as far as anyone in in the village was concerned. Kiki sat between the two men and faced her mother.

"You probably wonder why we called you here," Trinity said.

My goodness, did she need to drink so much whisky? Kiki could see her mother acting spacey. Did they really think she didn't already know and needed to sit down and air it out? Their auras gave everything away at that first meeting and Kiki hoped they'd just let it go. Why rock the boat now and upend perfectly peaceful relationships. Kiki glanced at George, worried.

"Out of respect for George, please do not talk about what we're going to tell you," Trinity said.

George rose suddenly. "You know, I've always loved you, lassie."

"Of course. I love you too, George." Kiki rose quickly and gave him another hug.

George smiled down at her, then turned to Trinity. "This changes nothing between us. Isn't that right?"

Trinity nodded.

Kiki stared at Dominique Diaz and felt incredibly upset. Who was this man to come and spoil George's peaceful life? Kiki always knew George wasn't her real father, but he always acted like he·could be and seemed proud at the possibility. George kept very close company with Trinity, for as long as Kiki could remember. He loved her mother deeply and naturally loved Kiki as well. He was loyal to Trinity, even when he married briefly once before. Kiki was sad to see her fake father walk out the door, finally and totally exposed. A connection was severed, and she realized they could never pretend he might be her real father again.

"Kiera. My green man, Mo Leannan. I want you to…"

"Mother, please be quiet for one second." Kiki sadly stared at the door George just exited. Then, she glanced at her mother gazing fondly at Dominique. If she had loved him so much, then why didn't she go with him? Or, why didn't he stay with her? "Just give me a wee moment to get over the one father."

Dominique became concerned.

"It is natural for you to feel this way. He has been here your whole life. You can still think of him as your father," Dominique said gently. His aura changed to soothe the air. "I just wanted to know you. And for you to know me, for who I am. No one else need know of these things, unless you want it. George has asked that we keep the status quo in the village."

Kiki smiled at him and took his hand.

"I've always known that George wasn't my real father and that you were out there somewhere. This is not so much of a shock," she told Dominique. "But, I didn't realize, until just now, that I've always taken George for granted. Maybe like a real daughter might, I suppose. And I'm sad about that, disregarding George. He always behaved like I was his little girl. But I'm happy to meet you too," Kiki said. "Tell me why I've never met you before?"

Dominique glanced at Trinity, then turned back to her. "I never knew about you. Trinity never told me. I suppose I did not leave a forwarding address," Dominique confessed. "Truthfully, I'm not sure what I would have done had I known. Your mother did not want to be burdened by a man or follow me on my quest. I invited her, I assure you, but she refused. Now my quest has led me back here to the both of you. Maybe it worked out the way it should."

They talked into the night. Her father was the son of a very wise woman, a woman who decided to teach both her son and daughter the pagan arts. His mother had once been the leader of their group in Turkey, so he had ancestors from Scotland. Kiki should know, she had three half siblings, all sisters. If she ever wanted to meet them, she was welcome. Just like Kiki, two of those sisters were marked by the demon spirit. Dominique was very determined to see those marks erased.

The next morning, Ian agreed to take Andrew to Castle Dunvegan with the crew. He didn't understand why Andrew needed to go, but Kiki said it was important coven business. As a MacLeod of the clan from Skye, Andrew had ties to that castle and could trace his linage to the laird of the land. George MacLeod always said that the MacLeods on Islay were closer to the seat of Dunvegan than the MacLeods left behind. Kiki suggested the crew interview Andrew directly in front of artifacts in the castle. Andrew was a very pretty man, very photogenic, and he could recite all the MacLeod stories. Plus, Emma seemed to have taken a shine to Andrew.

That meant Kiki and Janine could run through the summoning spells Gwen marked in Celeste's grimoire. Dominique, joined with them as they perused the book. He was very interested in charms written by a *dragoma*. Trinity avoided her that day. Sitting with her biological father, listening to his gentle nature, she wondered her mother might have been shaped differently paired with him. Instead of the radical town matriarch, she might have become a quiet, gentle, retiring, satisfied soul. Or bitter. One or the other. It made Kiki think about the detective.

"Have you spoken to many spirits?" Dominique asked Janine.

They lounged on the wall that connected the cottage to the Faerie Glen. It was near noon and a few tourists hurried past. The Faerie Glen had become very popular in recent years and it was worrisome. Janine read through verses Gwen marked, but no one knew what they meant and Janine proved to be very little help. She was preoccupied with euphoric feelings of love and pregnancy and could barely concentrate on serious matters. Janine flipped to a random page, not one Gwen marked.

"I really like this one. So short and simple. *Come wise soul, to us appear. Show yourself as we come near. Draw us in to make us three, so I command, so mote it be.*" She smiled at Kiki. "My type of charm, simple and sweet. I think she wrote it as a little girl."

Kiki felt a cold breeze and glanced at Dominique. Did he feel it too? His brow creased. Did he recognize the summons? Surely, the coven women would not let a man read Auntie Meg's book of happenings. Janine had hit directly on the charm Celeste used to call out the spirit of the wall. Janine recited it again, sitting right on that very wall.

Looking up and down the mossy rocks, Kiki expected to see an old woman, but all she saw were a few tourists. A woman by the old oak tree stood up and walked toward them purposely. She moved differently than the others and Kiki got a funny feeling about that woman. She stopped about three feet away and sat on top of the stones, glancing at them. She was young and beautiful. She pulled her long hair out of a ponytail and shook out the wavy tresses. Her aura had a shimmery, silvery outline to it. The woman nodded before tilting her head back to soak some sun onto her face. After acknowledging her, Janine and Dominique returned to their conversation about Janine's experiences.

"Good afternoon to you," the woman greeted Kiki. "I understand a couple of women live in that cottage over there and sell herbs and teas. Do you know anything about that?"

Kiki nodded. "Trinity Lovett and Annelise Batten. If you go around to the back blue door and knock, Annie should be in the drying room grinding herbs and taking photos. She's working on the web page. Have you seen it? The website for the cottage."

The woman nodded her head slowly, smiling sweetly. Kiki suddenly noticed her beautiful green eyes, her long dark lashes and porcelain skin. Mixed together, they gave her a striking appearance. Kiki felt an odd sensation. *Did the woman resemble Trinity a tiny bit?* No, her hair was auburn with a reddish tint, and she was tall and twig-like, *but her face.* When she spoke again, her voice had changed.

"A mix o' hemlock, nightshade, snakeroot 'n caster bean. Just a wee smear on each blade to touch the blood." The woman grinned at Kiki and her eyes sparkled beautifully. "That's how it's done." The woman nodded her head toward Janine. "She is meant tae be the last one, and th' Faerie Flag wilnae help her. But it may help ye. Ye tae take her stead can save that one."

That set Kiki's heart beating wildly, who was this woman? Kiki wondered why Janine and Dominique paid the woman no more attention than they would any other tourist sitting on the wall. Could they see her? Of course they could, they had greeted her. Kiki was very confused, but her throat felt too stiff and dry to speak. Her own eyes were locked and unable to move from the hypnotic green jewels gazing at her.

"Hey, babe!" A man trotted toward them. He waved to the woman. "Why'd you take off?"

The woman stood to greet the man. She turned briefly to nod goodbye, and Kiki noticed her eyes were no longer green and her face was no longer familiar. Kiki watched her walk away, holding the hand of her man. She was just a regular woman on an outing. Kiki searched the wall to where the woman had been before walking toward them, sitting under the old oak tree. *Had the spirit possessed her there?* She watched the couple walk toward the cottage and silently calmed her beating heart.

That was a message, wasn't it?

Janine patted her arm.

"Kiki, are you okay? Janine asked. "You look a little spaced out."

"Did either of you hear what that woman just said?" Kiki asked them.

"She was nice." Janine nodded. "Loved the web site, and I agree, Annie has an artistic eye."

Chapter 20
A Betrayal

Janine

It was another early morning and Janine decided to jog around the Faerie Glen. She wanted to go all the way to the top of Castle Ewen and back. She brought another offering of bread for the faeries and tucked it in the niche rock as she passed. She loved running over the gentle mounds and enjoyed the added fun of rocky obstacles. It was much more interesting than the flat surfaces of Davis back in California. She also figured out the faerie offerings. She spotted a couple of hooded crows hopping around the rock the previous morning, each eating crumbs. If she timed things right, she would get back just as Kiki and Ian rolled into the cottage from their *Spectral Analysis* investigation of the ruins of Castle Duntulm.

It was only a mile to the top of Castle Ewen, so Janine ran just outside the edge of the glen to add distance. Annie told her that the faeries would appreciate that. She took the winding narrow trail up the back side of the hill and was soon on top looking down at the glen. There were three spiral rock designs on the glen floor, looking very like a Celtic triskelion. Janine paused at the top to sip some water. It was then that she spotted him, a lone man standing far off in the hills, not moving. What was he doing out so early? Janine could barely see him, but it appeared like he was watching her. Something about his posture troubled her, he seemed familiar. *No, no, just a random traveler.* Janine ignored her paranoia and turned around to begin her jog back to the cottage, then she spotted them, the two hooded crows. They were sharing her bread crumbs. As she passed, one of the birds paused and carefully watched her movements.

She could hear the ruckus before she came over the hill. Ian and Kiki were in the parking area speaking with Roger McNally. They were not having a pleasant conversation. Everyone stared at Janine when she came over the last mound and jogged happily into the drive. Roger watched her for a second, then turned to Ian.

"You see, Ian? This is what I'm talking about." He pointed at Janine. "You let your young wife go running in the wee hours of the day, who knows what could happen in that wilderness? *That man* is still out there. You're busy here, lad, I should take the lass back to the manor. It's large, and it's protected."

"I'm fine. I just..." Janine was amused, but Roger McNally cut her off harshly with an upheld hand.

"Just be quiet there, lass," he said firmly. "Ian already had to settle a scuffle with one past fellow, I don't want any more of that happening. Hanging about with these women is bound to wrap you into even more trouble. I know their ways and I cannot sleep thinking about it, especially since your good news. Best if you come to the manor where I can help keep my eye on you."

"Not everyone is safer on that manor." Kiki glared at her uncle.

"You watch your tongue, Kiera," Roger glanced from Kiki to Ian. "I'll not have you spinning evil gossip. This discussion is not your business, it's a discussion between myself and my son. You mind your manners."

Roger held his hand up and he commanded silence. His Ian-shaped grey eyes froze on Janine.

"You can make this easy, lassie, and come along with me. You can run all you want on the manor, ride horses with Chloe, and have an easy time. There are several men that watch the grounds, so there'll be no trespassers to bother you."

Kiki shook her head and turned to the cottage entrance.

"And no leaving without permission. I can see you'll probably let those fellows tell you exactly what to do."

Janine watched Ian squirm. His soft blue eyes searched hers. He clearly hoped she would go back with his father, not because he wanted her to leave, but because his father insisted on it. Ian didn't want to lose the recent reconciliation they acquired. But Janine didn't want to go to the manor and be trapped there with Roger and silent Chloe. She enjoyed the chattering women in the cottage and hoped the coven would invite her to participate in the summoning they planned.

He will bend you to his will. Who will?

"I don't trust her influence on you," Roger said to Janine. "That one is just like her mother. Trinity relentlessly urged Celeste to disrespect me, and it caused a lot of confusion and pain in our lives. I'm just looking out for you, and Ian. It's been weighing heavily on my mind and I drove all night. You carry the McNally heir in your belly and we must protect you. We are obligated to take care of you. Why not make that easy for us? Make it easy for Ian. He's busy here."

Janine took Roger's hand and squeezed it, then glanced at Ian's blinking eyes.

"You mean well," she said softly to Roger. "But I'm going to stay here with my husband."

Then, she ducked into the house.

Trinity, Kiki, and Annie stood waiting with their hands on their hips. Kiki sighed, relieved to see her. Trinity seemed worried, like she wanted to go outside and tell Roger off, but felt it might be better to leave it alone. Annie nodded, then disappeared so as not to intrude. The door flew open and Ian stepped in. He swayed back at the sight of the three of them standing akimbo. He scowled briefly at his aunt, then turned to Janine.

"Are you sure?" Ian pleaded. "It'll just be for a couple of nights. I'll drive up day after tomorrow. We don't have to film anything at Dunvegan. We can wrap up early. He's just so set on it, on you going to the manor. It's nice that he's taken an active interest in my life again."

"Bollocks, Ian," Kiki said sternly. "The detective told us that the original text message came from a cell tower in Dornoch, and so he lied to you about that. What else is he lying about?"

"He's concerned," Ian snapped. "He drove up because he was worried about that text message too. He couldn't sleep and drove all night because of it. He thinks whoever send it was spying on us."

"She doesn't want to go, perhaps she can feel something is not right," Trinity said. "You know what happened out there before."

"I don't know," Ian snapped at her. "I had a dream, okay? You never should have told me my dream was real, I was a kid in mourning, Auntie. Angry at my father, and heartbroken about my mother. He was hard on us, everyone knows that. That made it easy to believe that dream."

Ian bit back whatever else he wanted to say. He looked at Janine.

"He's just trying to make amends. I like getting on with him more than hating him."

"Please, Ian," Janine said gently. "I just want to stay here with you. Is that okay? I want to be wherever you are."

Janine could see that he was disappointed, but he nodded. He told her he was going to take his father out for breakfast and try to explain it to him. Then, he banged out the door.

Janine let a breath go. She was very relieved that Ian didn't press her. She had been very close to giving in and she did not want to go back to McNally Manor without Ian. Janine glanced at Trinity and Kiki.

"I can't explain why I don't want to go back there."

"No need to explain it to us," Trinity said. "I'm just happy you followed your gut on it."

Kiki stayed awake to tell Janine about the ghost hunt in the old ruins. They sat in the overlarge kitchen, drinking coffee and eating fried eggs. Kiki told Janine that the remains of the castle were on a small cliff overlooking the North Minch. The ocean was very violent at night, and the crashing of the waves was scarier than any ghost. Kiki said it had been freezing cold and her teeth pretty much tried to chatter themselves out of her head. Her scanty lace up leather top was probably not the best outfit choice, but poor Emma and

Oliver, she chuckled. Sally designed some sort of furry animal suits for them. At least they were warm.

The wind made it impossible for Ian and his rotating new antennae and forget about any audio sounds in the howling wind. As for herself, she didn't feel any spirits. Kiki got the sense that any lingering ghostly energy faded with the elements long ago. She used her standard summoning charm, but it didn't urge a single MacDonald to come out to bicker. Only Emma and Oliver came out to bicker, over who would use which tools in the ruins. Did Janine know that the tech geeks had some sort of arm sleeve that they called *mellow-skin*? Janine couldn't stop giggling at the look on Kiki's face.

"I'm supposed to take it as a compliment," Kiki said. "But it's a little disturbing. Ian's crew was quite disappointed. Max is going to press for a request to film one night at Castle Dunvegan now. He's upset at the dud of a night we had on the cliff. Of course, if the sisters agree to filming the summoning, then we might be okay. Max plans to woo the old girls regarding that. My mother pretty much adores him, so it's very likely a done deal."

Janine's laughter subsided.

"Are you still involved with him, Max? He seemed pretty focused on you the other night. It's none of my business, and I'm not really upset anymore. I realize how gullible I can be. I've been quite a stupid girl when it comes to men."

"You're a trusting soul. My Auntie Celeste was the same way," Kiki told her. "I'm glad you put your foot down about going back with Roger. I half expected you to cave in. To answer your question, I'm trying to avoid Max."

"I am weak with men, I know it," Janine admitted. "But I felt something odd going on at that manor. Chloe is just too quiet, and I had weird dreams and strange conversations. Ian's father actually believes I did something to inspire the stabbing. He actually questioned me about it."

"I'm sure he believes Celeste caused everything he did to her," Kiki said. "Isolated her, institutionalized her. Maybe even…" Kiki let that last thought hang.

"Kiki, tell me the truth. The women have all discussed it here, I know they have. The redeemers for this curse of the charms, am I supposed to be the last one? Both the Mary spirit and the Ingrid spirit said it. The woods ghost gave me the charm and said there's a place to be filled and told me to fill it. Am I destined to fill a place in the redemption curse? Is that what everyone thinks? Because that's what I think."

Kiki moved away, and Janine could see it in her eyes. The coven concluded the same thing.

"It would make sense that a demon would mark a *dragoma* for death. Only someone like you can command it to listen and the curse won't end until the demon sits in witness to the stories of redemption locked in the charms. If there's a story in all twelve charms, then that's it. The demon must concede. That's what we're hoping."

"What about this talk of a last one?" Janine asked. "Even I know it must mean that one charm doesn't have a story to tell, and there's one place to be filled. What's the plan then?"

"There are a few ideas stewing in the cauldron. Not one of them include you wearing that charm. Everyone believes it's an obvious trick. Hoping we'll sacrifice the *dragoma* so there's no one to command it. Eva says there will not be a sacrifice. She was adamant that she would take on the last charm if there's no other way. She's old, very old, but still has a lover. She has tasked him to kill her if need be." *And then Andrew will make a wish on his faerie flag to bring her back.* Kiki raised an eyebrow. "Not really, though. It's a last resort, and not something anyone is seriously considering. Bertha, from Turkey, proposed a ritual that has worked before. No death, but one that calls on the blood of twelve or more sisters, a compurgation of sorts. A blood sacrifice. The shedding of blood works wonders against dark energy. There doesn't need to be a death, the blood of an entire coven united can do it. Very few of the sisters have actually participated in a blood sacrifice, so we're a little nervous."

"Is the coven going to ask me to help?" Janine asked.

"Trinity doesn't want you near a demon spirit and has pressed for not including you. She feels her sister's essence in your belly," Kiki told her. "She's very protective of you. But it's clear we need a *dragoma*, and so you may be asked."

"Well, I want to do it," Janine told her. "I'm not sure how effective I'd be, but I want to do whatever is needed to erase this nonsense. So, if anyone asks you, tell them I want to help any way I can."

Kiki nodded, then went off to bed.

After Ian returned and fell asleep, Janine escaped to the herb room to help Annie. Ian had been a bit grumpy and she didn't want to spoil her mood by arguing with him. He'd be better after a good nap. Janine enjoyed Annie's company, she was always funny and bright. Her artistic photos of the herbs in different states, fresh, dried, chopped, and pulverized were very pleasing. Plus, Annie filled her in on gossip from Trinity's den.

"I'm going to use a blue background for this one, that blue sheet over there." Annie pointed out the paper. "We want to bring out the reds in this powder. Blue will give it a softer, more romantic appearance."

Annie sprinkled the brownish powder on the slightly blue background. They watched the reds pop out, warming up the tones in her red clover. Annie used a digital camera suspended from a tripod to snap pictures. Her workroom felt cozy and warm. The hanging herbs created an interesting potpourri and Janine loved the ambience in that little room. She knew a larger drying room sat off the patio house, but it was not as cozy as Annie's nook off the kitchen.

"Kiki said you were an art major," Janine said. "Do you ever think about completing your degree? I finally completed mine this past December, so it's never too late."

Annie's wide eyes glanced up. "Don't tell Kiki. I finished my classes before we left on our Europe adventure. She was never going finish anything and we would have been stuck there forever." Annie shrugged sheepishly. She went to the window to adjust the light entering the room. "How's that?"

"Very romantic," Janine smiled. "Any more news on the summoning? Anything Kiki's worried about? She tends to treat me like a child about these things."

"You and everybody else." Annie passed the powder, and Janine transferred it back into a bottle. "She's a gifted girl, beyond compare. But she's does have her ego. Has she mentioned her fears about creating her own demon? No? Well, she's convinced that the demon spirit is placing people in such a way as to complete the curse, or to garner more victims anyway. She thinks your husband's father is being used to cause dissension in Ian."

"I don't follow. What does she mean by create your own demon? I thought a demon was a sociopathic or psychopathic person or something like that."

Annie nodded. "Kiki believes that people are being compelled to act outside of their normal nature. That we are puppets of the curse and will act out the roles written for us. Marked girls will gravitate toward the wrong men and then find an excuse to leave their lovers. Jilted lads will find themselves compelled to attack the lass that left them. Kiki's not the only one with such theories. The younger moon sisters agree, and so do the Turks. Even Sam and Andrew believe it to be so. Of course, I believe a person has free will. Just because a demon spirit compels a person doesn't mean they will act on it. Gwen is of the same mind as me, as are some of the older sisters. Andrew told me that he feels drawn to Kiera, but he is not going to touch her and become the demon's puppet. That's proof enough, don't you think?"

Trinity peeked into the kitchen. She advised Annie to take a nap, every woman in the coven would be needed at the summoning. She gathered up a tea service and lured Janine to her private den for a chat, she had a very important favor to ask. Janine was pretty sure she would be asked to participate in the night's ritual.

Chapter 21
The Summoning

Janine

Faerie Glen's upper parking lot was crowded with Doctor McNally's tech crew and their rental cars. The coven leaders gave permission for *Spectral Analysis* to film and monitor their ritual from the outer edge of the glen floor. The paranormal investigators received strict orders to avoid the main clearing and to stay off the rocky hill dubbed Castle Ewen. Annie meandered into the parking lot to bid the crew hello and to advise them on how to leave an offerings for the fae. Annie brought breads and dried petals in a large woven basket and wore a crown of flowers in her hair. She set the basket on the ground near one of their rental cars.

"Place your offering in an inconspicuous spot, near where you plan to sit," Annie instructed. "Make the offering yourselves, personally, just a wee crust of bread or a sprinkle petals will do. Always include a soft thank you. Doesn't hurt to compose a verse, the fae always enjoy a bit of a rhyme." Annie gave Janine a hug before walking off again.

"Is she for real?" Oliver scowled at her receding figure, brows lined. Ian's crew appeared unusually irritated.

"We're guests here," the doctor told his crew. "We'll follow Annie's directions and take them seriously. The locals truly believe in the faeries, so maybe there's something to it. It's smart to be discerning, but we must always keep an open mind. We are trying to record the paranormal, so let's assume something extraordinary exists in that glen. Don't forget what happened in the orchard back home."

"Boom!" Emma lambasted Oliver with a finger in the chest. "When in Rome, Oliver, when in Rome. We don't want to piss off the faeries. We are not talking about Tinkerbell or tooth fairy types. Highland Faeries are mean and harsh. Better to be safe than sorry, Ollie."

Oliver grimaced at Emma, Ian's students were not getting along. Janine noticed that neither of them took out the *mellow-skin* wrap, the opaque sleeve remained on the trunk floor of their rental car. Janine watched as they pull out other familiar gadgets. She itched to help, but remained off to the side, out of the way. Ian opened a map of the glen on the hood of the car. He already marked out the placement for equipment and observers. He grinned at Janine.

"For tonight, would you prefer to hang out with me near the stone wall," he pointed to a spot on the map, "or up here in the lot with Ben and the master controls? Max is going to be here with Ben, if that helps you decide."

Janine hadn't told him yet. She planned to be right smack dab in the center of the green meadow. She worried about his reaction to that information. She wrapped her arms around him and kissed him lightly.

"Don't be angry," she whispered into his ear and felt him stiffen. "It's just this once, that's all. I need to help with this summoning because of those Saint Comba charms. They were given to me, you know, so I have a stake in what's going on here."

"Janine." He stared right at her. "You realize that we are filming this. We need to use the footage in the show. If my father catches sight of you in that witches' ritual, he's going to feel betrayed. I assured him that you were not the pagan coven type. He'll think I'm either a total idiot or a total arse." His soft eyes pleaded with her. "Come on, lass, watch from the side with me, I promise you won't get bored."

Janine turned away because he could persuade her very easily with his beautiful eyes. But, she was the *dragoma* and she needed to help. Trinity revealed that since she entered the cottage, they've had all kinds of interesting occurrences. Did Janine realize the faeries were leaving trinkets in the offering rock? Coins, threads, shells. That rarely happened. They were appeasing Janine. Not just pagan sisters, but *them in the glen* valued a *dragoma* too. Did she realize she called on the spirit of the wall the other day? Kiki wrote out the encounter for the big book of happenings.

They needed her. Trinity didn't want to ask, but there was no other way. It made perfect sense that the demon marked Janine, only a *dragoma* would be able to command a bad spirit to sit, listen, and accept the testimony required to break the curse. The demon spirit wallowed in a state of resistance, and it grew greedy for victims. Surrounded by the fae, that glen was the safest place to meet a dark entity and command it. They needed her.

Janine resisted the urge to give in to her husband because Ian's arguments really came from Roger McNally, and whether he knew it or not, her father-in-law might be in league with the demon spirit. Janine would have to disappoint Ian and she stepped away.

"At least stay on the periphery of the crowd," Ian could see her mind was made up. "We might be able to splice you out of the picture."

Janine didn't know how to tell him that she would not be on the edge of the crowd.

"What if you get faint?" Ian said suddenly. He pulled her away from the tech crew and started walking her away from the cars. "Have you thought about that? This is bound to be a very intense paranormal event and you've fainted in intense events before. Aren't you worried about our baby?"

"It's only the first trimester," Janine said. "Trinity says—"

"What if I just say no, then? *No!*" Ian had a hold of her arm. It was unusual for him to be so forceful. "As your husband, what if I demand that you not participate? How am I supposed to protect you if you're down in the middle of it? I'm not allowed down there? Men are never allowed in the glen during a ritual."

His blinking eyes were breaking her heart. What drove this intense insistence of his?

"Are you joining the coven now?"

"Ian, you're overreacting. I'm not joining anything," Janine told him. "I'm just participating in this one summoning event. We've both done this sort of thing before, many, many times."

"This is different and... These women have been doing things for years, they don't need you to participate." His angry voice rose. "Crikes, Janine, I should get back over there and help set things up, you can see those two kids are at each other's throats, and I need to keep you and our baby safe. Don't forget you've fainted in paranormal situations! Why take that chance with our baby? You'll make me very happy if you change your mind and stand right next to me tonight, or stay in the cottage. You'll be safe and cozy in there."

Janine's eyes followed him as he walked away, the man she loved. She felt an uneasy lump in her gut as she remembered Annie's words. *Love, betrayal, death.* When Ian sees the significant level of her participation in the ritual, will he consider it a betrayal? According to Annie, a few sisters speculated that the demon nudged people to act out of character. Even so, Ian would never, ever harm her. She would not make that mistake again, letting her past fears paint him that way, and she tamped down her racing heart. As she turned back toward the cottage, Janine rubbed her arm where Ian had held it so tightly.

All twelve moon priestesses arrived in Uig Bay for the ritual plus many casual members of the coven. Bertha and Miranda were also present, and Dominique would be allowed to observe from a distance. Doctor McNally invited him to sit with Ben and Max near the control monitors. He thanked them gratefully.

Janine already met the three leaders of the coven, Eva, Trinity, and Cara, and one of the moon priestesses, Diana, but besides Gwen and Kiki, every other coven member was new to her. She tried to remember their names, Ginger, Roxanne, Kate, Lisa, Rebecca, and Elizabeth, as they congregated in Trinity's private den. The women studied Janine with obvious curiosity. Annie popped in briefly, with her bright eyes easing the mood. She wasn't a moon priestess, but she would lead the younger girls into the glen to set out offerings for the faeries. Trinity and Cara whisper instructions to her. Annie paused to nod encouragement at Janine before she left.

The coven women dressed in flowing skirts, silken scarves, and gemstones. They wore protective minerals as jewelry and sachets of protective herbs as belts or wrist bands. Gwen passed a familiar sachet to place over her heart and Trinity gave her a necklace strung with round beads and one hagstone. Trinity claimed that things were more easily seen through a small stone window. Then, each of the moon priestesses took turns handing Janine a piece of jewelry to wear. She soon found herself decorated with two anklets, four bracelets, three rings, and three strands of beads around her neck. Over the top of everything, Trinity delivered a red velvet hooded cloak.

"You don't think this is overkill?" Janine showed Gwen the rings.

Gwen smiled, "Everyone wants to be connected to the *dragoma*."

"I feel like everyone is staring at me," Janine whispered. "Does everyone know that I could be the last one? Is that common knowledge in this room? Or is it the *dragoma* thing?"

"A little of that, but more because everyone knows that you're Ian's new wife," Gwen whispered. "Half these girls had their eye on Ian McNally once upon a time. He was always a favorite lad around here." Gwen chuckled. "That's why a few of them are staring."

Eva called for a moment of silence. Janine was very familiar with Kiki stepping aside to "center" herself before a séance. *Deep breaths, and clear your mind with the exhale*, Janine told herself. Gwen hovered near Janine to comfort her. She felt glad, because she was getting nervous.

Miranda studied her from across the room. They met briefly, but Miranda still seemed a mystery. *Had she been fooled by Richard Wilkens as easily as Janine?*

Soon, the women began picking up the pieces of the alter. As they now had a *dragoma* present, Janine would be tasked to build it after leading them into the glen. Each priestess would hand her one small part and indicate where to place it. Earlier that day, Trinity led her to the exact spot on the glen floor to build that alter. It was in the same location many of the tourists chose to start a spiral rock design. Trinity laughed and said that the faeries guided hands on a daily basis in that glen. That spot happened to be a central location for faerie energy and the spiral was an ancient sacred symbol.

Janine donned her hood and led the women toward the glen with Gwen right next to her. The old crones following first, then the guests, then the rest of the moon priestesses. Kiki brought up the rear. Janine followed the low stone wall and wondered what Kiki wrote regarding her encounter with the wall spirit. The moon hovered overhead, well past the quarter stage, and the sky appeared banded with a greenish glow just on the horizon, the northern lights, beautiful.

Janine spotted Ian up ahead. He was not fooled by her low hood and stared directly at her with a disappointed face. His lips were pressed tightly. For a second, she feared he was going to stop her from walking past, but he didn't. *Keep going,* she urged herself. She hated the look on his face, but too many ghosts had warned her that she would be the *last one* and she didn't want to live with a curse hanging over her head for the rest of her life.

Janine meandered to the prescribed spot and stopped. She instantly spotted Annie among the women scattered in the glen and their eyes met briefly. Gwen gave Janine a wooden board to place on the center stone. A large spiral of rocks still lay on the ground and Janine used it for guidance.

Gwen stood just to the left of Janine, close enough to whisper an encouragement.

Trinity stepped up and delivered a three wick candle, which Janine placed in the center of the oak plank, then Trinity chose a spot to the left of Gwen.

The lovely grandmother, Cara, delivered a small ornate dagger with a carved wooden handle. Janine placed it on the far right edge of the plank, then Cara went to stand to the left of Trinity.

Weathered old Eva gave her twelve purple amethyst stones to circle the edge of the candle, then the old woman moved to the left of Cara. Janine could see that the women arranged themselves into the beginnings of an arc.

Bertha delivered twelve brownish smoky quartz stones. Janine would slowly build a design with those stones, a crystal grid, a twelve armed spiral to match the one on the ground. Bertha instructed her to place the stones in such a way that they curved and radiated outward, clockwise.

Gwen's friend, Ginger, brought twelve green jasper stones. She paused to kiss Gwen lightly on the lips and whispered something softly, then found her place in the circle.

Roxanne, with the dyed blue hair, delivered yellowish stones.

Tall, slender Kate gave Janine small black tourmaline chunks. *To ward against harm*, she whispered.

Lisa, a tired young mother, produced twelve selenite mini-pyramids, smiling shyly.

Rebecca, behind owlish glasses, surrendered polished corundum in reds and blues, blinking at Janine before she joined the circle.

Elizabeth, thick and sturdy, delivered a nervous smile and a stone carved with three triskelion spirals, which Janine placed at the left side of the wood plank.

Diana brought a stone carved with a trinity knot, which Janine placed on the right side of the wood plank. Diana gave her a brief hug.

Miranda delivered sticks of incense, which Janine placed on each of the carved stones. She also paused to hug Janine.

Kiki opened a silken scarf full of the Saint Comba charms and instructed Janine to place one at the end of each arm in her crystal spiral grid. She stood very close as she watched the charms being placed.

"It's not too late to bow out, my dear," Kiki whispered. "I can see your husband is fuming at us all, and I can't say he's totally wrong to be worried."

Janine didn't bother with an answer. She just stared into those feline green eyes of Kiki's and sent her to a place in the circle. Building that alter gave Janine an odd sense of power. She felt a surge of energy tingling below her skin and the hairs on her arms were standing on end. Then, she stepped aside for Gwen. It was the month of the Wolf Moon, and Gwen happened to be the Priestess of the Wolf Moon. In coven tradition, Gwen would lead any coven ritual during the cycle of her moon.

"On this night in winter's clutch, beyond the veil we seek to touch, I light the candle set for thee, so as it burns, so shall you be." Gwen lit the incense sticks and one wick of the candle, then delivered the taper to Janine.

"On this night in winter's clutch, beyond the veil we seek to touch, I light the candle set for thee, so as it burns, so shall you be." Janine lit the other wick.

"Come now, spirits, light it three," Gwen said softly.

"Come now, spirits, light it three, so I command, so mote it be," Janine echoed.

The third wick spontaneously ignited, and *something entered into the glen with them.*

Excitement permeated the air. By the way Kiki's eyes focused on the center of their circle, Janine knew it must be there. Many of the women noticed something and Janine spotted Trinity spying through a hagstone. It wasn't the demon, whatever it was, that much Janine knew. Gwen cleared her throat.

"We demand the spirit who tainted these charms to be obedient. Hold open your hands." Every woman in the inner circle opened their palms to the circle. Gwen looked to Janine and nodded. They chose three written charms from Celeste's grimoire and decided that Janine would choose one of them, whichever felt right at the correct moment.

"Come thee that spawned an evil deed, the blackened soul to which it feeds, witness now which was agreed, we call on you to now concede. So I command, so mote it be."

An audible gasp floated from several women in the glen, and the night became extremely still. Janine couldn't see anything, but clearly, others could. Kiki's eyes locked onto the center of the circle, and by the way her eyes tracked, Janine knew something moved around in there.

Janine resisted envisioning it. In the past, she lost precious energy trying to visualize a spirit, and it was too early in the ritual for her to lose energy. Earlier, Trinity advised her to remain aloof and ignore the taunts from the demon, her only goal was to command it. The coven women glanced at one another, and some frowned at each other. Janine couldn't see what caused the distress. Even girls outside the circle, the ones with Annie, were upset.

"What is it? What's going on?" Janine whispered to Gwen.

"The demon's mark." Gwen peered at her with gloomy eyes. "You have it, Kiki has it, Ginger has it. Nearly half the sisters bear the demon's mark. You can't see it?"

Janine shook her head. *Try not to see it*, she told herself. *Preserve your energy.*

"We shall summon the sisters of the charms to reveal each story of redemption," Gwen announced. "A blood sacrifice will be made on each charm, and the demon will be compelled to listen and accept them." Gwen nodded at Janine.

Janine addressed the inside of their circle.

"*Thee that spawned an evil deed, the blackened soul to which it feeds, witness now which was agreed, I demand that you shall now concede. So I command, so mote it be.* All that is present will witness the stories that absolve each woman who wore a charm. Every soul present will bear witness! After which, the curse will dissolve and each mark will be erased."

Gwen took up the short dagger and pierced the skin of her palm. She held the wound high over the alter and allowed several drops of her blood to spill onto a few of the charms.

"*With this blood, I call on your testimony*," Gwen said.

The entire circle moved counterclockwise, keeping the circle tight. Cara came toward the alter, and Gwen passed the knife to her. Cara spilled her blood and recited the charm, *with this blood I call on your testimony*, then passed the knife to Trinity as the circle moved steadily. After each high priestess made their blood sacrifice, the rest took their turn. Finally, at the end of the line, Kiki handed the blade to Janine. Gwen nodded to her. The dagger burned along Janine's palm and it brought a sting to her eye, but Janine was happy to leave a drop of herself on the charms.

"*With this blood, I call on your testimony.*" Janine watched her blood steadily drop onto the charms. She made sure to soil each one of them.

She returned the knife to the alter and took up the hagstone attached to her necklace. She slowly raised the hole to her eye and spied something dark and hunched in the center of the circle. It was the shadow of a person, bent over, curling into himself, but it shivered and had no discernable features. Janine noticed a red mark on Kiki's forehead, a glowing red light, not unlike the dot from a laser pointer. Janine turned to Gwen and saw that she did not have a mark. Janine dropped the hagstone and waited, breathing hard. She needed to calm herself and remain aloof.

Suddenly, one of the women in the circle began speaking in a loud voice. It was Cara, the beautiful crone.

"*I, Lillias Blar, met mah death at the haun o' mah lover, who did strangle me oan this very spot. His was the last eyes I glimpsed in life. And in his eyes, there wis na remorse fur whit he did, only anger at myself. And in death, I redeemed my own soul.*"

Then, another of the women called out, "*Anise Glindale, I was murdered because I refused to move far from home and my lover felt trifled with and betrayed. He slit my throat after dinner on the night I refused to leave, and he buried me in our backyard. And with my death, I redeemed a soul.*"

And then another, "*My name is Celeste. I was strangled on the front steps of my home by the one I loved. He bent me to his will, then held my throat until the world disappeared from me. He covered his foul deed by sending me over a cliff. With my death, I atoned for a soul.*"

Other women in the circle called out more names and stories. All of the women had been strangled, or stabbed by a lover, a husband, or fiancé. Freda Tod, Gillian MacDonald, Lisa Michelle, Abigail Kirkpatrick, Iona Fraser, Blaire Beasley, Jennifer Smith, and Holly MacLeod. Each told a tale of love, betrayal, and murder, and their deaths each redeemed a long lost soul.

Then came a long silence. Too long. No one recited a final story and that meant one of the charms did not have a redeemer. Janine searched Gwen's face.

"Order him to accept each testimony of redemption and to erase the marks," Gwen whispered.

"Hear me," Janine spoke to the center of the circle. "You will accept each story of redemption. You will erase every mark. You will accept the end of the curse. The blood we shed demands it."

The night suddenly grew darker. Patched clouds flowed in to cover the moon. Janine reached for the hagstone and again put it to her eye. She could see the dark figure squirming, moving quickly toward the alter and Janine dropped the stone, heart suddenly racing.

"Calm, Janine, breathe easy," Gwen whispered. "Dinna let it know you're afraid. Now tell the demon again what you want. Search your core, and latch onto a strength."

Janine took a deep breath. She glanced toward Ian and thought about their baby. She knew that even though he was upset with her for being in that glen, Ian would always come running to catch her if she should fall. He was an expert at catching falling women, and she had nothing to worry about, not with him close by.

"You will accept each story of redemption. You will erase each mark. You will honor the end of this curse!" she said firmly.

Another of the grimoire charms suddenly blazed into her head, the words glowed behind her eyes. Her voice took on a calm commanding tone.

"Blood for blood, life for life, we now seal up this seam. Eye for eye, nose for nose, fading to a dream. Ear for ear, tooth for tooth, wound for wound is cleaned. Each weak soul is now atoned, each dark soul is now reformed, and each lost soul is now redeemed. All in witness here to see, So I command, so mote it be."

Something happened, because the women in the circle let out a collective sigh of relief. Janine raised her hagstone, but she could no longer see the dark figure. She turned to Kiki and could no longer see the red mark. Janine maneuvered the small stone around and could not see any of the marks. Her heart felt tremendously lighter.

As she maneuvered the stone toward the alter, she jumped. Through the hagstone hole, two beady red eyes glared at her. Then, the dark shadow moved close to her, turned, and blew out the candle. It instantly vanished with the flames.

Gwen began chanting in a thick accent, a simple song, and soon, all the women in the glen joined the chanting. Janine stood quietly, steadying her heart, not understanding the old language. Gwen kept hold of her hand, clutching it firmly, sending her calming energy. When the chant dimmed away, Gwen turned and hugged her tightly.

The pagan circle broke up and Eva, Cara, and Trinity moved quickly to the alter and searched the charms. Kiki also hurried over, her green eyes glowed with concern. Janine's heart rate pounded at top speed and though Gwen stopped hugging her, she did not let go of her hand.

"Do we know which one?" Cara whispered.

"It's this one." Eva pointed to one of the charms. "I feel that it is this one."

Kiki gather the charms from under the old women's noses and they started moving back toward the cottage. As they passed Ian, he avoided her eyes, still fuming. Not only would his wife be a prominent figure in the summoning shoot, but a nice story about how his mother was strangled by a lover on the front drive of McNally Manor would make it into the clip. Janine didn't blame him one bit for being upset. Gwen and Kiki walked closely on either side of her as they passed him.

"Maybe you'd like to hide in my room," Kiki whispered.

"I didn't see or hear hardly anything. Just those women reciting stories," Janine told her. "Were we successful? What happened? It looked like we were successful."

Kiki and Gwen exchanged glances.

"Pretty much successful," Kiki said. "The demon accepted all the stories of redemption and erased every single death mark as you ordered. The blood ritual worked."

"Pretty much?" Janine said. "What does that mean? Is the curse over or not?"

Kiki and Gwen led her around to the back of the cottage, away from everyone else. They stood under the lattice patio, just outside the kitchen nook doorway in the shadows.

"There's still one more thing I need to do," Kiki rummaged around the silk scarf.

"All the marks were erased, as you commanded." Gwen stared straight into her eyes. "But then he came close and left his mark on you again. Don't take it personally, it's probably because you're a *dragoma* and forced it to listen. It's a trick."

Kiki told Janine everything she saw. Every mark was erased and as long as a final redeemer fills the empty spot, there will never be another mark. But the demon wouldn't wait forever, only until the last cusp of the full moon, when the blood they shed dispersed, dried, and flaked away. If the final witch wasn't redeemed by then, then marks would begin to appear again. Hide the charms if they must, but the dark magic would seek out victims sooner or later.

"Give me the charm," Janine snapped. *So, the demon still wanted Janine to be the last one.*

"No." Kiki clutched the scarf to her chest. "You're not wearing that charm. No one with a brain expects you to wear that charm. It's a ridiculous attempt to get us to sacrifice our *dragoma*. The demon doesn't understand that we would never sacrifice anyone. That's not going to happen."

"I don't want anyone wearing it," Janine demanded.

She was a lot taller than Kiki, and stronger too. She was not letting Kiki walk away with that charm.

"You already told me what Eva planned as a last resort. She wants to wear it and end the curse, and I won't have it. So, give me the charm, Kiki, I mean it. It's mine, you know it. Don't worry, I won't wear it, but I'll not have someone else wearing it, either. Give it to me so I know it won't be used for something stupid. Clearly, I'm supposed to be the last one. No one else is marked now, so no one else needs to touch it. Until we figure something out, something that makes sense, I'm keeping the charm with me. The full moon is when? Day after tomorrow? That gives us at least three days to work something out."

Kiki opened her scarf full of charms. They were still stained with blood. She wiped one of them off and gave it to Janine.

"Even if you don't wear it, you're still in danger," Kiki said gently. "The demon is trying to find a way to work around us, Janine. Ian is very angry. Everyone could see it. It's out of character for him to be so angry. Maybe you should hide from him for a day or so, until he cools off."

"I'll never hide from Ian. He may be angry, but he would never hurt me. I'm safe with him. You're being absolutely ludicrous."

Gwen seemed very upset, her face was red.

"Kiki what is going on in your head? You're making me nervous, please don't disappear without telling me." Gwen could see the lights go on in the cottage. "We'll need to go in. Bertha and Miranda will want to discuss storing the these, and the old crones will want to discuss everything, and I need to get back to Inverness tonight. Why don't you come back to the city with me? Get a little distance from this."

Kiki hugged Gwen quickly and then passed the scarf of charms to her. They went in through the back kitchen door and Kiki paused inside the herb room. She desired to make a special tea to calm her nerves and urged them go ahead. Gwen did not want to leave Kiki in the kitchen, but as the Wolf Moon Priestess, Gwen was needed in the den to discuss the ritual right away, and she was required to add an entry into the old book. Kiki pushed Janine to follow Gwen and pulled a cup from the kitchen shelf.

Chapter 22
The Faerie Flag

Kiki

Kiki found Andrew MacLeod in the pub. She rushed over to grab him and all the old men chuckled as they watched her drag him out the door. It wasn't uncommon for a witch to seek out a lad following a special ritual. She could hear the laughter follow them out bar, but she could really care less. They needed to resort to plan "BFF," Bring on the Faerie Flag. Eva's plan would not work, as the demon demanded the *dragoma*, or a maiden in bloom. In the eyes of some of those women, Kiki could see they felt the needs of the many outweighed the needs of Janine. There was no way she would allow Janine be a Comba Charm victim, or to continue mixing in this dark business, not with her Auntie Celeste's grandchild growing inside of her. Kiki could already see the baby's aura. She was already a beauty. They should never have allowed Janine to participate in their ritual!

The wall spirit said that the Faerie Flag could not help Janine, but it could help Kiki.

The wall spirit had been instructing her. Perhaps there was a reason Janine always shunned those charms while Kiki constantly itched to wear one.

Andrew followed Kiki to his room around the corner. When he went to the Castle Dunvegan with Ian's crew, Andrew swiped the Faerie Flag. He replaced it with a replica flag he had treasured since he was a boy. As long as no one looked closely, it would be okay until he could return the original. The crew planned to go back to the castle the next day, and that was when Andrew hoped to switch the flags back.

Kiki could clearly see an aura radiating off that flag. It pulsed with faerie energy and was definitely the real thing. Kiki watched it glow brighter in Andrew's hands. It knew Andrew as a true MacLeod. Kiki had no doubt her plan would work, as long as she could get her lover to kill her.

"I don't know about this Kiera, something happened." Andrew shrugged. "Suddenly, I'm not as obsessed with you like I was. I think the summoning was a success. It's like that vise that had me locked down is gone. Maybe we dinna need to use the wish. Maybe everything will turn out okay."

"It's temporary," Kiki told him. "The marks are erased for now, but after the full moon comes and goes, the marks will be back. If the demon tried to use you before, he'll likely try to use you again. It's not like anyone is ever going to use that last faerie wish, Andrew. You're a MacLeod, right? Tied to the women in the coven through hundreds of years of history. There needs to be one last victim. Maybe that wish was waiting for you. We don't want a real victim, do we? Don't you want to help destroy a curse that has plagued our kin for hundreds of years?"

"I'm not laying my hands on you, lassie. That part I'll not do."

"Dinna worry about that," Kiki said. "I only have one lover in the world and I think I can easily trick him into cutting me with a poisoned knife. How's that for a betrayal? If that doesn't work, then he's already upset at me, regarding you. I can lure him into the glen and get him very riled up if needed. If the demon wants a victim, I can make that happen. I just need you to be ready with the flag. To wish it away."

Kiki coated a dagger with poisons she stashed in a lower drawer in the herb room. The spirit of the wall instructed her to poison a knife for a reason. That spirit knew what must be done, and it made total sense.

Max Colliers had been obsessed with Janine's knife marks. He imagined the scars had come from some sort of risky sex play and his curiosity had been inflamed. He practically begged Janine to allow him to participate in that type of play, even tried to coerce her. Kiki could easily lure Max into the glen with an invitation he couldn't resist.

It was the perfect place to end the curse, because the faeries had attended the summoning and desired an end to it as well. Andrew could be waiting in the wings with their Faerie Flag, and as a MacLeod, he could make a wish. He could wish the poison out of her system and bring her back from death. Kiki also brought a portable, personal defibrillator to help. Trinity kept one in the herb room in the case of an accidental poisoning. Kiki told Andrew that he probably wouldn't need the electric shock machine, as the flag would probably be enough, but it was there, so she brought it. Didn't hurt to hedge their bets. If she was completely wrong about all of it, then so be it. At least an ancient curse would be put to rest.

Perhaps that's why things didn't work out with the detective. Perhaps Kiki was never meant to transition from maiden to mother or to crone. Her carefully nurtured core might be the final sacrifice needed to satisfy the thirst of this ancient curse.

"I'm going to take him to the top of Castle Ewen. It might get dicey if he sees you, so hide out in the glen, or in that little cave just below. You need to be close enough to hear what's happening so you can come up as soon as I'm a goner and use the flag."

Kiki took another look at the Faerie Flag. It definitely glowed with energy. *If she survived, she was going to go to Chicago and do whatever was needed to win that stubborn detective back and make her baby.*

"I'm counting on you, Andrew. Meet me in one hour. If the plan falls through, I'll call you."

Kiki had no problem contacting Max. He picked up on the first ring. She knew that he was waiting for her call. He had been hanging around the cottage, and he dropped in to visit her mother more than once. He had sent Kiki flowers with a cute note that said, *okay, there's nothing here, I promise. You should call me.* Kiki hated to use Max in this awful event, but she needed him, and he was just the sort of rogue that would come through for her, reckless, spontaneous, and full of passionate base energy.

Max once yearned to cut a design on a lovely bosom. The wall spirit knew that and then practically instructed her to poison a knife.

"Well, Kiki, I'm not sure if I can meet you right now. I'm actually having drinks with someone, and it's very late. Maybe we can get together tomorrow."

So, Kiki thought, he was going to play hard to get, make her wait and squirm. How charming. But she didn't have time to wait. At the cottage, they likely figured out that she took a charm from the pile and would be wondering what she was up to. They'd wonder if she passed the right one to Janine or kept it for herself. Only Gwen knew how that transaction went and she wouldn't keep quiet forever. She would expect Kiki to wait until the full moon before trying anything, so she couldn't wait another night.

"No problem, lover," Kiki purred into the phone. "I'll just ring Andrew. He's quite young and vigorous, a prime stud. That summoning really stirred me up. It reminded me of our night in the sacred valley, was it the same for you? Before the sunrise, I hoped to reenact a little of my awakening, and, perhaps, add a little extra spice into the mix. What do you think about a little erotic knife play? A wee blood ritual on the top of Castle Ewen with our reenactment. I recall that you once yearned to try something like that, carve your mark on a bosom. Well, my bosom is screaming for you, Max. But if you're too tied up with someone else, I can call Andrew. He's always ready to please a lass in need."

She could hear him swallowing. He must have dropped something.

"Are you pulling my leg?"

"You know I'm not pulling your leg, Max." Kiki used her special sultry voice. "But I can certainly pull something if you meet me. My base door has been thrown wide open and I'm fantasizing about you. You know I can't control my desires when that happens. Will you come? You can make a nice design between my breasts with my silver dagger, I'm very set on it. Tell me now if you can't, so I can ring Andrew. I'm in a heated state and need to be satisfied soon. I'm dying for you, but Andrew can easily step in if I need him."

"Don't call Andrew." She could hear Max shuffling around. "I'll meet you. You say on that little rock tower in the glen? No one's going to be out there?"

"No one should be out there, but I don't care if they are. I'm not planning to be shy."

Kiki texted Andrew that they were on schedule. He texted back that he would be there with the flag. She avoided the main cottage on the way to the glen. She found a few soft wool blankets in the outer herb house and snuck away quickly and quietly. Although the house appeared dark, someone might still be up and about. Likely, a fair amount of whisky had flowed in Trinity's den, then many of the women probably found warm arms to settle into. Kiki wondered if her mother gravitated to the attentions of Dominique after that ritual. For some reason, Kiki was rooting against that. She was rooting for George.

The waxing gibbous moon dipped well past its apex but still illuminated the area well, even with the clouds. She was happy it wasn't too cold.

Kiki observed someone skirt across the glen and jump into the trees. How did Andrew beat her there? The crisp night air carried sounds well and Kiki heard a far off car engine. She hurried toward the narrow trail that led to the top of the rocky hill. She wanted to be up top, waiting for him. Andrew, in the trees, ducked down when she glanced over. Hopefully, he'd be prompt with that Faerie Flag when she needed it. Why was he so far inside the tree line anyway? She asked him to be just below the top of the hill or in the little cave. She texted him to get closer. In the distance, she heard the car door slam and knew Max was on the way.

At the top of Castle Ewen, Kiki laid out wool blankets to make a warm nest between two large boulders. She carefully placed the poisoned dagger on one of them. She retrieved the Saint Comba charm and clasped it around her neck. The metal felt cool against her skin. It felt right. It calmed her. It was the charm Janine had asked for, the one from Gram's attic box without a redeemer, Irene Lumen's charm.

The night was mostly clear. She had a beautiful view of the valley and cottage roof. She watched Max hurry across the glen floor and felt a little jolt of something in her chest. Here he was, running to meet her again. She could not take her eyes off him. He carried a blanket, or a bag, or something.

After a few minutes, Max appeared at the top of Castle Ewen. He slowed down when he spotted her and began to swagger toward her. He glanced around, then fixed his eyes on hers.

"Another great spot." A handsome, mischievous grin spread across his lips. He pulled a bottle from his pack. "I remembered to bring gifts. Whisky and cheese. Does the lady desire a little nip?"

Kiki couldn't help smiling at the rascal and accepted the whisky. Now that she was no longer rushing, her brain had slowed down to think.

What was she doing? Would Andrew make it in time with the Faerie Flag? He should be just below the top, listening.

Kiki suddenly felt tired and all she really wanted was to lay down with Max, cuddle him, and fall asleep in that soft wool. But neither of them climbed the towering rock for that. Max bent down to initiate a slow, sensual kiss that stimulated a tingling in her core. She felt her knees give out. *Holy crap*, she thought, *he's mixing love with that kiss*. Some part of her began to yearn deeply for him. Kiki pushed him away.

"Come on now, don't get romantic on me," Kiki chided him. "I'm looking for my bad boy. Come lay down with me on these blankets and we'll put on a nice show for the faeries."

He grinned. "I feel inspired to romance you, Kiki."

He followed her onto the wool blankets and kissed her passionately. He moved very differently than before and sent her more than just passion energy. Thing were not going the way she expected.

She pushed him aside again. *Keep that door shut.*

He pulled her back and kissed her again, taking his time, caressing her skin. She felt a creamy bit of warmth coat her core and she imagined tumbling into those blankets, kissing him deeply, and straddling his engorged… Kiki did not like how things were playing out. Max was chipping away at her resolve. If he kept up his loving caresses, she might not be able to follow through with the plan.

But she had to, because back at the cottage half those witches were hoping Janine would slip the charm around her neck and *be the last one.*

Kiki squirmed out of Max's arms and glared at him.

"Come on now. Let's get this going"

Kiki unbuttoned her top and exposed a generous portion of her voluptuous assets. There's the reaction she wanted, much more lustful. She grabbed the dagger and handed it to Max.

"Go ahead. Carve in your mark. Do a good job now." She helped him unbutton his shirt.

Max put the knife down and focused on kissing and caressing her instead. Kiki took up the dagger and pushed it into his hand.

"Max, don't make me wait. Let's get this blood sacrifice going. I want you to hurt me like I've hurt you. I want to see my crimson red smear across your chest while we kiss. Aren't eager to make your mark on mine? I know it's a fantasy of yours. If you make the cuts deep enough, they'll always be there, and I'll always think of you whenever someone touches them."

Max chuckled and put the knife aside, shaking his head.

"I like the sound of that, but I don't want to cut you, Kiki, I wouldn't dare. I just want to make love. I've been dreaming of this moment for a long time." He started kissing her all over again. Kiki pushed him aside.

"Max. Would you please cut me? I know you've always talked about doing something like this, do it to me." She pushed the knife back into his hand. "Please."

Max sat up. He tossed the knife away. *The idiot!* He stared at her and his expression turn serious. *Where was the roguish Max Colliers she was counting on?* He actually gazed sweetly at her, longingly, core aura pulsing blue.

"I don't want to cut you and I don't want anyone else to touch you. I know you keep saying that we're not a thing, but maybe we could be. Can't you feel it a little bit? This thing between us? I can't even look at another woman without thinking about you. I think… I think we should do something drastic." He chuckled softly. "I mean, drastic."

Kiki sat up and pulled her clothes back together. So, he wasn't going to cut her. Then, she'd have to humiliate him into strangling her or something. That was probably best anyway, it followed the curse better. Why did he have to bring love energy into it? How had he even mustered that up? It made the effort to push him into anger much harder. She actually enjoyed his romantic overtures, they felt so nice. She couldn't look at him or she'd waver. Kiki took a deep breath.

"Don't be an idiot, Max." Kiki grabbed her phone. "I guess I'll just give Andrew a ring. You may have heard around town, the MacLeod tool is legend. He'd be more than happy to carve something on me and satisfy this craving of mine. I probably should have called him to begin with, instead of a squeamish prat like you."

Max stared at her and she could see the light dimming from his eyes. She hated herself.

"Kiki, I think I love you. Does that mean anything to you?"

No, no, no! She couldn't lose her resolve now. She kept her eyes glued to her phone.

"Don't be such a sap." She made herself laugh, and it sounded hollow. "I'm sorry, but you're just not love material, everyone knows that. And what I need from you, maybe Andrew is a better bet after all."

"I can't believe you said that." Max pulled his shirt together. "Are you trying to make me lash out at you?"

Then, she saw him flinch with understanding. Max drew himself up to sit on one of the rocks, considering her.

"What's going on? What are you playing at?"

Well then, Kiki thought, he's not going to fall for her game. Kiki grabbed his bottle of whisky and had another taste. Then, she set it down. She was fingering the Saint Comba charm dangling from her neck.

"There needs to be a final victim, before the end of the full moon. I know you don't believe any of it, but many women will be marked for death if the curse isn't broken. You can help me here, as my lover. I've betrayed you terribly, don't you agree? If you would just strangle me, or cut me with the poisonous knife you tossed away, the curse will be over. Don't worry, I won't be dead long. *We have a plan.*

Andrew is waiting down the trail with the Faerie Flag. He's a MacLeod and can make a wish on that flag. So you see, no problem. I'll only be dead for a few minutes, but it should be long enough to break the curse."

He stared at her as if she were crazy. He picked up the whisky and took a long sip. Then, he stood up and buttoned part of his expensive tailored shirt.

"Andrew is down that trail, waiting for me to kill you? And then he's going to run up here with a Faerie Flag and wish you back to life?" Max summed it up out loud.

He started laughing in a mean way. Stumbling and laughing. He finally got a hold of himself and glared at her.

"You're being serious. That numbskull is waiting just down the path with his magical Faerie Flag? And this is what you think of me? You actually believe that I could harm you. I'm the villain." He looked completely brokenhearted. He threw the whisky bottle and after a long moment, the crash echoed in the glen.

"Under the influence of the demon," Kiki said softly, realizing her folly.

She could see his sadness transform into anger. Then, he moved toward the trail and started hurrying down, growling for Andrew. Kiki could hear a scuffle just over the rise. It was a disaster. They were fighting down there.

In her head, Gwen was calling her an *eejit*. *You cannot turn someone into a demon.* Why did she think she could get Max to kill her? Gwen would say they needed to be patient and find another way. Well, she tried. The plan would have worked with the right man. *The right man, or the wrong man?*

Kiki stood up and gathered the wool blankets together. She could see the moon had grown huge as it dived toward the western horizon. It was close to dawn and people would come around soon. She hoped Andrew and Max were not hurting each other down on the path.

Kiki faced the trail and saw someone's head popped up. It wasn't Max, and it wasn't Andrew. She had seen that aura before, and it lacked a core with a frightening emptiness. Richard Wilkens, bright eyed and handsomely flushed, stared at her. Kiki clutched the blankets and searched around, but she knew the top of that rocky hill well. There was only one way up and one way down, and that soulless man was blocking her exit. She suddenly felt terrified. Clearly, he could see it.

"I was watching you," he said softly. "I asked about you in the pub. You have everyone fooled."

"What do you want?" Kiki asked.

"I want what's mine," he said softly. "And to clear up what was done."

"Well then, I'll leave you to that." Kiki moved forward to pass, but he stepped in her way.

"I don't think so." He tilted his head slightly, looking at her cleavage. "You're wearing my mother's necklace. My sister will want that back."

He stepped over and grabbed her neck with a fast firm hand. He held her high so she had to roll to her tip toes. He grabbed the charm and yanked it off her neck. The chain burned as it cut through her skin. He tucked the necklace into the deep layers of his clothes, next to his heart, while keeping a firm, strong hand on her throat. He squeezed her neck as his lips bent into a tense smile and his eyes narrowed.

"You corrupt people, do you know that?"

She could not answer. She could not even gasp. His grey eyes were like glass and she could see the reflection of the moon perfectly.

"I followed you around Inverness a bit. You enjoy toying with people, don't you, like those two losers down on the trail? And what you did at that river. It was your influence that caused it, don't try to deny it. That child was my daughter. My beautiful little girl." He put both hands on her neck now. "I saw you at my parole hearing, sitting behind her and urging her to keep blaming me… and you continue to confuse her, just like her sister. Did you tell her that she could talk to ghosts? You did, didn't you? You enjoy playing these games, don't you? You led me here."

Kiki suddenly had an *aha* moment as she recognized the scene. Winter heather edging the hill top. A swollen moon descending toward the horizon. The soft breeze flowing over the grass as the stars dimmed. Kiki recognized her alternate vision from that night in the Graceland Cemetery in Chicago. The interwoven death vision she experienced as she stared into the metal face of the statue of death.

The moment of her death was at hand!

Well, how about that Gwen Murphy! Kiki experienced a bona fide vision of her very own future and not just a spirit's jumbled message. She clearly foresaw this very event. Kiki felt so pleased with herself. She really was the most gifted sister in the coven, *ha!*

Rick continued to squeeze her neck and she began to choke. He continued talking, but her ears were no longer listening. He forced her slowly to the cold ground. The interwoven images made sense now. The glen for Kiki, the woods for his mother. The moon in the sky for Kiki, the moon reflected in the pond for his mother. Heather for Kiki, cattails for his mother. The son for Kiki, the father for his mother. Kiki tried to struggle, but she already knew how it ended and it was no use. She found herself following the script, look at the moon, then to his eyes, then at the stars. Soon, the light would narrow into pinpoints before going out. Kiki realized that she hadn't drawn a breath of air for a very long time and her field of vision had grown incredibly small. Her hands gripped his wrist, trying to pry his fingers from her neck, but Richard Wilkens was a very strong and determined man. If there was something she forgot to do, it was too late now.

She remembered everything clearly, faeries lighting up the night by a loch in the glen, her auntie in the garden showing her how to arrange the weeds, her mother holding her hand as she went to school that very first day, realizing the man in that boat on Uig Bay was really a ghost, her cousin blinking as he coached her on how to throw a dagger, Gwen's freckled face laughing hysterically, the Nimble Men dancing across the winter sky on her fourteenth birthday, herself dancing at a fire festival, and on and on the clips flashed through her mind, right up to Max's brokenhearted eyes staring at her, sparking an unexpected feeling deep inside her core. Her lover possessed a heart after all. Fascinated, Kiki watched her world view grow smaller and smaller and smaller, until there was nothing left but silence.

Chapter 23
The End

Janine

Ian slept on the living room couch. He accused her of completely disregarding his feelings, not only had she participated in the ritual, she had been a key player in the ritual. There was no way to block her image on the screen and his father was sure to watch the show. And Roxie, calling out his mother's name, did Janine know she was going to do that? Why did Janine insist on helping him make amends with his father if she was just going to dash it all to pieces immediately afterward? He didn't understand her vacillating attitude regarding his father. Ian had been so annoyingly righteous that Janine finally attacked back.

Sit on his high horse all he wanted, but when did he plan on telling her that he knew half the girls in that ritual once upon a time? They were all very curious about her and she got very distinct vibes that a few of them had known him pretty darn well. Was that the real reason he didn't want her mixing with the coven women, afraid they might gossip about him? He should leave her alone or just fess up.

But she didn't really believe any of that, and when he stomped away, she instantly missed him.

Janine couldn't sleep with worrying about it. Then, like clockwork, she was wide awake an hour before the sunrise.

Every day in Scotland the early morning called her out to run. Why stew in bed? She'd sneak downstairs to check on Ian. If he was still awake, she'd try to make amends; if not, she'd go for a run and wake him when she got back. She needed to pump some endorphins into the baby before she got too far along in the pregnancy.

Janine heard Ian's gentle snores before she got to the bottom step. Run first, talk later. She quietly left the cottage and began a trot. Her thoughts went to the summoning. Many of the women were both happy and upset at what occurred in the glen. Like Janine, not everyone had been able to witness things. Many needed Gwen and the older ladies to repeat what had happened.

But everyone did wonder about Kiki disappearing. Where had she gone so suddenly? Someone claimed she ran off to meet a man, and the fellows at the pub confirmed it. Gwen believed Kiki had a very bad idea brewing and hated leaving with the carpool back to Inverness. But Gwen had obligations that needed attention, and she couldn't control Kiki anyway, even if she did find her. Not to worry, she'd return before the full moon and intervene in whatever nonsense Kiki was hatching.

As Janine passed over the last mound into the Faerie Glen, she spotted activity in the distance at the top of Castle Ewen. Two people already climbed the hill, even though the sun had not yet popped over the horizon. Maybe they wanted to watch the sunrise.

Janine gazed at them and realized that one of them was Kiki. Who was the other? She didn't know, but his posture seemed familiar. Was it the guy in the hills she had seen the day before? Something set off an alert in Janine's head. Kiki's stance suddenly appeared defensive. Instead of taking the long way around the glen, Janine decided to cut across instead. She lost sight of the two on top as she went around to the trailhead.

She found Max sitting near a rock, holding his brow. Blood trailed down his neck and he was trying to stand up. Another fellow lay a few feet away, it was the dark eyed guy, Andrew MacLeod. Janine ran over to check on Andrew. Someone broke his nose and the front of his head was bloody. She noticed the bloody rocks and glanced at Max.

"Did you guys bash each other with rocks?"

"No," Max wobbled, but sat up straighter. "Andrew was already like that. There was another guy. He looked like that guy," Max spoke sluggishly. "That guy, you know, *the* guy!"

He was obviously very disoriented and upset. Janine picked up a rock and ran up the trail. Whoever bashed rocks into Max and Andrew was up top with Kiki. She sprinted to the top and saw someone bent over Kiki with his hands on her throat. She only saw the back of his head, but she knew it was Richard. An ice cold fear froze her for an instant, then she stepped on something, a witch's dagger. Janine traded the rock for the knife and felt dizzy, but she looked up anyway and yelled,

"Get off her!"

Richard turned quickly and rose to a full standing position. His grey eyes brightened at the sight of her. He broke out in a grin, happy to see her. Janine noticed that Kiki remained limp and made no sounds. What did he do to her? Richard took a small step in Janine's direction and she waved the dagger in a threatening way. He paused.

"There you are," he said. "Right on schedule. You always loved to run just before the sunrise. I didn't want you to see me like this, to meet this way. I'm sorry about this, but you can see that I didn't plan this, right? This is not my fault. They were here already, doing these things. I didn't expect any of these people. I only came to meet you during your run and they were already here." He glanced guiltily at Kiki, then back again. "I was defending myself. Those guys, they both tried to jump me, and she… she's responsible for —"

"Stop. Back up."

He stared at the knife in her hand and Janine felt a terrible déjà vu, they had done this before. For a moment, she felt the resolve drain from her limbs knowing what came next, but she stopped herself. She stood her ground instead of shrinking. She wasn't weak and feeble, she was strong and capable. There was nowhere to hide anyway and she needed to get to Kiki.

"Please put that down," he pleaded with her. "You're completely confused and you remember everything wrong, you do. We could rewrite our story, Janine, we… We had an unfortunate episode, but we can put that behind us and forgive each other, we can get past it. We're soulmates. There hasn't been a single day that I haven't thought about you, and it's no use fighting fate. These people, they have been poisoning your mind for a very long time."

He took another step toward her and she waved the knife wildly at him. It sliced him on the hand making a cut similar to her wound from the blood ritual. Did it sting him? He flinched back. His slate grey eyes began to darken as he took another step toward her. Then another. And another. His eyes fixed on the dagger in her hand, and she felt herself wavering. Just like before, she knew she couldn't stab him. She swiped at him again and made another cut. It only angered him as he howled at her. His eyes were in agony. She would not be able to drive that knife into flesh, she knew it. So, she threw the dagger far away instead and his eyes tracked it flying through the air. It went over the edge of the drop off, out of reach.

She decided to ram him instead. She was strong and fast, and had been studying Ian's violent rugby matches. In her head, she practiced a rugby front tackle for weeks in anticipation of being asked to play.

This time, when Richard sprang toward her, she bend down to take the hit with her shoulder, crashed down, and caved backwards while twisting so that they hit the ground with Janine on top. A surprise move that he didn't expect. Janine instantly sprang up and sent her foot into his crotch as hard as she could, as if she were making a long pass in soccer. She made a good connection with his balls and watched his face cave in agony. He was sweating profusely, and his face went terribly red. Her tackle couldn't have been that effective. Why was he gasping oddly and writhing in pain like that? He was precariously close to the edge of the plateau and squirming crazily. He was going to fall off. She didn't care and ran to Kiki.

Kiki felt completely limp. Janine checked for a pulse and couldn't find one, nor could she detect any breathing. Her own pulse pounded in her head and her vision tunneled into total panic. Janine heard herself yelling at Kiki to wake up, to open her eyes. Then, Max stumbled up the trail and the sight of his wobbly steps calmed her a little bit. She watched him use a foot to help send a motionless Rick over the edge of the hill top. They heard a sad thump as Rick hit the floor of the glen. Janine yelled at Max.

"She's not breathing and I don't feel a pulse!"

Janine opened Kiki's airway and gave her thirty chest compressions. Then, she gave Kiki two large breaths and more chest compressions. More breaths, more compressions. Crap, she thought, how many compressions was that?

Max's voice boomed next to her ear. It took a moment to comprehend what he was saying. He yelled into his phone, then he yelled down the trail as Janine gave Kiki more breaths and more chest compression. She kept losing count and needed Max to *shut up*, but she didn't have the breath to tell him that.

"Andrew!" Max screamed. "Get up here with your fucking Faerie Flag and make your wish right now! We need that flag!"

Janine stared at Max and could feel the sweat on her brow. *Did she hear that right?* Then, Max reached over, gently moved her hands aside and spoke softly in his gentleman's voice.

"You need a break, I got it." Max gave the next two breaths and started compressions.

Janine counted out loud for him, and he nodded a thank you to her. When she got to thirty, he paused to give more breaths, then went back to the compressions. He seemed calm and focused, even though she knew he had a concussion. She could see the dried blood on his neck, and his pupils were each a different size.

"Come on, Kiki," he said softly with the rhythm of his movements. "Just breathe. Come on, I dare you. It's a win-win for you. Whatever you want, just breathe."

Then, Andrew MacLeod was there with laggard movements. He stumbled in close and emptied out his bag.

Janine watched a small square portable medical device tumble out.

Was that a defibrillator? She had just been wishing for a defibrillator.

Andrew ignored it and placed a ratty cloth on Kiki's stomach instead. What in the world was he doing? He threw his head back and yelled into the air.

"I, Andrew, of the Clan MacLeod, call on the faeries of Skye! I hereby use the third wish of this flag, given to my clan, the Clan MacLeod! Bring her back! I wish it! I wish it!" Then, he fell over from the exertion, breathless.

Janine grabbed the portable defibrillator and tore it open. She stopped Max in his compressions and attached the pads to Kiki's chest. Then, she plugged the leads into the device and waited for the full charge light. When the green light blinked on, both Max and Janine moved back a tad. Then, she shocked Kiki. Her whole body convulsed.

Andrew struggled to a sitting position and asked if it worked. But Janine wasn't watching him. She was watching Kiki's chest and trying to find a pulse in her arm. Just in case, she set the defibrillator to charge again. How long should they wait? How many more charges did they have? She glanced at Max and could see him crying. It made her want to cry, but she didn't, not yet. Janine restarted CPR and stared at Max.

"After two minutes of CPR, we'll try it again," she said, and Max nodded.

"Thirty," Max sobbed, and she was grateful because she hadn't even been counting.

She gave the two breaths and then went back to the compressions. Max counted softly. Then, they shocked Kiki again as Andrew shouted out his wish again. Janine whispered to the faeries to please listen to Andrew and his wish. As Max and Janine searched for a pulse, the sun cast the first beams of morning light over the Faerie Glen and started a brand new day.

Richard Wilkens and Kiki Mellow both died in the Faerie Glen just prior to dawn. Kiki from suffocation, and Richard from cardiac arrest caused by the toxins coating Kiki's dagger. They were both evacuated by helicopter to the nearest hospital. Max Colliers and Andrew MacLeod were also taken to the hospital, but they were ferried away by ambulance and treated for concussions. Janine spent a couple of intense hours answering questions from authorities before she could finally escape into her husband's embrace.

"I'm sorry, Ian," she sobbed uncontrollably as he held her. "I should have listened to you. Your father's instinct was right. He was here."

"Oh no, lass, I never should have snapped at you." He was crying too. "You took care of yourself pretty good. Maybe even… maybe we can hope Kiki's okay. Let's not ever fight about anything ever again."

Ian, Janine, and Trinity drove to the hospital the moment the authorities released Janine from questioning. She would have to stay in Scotland for a while, but for all intents and purposes, it appeared to be a case of self-defense in the alleged death of Richard Wilkens.

Max and Andrew sat draped over seats in the hospital waiting room. Gwen sat with them, speaking softly to Max. She jumped up and ran over to embrace Janine and Trinity the moment they entered the room. Then, Gwen escorted Trinity and Ian to the nurse's station to alert the doctor that family had arrived. After a moment, all three of them disappeared behind the big doors separating the waiting room from the patients and medical staff.

"No one is telling us anything," Max grumbled. Both Max and Andrew wore matching head bandages. Neither of them opted to be admitted for observation. "They were waiting for family, for her mother. I'm afraid to get my hopes up, but why wouldn't they say anything?"

Janine sank onto the seat next to Max and gently took his hand in hers. He peered at her with a terrible sadness in his eyes.

"Thank you for trying so hard." Janine squeezed his hand.

Max nodded, trying to be brave, but he looked like a lost boy without his glasses. Andrew had his head tilted back. A torn yellow cloth covered his eyes. *Did he swipe the fabled Faerie Flag from that castle the other day?* He wasn't moving, and it was hard to tell if he was awake or asleep. Janine put her arm around Max because he was shaking. What were they waiting for, a final confirmation? Kiki did not have a pulse on that rocky mound and Janine had resigned herself that the worst had surely occurred. She felt completely numb.

Then, Gwen burst from big double doors. Her eyes were big and bright, and Janine's heart started racing. What did that face mean? All three of them jumped up expectantly to greet her, afraid to hope.

"It's a miracle!" Gwen's big eyes bore right into hers.

"She's alive?" Max asked tentatively, and Gwen nodded vigorously.

Max and Andrew began jumping up and down.

"It worked!" Andrew yelled. "I can't believe it, it worked! Thank the faeries and their flag, it worked!"

The guys hugged each other and then hugged Gwen and Janine. The adrenaline rush felt overpowering, Janine couldn't possibly sit down. She wanted to run through those big doors and see what was going on.

"Is she awake? Can we go see her? Is she okay? Did she say anything? What's the prognosis?" Max asked his questions in rapid succession. "Will they let us go back there?"

"She can barely say a word or open her eyes." Gwen chuckled. "But her ego is bigger than ever."

She stared gleefully at Janine.

"She turned right to me, pleased as punch with herself. Guess what she was babbling about. She was bragging that she had a vision, not a message from a spirit, but a vision, perfect and acted out according to script. More accurate than any of the sights I've ever had, she bragged. She claims to be the new mistress of prophecy now. Can you believe the ego on that wee lassie?"

Tears were rolling down Gwen's freckled cheeks as she spoke.

"Then she begged Ian to fetch her a wee dram to coat her throat, but I don't think she's going to get it."

Kiki Mellow returned from the dead with only the bruise marks on her neck to show for it. The doctor placed her on blood thinners to alleviate possible blood clots and her voice was weak for about a week. The doctor lauded the chest compressions for keeping her brain cells alive, and the paramedics couldn't say how her heart restarted. When the helicopter got into the air, they suddenly detected a pulse. By the time they made it to the hospital, Kiki had become quite stable. Kiki couldn't tell them anything about being dead. No bright lights, no lost relatives, all she remembered was blue-green sparks similar to the light glow worms emit around the lochs in the glen. She winked when she said it.

Epilogue

Kiki

Four months later, Kiki and Gwen were excited that Janine and Ian were staying for the Beltane Festival. They met at the cottage on Skye and crowded the grounds with friends. Gram and Leone both came from California, as well as Emma from the show, and Gwen's partner Bridget was there, plus a few locals, George, Andrew, and Sam, and several other coven families.

Kiki invited two men to the Beltane that year, Detective Bob Anderson and her boss Max Colliers. After recovering from her hospital stay, Kiki found herself quite confused on matters of love and could not resolve which man should sire the baby she desired. She decided that if they both showed up, she'd sample each of them, then let her egg decide on the father.

The coven women and the visitors from Turkey agreed that the demise of Richard Wilkens satisfied the 300-year-old curse placed on their ancestors. Gwen reasoned it out to Janine. Richard Wilkens passionately loved her, then he completely betrayed her, and while in possession of the last charm, Janine dealt him a fatal blow. Janine became the last one to vindicate the Comba Ladies and fill the empty spot of redemption. Not by being a sacrifice, but by delivering the fatal blow. The dictum never required that the victim be a woman, and the killer be a man.

Every spirit had always been right about Janine. She was, indeed, the last one.

The End

Did you miss parts one and two of the trilogy? Do you wish to discover the back story to Janine and Kiki's friendship and read of their budding romances?

Turn the page for information on the missing pieces of the *Spectral Analysis* puzzle…

Reviews Help Authors

Thank you for reading. If you enjoyed this story, consider leaving a review on Goodreads, Amazon, B&N or your favorite bookstore

Spectral Analysis-Part 1

Seeking Lost Souls

A fractured past, entwined with a new inflamed desire, is the perfect combination to aid skeptical Janine into believing the paranormal…but will her enlightenment occur in time to subvert a tragedy?

Don't believe in ghosts? Well, neither does Janine Stinger, even though she operates some of the tech equipment on a ghost hunting TV show. Apparently, her new and passionate romance with Ian McNally has triggered some unsettling flashback emotions and… she thinks she feels something, and hears something, and eventually sees something that might be a ghost. She doesn't want to believe in ghosts, but if she doesn't believe, that means she's screwed-up in the head, and her violent past still haunts her. But then again, if she does believe, that means the ghost is coming after someone precious to her. What will she lose? Her fragile psyche, or a precious child?

Spectral Voices- part 2

Someone is Speaking Spirits

As fate forces her to face some startling mystic abilities, Janine grapples with how she fits into the greater scheme of things, all while facing unresolved feelings for the man she scorned.

From across the void, faint whispers tease the paranormal investigators of *Spectral Analysis*, could one of them, perhaps skeptical Janine, actually be speaking to spirits? Spiritualist and self-proclaimed witch, Kiki Mellow, thinks yes. As the ghost hunting crew seek out paranormal activity in the windy city, they stumble upon an ancient curse linked to a charm necklace, a coven of witches, and to Janine Stinger. As Ian McNally shares his scientific theory on paranormal energy, Janine becomes emotional entangled all over again; with the doctor, the paranormal, and with her violent past. Will she take the leap of faith and embrace Kiki's pagan philosophy?

If she does, one sinister spirit might just excise her of her own ghosts, and that could lead to her own demise, or, her happily ever after…but who knows what dangers manifest when reaching across the void?

About the Author

Joanne Alain Cook is a mother, wife, sister, teacher, artist, officer, and writer. She retired from the USAF after serving both in the active duty and reserves as a C-130 navigator, executive officer, and maintenance officer. Joanne is of Korean/American heritage and has lived in Texas, Japan, Georgia, and California. Her adventures have taken her to every hemisphere on Earth, and she has spent many hours flying in the air and scuba-diving under the sea and lounging on her sofa while reading. Joanne currently teaches science in Northern California. She lives in Sacramento with her handsome husband of twenty-plus years, beautiful brainy daughters, goofy Labrador, angry bearded dragon, frightened chickens, and clueless fish.

Art by Alaina Grace Batten

www.ingramcontent.com/pod-product-compliance
Lightning Source LLC
Chambersburg PA
CBHW061302190726
48288CB00002B/315